Praise for
TEMPER

"For potboilers, nothing comes close to *Temper*. . . . There's violence here, but it's not only physical; it's emotional and psychological—even intellectual."

—*The New York Times Book Review*

"*Temper* is raw, ingenious, and utterly fearless. I devoured every word as the story bent and twisted in ways I did not see coming. Layne Fargo delivers psychological suspense at its very best—without tricks or misdirections, just brilliant storytelling and profoundly astute observations about human emotions and relationships. *Temper* is the real deal."

—Wendy Walker, *USA Today* bestselling author of
The Night Before

"The theater is a tempestuous, bloody place to be in Fargo's prickly debut. Fargo's propulsive writing style and Joanna's and Kira's dueling narratives drive the increasingly frenzied chain of events that play out. . . . Fargo is an author to watch."

—*Kirkus Reviews*

"Twisty, sexy, and so believable it's scary, the pages of *Temper* bleed an irresistible blend of voice, subculture, and character. Compulsive reading for fans of *Black Swan*, *Mozart in the Jungle*, or (dare I say it?) real-life backstage theatrics."

—Jessica Strawser, bestselling author of
Forget You Know Me

"A twisted tale of what happens when violence, ambition, and the taste for blood take center stage. . . . [*Temper*] builds a sense of danger and suspense that will keep readers guessing, literally until the last page. Fargo's first novel features complicated female characters and will be well received by fans of Gillian Flynn and Tana French."

—*Booklist*

"Utterly compelling. A fascinating look at our willingness to accept the destruction of others for the sake of artistic genius."

—Victoria Helen Stone, bestselling author of *Jane Doe*

"Layne Fargo's theater noir debut *Temper* is a suspense novel paced to make readers twitch in their seats waiting for the final curtain. Sexy and sinister."

—Lori Rader-Day, award-winning author of *Under a Dark Sky*

"Addictive . . . The novel's violently sensuous suspense careens toward a chilling conclusion you'll never see coming."

—*BookPage*

"Layne Fargo's dangerously seductive debut about ambition, obsession, and the capacity for violence will bewitch you from the start and keep you in its thrall until long after you've turned the final page."

—Kathleen Barber, author of *Follow Me* and *Truth Be Told*

"Fargo maintains a scalpel-like control over her characters, even when they themselves are out of control."

—*Chicago Tribune*

"In her dark, sultry debut, Layne Fargo delves deep into the psychological war zone of the theater, perfectly capturing its hothouse world of rivalries, dalliances, and duels—both onstage and off. Toying with the line between victim and villain, real life and fantasy, *Temper* revels in its mind games, delivering twist after twist as it races toward a Shakespearean climax. The final page will leave you gasping."

—Amy Gentry, author of *Last Woman Standing*

"This sinister, of-the-moment novel focuses on the power struggle between an ambitious actress and an abusive director, but you don't have to be a theater buff to enjoy it. The story brims with complex female characters, psychosexual manipulation, and plenty of drama on and off the stage."

—*Chicago Review of Books*

"*Temper* is a completely compelling read in which anger and passion fizz off the page. It is a strong and timely story, with two unflinching heroines whom I was totally rooting for, especially as they revealed their most unabridged selves."

—Araminta Hall, author of *Our Kind of Cruelty*

"*Temper* is the kind of debut people are going to remember: intense, well crafted, and emotionally blistering."

—*CrimeReads*

"Ambitious women and behind-the-curtain theater drama? Sign us up!"

—*Book Riot*

"*Temper* dances the reader through the tangled, incestuous, and artistically volatile network of Chicago storefront theater with ferocity and ambition. Part noir, part mystery, part feminist manifesto . . . The result is a fast-paced, tempting, hard-to-put-down story with vivacious characters, an unpredictable plot, and a narrative climax worthy of the stage."

—*Newcity Lit*

TEMPER

Layne Fargo

SCOUT PRESS

New York London Toronto Sydney New Delhi

Scout Press
An Imprint of Simon & Schuster, Inc.
1230 Avenue of the Americas
New York, NY 10020

First Scout Press trade paperback edition April 2020

SCOUT PRESS and colophon are registered trademarks of Simon & Schuster, Inc.

For information about special discounts for bulk purchases, please contact Simon & Schuster Special Sales at 1-866-506-1949 or business@simonandschuster.com.

The Simon & Schuster Speakers Bureau can bring authors to your live event. For more information or to book an event, contact the Simon & Schuster Speakers Bureau at 1-866-248-3049 or visit our website at www.simonspeakers.com.

Interior design by Jaime Putorti

Manufactured in the United States of America

10   9   8   7   6   5   4   3   2   1

The Library of Congress has cataloged the hardcover edition as follows:

Names: Fargo, Layne, author.
Title: Temper / Layne Fargo.
Description: New York : Scout Press, 2019.
Identifiers: LCCN 2018028225 | ISBN 9781982106720 (hardcover) |
    ISBN 9781982106737 (ebook)
Subjects: LCSH: Actresses—Fiction. | Ambition—Fiction. | Violence in the Workplace—
    Fiction. | Chicago (Ill.)—Fiction. | GSAFD: Noir fiction.
Classification: LCC PS3606.A685 T46 2019 | DDC 813/.6—dc23
LC record available at https://lccn.loc.gov/2018028225

ISBN 978-1-9821-0672-0
ISBN 978-1-9821-1250-9 (pbk)
ISBN 978-1-9821-0673-7 (ebook)

For Nate, the anti-Malcolm Mercer

TEMPER

KIRA

THE ACTRESS EXITS THE THEATER IN TEARS.

It takes her a few seconds to realize she has an audience. My audition is the last of the day, so I'm the only one left waiting in the row of mismatched chairs set up against the lobby wall. When our eyes meet, she takes a small, hiccuping breath, choking back her emotions like vomit.

I don't remember her name, and I'm not sure she ever knew mine, but we did a play together once. Years ago, one of my first jobs in Chicago. She was the heroine, and I was the slut who seduced her boyfriend. (It wasn't a very good play.) I've seen her a few times since then, on posters for shows at Lookingglass, the Goodman, Steppenwolf—the type of theaters I can't afford to go to unless I know someone who can hook me up with comp tickets.

She was always so poised, one of those classic ingenues with perfect ballerina posture. But right now she's a wreck: shoulders hunched and shaking, lightning-strike lines of mascara cutting down her face. She didn't just lose it on the way out, after the audition was over. No, she's been going for ten minutes, minimum. Which is about the same amount of time she was inside the theater.

What the hell happened in there?

Before I have a chance to ask, she hurries toward the door, ducking her head so her hair sweeps across her cheekbones like closing curtains. Even the sweltering wind blowing in from the street outside can't stop me from shivering. As if I wasn't already nervous enough about this damn audition.

The door separating the lobby from the theater swings open again, and a dark-haired young girl wearing crooked cat-eye glasses comes out. She stops on the threshold, holding the door ajar with her hip, and looks down at the clipboard in her hands.

"Kira Rascher?"

Here we go. Whatever went down in that room, it's my turn now.

I hand her my stapled-together headshot and résumé, and she stacks them on top of the clipboard. Her fingernails are bitten down to the quick, what's left of them covered in chipped black nail polish.

"After you," she says.

The temperature inside the theater is at least a ten-degree drop-off from the lobby. All my exposed skin—arms, shoulders, the sliver of leg bared by the slit in my long skirt—prickles with goose bumps. The lights are on full, but the black paint on the walls swallows up their brightness.

The Indifferent Honest Theater Company is a typical Chicago storefront theater: a former retail property hollowed out and turned into an intimate performance venue. *Intimate*, of course, meaning claustrophobic. The space holds fewer than fifty seats, and the stage is just a scrap of bare floor in front of them.

Sitting dead center, a few rows up, is Malcolm Mercer—the man I'm here to see.

It's so surreal to be standing here in front of him, for him to play the role of spectator. We've spent hours together in this room, but this is the first time I've ever seen him out of character. Last time I saw him perform, he had his hair buzzed short to play a soldier with PTSD. It's growing back in now, long enough to show the curl in it again, but he used to wear it even longer, skimming his jaw. He'd use it almost as another prop, raking his fingers through it, flipping it out of his eyes, seizing it at the root.

In addition to directing, Malcolm plays the male lead in every Indifferent Honest show—the perks of being artistic director. The play I'm auditioning for is a two-hander, so if I get the part, he'll be both my boss and my sole costar.

Intimate indeed.

Only his eyes move, tracking me as I take my position at center stage. You'd never guess he'd just witnessed—or maybe caused—an emotional meltdown. He seems entirely at ease, legs crossed at the knee, steepled fingers resting on his thigh.

The clipboard girl tries to hand him my headshot, but he ignores her. The blond woman sitting next to him—Executive Director Joanna Cuyler, the other half of Indifferent Honest—takes it instead. Joanna is intimidating in her own way, with her razor-sharp bob and wide-set feline eyes. She spends a few seconds glancing from the picture to my face and back again, like she's checking my ID at airport security, before tucking it under the spiral-bound notebook in her lap.

Malcolm's lips are slightly pursed, as if he's on the verge of speaking, but Joanna is the one who prompts me to begin. "Whenever you're ready, Ms. Rascher."

There's a certain facial expression I'm used to seeing in audition rooms: a mask of polite detachment, not quite bored, but not too interested, either. That's the way Joanna looks at me when I start my monologue.

But that's not how Malcolm looks at me.

I'm being ridiculous. Of course he's staring at me, I'm standing on a stage doing a monologue. He's paying close attention to my audition—it's his job, for fuck's sake.

But I've done hundreds of auditions, far too many of them for creepy assholes who leered at me, asked me to twirl, bend over, take off my top. And none of them ever looked at me the way Malcolm Mercer is looking at me right now.

His gaze is hard. It has weight and heat, and it seems to touch my whole body at once. I've known since I was thirteen what it feels like when a man mentally undresses me, and this is something else.

It's like he's stripping off my skin instead of my clothes, peeling it all away so he can see the blood and bone and sinew underneath. So he can expose every piece of me.

I reverse two words of one line and stutter over another. A drop of sweat traces a jagged path down my back despite the chill. My voice is getting higher, smaller, a tremor under every syllable knocking the words off-balance. The pressure of his stare feels like fingers around my throat.

This fucking bastard. I had him all wrong. When I walked in here, he wasn't relaxed. He was coiled, lying in wait. He must enjoy this—making people uncomfortable, pinning them down like specimens in a display case and watching them squirm.

Well, if this is how he made the last girl cry, it's not going to work on me. Crying is easy. Anyone can cry. Hell, I've been able to make myself do it on command since my first acting class. The more he stares, the more I want to get through my monologue just to spite him.

So I do the one thing you're never supposed to do during an audition: I stare back.

At least it's in character, since my audition piece is a blistering speech given by a woman who just found out her lover has been cheating on her. I look Malcolm dead in the eye and pretend he's every man who's ever pissed me off. Soon I've lost track of where my simulated rage stops and my actual anger begins. But it doesn't matter, because with each line I'm gaining strength, shaking off his grip. The air between us seems to crackle.

By the time I reach the end, the words are spilling from my mouth like they're my own, raw and real rather than rehearsed. I let a beat go by after the last line, then drop character and lift the corners of my lips, the way I practiced in the mirror at home. My natural expression is the kind that inspires passing strangers to tell me to cheer up, so I have to rehearse my smiles almost as much as my lines.

For the next few seconds, the only sound in the theater is the scratch of Joanna's pen in her notebook. She draws a long line across the page, emphasizing something or striking it out, I don't know which.

Malcolm doesn't move, doesn't speak, doesn't even blink, so neither do I. I want to look away from him—to look anywhere else, really: the floor, the emergency exit sign, my own feet—but breaking eye contact now would feel like conceding territory, admitting defeat.

It's Joanna who interrupts the silence. She seems to do all the talking around here.

"Thank you very much, Kira."

She glances over at Malcolm and raises her eyebrows. He leans back a little in his seat. Not a word spoken, but something has clearly passed between them.

Finally—*finally*—his eyes move away from mine, and I feel like I've won whatever strange game we were playing.

But my triumph is short lived. His gaze slides down my neck and along my collarbone, coming to rest on the swell of my chest, and I can feel my smile decomposing.

He's not evaluating my talent or weighing whether I'm right for the part. He's trying to decide if he's interested in sleeping with me.

Fuck this guy. I should tell him off and storm out. I've wanted to do that every time this has happened before. Now is my chance.

When Malcolm lifts his eyes to meet mine again, I'm ready, a whole battery of retorts locked and loaded. But before I can unleash them, he disarms me completely.

"You're bleeding," he says.

2

JOANNA

OF COURSE, I SAW THE BLOOD AS SOON AS SHE WALKED IN. A small red streak on her right breast. I'm surprised it took Mal so long to notice, the way he's been staring at her.

"Excuse me?" Kira says.

"You're bleeding," Mal repeats.

She looks down at her chest. So does he.

For God's sake. He could at least attempt to be subtle about it.

I'd guessed that the mark was a cut or a scratch. Then it occurred to me it might be stray lipstick; the color is similar enough to the stop sign shade she has on her lips (a little much, and not just for an audition).

"Oh, that's just—it's stage blood," she says. "I'm a teaching artist. With the Will Power program?"

I noticed that on her résumé. I also noticed she left off the exclamation point at the end of the name. The program coordinator and I dated, briefly, and she always had extra promotional flyers and postcards scattered all over her coffee table. A creepy cartoon Shakespeare head and the words *WILL POWER!* in cheerful comic-book text.

Now Kira's cheeks are burning almost as bright as the blood-stain. But she doesn't try to cover it up or wipe it away. Mal will like that. He likes her already, I can tell. He liked her as soon as she walked in, before she'd even begun her monologue (which I'll admit was good, even with those minor mistakes at the start). He gets a certain shine in his eyes, like a starving tiger spotting its next meal.

Too bad she's all wrong for the part. I told Mal we should have put more in the audition notice than a gender and age range. He loathes typecasting, but it has its uses. Mara is supposed to be a tight, contained character, full of secrets. Kira is just the opposite: an open book, everything she's feeling at any given moment broadcast in Technicolor across her face. Did she think she was fooling anyone with that rictus of a smile?

And then there are her looks. She's beautiful, to be sure, but in an obvious way. Nearly vulgar. Her long black dress isn't revealing, but a body like hers can't help drawing attention to itself. As she talks, she keeps shifting from one leg to the other, jutting her hips out, which pulls the fabric over her breasts so taut it's practically see-through. She looks like she should be on the cover of a 1950s pulp novel with a pistol in her hand.

"We're doing our *Macbeth* workshop this week," she's saying now—vamping, desperate to fill the silence. "The, uh, dagger scene was today, and I came straight from there, so . . ." I should put her out of her misery. If I leave it up to Mal, he'll let her twist just to watch her unravel.

I raise my hand. She falls silent, but her lips stay parted, showing the wet point of her tongue.

"Thank you for coming in, Kira. We'll be in touch." A polite lie I've told so often, I don't even feel guilty about it anymore.

She smiles again—even less convincing this time. "Okay. Thank you."

I watch her go. Mal doesn't. He keeps staring at the spot on the stage where she was standing a moment ago, as though he can still see her there.

"Was she the last one?" he asks.

"For today. We have a couple more scheduled for tomorrow afternoon."

We've been here since eight this morning, and we haven't had anything to eat since Mal sent our intern, Bryn, out to pick up breakfast at Chicago Bagel Authority. I'm more than ready for a proper meal. After a day of auditions, Mal and I always go out for dinner and talk through our options. I was thinking La Crêperie on Clark Street, but I'll see what he's craving.

Bryn hands me the clipboard with the audition list. She's done a decent job today, though I'm not about to admit that to Mal. He's the one who hired her—his idea of helping me, when I made the mistake of complaining about my workload in the ramp-up to the new season. So now, in addition to doing all my own work, I have to supervise hers. But it was a nice change, not having to run back and forth to the lobby and corral all the actors and their assorted neuroses on my own.

Mal wants Bryn to stage-manage, too. He says she has experience. I'm guessing said experience is limited to high school plays performed on a stage stuck to the end of a basketball court. *Temper* isn't a very complex show, though, from a technical standpoint. One set, minimal props, all costume changes done onstage. She'd have to really be trying, to fuck it up.

"Should I cancel the others?" I ask him.

We may have ended on a weak note this afternoon, but several of the women we saw earlier in the day were excellent. Exactly what we're looking for. It's unfortunate about the actress who auditioned next-to-last. I had high hopes for her; she was fantastic in the adaptation of the Persephone myth the Hypocrites did last spring. But someone who breaks down crying during an audition isn't going to last a minute in rehearsal with Mal.

He stands and stretches, rolling his neck from side to side until it cracks. The hem of his shirt lifts, exposing a strip of bare skin above his belt.

Then he reaches for my notebook. I grip the sides, the metal binding cutting into my palm. But he isn't trying to flip it open, just tilt it up. So he can slide Kira Rascher's headshot out from underneath.

He holds the picture up to the light and stares at it for a long moment, his lower lip caught between his teeth. There's a vein in the center of his forehead that always stands out when he's concentrating. Right now it's throbbing, steady as a metronome.

"Sure," he says. "Cancel them."

However much he may have liked her, there's no way he'll pick her. Not for the play, anyway. Mal prefers to sculpt from more pliable material, and Kira Rascher seems like the type who would snap before she'd bend.

The longer he keeps staring at her picture, though, the less certain I feel. Mal can say more with a pause than most people convey with a torrent of words, and usually I can interpret his silences like a second language. But for the first time in the dozen years we've been working together, I have no idea what he's thinking.

3

KIRA

AFTER THE CHILL OF THE THEATER, THE OUTDOORS FEELS even more like an oven. We're having one of those sweltering late-September weeks Chicago suffers through every year before the weather turns for good—the last gasp of summer breathing down the neck of fall. The heat rising from the sidewalk on Belmont Avenue wraps around my ankles and slides up under the hem of my skirt.

The first thing I see, once my eyes adjust to the sunlight, is my roommate's black Jetta, parked right outside the building in defiance of the loading zone signs. When Spence dropped me off for the audition, I told him not to wait for me, so of course he's still here. I should have begged him to stay, then I'm sure he would've gone straight home.

Spence is leaning against the passenger-side door, holding a cup of iced coffee in each hand. His sunglasses are low enough on his nose to show off the dense slashes of his dark eyebrows. He looks like a charming serial killer trying to lure unsuspecting women into his vehicle.

"So?" He offers me the fuller of the two cups. "How did it go?"

As I reach for the coffee, his eyes snag on the same spot that caught Malcolm Mercer's attention. "Oh, shit," he says. "You've got a little bit of—"

He swipes his fingers through the condensation on his coffee cup to wet them, then rubs at the top of my right breast.

"There, got it. Don't worry, I'm sure they didn't even notice."

I try my coffee. It's so sweet it makes my teeth hurt.

"He noticed," I say.

"How do you know?"

"That's the only thing he said the whole time I was in there. 'You're bleeding.'"

I hate my job every day, but I especially hate dagger day, when my teaching partner and I act out the murder of King Duncan by smearing a mixture of dish soap, chocolate syrup, and red food coloring all over a pair of plastic Halloween-store daggers. The high school students love it, but it makes a hell of a mess. Sometimes I'll find sticky red spots on myself days later—under my elbow, in the shell of my ear, between my toes.

Maybe I should have said "The Scottish Play," rather than *Macbeth*. I'm not superstitious about saying the M— word in a theater, but Malcolm seems like the type who might be.

"I bet it went better than you think," Spence says.

Easy for him to say. When Spence talked me into moving to Chicago with him after college, he was a pathetic struggling actor like me, but now he's a professional fight choreographer—one of the most in-demand in the city. He's already been hired to do the fights for all four shows in Indifferent Honest's season.

I'm pretty sure his connection has something to do with how I got on the audition schedule despite my less-than-illustrious list of credits. It's almost unheard of for Indifferent Honest to hold open auditions at all. They usually stick to hiring performers who have an existing relationship with the company. Spence swears he didn't pull any strings, but the more he denies it, the less I believe him.

Not that I give a shit. I may be sick of playing the same old bimbo and bad girl parts, but now that I'm over thirty, even those opportunities are likely to shrivel up soon. I'm not above riding Spence's coattails if they'll get me where I want to go.

A CTA bus lumbers by, hot wind gusting in its wake. I take another sip of coffee, biting down on the straw. "The girl who went before me came out crying."

"Well," Spence says. "Then we know at least one other audition was worse than yours."

I glare at him over the lid of my coffee cup. He keeps right on grinning. After all these years, he's developed an immunity to even my most poisonous looks.

"Come on." He loops his arm around my shoulders and presses a kiss to my temple as he steers me toward the passenger door of his car. "You deserve some day drinking."

WE HEAD FOR LADY GREGORY'S, SPENCE'S FAVORITE NEIGH-borhood drinking spot. He would say it's because of the ambiance, but really it's because the place is within easy stumbling distance of our Andersonville apartment.

Spence requests a seat in the Library, the section at the back of the bar set up like an English nobleman's study complete with a fire-place, built-in bookshelves loaded with leather-bound books, and a stained-glass dome set into the ceiling. This is how Spence would decorate our place, if he had the money.

Since it's a Wednesday between the lunch and dinner rushes, we practically have the place to ourselves. The hostess gives us one of the tables by the picture windows looking out on Berwyn Avenue, where the weekly farmer's market is setting up.

I sit on the bench seat with my back to the window, and Spence slides in beside me. Like always, he decided what he wanted to order before we even walked in the door, so while I browse the menu, he stares off into space, twisting his fingers in the ends of my hair.

Then suddenly he sits up straighter and stops touching me, slid-ing over so there are a few inches of space separating our hips. I know what that means: target acquired.

I follow his gaze across the restaurant. He's staring at one of the waiters, a young guy with curly brown hair and a splash of freckles across the bridge of his nose. He's cute. A little innocent-looking for my taste, but Spence likes that kind of thing, at least in men.

There's something familiar about him. Spence sees it too.

"Hey," he says. "Isn't that—"

It is. The actor who played Horatio to Malcolm Mercer's Hamlet.

Hamlet was the first Indifferent Honest production Spence and I ever saw, back when the company was still operating out of Malcolm and Joanna's Ravenswood loft. The audience had to stand for the whole show, our backs against the crumbling walls, and the set was nothing but a couple of folding chairs and some mismatched, overlapping thrift store carpets. It was grungy and chaotic, and they were probably violating about a hundred different fire and safety regulations, but to this day it's one of the best pieces of theater I've ever seen.

Spence claps his hands together. "It's a sign! We have to talk to him."

"No, let's not—"

But it's too late, Spence is already waving him our way—and, at the same time, scooting over another inch so we look as platonic as possible.

The waiter comes to stand beside our table, gripping the back of one of the empty chairs across from us. He's grown a little thicker around the waist since we saw him onstage years ago. Otherwise, he doesn't seem to have aged a day. He has one of those faces that will probably look boyish when he's fifty.

"Hey. Everything okay here? Molly will be over in a minute to take your—"

"We loved you in *Hamlet*," Spence says. Speaking for both of us.

The waiter's standard service-industry smile glitches a little. "Wow. Good memory."

"Maybe you're just memorable. I'm Spence."

He sticks out his hand—not for a handshake, like a normal person, but with his palm turned down and his wrist bent, like he's a sovereign offering his signet ring for a kiss. The waiter shakes it anyway, wrapping his hand around the tips of Spence's fingers. He has a cuff bracelet on his wrist, thick brown leather with a tooled design. Spence can't stand it when men wear jewelry, but he must think this guy is attractive enough to merit an exception.

"I'm, uh, Jason." He says his name like he's not quite sure he's got the right answer. He's blushing, too, his milk-and-cookie-crumbs complexion flushed feverish pink. Spence tends to have that effect on people. "Jason Grady."

"Nice to meet you, Jason Grady." Spence cocks his head toward me; so he hasn't forgotten I'm here after all. "This is my roommate, Kira. She's an actor too. She actually had an audition at Indifferent Honest this afternoon."

"Oh?" Jason looks to me for confirmation.

I nod, once—the bare minimum. I don't want to talk about this, especially not with a stranger. Leave it to Spence to turn cheer-me-up drinks into a chance to get himself laid.

Spence leans forward and drops his voice to a stage whisper, like he's about to reveal a secret. "For the new show Malcolm Mercer's directing."

Jason doesn't let his smile slip this time, but it stiffens and leaves his eyes. "Oh wow, that's . . ." He shakes his head, quick and violent like he's trying to dislodge something. "Well, good luck. Can I start you guys off with something to drink?"

Jason keeps on smiling and even trades a few more flirtatious quips with Spence while he's taking our order. But as he writes, I could swear his hands are trembling.

BY THE TIME SPENCE IS READY TO GO HOME, OUR DAY DRINK-ing has turned into night drinking. It's not so late—a little past seven—but it's already fully dark outside. Soon enough it will be pitch-black before five p.m.—my least favorite part of the year.

Our actual server, a wholesome-looking redhead with wire-rim glasses, is the one who brought the drinks—red wine for me, a whiskey cocktail with the melodramatic name "Gods and Fighting Men" for Spence—and then took care of us as we lingered over dinner, dessert, and several more rounds from the bar.

Jason hasn't set foot in the Library again. More than once, though, I've noticed him glancing in our direction as he's carrying a tray from the kitchen or ringing up a customer's credit card at the cash register. At first, I figured he was just reacting to the less-than-subtle *come-hither* signals Spence kept sending his way, but that can't be it, because whenever his eyes passed over our table, he wasn't looking at Spence. He was looking at me.

I head downstairs to the bathroom so I can avoid the awkward moment when I offer to pay my half of the bill, and Spence refuses to let me. I have to grip the banister to steady myself as I descend the winding wooden steps. I'm nowhere near drunk—despite Spence's best efforts to be a bad influence, I limited myself to two glasses of wine and a sip of his cocktail—but I still feel unsteady, the caffeine and alcohol warring with the leftover audition adrenaline thrumming through my veins.

That fucking audition. Over the years, I've gotten pretty good at shrugging off even the worst audition experiences. That shit will break you, unless you can shed it all like a snake skin as soon as you walk out of the room.

Usually, though, I leave with at least some sense of how I did, whether the director liked me or not. But Malcolm—he might have been blown away by me, or he might think I'm the worst actress in Chicago. Those dark eyes of his are like inkblots, open to any interpretation. I swear I can feel them on me even now.

I'm so lost in thought, I'm pushing open the bathroom door before I register that I've made it down to the basement. So I don't notice the person moving in the shadows over my shoulder until their hand is already on my elbow.

It's not a grab or a grip, just a light touch to get my attention. My heart starts hammering anyway.

I whirl around and find Jason Grady standing next to me. He's still wearing his ugly beige polo shirt with the Lady Gregory's monogram stitched on the chest, but he's taken off his apron. It's gripped in his fist, the strings wound tight around his knuckles.

"Can I talk to you for a second?"

The words rush out of his mouth like he's over-rehearsed them in his head. When I don't answer right away, he looks down at the floor and scratches at the nape of his neck. He might even be blushing again, but I can't tell in the dim light of the basement.

I readjust my purse strap and fold my arms across my chest. "Okay."

Jason frowns, and for a moment he looks his age, maybe even a little older. Shadows settle into the hollows under his eyes, etch out the fine lines around his mouth.

"How well do you know Malcolm Mercer?" he asks.

"I don't."

"But you've heard about him?"

I nod, though I'm not entirely sure what he means. Of course I've heard about Malcolm. Anyone with even a vague connection to the Chicago theater community at least recognizes the man's name. He does have a reputation for being intense—well deserved, if what went down during my audition was standard behavior—but as far as I know, it's just typical macho Method acting bullshit. Nothing I haven't dealt with before. Last year I did a show with a guy who stopped showering and picked bloody pockmarks into his arms so he could really "understand" his schizophrenic character. If I could kiss him on the lips every night for eight weeks straight, I can put up with anything.

"Whatever you've heard," Jason says. "Trust me, the truth is worse. Mal and I were involved for . . . well, way longer than I'd like to admit, and not just professionally."

So Malcolm Mercer likes men, too. Spence will be thrilled; he's always complaining he never meets any guys who occupy the same section of the Kinsey scale as him.

Malcolm's sexuality may be news to me, but the fact that he's an asshole isn't. Most directors are, in my experience. They're either tyrants who run their rehearsals like boot camps and scream themselves hoarse if you drop a line, or lechers who try to stare down your shirt and give you unnecessarily slow shoulder rubs backstage to help you "loosen up."

If you're really lucky, of course, you get a director who's both. But still: nothing I don't know how to handle. Learning to cope with men like that is a foundational skill for any actress, like knowing stage right from stage left.

I smile at Jason. It's condescending, but so is this little speech he's giving me.

"Look, I appreciate the heads-up, but I can take care of myself."

Jason takes another step toward me. He was already too close, well into my personal space, but he's so thoroughly unintimidating, with his narrow shoulders and wide blue eyes, that even though he's got me backed against the wall with his body between me and the only exit, I can't talk myself into feeling threatened.

His Horatio seemed sweet at first, too. Jason played him as an anxious romantic, burning with unrequited love for his best friend, the Prince of Denmark. But by the end of the play there was something sinister about him, a sick jealousy seething under all his smiles that made you wonder whether he might have pushed the fair Ophelia into that weeping brook himself.

"You don't have to take my word for it," he says. "Ask anyone who's ever worked with him."

"What, do you guys have a support group or something?"

Jason reaches for my elbow again. This time his fingers dig in around the bone.

"Mal hurts people," he says. "He'll hurt you, too."

All the stammering schoolboy sweetness from earlier is gone. Or maybe it was only an act to begin with.

I start to wrench my arm out of his grip, but he's already letting go, backing away from me—slowly, like he's afraid I'll bite. I always look angry, so when I'm pissed off for real, I come across downright murderous. Spence told me once that when I'm mad I look like an actual Fury, like I could strike a man dead with my eyes.

But Jason doesn't flee. Not yet, anyway. He's reaching behind his back, fumbling for something.

"At least take this." He pulls his order pad out of his pocket. The top sheet already has a phone number scrawled across it. He rips it off and holds it out to me. "If you need help or—or anything. Call me."

"I told you, I don't need your help."

"You will." He stares at me for a moment, then shakes his head. "God, you're just his type."

I may have only officially met Malcolm today, but I've known plenty of men like him before, and their "type" is almost exclusively sweet little things young and stupid enough to worship them as the gods they wish they were. Jason must think I'm stupid, then, because I'm obviously not that young anymore.

But I know what I'm getting myself into. I know how to handle men like Malcolm Mercer. And if just exchanging stares with him could spark the performance I gave today, imagine what sharing a stage with him would do.

4

JOANNA

FIVE MORE MINUTES UNTIL MAL GETS HOME. MAYBE LESS.

Morning people are rare creatures in the theater community, but the start of the day is always when I'm most productive. I can usually get a couple of hours of work in before Mal wakes up, then another hour while he goes for his daily run. He does a few miles most days, down the lakefront trail and back again.

My hands are starting to cramp, but I keep them hammering over the laptop keys. Answering emails, logging expenses, adding new items to the to-do list in my notebook faster than I can check off the old ones. Ignoring the hollow roar of my stomach. Eating breakfast just slows me down, so I subsist on coffee until I leave for the theater.

There's never any food here anyway. Neither of us cooks, so the kitchen has become my de facto home office. It's the one area of the apartment we haven't gotten around to remodeling, so it still has the same checkerboard linoleum floors and sagging cabinet doors that were there when we moved in. But it has a window, which is more than I can say for my office at Indifferent Honest. A barred, grimy window that looks out on the brick side of an adjacent building, but still. Better than nothing.

The screech of the gate, then footsteps on the stairs. He's back.

I shut my laptop just as Mal walks in. The dining table wobbles when I stand up. Like most of our furniture, it's left over from a show: the strip club set of our production of Patrick Marber's *Closer*, five years ago. Or was it six? It's hideous, made of scratched-up Lucite, but the top is always scattered with enough unopened mail and theater-related detritus to render the clear surface opaque.

I get a clean mug out of the cabinet and pour Mal some coffee from the scorch-marked glass carafe. Our morning routine.

He takes his coffee and sips, without looking at me. I don't think he's looked directly at me since he came in. I'm used to his moods by now, but this feels different. He seems distracted, detached, like his body is here with me, but his mind is elsewhere.

A triangle of sweat darkens the front of his gray T-shirt. He strips the shirt off and uses it to sop up the perspiration on his forehead and the back of his neck. He misses a spot: one bead of moisture traveling down his spine, disappearing into the waistband of his shorts.

I lean against the counter, the peeling edge of the laminate digging into my hip, and fold my arms. "Have you done any more thinking about—"

Mal nods. A little sharp—he's annoyed with me. This is far from the first time I've brought the subject up. Every time I do, if I get any answer at all, it's just that he's *still thinking*.

But I shouldn't *have* to keep bringing it up. Usually I need to cut Mal's callbacks off before they get out of hand, not harass him to schedule them in the first place. Mal loves auditions. He'd make every last actor in Chicago parade across our stage if he could.

Not me. I hate the fear, the desperation, the naked longing on their faces. It taints the air. I can feel it all over me, sometimes for days afterward, like a film on my skin. It's not that I'm judging them or pitying them. I know all too well what it's like to feel that way, to want something so much and have no control over whether or not you get it.

That's why, whenever possible, I try to talk Mal into limiting audition slots to people we already know. Usually that means the best roles go to whichever actors or actresses he happens to be fucking at the moment, but right now he's between conquests. So here we are.

"We really need to make some decisions, narrow the field."

Mal doesn't respond. He's drinking his coffee. Still not looking at me.

"Why don't you go shower," I say. "And then we can sit down and talk through the rest of the—"

"I have to go out for a while."

"Right now?"

No point in asking him where he's going. If he wanted to tell me, he would.

"We can talk as soon as I get back. I promise."

He drains his coffee, then reaches across me to set the mug down on the counter.

He's so close to me now I can smell his sweat, feel the heat rising from his skin. I don't move, but every molecule in my body strains toward him like a dog at the end of its leash. It's been three days since he last touched me, and that was accidental, his fingertips brushing mine as I handed him the preliminary plans for the set.

"Okay," I say.

A rare broad smile, the skin around his eyes crinkling like paper. He brushes a kiss across my cheekbone—so quick I feel his breath more than his lips on my skin—and then heads for the bathroom.

There's a little liquid left in his mug, just enough to coat the bottom. I tip my head back and let the coffee trickle onto my tongue and down my throat, before placing the mug in the sink.

I try to corral the papers strewn over the table so they're compact enough to carry back to the theater. As I'm stuffing the stack into my laptop bag, something slides out and off the edge of the table. I bend down to pick it up.

Kira Rascher's brown eyes stare back at me.

Her headshot shouldn't be here. Bryn was supposed to file all the materials from the auditions days ago. I watched her do it, bent over the bottom drawer of the filing cabinet in my office for far longer than should have been necessary for such a simple task. Mal must have taken Kira's or asked Bryn to get it for him. Brought it home with him, left it *here*. Where he knew I would find it.

I don't understand. He hasn't even mentioned Kira to me. Not once. When we went to dinner after the auditions, I brought the collection of headshots like I always do, sorted them into piles on the table between us. He didn't raise any objections when I put hers into the *no* pile.

There are fingerprints all over the glossy paper. Not only around the edges. Over her lips, the curve of her cheek. All the places he touched.

I want to rip her down the middle.

5

KIRA

WHEN I SWITCHED ON MY PHONE AT LUNCHTIME AND SAW A message waiting for me, I got embarrassingly excited. But it was only an all-caps text from Spence, telling me to STOP CHECKING YOUR DAMN PHONE, WOMAN.

Last night, when I'd gotten to the point of poking at the home button every ten seconds like a lab rat pushing a lever, Spence resorted to wrestling the phone out of my hands and hiding it. I stole it back from him after a few hours, though, and then spent most of the night switching off between staring at the glow of the screen and the ceiling of my bedroom.

At least I have a place to hide out during my lunch break. Usually we end up eating in the faculty lounge (that's where my teaching partner is right now; Tim is a freak of nature who actually enjoys small talk), but at this school the teachers have little offices attached to their classrooms. The English teacher whose class we're commandeering this week let us use hers as our "backstage" area. It's pretty much a glorified closet, papered with posters of kittens spouting inspirational slogans and B-list celebrities imploring you to *READ*, but it's better than nothing.

Sometimes I can't believe I voluntarily set foot in a high school every day, after hating it so much the first time around. My mother always insisted her high school years were the best of her life. Sure, maybe when you're class president and captain of the volleyball team and on homecoming court four times in a row, like she and my sister were. But when you're a straight-C fuckup who gets sent to detention at least once a month because the boys in study hall won't stop trying to unhook your bra, it's not such a fun time.

My Lady Macbeth gown is in a heap on top of the duffel bags we use to transport all our props and costumes. They're big enough to hide human bodies in, so even stacked they take up most of the floor space in here. I'm still wearing leggings and the black camisole our boss, Lauren, insists I keep on under the dress. She's concerned the neckline might prove too "distracting" without it. Which is ridiculous—if I learned anything in high school, it's that teenage boys will stare at my rack whether I'm wearing a wet T-shirt or a nun's habit.

After Lauren instituted this rule, I asked Tim if he agreed with her. He just shrugged and said he didn't think of me that way. Tim is my age, but he's been married for ten years already, and he's one of those guys who acts like women other than his wife don't even register as sexual beings. The two of them are revolting together. She packs his lunch for him every day and leaves a note inside, like he's a third grader and not a thirtysomething man.

Alas, I don't have a wife—or a husband, as my mother and sister never tire of reminding me—so my lunch consists of two granola bars and a Diet Coke, all from the vending machines in the cafeteria. I take a swig of Coke to wash the granola grit out of my mouth, then lean against the edge of the teacher's desk and swipe past Spence's message to open the browser app. I tap the letter *m* with my thumb, and I don't even have to type in the next letter for it to autocomplete *malcolm mercer*.

I am so fucking pathetic.

The top news result is a *Trib* article—posted a few hours ago, so I couldn't have read it during any of my shameful Google-stalking sprees last night. "Indifferent Honest Debuts New Work by Mystery Playwright," the headline reads. By Robert Kenmore.

My ex has been writing for the *Chicago Tribune* for several years now, but seeing his name in print still catches me off guard. Our breakup was fresh when I heard Rob got the newspaper gig, and my first thought was to wonder what it would be like to have him critique my work, to see all the things he was too nice to say to my face written down for the whole city to read.

But I shouldn't have worried. In all this time, I haven't done a single show worthy of Rob's notice, let alone his criticism.

> This fall, Lakeview's Indifferent Honest Theater Company will present the world premiere of *Temper*, a new play by L. S. Sedgwick. Ms. Sedgwick has no previous professional credits, but the company's press release about the upcoming production describes her as a "bold new voice" based in the Midwest.

Well, that explains why my search came up empty when I tried to find other L. S. Sedgwick plays to read for potential audition pieces. If she'd done so much as a fringe festival one-act before, Rob would have found out about it. Not only is he a professional journalist, he's a total nerd who does research for fun. We met when he was dramaturging a Victorian play I did at a now-defunct storefront company in Uptown, and he dug up every obscure fact the director asked for, from what our characters would have eaten for breakfast to an appropriate period print for the wallpaper decorating the set.

In lieu of a picture of the mysterious playwright, Rob's article is accompanied by a moody shot of Malcolm in a black turtleneck. He has his chin propped on the heel of his hand, and he's staring off into the middle distance, no doubt having Very Deep Thoughts. I should find the picture ridiculous, laughable, pretentious—and if Spence were here, I'd pretend I did—but the truth is, it fills me with a strange, stomach-twisting jealousy. All I can think is, *No one will ever take me that seriously.*

Tim returns from lunch with a paper napkin tucked into the collar of his puke-green polyester doublet, eating cookies out of a Ziploc bag.

"There you are," he says. "Being antisocial again, I see."

I don't know how he stands it. The teachers always ask the same questions, at every school: what it's like to be a professional actor, if I've been in anything they would have seen, whether I know this or that famous person. They think what we do is so glamorous, but in reality, it's just a different kind of drudgery.

The worst are the ones who had artistic dreams of their own at some point. Maybe they played Adelaide in their high school production of *Guys and Dolls*, or they took an improv comedy class at Second City once—or even worse, they actually tried to make it, spent six months to a year waiting tables and going to cattle calls in New York or LA before giving up and getting a real job and a house in the suburbs. Those ones always act like they know me already, like we have something in common, and it makes me want to run away screaming.

Tim holds the bag out, offering me a cookie. They're lumpy and brown—made by his wife, too, no doubt, which means they're "healthy" and probably taste awful. But my sorry excuse for a lunch has left me hungry enough to take the chance.

"Any news?" he asks.

He asked me the same thing this morning when he picked me up for our break-of-dawn drive to the suburbs, and my answer was identical then: "Nope. Nothing yet."

I shouldn't have told him about the stupid audition in the first place. He'll probably keep asking me if I've heard back yet until the show's goddamn opening night.

"I'm sorry," he says. "But hey—life of an actor, right?"

He grins at me, eyebrows raised, waiting for me to smile back. I do—a little too broad, top teeth showing. In my experience, this is the easiest way to get him to shut up.

Tim pops another cookie into his mouth and mumbles through crumbs, "Hey, do you know who that guy is?"

"What guy?" I take a nibble from the edge of my cookie. Yep, just as I thought: tastes like chocolate-flavored cardboard.

"The one talking to Ms. Clark. He doesn't look like a teacher."

I bow my head over my phone again so Tim won't catch me rolling my eyes. I find it absurd that he insists on calling all the teachers "Ms." and "Mr." even when we're not within earshot of the students.

Tim gestures in the general direction of the hallway. "Him. In the gray jacket."

I stick the rest of the cookie into my mouth—best to get it over with—and peer around the office door.

The teacher is standing outside the classroom, hugging a stack of folders against the front of her cardigan. She's so young-looking, she could pass for a student if it weren't for her dowdy outfit, which looks like something my mother would put right back on the rack at a central Ohio outlet mall.

Next to the teacher, straddling the threshold between the room and the hall, is a dark-haired man wearing a vaguely military-looking canvas jacket. She's smiling up at him with some serious *fuck me* eyes, so my guess is he must be her boyfriend, paying her a visit on her lunch hour.

Until he turns his head.

How the hell does Tim not recognize Malcolm Mercer? And more important, what the hell is Malcolm Mercer doing here?

"So?" Tim asks. "Do you know who he is?"

I shrug, without taking my eyes off Malcolm. "Must be a friend of hers."

They *do* seem pretty friendly. He's standing close to her, leaning in, and she keeps touching his sleeve to punctuate her words.

Maybe my first assumption was right—he could be fucking her, and the fact he's here at the same time I am is only a coincidence.

I've just about managed to convince myself. Then he turns and looks right at me.

He's not surprised to see me. His expression doesn't ask: *Why are you here?* It says, in no uncertain terms: *You know why.*

And then I realize—this is it. This is my callback.

"Shoot." Tim points to the clock above the chalkboard. "We're running late."

One whole minute, but who's counting? He tugs the napkin free from his collar and tosses it into the trash can.

"You coming?" he asks.

I pick up my dress, shaking out the crumbs of granola scattered over it. "I'll be out in a minute."

Tim takes his place at the front of the class, and I spy around the edge of the office door again. Now that the students are filing in, Malcolm and the teacher have moved out of the doorway. She offers him her padded swivel chair, but he demurs, heading for one of the empty desks by the exit instead.

I don't want Malcolm to see me this way. It isn't just my crushed-velvet monstrosity of a costume (though that doesn't help), it's the performance I'm about to give.

Lady Macbeth has always been a bucket-list role for me. That was one of the main draws when I applied for this job, that I'd finally get to play her. On the first day of rehearsals, I showed up off-book and abuzz with excitement. Then Lauren stopped me a stanza and a half into my first scene. My performance was "too sexy," she informed me, not "appropriate" for the students. As if they aren't Snapchatting naked pictures to each other all the time anyway.

So I tried out another version of the character. Then another. No matter how I played her, Lauren deemed my Lady M. too *something*—too loud, too dominant, too intense, too much. By the time we reached the end of the rehearsal process, I'd adjusted my performance so much it felt like a puppet show, all the blood leeched out. It still feels that way most of the time, like Lauren's sticking her hand up my ass and making my mouth flap.

I wish I could approach Malcolm and apologize in advance. Maybe I should—tap him on the shoulder, tell him this isn't the way

I want to play Lady Macbeth, that I'm capable of so much more. But he has no reason to believe me.

Unless.

Unless I show him. Forget about everything I've done before, forget what Lauren thinks is appropriate. Play the part the way I've always wanted to.

I ease the office door shut and lean against the back of it, eyes closed, thinking. Then I stop thinking and my hands go to the hem of my camisole. I strip it off and stuff it into my purse. When I put the dress back on, my cleavage bulges over the low scooped neckline.

If Tim notices my costume alteration when I join him at the front of the classroom, he doesn't give any indication. He's already launched into his start-of-class introductory spiel. He always does this part by himself. We tried doing it together at first, trading off lines like a comedy duo, but his genuine enthusiasm just made my lack thereof all the more glaring. Tim is as energetic as a children's show host, and his voice has that same shiny-plastic gleam.

Malcolm watches him, hands folded on his desk, polite and attentive as one of the suck-up honor-roll students. I'm not fooled. His showing up here isn't a friendly gesture. It's a challenge. A dare. He must have seen something he liked in my audition, but it wasn't enough to convince him to cast me. So now he's giving me one more chance to impress him, to make up his mind.

I have to take it.

For this scene we need one student to play the messenger who delivers Macbeth's letter to me. There aren't any volunteers, so Tim steps in to pick someone. He points toward the back of the classroom, and for a second I think he's calling on Malcolm—an absurd idea, though it still makes my chest clench like a fist—but he's actually pointing at the student sitting right in front of Malcolm. One of the popular kids, an almost cartoonishly handsome boy with messy-on-purpose hair and a cleft chin.

The boy groans, but he slides out of his seat and accepts the script pages. We start the scene, and he rushes through his lines in a mumbly monotone. Then, with all of five words left to go, he trails off, staring at my tits. A few nervous giggles bubble up from the edges of the classroom.

"Give him tending," I say, skipping over the messenger's last line. "He brings great news."

I nudge the boy back toward his desk—and steal a glance at Malcolm. He's leaning back in his seat, hands folded on his stomach, his heavy-lidded eyes slightly unfocused. I can't blame him; I'm bored, too. I've done these scenes so many times, the words feel meaningless.

Now I'm all alone at the front of the class. I press the crumpled piece of notebook paper standing in for Macbeth's letter to my chest and start my soliloquy.

"The raven himself is hoarse that croaks the fatal entrance of Duncan under my battlements."

My eyes are open, but I don't see my mundane surroundings. Instead, I picture myself standing on the rampart of a castle, staring out to the horizon. I visited the Scottish Highlands once—a long time ago now, a weekend trip during a summer drama program Spence and I did—and I call on those memories to color in the setting in my mind: the bruise-colored sky meeting the wind-scoured moors, the air so laden with moisture you could sip from it. I fantasize away my shitty synthetic dress, too, replacing it with a fine brocade gown and a fur-lined cloak. Just imagining the feel of a corset cinching my waist and fur brushing my collarbone makes me draw up into a more regal posture, changes my breathing, deepens my voice.

"Come, thick night, and pall thee in the dunnest smoke of hell."

As I approach the end of the speech, I start to imagine wind swirling around me—the violent kind that signals a coming storm—whipping up the hem of my skirt, the ends of my hair. My voice keeps mounting in power, too, reverberating like it's echoing off centuries-old stone rather than drywall and linoleum.

When Tim makes his entrance as Macbeth, I stride right up and embrace him. This isn't part of the blocking—we aren't supposed to touch each other at all until the end of the scene, when we clasp hands to seal our pact to kill the king—but it feels right.

"Great Glamis! Worthy Cawdor!" I take a step back and cup Tim's face in my hands. "Greater than both, by the all-hail hereafter!"

"My dearest love." Tim's voice is pitched higher than usual, sliding up at the end like he's asking a question. He hooks his fingers under my elbows, like he's thinking about pushing me away, but he doesn't do it.

His next line comes out steadier. "Duncan comes here tonight."

"And when goes hence?" I turn away from him. This is part of our normal blocking, but I've never been able to justify it before, I just did it because Lauren told me to. This time, though, I rub my hands together and let a look of pure, naked greed pass over my face like a shadow, and it makes total sense. I'm turning away because I don't want to expose this side of myself, the extent of my cunning, to my husband. Not until the time is right.

Moving away from Tim also gives me another chance to check on Malcolm. He's leaning forward in his seat now, elbows propped on the desktop. His expression is still difficult to read, but one thing's for sure: he's no longer bored.

As I tell Macbeth to "look like the innocent flower, but be the serpent under it," I weave around Tim, sinuous as a cat, my fingers skimming over his chest, his shoulders, up to the nape of his neck and into his hair.

This is the Lady Macbeth I love, the one who's existed in my head since the first time I read the play. The seductress who's so much smarter than her husband, who holds him in sexual thrall, manipulates him into doing her dirty work. Playing her this way is as natural as breathing.

The hardest part is pretending to be attracted to Tim. I call up the castle in my mind again and picture him standing there with me, his garish doublet replaced with a gore-stained kilt, fresh from battle. I concentrate on the image until I can smell the musk of his sweat, the coppery tang of the blood painting his brow, feel the heat of his body beside me, mixing with the misty chill of the Highland air. Tim's eyes are his best feature—pale blue, like Lake Michigan on a winter morning—and I try to imagine how blue they would look against the backdrop of the stark Scottish sky.

"We will speak further," Tim says—Macbeth's last line. The rest of the scene is mine.

"Only look up clear; to alter favor ever is to fear." I stop circling and stand facing him again, my palms flat on his chest. His breathing quickens, and I'm so close to him now I can feel the heat of it on my face.

"Leave all the rest to me."

My voice is a sultry hiss. It sounds like it belongs to someone else. I feel possessed. And I know what I have to do. What Lady Macbeth would do now, in this moment.

So I kiss him. I kiss him like I've been longing to do it for months, like I'm hungry for him, like I love him with all my soul. The full length of my body is pressed up against his, but instead of Tim's soft belly, I'm imagining battle-scarred armor—a stiff leather breastplate, the hilt of a sword hitting my hip bone.

And then I'm not imagining Tim at all anymore. In my mind, Malcolm Mercer becomes my Macbeth, and it's Malcolm's mouth moving against mine, Malcolm's hair threading through my fingers, Malcolm's hands gripping my waist, the wind surging around us both, a tempest howling in my ears—

The students erupt into a chorus of *oooooo*s like a sitcom audience, and the teacher stands up and slams her hand down on the nearest desk.

"That's enough," she says. *"Enough."*

The kids go silent. I release Tim and rock back on my heels. The teacher dismisses the class, even though the bell won't ring for another ten minutes. But one member of our audience stays put. The only one who matters to me.

Malcolm is leaning back in his chair again, palms laid flat on the desk. He licks his lips, presses them together, and then parts them slightly, like he wants to say something but he can't find the words. As if I've rendered him speechless.

The smile starts at one corner of his mouth and spreads to the other, like a slow-burning fuse. It's better than any standing ovation I've ever received. I smile back—a real smile, not one I had to rehearse in the mirror—and take a step toward him.

Tim grabs my elbow. His whole body is shaking. I've never seen him so angry before—never seen him angry at all, really, unless he was in character. It hardens the planes of his face, makes him almost handsome.

I wrench my arm out of his grip. "Let go of me."

Total hypocrisy, but I don't have time to explain. My whole body is buzzing with energy, like I could lift out of my shoes and ricochet off the ceiling. All I can think about is Malcolm, the look on his face, that smile. I have to talk to him.

But when I turn back, I find nothing but empty desks. He's gone.

6

JOANNA

I THOUGHT I MIGHT ACTUALLY FINISH WORK AT FIVE O'CLOCK like a normal person today. I worked straight through lunchtime without stopping, leaving the Potbelly sandwich Bryn brought me still in its wrapper on my desk. But Mal always knows the perfect time to make an entrance. At 4:59 sharp, he bursts through the door of my office.

I heard his heavy footsteps on the stairs leading down to the theater's basement, but Bryn, as usual, has her ears ensconced in enormous black headphones, so she starts when Mal appears in the doorway. Whenever she's here, we have to share office space; it's that or banish her to the hallway. She doesn't even have a proper desk, just a card table and a folding chair set up in the corner.

Mal seems agitated, but he's not upset. He has that hungry shine in his eyes again, though, and I have a sinking feeling I know exactly what this is about. Or rather, who.

"Bryn," I say. She doesn't answer at first, so I say her name again, louder. *"Bryn."*

She lowers the headphones so they collar her neck. They're turned up loud enough that some of the sound leaks out. Screeching guitars, the thump of electronic bass.

"I'll see you tomorrow," I tell her.

She nods and shuts her laptop. The music cuts out, but she still puts the headphones back over her ears before heading for the door. Mal doesn't step out of the way to let her pass. She has to curve herself around the doorframe like a cat to keep from brushing up against him.

Bryn is pretty, though it would appear she has no idea, from the way she dresses; all her clothes are black or gray and ripped in at least one spot. But she has that Snow White coloring, rosy lips and raven hair, wide eyes like a woodland creature. It's probably for the best she seems a little scared of Mal.

"Are you ready to schedule callbacks?" I ask Mal as soon as she's gone. "If we do them later than tomorrow, we'll probably have to push back the read-through, too, but since it's such a small cast, it shouldn't—"

"We don't need to have callbacks."

He's started pacing, making a circuit around the room. There are boxes and piles of equipment everywhere, but he sidesteps them without even looking.

"What do you mean? We always have callbacks."

"I don't need to see anyone else."

All these days of reticence, and now he's so sure. I'm fine with deferring to Mal on final casting decisions. He is the artistic director, after all; he leaves the management to me, and I leave the art to him. But usually he at least discusses them with me first.

I wonder where he went today. I wonder what she did to make up his mind.

"How about this," I say. "We can bring in a couple of different actresses, including Kira, you can read with each of them, and then—"

"No."

"I'm only talking two other people." Mal is already shaking his head. "Three at most."

"We would be wasting their time. And mine."

"It wouldn't take more than an hour, and that way we could see—"

"I told you. I don't need to see anyone else."

He's still pacing, his footfalls rattling the picture frames on the walls. Posters, for every show we've ever done together. There are so many now, I'm running out of room. I'll have to start hanging them out in the hallway. I'll keep my favorites in here, though. The ones from when we were first starting out, when my name was listed next to Mal's. We always went by alphabetical order, so I was first. *A New Production by Joanna Cuyler & Malcolm Mercer.*

"It's just, she's not very experienced, Mal. You saw her résumé."

His lips curl into a sneer. "Really, Jo? Her résumé? This isn't a fucking investment bank."

No, but it is a business, which he forgets far too often. Making art is all well and good, but no one's going to see it if you can't pay your damn electricity bill.

Mal finally comes to a stop, standing behind my desk, leaning against the chair and gripping the back. His knuckles brush my shoulder blades and his breath stirs the hair on the back of my neck. He used to stand behind me like this whenever we pulled all-nighters, drafting season announcements or hashing out production concepts. Back in the early days, before we had our shit together. When we started Indifferent Honest, we were only a year or two older than Bryn. Hard to believe I was ever so young.

"Kira has never done anything even remotely like this before," I say. "And I'm concerned that—"

"She can do it," he says.

Maybe she can. But it's a risk, and one we don't need to take. We do well enough, but small companies like ours always sit on the razor's edge of ruin. One bomb could throw our bank account into chaos for seasons to come. If the company goes under, Mal could always move on to another theater, even try for TV or film. But Indifferent Honest is my life's work. Without it, without *him*, I have nothing.

She's not the right choice. But I can't put it into words why. Usually we agree about things like this, so there's no need to.

He's leaning down now, his mouth next to my ear. "I can get it out of her."

Get it out of her. As though her performance is something he can pry from her chest cavity with his bare hands and toss onto the stage, bloody and throbbing.

He rubs my shoulders, his thumbs tracing the outline of the bones. He used to do this, too. Massaging my neck when I got too tense, pressing his fingers into the base of my skull. Back when it was just the two of us, taking on the world.

I feel a twinge in my top lip and realize I've been chewing on it. Not hard enough to draw blood. But almost.

"If you're sure," I say.

I don't have to turn around to know he's smiling.

"I'm sure," he says.

7

KIRA

FOR OBVIOUS REASONS, TIM WASN'T KEEN ON CHAUFFEURING me home today. Getting back from the suburbs on my own required three separate buses, which gave me plenty of time to think about what I'd done.

When I finally get home, I find Spence reclining on the scuffed leather sofa in our living room, reading the latest issue of *Esquire*, a plate of Brie and green grapes balanced on his stomach. His hair is damp, as if he just got out of the shower (a distinct possibility, even though it's nearing sunset).

"Long day?" he says, without looking up from the magazine.

I drop my purse on the floor behind the sofa and kick off my shoes, so hard they rebound off the cracked baseboard. "I think I lost my job."

"What?" Spence sits up to stare at me. A single grape rolls off his snack plate and onto the scraped-up hardwood.

I'm starving—my vending machine lunch wore off before I boarded the second bus—so I pick up the grape and pop it into my mouth. I can tell my announcement has truly shocked Spence, because he doesn't give me any shit for how gross I'm being, eating off our rarely-vacuumed floor.

"Malcolm Mercer came to see me today."

"What?" Spence says again, but now there's a slight waver in his voice. He's avoiding my eyes, too, and twisting the corner of the sofa cushion between his thumb and forefinger.

"You knew," I say.

He doesn't deny it. I make a fist and hit him in the arm—not hard enough to do any real damage, but with too much force to be considered playful. Spence *oof*s and winces, acting like I've actually hurt him.

"Bastard. You could have at least warned me."

"I was there the other day signing my contract, and he asked me about your work schedule. I thought he wanted to know the best time to call you, so they could set up a callback. I swear, I had no idea—I mean, what happened exactly? He just randomly showed up at the school?"

I nod, crossing my arms over my chest.

Spence's eyebrows slant to an even steeper angle as he mulls this over. "Maybe he thought if he took you by surprise, he'd get to see a more authentic performance?"

"Oh, it was fucking authentic, all right."

Spence leans over the low back of the sofa and pries one of my hands free, pressing it between his own. He brings my knuckles up to his mouth and kisses them, then presses his lips to my fingertips, the center of my palm, the inside of my wrist.

"Tell me everything," he says.

He keeps ahold of my hand, tracing spirals on my skin with his thumb while he listens. By the time I get to my sexy Scotsman fantasy, the corners of his lips have started to quirk up with unmistakable delight.

I jerk my hand away, crossing my arms again. "Stop smiling."

Spence schools his features into a serious expression of concern, but I can still see amusement shimmering in his eyes. "Go on," he says.

"And then I kissed Tim."

"Kissed him? How?"

I demonstrate. Unlike Tim, Spence kisses me back, his tongue darting out to meet mine, his hands squeezing my waist. Usually I have to go up on my tiptoes to reach Spence's mouth, but standing on his knees on the sofa he's only an inch or so taller than me. About Malcolm's height, in fact. I didn't realize how short he was until I saw him next to the teacher today. He seems taller onstage—the sort of person who takes up more than his fair share of space.

When I pull away from Spence, his lips curl up in a wolfish grin. "Jesus, woman." He slides his hands down from my waist to my ass. "You are *so* fired."

I haven't officially been fired yet, but I know the call is coming. Lauren's been looking for an excuse to get rid of me for a long time now, and she won't waste this chance.

I did try to apologize to Tim—once in the immediate aftermath, and then again while we were packing up at the end of the day. He just kept saying the same thing, over and over: *I don't believe you.*

And he was right. I'm not sorry. I'd do it again. Given another chance, I might even take things further, since I'm not sure what I did was enough to seal the deal with Malcolm. Which means I may have traumatized Tim and tossed a grenade on my only source of gainful employment for nothing.

"Hey." Spence pulls me closer, squeezing my arms. "You hated that job anyway."

"I needed that job."

"You know I would never let y—"

"Don't."

I'm not in the mood to have this conversation again. Spence has always been better off than me, in part thanks to his parents, who are far more supportive of his artistic ambitions than my family has ever been of mine. But my acting career has stagnated, while his profile as a fight choreographer keeps on growing, and every month the financial gap between us feels wider. Letting him treat me to dinners and drinks is one thing. Taking money from him to pay for basic living expenses is something else.

Spence makes the wise decision to change tactics. "Let me cheer you up," he says, already grabbing me by the waist and hauling me over the back of the sofa.

Finally—this is what I've been wanting since I walked in, the one surefire way Spence and I can always raise each other's spirits. Before I've even landed on top of him, we're kissing again, his fingers tangling in my hair, my hands sliding between his shirt and his skin. I breathe in his smoky, familiar cologne—tobacco and black pepper with a hint of something sweeter underneath—and block out everything beyond his body and mine.

AFTERWARD, SPENCE FALLS ASLEEP. I LIE AWAKE, CHEEK pillowed on his chest, staring at my distorted reflection in the television.

Fucking Spence is usually more than enough to take my mind off any problem. I came—twice—but I still feel unsatisfied, my skin humming with unspent energy. If I close my eyes, I see Malcolm, leaning forward in his seat, that slow smile spreading across his lips. From someone like him, that was high praise, I'm sure of it.

Except I'm not sure at all. When it comes to Malcolm Mercer, I'm sure of nothing. My initial audition must have impressed him, at least on some level, or he wouldn't have gone to the trouble of tracking me down. But for all I know, I humiliated myself today, and in two months' time I'll be stuck sitting in the audience with Spence, swallowing thick lumps of jealousy like bile while I watch someone else play yet another amazing part that slipped through my fingers.

I stir and stretch, just enough to rouse Spence. He smiles before he opens his eyes.

"Hey." His voice is always gravelly, but sleep makes it thrum like a rumble strip. "Feeling any better?"

I nod, but I look down while I do it so he won't be able to tell I'm lying.

"I need a shower," I say.

"You sure do, you dirty—"

I sit up and press my hand over his mouth. He nips at my palm, then kisses it.

"I'll go pick up some takeout and hard liquor," he says.

My response is immediate, automatic. "I really shouldn't, it's—"

"What?" he says. "A school night?"

Good point. I'm guessing I don't have to worry about getting up early to teach tomorrow, or any other day from now on.

I unravel my naked limbs from Spence's and stand up, sidestepping the snarl of discarded clothes between the sofa and the coffee table. Knowing us, we'll leave them lying there until someone runs out of underwear and has no choice but to do laundry.

Spence stares after me. I glare at him over my shoulder, eyes narrowed and lips pursed, pretending to be annoyed. "Creep."

"Slut." He blows me a kiss.

My purse is on its side behind the sofa, my tangled earbuds sprawling out onto the floor. No point in putting this off any longer. I crouch down and fish out my phone. It's still on vibrate, I never switched the ringer back on after class.

Two missed calls and a voice mail from Lauren. No other messages.

I glance back at Spence. He's gotten as far as putting on pants (though his boxer briefs are still lying on the floor between my shirt and my bra). I don't feel like dealing with this in front of him, so I head for the bathroom, pressing the phone against my thigh.

"Any food or drink requests?" Spence calls after me.

"Surprise me."

The overhead light in our bathroom has been burnt out for at least a month. The bulbs above the medicine cabinet do work, but I'm sure I look like shit—mascara smeared, a storm cloud of frizz around my skull, Spence's chest hair imprinted on my cheek—so I'd just as soon stay in the dark. I feel my way to the tub and turn on the water, then pull one of the ratty red towels off the rack on the back of the door. I can never keep straight which one is mine, so I just use whichever happens to be drier when I'm ready to shower.

I wrap the towel around myself and start pacing back and forth on the little strip of floor in front of the sink. I should just listen to the message. Rip the Band-Aid off. Waiting isn't going to make this any easier.

But what the hell am I going to do now?

I sit down on the edge of the tub. The porcelain is freezing against the backs of my thighs, but I've stalled long enough the water's gone from lukewarm to scalding. Steam curls along my spine as I tap my phone on, then off, then on again. The blinking screen casts an eerie blue glow over my bare legs.

Then it lights up again, without me touching it. Someone is calling—a number I don't recognize. A number with a Chicago area code.

The phone buzzes again, and I stop breathing. I shouldn't get my hopes up. It's probably a wrong number. Or a fucking telemarketer. It could even be some higher-up from the foundation that sponsors the school program, calling to inform me I should be ashamed of myself, and I'll never do Shakespeare in this town again.

It's like I'm back in high school, staring down at my shoes as I try to summon the courage to look at the cast list taped to the classroom door. Gut writhing like a pile of snakes, ears pounding with the rush of my own blood. I hated that feeling then, and I hate it even more now. But I suppose it's good to know I'm still capable of wanting something this much.

Screw it. In the middle of the third ring, I shut my eyes and answer the call.

"Hello?"

"Hello, Kira."

He doesn't say his name. So arrogant. But the truth is, I knew it was him before he said a word, from the sound of the breath he took before he started to speak.

I cradle the phone against my cheek. A smile spreads across my lips—slow and sparking like a lit fuse, the same way he smiled at me in the classroom. I did it. I'm in.

"Hello, Malcolm."

8

JOANNA

SHE'S LATE. ONLY TWO MINUTES, BUT THAT STILL MAKES KIRA the last to arrive for the read-through. Except for Bryn, but Bryn has an excuse; she's down in my office making photocopies of the contact list.

Of course, Mal isn't ready to start. He pulled me onstage with him so we could have one of his impromptu, last-possible-second business meetings to hash out the decisions I've been harassing him to make all week: when to hold the first run-through for the designers, whether we really need a full five nights for tech or we can get away with fewer. It's a compressed rehearsal schedule as it is, a little over a month. We've had worse, though, and we always make it work.

Three minutes. Maybe she won't show at all, and Mal will have to admit I was right for once. But then we would have to cancel the read-through, find a new actress, reschedule everything. And I'd have to wait even longer to finally see Mal play this role, when I've already been waiting for months.

Mal was in character when I met him—a character I created, in fact. My senior year of college, I was one of five students chosen as a finalist in a nationwide one-act play competition. Our prize was a trip to Chicago to see staged readings of our scripts done by local actors. Mal played the male lead in mine. He'd been in the city about a year then, scraping by with odd jobs and occasional acting work. Mostly experimental stuff: site-specific Shakespeare performances at warehouses in the West Loop, a living art installation at a gallery in Pilsen.

When he read my play, it was the first time I'd heard the lines out loud the way they sounded in my head. He was so far beyond the boys back in the University of Michigan theater department, who slouched and mumbled through every scene because they thought it made them Brando-esque (as if they even knew what that meant). I'd seen professional-caliber theater before, thanks to the semi-annual trips my mother and I took to New York City and the Stratford Festival when I was a teen, but there was something different about Mal. Something more.

I thought he was handsome, of course—those dark, penetrating eyes; that thick curly hair, black all the way through then instead of flecked with silver at the temples like it is now. He looked timeless, placeless, like he could hail from any era, any number of ethnicities. But that wasn't what drew me to him. Talent radiated from his body like a force field. Even sitting still, he seemed dynamic. I wished I could take him back to school with me, have him stand over my shoulder while I wrote, whisper every word in my ear as I typed it.

Everyone thought I was crazy, moving to a strange city to start a theater company with a man I barely knew. It may not have turned out quite the way I thought it would, but no matter how many times I see Mal onstage, it's still as thrilling as the first time. That's what makes it all worth it.

Four minutes. Mal's gaze keeps sliding away from me, toward the door. He's not annoyed that she's late. He can't wait to see her again.

Mal and I built this place together. Every screw, every brush of paint. He may be fascinated by Kira now, but he'll tire of her soon enough. Just like the others. And then I'll have him all to myself again.

I just have to be patient.

Good thing I've had years of practice.

9

KIRA

"LIPSTICK," SPENCE SAYS.

We're at a stoplight, stuck in the Cubs pregame traffic snarl several blocks from Indifferent Honest. The start time of the first *Temper* read-through has already come and gone. I take a black bullet-shaped tube out of my purse, and Spence twists in the driver's seat so I can use his sunglasses' reflective lenses as a mirror.

The lipstick is the most dramatic shade I own, shiny black-crimson like the skin of a cherry. Putting it on always feels like donning armor. I'm wearing the earrings Spence got me for my thirtieth birthday, too: stainless steel spikes that look like they're stabbing through my earlobes.

More armor. I need all I can get today.

The light turns green while I'm still rounding the curves of my Cupid's bow. The driver behind us honks. Spence sticks his arm between the seats to flip the guy off, which gets us another honk, louder and longer this time. I snap the cap back on the tube, pressing my lips together to blend, and Spence squeals through the intersection.

I still can't believe I got the part. I'm hoping it will feel real once I say the lines in front of other people. (Spence has helped me run lines a couple of times already, but he doesn't count as other people.) It certainly didn't feel real during my phone call with Malcolm. By the time we hung up, the hot water had run out, and I ended up taking a cold shower. Not a bad idea after a few minutes with that man in your ear. His low, polished voice makes everything sound poetic, even phrases like *boilerplate non-Equity contract* and *Sunday at seven o'clock*.

The night of The Call, Spence returned laden with a bottle of ginger-infused vodka and two sweating paper bags full of Thai takeout. When I rushed to the front door to tell him the news, he dropped the shopping bags so he could sweep me up in a congratulatory hug. My towel slipped to the floor, and by the time we finished celebrating, our dinner was as cold as my shower.

I waited until I was fortified with food and one of Spence's famous cocktails before listening to the voice mail Lauren left me. I was—like I'd figured—*so* fired. She kept the message professional, but I could picture the look on her face, that pinched, ferrety expression she gets when something or someone makes her the slightest bit uncomfortable. I didn't bother calling her back.

Spence passes the theater, turning down a side street to find parking. As soon as he's muscled his way into a tight spot in front of a redbrick courtyard building, he slides his hand under my hair to squeeze the back of my neck. So I guess I'm doing a shit job of hiding how nervous I am.

Spence's presence isn't required at the read-through; usually the fight choreographer comes in later in the rehearsal process. He might claim he's only here for moral support, but I know better. He wants to see Malcolm Mercer in action.

"Ready?" he asks.

I suck in a breath and hold it.

"You're going to be great," he says. "You're perfect for this part."

"How do you know? You haven't even finished reading the script yet."

"Well, you and your character *do* have a few things in common."

He means the fact that she spends most of the play in the throes of a medical abortion, which she tries to pass off as a miscarriage.

Not exactly the sort of personal experience I can put in the "Special Skills" section of my résumé.

Spence leans across the center console to kiss me. I put my hand up to stop him.

"Lipstick."

He kisses the air above my left cheekbone instead, and we head inside.

10

JOANNA

IT'S FIVE AND A HALF MINUTES PAST THE HOUR WHEN KIRA Rascher finally graces us with her presence. The fight choreographer, Spencer, walks in with her. Right behind, hand on the small of her back. So he's late too, but since he isn't required to come to rehearsal until after we've finished the initial blocking next week, I can't technically count it against him.

They take seats in the last row. The bad kids in the back of the class.

I knew the two of them were acquainted—they listed the same address on their contact forms—but I wasn't sure if they were a couple. Now that I see them in the same room, though, it's obvious they are, at the very least, sleeping together. The shirt she's wearing must be his. It hangs way too large on her, the hem covering her ass, but the buttons strain against her breasts. The black fabric is wrinkled, like she fished it off the floor after fucking him. Maybe she did.

The sexually explicit elements of the play are the only part I'm certain Kira will have no trouble with. She and Mal are playing a married couple, Mara and Trent. There's tension between them from the first page. Something rotten at the core of their relationship, eating away at them both. But as tense and unhappy as they seem, they still share a torrid sexual connection.

The first act stays at a simmering slow burn, but in the second act, Mara's rage at Trent boils over into violent reveries, where she acts out what she really wants to do to him. After each reverie, there's a blackout, and the scene rewinds to show what actually happened between them: Mara swallowing her anger, biting back her curses, smiling tight enough to snap bone while Trent stays oblivious to just how much she hates the fucking sight of him.

I have no doubt Mal can handle the sharp turns from brutality to control and back again. But I'm not so sure about her. Who knows, maybe she'll surprise me. But no matter what happens, I'm not going to let her ruin tonight for me.

As I take my seat, I steal another glance at Kira and Spencer. He's leaning over, whispering something to her, so close his lips touch her earlobe. She slouches down, pressing the soles of her shoes into the chair in front of her. Leaning into him so her hair spills over his shoulder. Apparently whatever he's saying is hilarious, because she puts her hand over her mouth and laughs into her palm.

This is exactly what I was afraid of. She isn't taking this seriously. She has no idea what she's getting herself into, the type of commitment Mal expects.

Well. She'll find out soon enough. And I have to admit: I'm looking forward to that, too.

11

KIRA

ONE THING I LOVE ABOUT THE THEATER—IT TENDS TO RUN even later than I do.

Malcolm and Joanna didn't seem to notice us slipping in. They're standing together at the edge of the stage, talking in tones too hushed to carry to our seats at the back of the theater. While we wait, Spence tries to calm my nerves by whispering in my ear like an aide filling a politician in on the people she needs to greet during a fundraiser.

"That's the sound designer, Austin." He nods toward a twenty-something guy with an auburn longshoreman beard and blocky black glasses. "Actually, I think he might be doing the lighting design too. He's great. I worked with him at Boho last year."

I caught Austin checking me out when we walked in, but once he saw Spence looming behind me, he suddenly found the toes of his combat boots extremely fascinating. Letting people assume Spence and I are a couple saves me from fending off a lot of unwanted male attention. Of course, sometimes he frightens off wanted male attention too, but overall it's a fair trade.

"And her?" I point to the dark-haired young woman who just walked in—the one from the audition. She's carrying a stack of papers rather than a clipboard now, but she's dressed almost identically. The only difference I can spot is that her oversized sweatshirt is dark gray today instead of black.

"That's Bryn," Spence says. "She's Joanna's intern, but she's going to be stage managing, too."

"Stage managing, seriously? How old is she?"

"Nineteen, I think? She told me she was a 'rising sophomore' at DePaul." He does air quotes around the term "rising sophomore."

"Is that like being eight and three-quarters?"

Spence snickers. "Pretty much."

Malcolm and Joanna are still deep in conversation, ignoring the rest of us. They've got matching creases between their eyebrows, like little hash marks carved with a knife tip. His head is bowed toward hers, his hand between her shoulder blades, but he's not touching her. His palm hovers an inch or two away from the back of her jacket.

Joanna is dressed better than anyone else in the room, in dark-wash designer jeans and a black blazer tailored to her small frame, similar to what she had on the day of the audition. I suddenly feel sloppy in the outfit I chose: one of Spence's button-downs over faded leggings and ballet flats with holes in the bottoms.

I wonder if Malcolm and Joanna have ever fucked. There's something between them, something deeper than friendship or business partnership, a vibration in the air when they're near each other. Then again, men like Malcolm seem to have sexual tension with everyone. Everything, even. Brick walls. Lamp posts. Their own reflections.

But I can't quite see them as a couple. It's not that Joanna isn't attractive. She just seems so serious, studious almost. She reminds me of the few girls who were nice to me in high school. They weren't paranoid about me stealing their boyfriends, because they didn't have any to steal. Not due to lack of interest from the boys, they just had more important things on their minds.

Finally they break apart, and Joanna takes a seat in the front row, a few chairs over from where Bryn has settled in with her stage management binder. Then Malcolm looks up at me.

"Kira."

No moment of searching. He knew precisely where I was sitting, even though he didn't even glance my way when I walked into the theater.

On the stage behind Malcolm are two folding chairs. He gestures toward the one on his left. Usually read-throughs happen around a big table like an awkward family dinner, but since it's just the two of us, I guess he decided to do without.

Everyone has fallen silent now, twisting around to stare at me. Spence's legs are blocking my path to the aisle. I climb over his knees, clutching my copy of the script, and he puts his hands on my hips to steady me.

Once I'm where he wants me, Malcolm turns to face the rest of the production team. "Thank you so much for being here tonight, everyone."

He doesn't speak loudly, like he's giving a speech. His voice is calm and low enough to force his audience to lean in and listen carefully. Even though I'm sitting the closest to him, I find myself leaning forward too. It's like his voice has its own gravitational pull.

"Some of you I've had the pleasure of working with before." He nods toward a woman in the second row with silver-streaked hair—the costume designer, Dawn, according to Spence. She's been working with Indifferent Honest since *Hamlet*, though their costumes for that show were simple street clothes. Malcolm had worn a hoodie and ripped jeans and still managed to look every bit a prince.

"But many of you I'm working with for the first time," Malcolm continues. "I'm sure we'll all have the pleasure of getting to know one another much better over these next few weeks, but I want to start off by saying one thing: I don't want you to think of me as the director."

He lets this statement hang in the air for a few seconds. My first instinct is to scoff—in my experience, it's the directors who pay lip service to this kind of artistic equality who turn out to be the biggest assholes—but everyone else seems to be buying what Malcolm is selling. Even Spence. I try to catch his eye, to exchange a *can you believe this guy?* look, but he's totally engrossed in Malcolm's speech.

"This play is something all of us, every person here in this room tonight, is creating together."

As he says this, Malcolm makes brief but intense eye contact with each person in the room, finishing with a glance back at me. It's like he's trying to put us in a trance.

"All right, then." He smiles. "Without further ado: *Temper* by L. S. Sedgwick."

He sits down in the other chair on the stage and crosses his legs, then motions to Bryn. She clears her throat and starts reading the opening stage directions. She has a creaky alto voice, vocal fry crimping the end of each sentence, and she twists the corner of the page with her fingernail as she reads.

"'Lights up on a hotel room somewhere in the American Midwest. Not luxurious, but not too shabby, either. Trent and Mara enter from the hallway. They've just checked in; they're there to attend the wedding of a mutual friend. Mara makes a slow circuit of the room, inspecting it. Trent watches her, still holding their luggage.'"

Malcolm stares at me. At least the gaze is in character this time. And he won't be able to keep it up, he'll have to look away to read his lines. He has the first line in the show, so I won't have to put up with this much longer. Tonight won't be anything like the audition.

I keep my eyes on my script, following along with Bryn, and doing my best to ignore Malcolm. But when he delivers Trent's first line—"Are you sure you're okay?"—his eyes stay fixed on me.

I steal a glance over at his lap, which holds only his folded hands. He doesn't have a copy of the script. He must have already memorized all his lines.

Shit. Was I supposed to be off-book too? Well, it's too late now. *Just read the lines. Stay calm. Pretend he's not there. Just read.*

"I'm fine." My voice only wavers a little, but I'm sure Malcolm noticed.

"Because we still have time to go to the hospital," he says.

"No, we don't."

"'Trent puts his hand on the back of her neck,'" Bryn reads. "'She tenses.'"

Malcolm doesn't touch me. It doesn't matter. Everyone in the room is looking at me, but his eyes are the only ones I can *feel*. Those goddamn eyes. I thought they were the same color as mine, but up close I can tell they're darker, so brown they're almost black, the color of saturated coffee grounds.

"The wedding's in an hour," I say.

Malcolm curls his hands into fists. "That little bitch, I should have—"

"It was an accident. She was a teenager."

The words are coming out steadier now, but my mouth feels desert-dry. I brought a water bottle, but I left it in my bag on the seat next to Spence, so I can't get it until Malcolm gives us a break—which won't happen until the end of the first act, if then.

I swallow, and the saliva seems to stick to the sides of my throat. "I bet you were a shitty driver when you were a teenager too."

"I never rear-ended anyone. And on a goddamn highway on-ramp, for fuck's sake!"

" 'His voice keeps crescendoing,' " Bryn reads. " 'It's clear he has a temper, and it's equally clear Mara is used to being the one to defuse it.' "

He's leaning forward in his seat. I have to contract my leg muscles to keep my knee from knocking into his. This is the closest I've ever been to him.

But then I remember—no it isn't.

During the *get thee to a nunnery* scene in *Hamlet*, Malcolm pushed the actress playing Ophelia to the floor, and she landed right at my feet. Spence was standing beside me, and I felt him seize up, like he was resisting the urge to bust through the fourth wall and come to Ophelia's aid. It felt so real, like it was an actual argument rather than a rehearsed scene.

As he delivered the line *why wouldst thou be a breeder of sinners*, Malcolm got down on the floor with her, caging her body with his arms. He was so close then I could have touched him, reached out and run my fingers through his hair.

" 'Mara crosses to the bed,' " Bryn reads. If only I could do the same. Just stand up and turn my back on him and walk away.

When Malcolm stood back up after that exchange with Ophelia, his sleeve brushed my ankle and a shiver passed through me. I realized then: this was what I wanted to do. Make theater that was raw, immediate, visceral, that broke down the barriers between the audience and the actors.

And now I'm finally here, sharing a stage with Malcolm Mercer, and I'm failing. He's hemming me in, holding me down with nothing more than a look. I might as well have let him tie me to this chair. I cannot sit here with him looking at me like this for the next two hours, I will fucking scream.

"We'll call the insurance company in the morning," I say. "There's nothing else we can do for now."

But I'm not tied down. I could stand up. Rebel against all the rehearsal rules drilled into me since my first high school play, wrest control away from Malcolm and take the scene into my own hands. What's the worst he could do?

My next line is: "We should get ready." I'm not ready, not at all, but my thigh muscles are already tensing, my fingers curling around the metal edge of the chair—my body knowing what I'm about to do before my mind has even decided.

What's the worst he could do? I guess I'm about to find out.

12

JOANNA

THE LEGS OF KIRA'S CHAIR SCREECH AGAINST THE FLOOR, drowning out the first few syllables of her next line.

She stood up. Why would she stand up? What the hell is she doing?

She's still holding her script, but she's dropped it to her side, resting against her thigh. She walks upstage left, then stops, tossing a look over her shoulder at Mal, the same spark in her eyes she had at the audition. As if she's challenging him to a duel.

I grip the top of my notebook, bracing myself. Bryn should be reading the stage direction following Kira's line—*Trent comes up behind her*—but she seems to have been stunned into silence as well. She's only known Mal for a few weeks, but that's long enough to learn what he can be like.

The last time someone openly defied Mal in rehearsal, they were replaced within the week. Not that Mal fired the guy. He didn't have to. As I recall, the last straw was when Mal berated him for gesturing too much during a speech, and then, to remedy the problem, lashed his hands behind his back with a length of rigging rope. The actor lasted an hour before storming out of the theater with rope burns on both wrists, never to return.

Mal still hasn't taken his eyes off Kira. And now he's smiling.

"What are you doing?" he asks.

His tone is even, but then, he rarely bothers with yelling. Why would he, when there are so many other, more creative ways for him to express his displeasure?

I can't believe she made him break character.

"I thought we could try it on our feet," she says. "See how it feels."

Silence. I think everyone's holding their breath. Everyone except her.

Then Mal stands too. He picks up his chair, and Kira's, and moves them both offstage. Once the stage is clear, he turns to her.

"Excellent idea," he says. Still smiling. "Do you want to take it from your last line?"

It's like watching someone scratch a wild animal behind the ears. Kira has no idea what a feat she's pulled off. She nods and says her line, and then they're back into the scene, like nothing happened at all. Like she didn't just flout Mal's authority in front of the entire company.

I give Bryn a soft nudge in the arm, and she clears her throat and resumes reading the stage directions. This is the most I've ever heard her speak, and it makes me grateful she's usually so quiet. Her voice has that grating, monotone quality I can't help associating with her age, the uncertain upward lilt at the end of each sentence. I spent years training myself not to speak that way, modulating my tone, extracting all the *like*s and *um*s from my vocabulary so no one could use them as an excuse to not take me seriously. Mal used to call me out on my immature verbal tics. "You're not asking a question," he'd say. "You're sure. So sound like it. Commit."

"'Mara turns,'" Bryn reads, "'so Trent can unzip her dress.'"

Kira gathers her hair in her fist. Mal presses his knuckles into the space between her shoulder blades, and she lets her hair drop. Her dark curls seem to devour his fingers. He drags his hand along her spine, miming pulling down a zipper.

They look good together onstage—about the same height, the same coloring, a matching set. Like they could be related, except for the way they're looking at each other. There's a heat between them now that wasn't there when they were seated.

"'She kisses him,'" Bryn says.

Kira turns and puts her hands on his chest. But when she leans in to touch her lips to his, Mal sidesteps her, skipping ahead to his next line. Her expression darkens for a second, like a storm cloud passing over her face. It could be in character, but I know better.

More important, I know Mal. One way or another, he always makes you pay.

13

KIRA

MY FIRST NIGHT OFF IN OVER A WEEK, AND I'M SPENDING IT IN bed with Spence. I'm on top, straddling his waist. I slide my hands up his chest, knees squeezing his ribs, and lean over him, until my face hovers inches above his, close enough to kiss. Our eyes meet.

Then I wrap my hands around his throat.

He takes ahold of my wrists and writhes underneath me, groaning and gagging. I keep staring into his eyes until he shuts them and goes still.

If this were real, it would take much longer for him to pass out—over a minute. That's the kind of weird shit you know when you live with a fight choreographer.

I let go and sit back on his stomach. He opens his eyes again, already grinning.

"Awesome," he says. "Keep your fingers a little looser, though—there shouldn't be any pressure at all on the neck. Show me the hand position again?"

I put my hands in a U shape, one thumb crossed over top of the other, and hold them out for his inspection. Spence makes some small adjustments, then draws my hands back toward his neck, lining up my index fingers with the underside of his jaw. He tilts his head down so his chin is braced against my overlapped thumbs, keeping me from actually pressing on his throat.

"There you go. Perfect."

"You want to try it again?" I ask.

This extracurricular practice session is more for me than for him. I know he's had his choreography planned out for weeks already, whereas I'm more than a bit rusty on the stage violence front. In my teaching job, the only fight scenes we did involved fake swords made from pool noodles.

"Nah," Spence says. "I think you've got it."

The fighting in *Temper* is all unarmed. The strangling comes at the close of the show, and it's the only one of Mara's violent acts that isn't clearly all in her imagination. The play ends with Trent lying on the bed, his eyes closed, and it's left ambiguous whether he's only sleeping, or if Mara really choked the life out of him.

In the past when I've done fight scenes, I've been the victim— the one pretending to be smacked in the face or pushed around the stage, while actually dictating the timing and intensity of every move. But in *Temper*, Mara is almost always the attacker, which means Malcolm will be the one in control. Though it's tough to think of Malcolm Mercer as a victim, in this or any context.

I climb off Spence and stretch out on the mattress. The bedding is disheveled from our fake tussle, but it still looks more orderly than my own next door.

He reaches over me to grab his battered brown Moleskine from the bedside table.

"Seven p.m. call tomorrow, right?"

I nod. "It'll be nice to finally have someone to talk to at rehearsal."

He makes another note, then shuts the pen inside the notebook and returns them both to the table. When he lies back down, he stays facing me, his head resting on his hand. "He's still pulling the strong-and-silent-type routine, huh?"

Working with Malcolm Mercer has been nothing like I imagined. I was ready to deal with unreasonable demands, withering disdain, or even outright cruelty. But so far, he's barely spoken to me. What little direction he's given me has all been surface-level.

Try crossing downstage instead of upstage.

When you say that line, put the emphasis on the second word instead of the first.

Do it again, but faster.

So his reputation is all a bunch of bullshit, or he's holding back because he thinks I can't take whatever he's dished out before. Either way, it's fucking infuriating.

I'm not sure if Spence's presence at rehearsal will help or hurt matters. We're not great at acting professional around each other—which was fine back when we were in college. The day I walked into my first acting class at Ohio State and saw him slouched in the back row, there was an immediate connection between us. His long legs were sprawled across the aisle, like he didn't give a damn who he might be inconveniencing, and I climbed over them so I could sit next to him. I kept staring at him, first trying to figure out if he was wearing eyeliner (he was), then whether he was straight or gay (he was neither). We paired up as scene partners, and we've been a clique of two, inseparable and impenetrable, ever since. The sex was secondary—one more way we had fun together, when we felt like it. We were just as likely to stay up all night eating pints of ice cream and mocking terrible BBC Shakespeare productions in each other's beds.

I roll onto my back. Spence starts running his fingers up and down the inside of my arm. I would never tell him, but I love it when he touches me this way, petting me like a cat.

"He still won't kiss me," I say.

"Seriously?"

"Seriously."

There's a scene, right before the strangling, where Malcolm and I are supposed to have an intense, seconds-from-penetration make-out session on the hotel bed. But we haven't even blocked that yet. I'm talking about the several quick, casual kisses called for in the script. Like the one I'm supposed to give him after he unzips my dress. At the read-through, I figured I caught him off guard, but now that we're well into rehearsals, it's getting fucking bizarre. For most actors, that type of stage kissing is merely a matter of mechanics, no more sexual than touching someone on the shoulder or taking their hand. But every time I've gone in for so much as a peck on the lips, Malcolm has dodged me or found some excuse to stop the scene and start over. After a few days, I gave up trying.

"Maybe it's against his religion," Spence says. "Or maybe . . ."

I look over at him. "What?"

He takes my hand, staring solemnly into my eyes like he's a doctor about to convey a fatal diagnosis. "Maybe . . . you have terrible breath."

I yank my hand free so I can use it to smack him in the chest. He laughs and catches me up in a hug, pinning my arms against my sides. I stop struggling and relax into him, my face pressed against the front of his shirt. He loosens his hold and starts rubbing my back, making slow circles with the heel of his hand.

We lie there for a few seconds before I tilt my head back so I can kiss him on the throat. Then on the end of his chin. Then on the mouth.

He kisses me back—out of habit, if nothing else—but only for a few seconds before pulling away. "I have to leave in twenty minutes."

"That's plenty of time."

"Sorry, doll. Not tonight."

He stands up, then leans over the side of the bed to give me another kiss—this time a chaste one in the center of my forehead. I scowl and stretch, draping my bare legs over the space he just vacated.

"Okay. Who is he? Or is it a she this time?"

"I have no idea what you're talking about."

Spence may be a decent actor, but he's an awful liar. He must really like this one, though, whoever he or she may be. Whenever Spence is seeing someone new, I typically get the full TMI rundown whether I want it or not—including but not limited to: scandalous personal stories, ill-advised body art, and any weird sounds they make during sex. I can't remember the last time he was enamored enough with someone to keep secrets.

Spence shuts the bedroom door so he can check himself out in the full-length mirror hung on the back. Usually when he looks in the mirror, he preens like a peacock or combs his hair back like a 1950s greaser, but this time his lips twist to the side. I know that look: he's mentally flicking through the contents of his closet, trying to decide whether or not to change his clothes.

"Wear your red button-down," I say. "It makes you look like an evil prince."

He meets my eyes in the mirror and smiles. Once he's swapped out his plain black shirt for the recommended red one, he turns to me, arms out, awaiting inspection.

He looks devastating. I want to peel the shirt back off his shoulders and pull him into bed with me again. But I settle for giving him an unsarcastic thumbs-up.

"I'll see you at the theater tomorrow," he says.

So he's not planning on coming home tonight. Interesting. Spence has never been the sleepover type; even I get kicked out of his bed and sent to my own room after we fuck. Which is too bad, because I've always liked Spence's room more than my own. The walls are painted a deep, kingly burgundy (despite the no-painting clause in our lease), and he has a leather headboard with nailhead trim and I-don't-even-know-how-high thread-count sheets. And then, of course, there's the floor-to-ceiling rack of weapons by the bed. Spence has been building his collection for years. So far it includes a broadsword, a set of rapiers with ornate basket handles, a dagger with a fake ruby in the hilt, and a variety of small swords.

I'm making it sound fancier than it is—the sheets are from Nordstrom Rack, he found the headboard in an alley, and most of the weapons are theater company castoffs he's rescued and refurbished—but it's a hell of a lot nicer than my room, where most of the furniture is from Ikea, and the closest thing to an accent color is the rusty water stain on the wall above the bed.

"See you tomorrow," I say.

I stay in his bed for a while after he's gone, watching the light through the window bloom orange and then wither to gray. I curve my fingers into the position Spence showed me again and extend my arms, pretending to strangle the empty air above me. Then I reverse the grip and bring my hands to my own throat.

At first, I do it the way he told me to: no tension in my fingers, chin braced against my thumbs. But I'm curious, and now Spence isn't here to stop me from jutting my jaw out, stiffening my hands, pressing down.

I squeeze until my vision starts to blur and spark, until I can't hold on any longer and I have to let go, gasp in a breath, blink the black stars out of my eyes.

If Malcolm Mercer thinks I can't take it—can't take *him*—well then, I'm going to have to find a way to prove him wrong.

14

JOANNA

"YOU FUCKING LIAR."

"Listen to yourself."

"I saw you."

"If you're not going to be reasonable, I can't—"

"I saw *both* of you."

"I don't know what you think you saw, but—"

Mal stops, dropping character and turning to the audience, which tonight consists only of myself, Bryn, and Spencer. "So that's when she's supposed to shove me."

"Got it," Spencer says. He's been pacing back and forth across the foot of the stage, watching the scene from several different angles—and occasionally blocking my view.

Kira calls him "Spence," like he's some kind of film noir detective (though with his dark good looks, he seems more like the murderer the detective would stop at nothing to track down). I hired him after seeing his work last summer—a production of *Coriolanus* in a Wicker Park basement. His choreography made use of every square inch of the cramped space. I could see the technique in it, the precision, but the way the other audience members reacted, I knew it felt real to them. Dangerous, like they could be run through with a blade at any moment.

Mal hates anything that feels too safe onstage, so I thought Spencer's style might be a good fit. He had creative differences with the woman who did the fights for our military play *The Thousand-Yard Stare* last season and ended up re-choreographing the whole thing on his own a week before opening. I swear, if he could clone himself, he'd do every job in the theater company, from building the props to sewing the costumes to running the lights. Everything except the boring office work; that, I'm sure he'd still be more than happy to leave in my capable hands.

I have a stack of said boring office work sitting in the seat next to me, and my notebook open on my lap. Trying to multitask, make sure Mal is playing nice with Spencer while also checking a few more items off my to-do list. The short rehearsal period has me feeling like I'm falling behind already. Bryn isn't entirely useless, but she still stares at me with that fawn-in-the-headlights look every time I ask her to do something new. Sometimes I wish I could clone myself too. Or that we had the steady nine-to-five schedule and administrative staff of an Equity theater. But if we rehearsed during the day, I'd probably still end up spending most nights toiling away in my office. There's always more to be done.

Spencer makes some notes in a small brown notebook, then tosses it onto a seat at the end of the front row. "Great," he says. "Why don't we start with—"

"Just one second, if you don't mind." Mal turns to Kira.

She has her hair gathered up in a knot on top of her head today, a few curls escaping to frame her cheeks. Her face is shaped like a heart, the hint of a dimple softening the point of her chin. The sweetness of it somehow makes her look even more like a femme fatale. The type you wouldn't see coming until she'd already ruined your life.

"I need you to make the escalation clearer," Mal says. "Even though Mara's only imagining this, her actions can't come out of nowhere. There has to be a natural progression. You see what I'm saying?"

She nods, pursing her lips. No lipstick today, but they're naturally stained red, like she's been eating berries. (Or sucking blood.) "Do you want me to do it again?"

"No, no, that won't be necessary. Just try to be mindful of it next time, okay?"

Mal waits until Kira nods again. Then he turns back to Spencer with an expectant look. As though he, not Mal, is the one who's been holding up the proceedings.

"Right. Okay." Spencer is flustered, trying to hitch back onto his train of thought.

"Should I start the shove as he's saying 'but'?" Kira asks. Trying to help him out, be a good friend, or whatever they are to each other. "Or after?"

"Let me hear those last couple of lines again," Spencer says.

"Sure," Mal says. He turns away from Kira, and then he's back in character. I can see the moment it happens. It's like flipping a switch for him; no need to ramp up or come down.

"If you're not going to be reasonable, I can't—"

"I saw you." Kira takes a step toward him. "I saw *both* of you."

Her voice lowers. There's no edge of hysteria. She sounds dangerous. The way I wish I could sound, the way I imagine myself sounding when I obsess over what I should have said to someone after an argument. In the moment, I'm hopeless. Words fail me.

But she said those lines out of order. I make a note. That's really Bryn's job, but I haven't seen her do anything with her pen today except chew on the cap; she has a disgusting habit of gnawing her nails down to ragged stubs, too.

"I don't know what you think you saw, but—"

"Okay," Spencer says. "May I?"

He indicates he wants to switch places, like Mal and Kira are dancing and he's cutting in.

"Put your hands on my chest," he tells Kira. "We're going to do a shared-energy push for this, so you'll actually shove him, but you only need to give him a little energy to get him going. He'll do the rest."

I'm trying to draft an updated company description for the *Temper* program. Mal asked me to write a new one; he said the old one was getting stale. The picture of the two of us accompanying it certainly had. We'll have to get a new one taken, though I don't know when we'll find the time. I should have had the photographer who shot the image for the *Temper* poster last month take a picture of us while she was at it, but that photo shoot ran far too long as it was.

The poster is relatively simple: a woman's hands scratching down Mal's back, their skin bathed in blood-red light. But Mal was obsessed with getting the position of her fingers just right, and since he couldn't see them himself, we had to stop after every few shots so he could review the images with the photographer and then reset, until he was satisfied. The model was fighting back tears by the end of it. But you can't see her face in the images anyway.

> *The Indifferent Honest Theater Company has brought challenging new works and cutting-edge reinventions of classics to the Chicago theater community since—*

My attention drifts back to the stage. Mal keeps touching his face. He started by tapping his fingertips against his chin, and now he's running his thumb over his lower lip. He's not really listening, just making a show of it. Paying attention, but not to Spencer's words. Shoving is stage combat 101, so none of what he's saying is new information to Mal. But how Spencer interacts with Kira, the casual possessiveness in the way they touch each other—I'm sure Mal is very interested in that.

"Great. Now if you two could move back to your marks at the end of Trent's line." Spencer steps aside so Mal can retake his position on the stage. "Remember, Kira, as the attacker, it's up to you to establish eye contact with the victim beforehand."

Kira locks her eyes on Mal's. That heat rising between them again. I look back down at the notebook page.

We champion work that's unafraid to explore the dark side of human nature . . .

I glance up again, right as Kira pushes her palms into Mal's chest. He stumbles backward as though she's shoved him much harder, but it's not especially convincing.

"That was good," Spencer says. "But next time, position your hands a little lower."

He puts his own hands on Kira's chest to demonstrate. Any lower and he'd be groping her.

"Avoid the clavicle, target the pecs—you want to hit muscle, not bone. Let's try it again."

Indifferent Honest's twelfth season starts off with a world premiere by—

Twelfth season—that's embellishing a bit, since our first two years were a series of random experimental performances and staged readings, most of them put on in the living room of our loft with the help of friends we paid in bottles of Goose Island beer. Not proper seasons by a long shot, but Mal insists we should count them. And we threw a tenth-anniversary fundraiser two years ago, so I guess now we're committed to this timeline.

Spencer takes them through the sequence a few more times. Then Mal drops out of character and says to Kira, "You can do it harder. I won't break."

He smiles, like he's just told a joke, but Spencer isn't amused.

"She's doing it hard enough. It's up to you to sell it. If you react like she shoved you with all her strength, the audience will believe it."

"I get that," Mal says. "It's just tough when she's giving me so little energy."

He turns to Kira, cutting Spencer out of the conversation. That didn't last long.

"Let's just try it once with a little more force behind it," he says.

Spencer shakes his head. "I don't think that's—"

"If it's too much, we can dial it back." Without giving either of them a chance to argue further, Mal launches back into the scene. "If you're not going to be reasonable, I can't—"

Kira hesitates, looking to Spencer like he's still in charge here. Like he ever was. He's glaring, a muscle in his jaw jumping, but he doesn't try to interrupt.

"I saw *both* of you."

Less conviction this time. She can't switch it on and off like Mal can.

"I don't know what you think you saw, but—"

She shoves him. Maybe not with all her strength, but much harder than she did before. Mal reels back so far I think he's going to hit the floor. My stomach leaps into my throat. If he breaks his ankle or his tailbone or his *anything*, we are so fucked. There are no understudies, and we open in just a few—

But he catches himself, and when he straightens up, he's already smiling.

"That was better," he says.

"That was way too hard," Spencer says. "She almost knocked you on your ass."

"No, it just looked that way," Mal says. "I was in control the whole time. Let's do it again, Kira. Same level of intensity." He smiles at her. "Don't hold back on me now."

I shouldn't have worried. Of course he was in control the whole time. He always is.

15

KIRA

BY THE TIME WE GET TO THE END OF FIGHT REHEARSAL, Spence is so pissed off, the anger shimmers around his body like a heat mirage. He's been watching Malcolm and me from the foot of the stage for the past hour, his arms crossed over his chest. Silent.

He may be a bit morally flexible in his personal life, but when it comes to his profession, Spence has always been obsessed with doing things the right way, following safety protocols to the letter. He'd rather make sure people are safe than make sure they like him. Even on his first-ever fight gig—a terrible outdoor production of *A Midsummer Night's Dream* we did together the summer after we graduated from Ohio State—he didn't hesitate to ream out the girl playing Hermia in front of the whole cast after she accidentally scratched Helena on the neck and drew blood during their Act III tussle.

But now he's just standing by, letting Malcolm tread all over him. Spence might as well not even be here. I'm pretty sure that's what Malcolm would prefer anyway. There were a few moments when I thought Joanna might intervene. This is the first rehearsal she's stayed all the way through, instead of bustling in and out of the theater typing on her phone or holding stacks of file folders propped against her hip. But she's just been sitting there, teeth worrying her lip as she splits her attention between the stage and whatever she's writing in her notebook.

Malcolm turns to Spence. "You'll be joining us again on Sunday, yes?"

Next up on the stage combat agenda is the scene where I slap Malcolm across the face. Spence looks like he might want to get in some early practice right this minute.

"Right." Spence's teeth snap down on the word. "Same time?"

Malcolm looks to Joanna for confirmation.

"Thank you for your expertise, Mr. Spencer." Malcolm claps Spence on the shoulder like they're old friends, sticking his other hand out for Spence to shake.

Spence hesitates before accepting, like he isn't sure whether Malcolm is being genuine or making fun of him. To tell the truth, I'm not sure either. I was concerned about Spence trying to flirt with me or tease me or otherwise make me look unserious and unprofessional, but I could never have predicted he'd let Malcolm steamroll him like that.

I go to the seat in the front row where I left my bag and start packing things back into it—my script, my water bottle, the wrapper of the candy bar I ate during our last break.

Spence sidles up to me as I'm pulling the elastic out of my hair. He leans in like he's about to whisper something in my ear. Without looking up at him, I shake my head. My hair tumbles over my shoulders, and I rake my fingers through it to loosen the curls.

"Later," I tell him.

"You don't even know what I was going to say."

I glance at Malcolm, then back at Spence, one eyebrow raised. Malcolm is occupied at the moment, discussing something with Joanna and Bryn on the other end of the row of seats, but why take the chance when we can vent in the privacy of our own apartment?

"Fine," Spence says.

I hoist my bag onto my shoulder. "Want to pick up some food on the way home?"

Spence smiles and looks down, shuffling his shoes against the floor like the shy schoolboy he's never been. "Actually . . ."

Two nights in a row? That might be a new record for him.

"Fine. More for me." I'm a little disappointed, I was actually kind of looking forward to one of his epic rants. "Have a good night."

"Oh, I will." His voice is thick with innuendo.

I roll my eyes, but he doesn't see it because he leans in to kiss me—not on the mouth or the cheek, but somewhere in between, his lips brushing the corner of mine.

He heads for the door, not looking at Malcolm on his way out. I hitch my bag up higher on my shoulder, getting ready to leave too, but I'm not quick enough. Joanna intercepts me, breaking away from her conversation with Malcolm and Bryn.

"Hey, Kira," she says. "Great job tonight."

"Thank you." I shift my weight, hiking my purse strap up higher. That's the longest sentence she's said to me since the audition.

"Dawn left some costume pieces for you to try on. Think you could take a look at them before you leave?"

I'd really rather not—I'm already fantasizing about an order from Insomnia Cookie I don't have to share with Spence. But the way Joanna asks the question, it's clear the only acceptable answer is *Sure, no problem.*

"Bryn," she says.

Bryn and Malcolm both look up from the page they were studying in her stage management binder. He has his foot up on the seat next to her, and he's leaning into his knee, stretching out his hamstrings. I try not to notice the way his black workout pants pull across his ass.

"Can you show Kira where those costumes are?"

"I'll do it," Malcolm says.

The corner of Joanna's mouth twitches—or did I imagine that?

"Okay. Thank you," she says. "Just let me know which ones fit, okay?"

She exits into the lobby, Bryn following close behind.

"Come on," Malcolm says, already heading for the doorway that leads backstage. "Everything's in Dressing Room B."

It's not until he switches off the lights in the theater, plunging me into darkness, that I realize this is the first time we've ever been alone.

I follow the sound of Malcolm's footsteps into the narrow hallway behind the stage. Indifferent Honest has two dressing rooms— a rarity for storefront theaters, which sometimes don't even have one—but they're far from luxurious, each about the size of a walk-in closet. Dressing Room B is outfitted with a rough wooden table splattered with black paint, years' worth of eyeshadow dust ground into the grain. There's a wide mirror propped on it, some lights screwed into the wall above, and a rusty folding chair in front.

Sitting on the chair is a shopping bag overflowing with black satin—different versions of the slip Mara wears for most of the second act of the play. I start pulling them out and draping them over the chair.

"I actually wanted to talk to you about something also," Malcolm says. "So once you're done—"

"Stay." I meet his eyes in the mirror. "We can multitask."

He looks surprised. Good.

I unbutton my sweater and shrug it off my shoulders, letting it fall to the floor. Then I peel off my tank top, exposing the black bra underneath. It's not particularly sexy—I wore the closest thing I have to a sports bra, since we were working on combat stuff—but it still creates impressive cleavage.

"Should I shut the door?" He's still hanging back on the threshold, leaning with one shoulder against the doorframe.

I shrug. "If you want."

He takes a step inside, pulling the door closed behind him.

"What did you want to talk about?" I ask. I've shed my leggings now, too, and I hold the first slip up to the light to examine it. Taking my time. He likes staring at me so much? Now's his chance to get a good long look. If he thinks I'm going to get embarrassed, blush and stammer, try to cover myself up, he's sorely mistaken.

"Have you ever been married?" he asks.

Okay. Not quite the line of conversation I was expecting.

"No," I say. "Have you?"

He acts like he hasn't heard my question. "You have a boyfriend, though?"

"Not at the moment."

"Really? I was under the impression you and Byron were involved."

It takes me a second to realize he's referring to Spence. No one calls him by his old-fashioned first name, not even his parents back in Pennsylvania.

"We're roommates," I say.

"But you fuck each other."

I almost say yes, but I stop myself. Why should I answer? He didn't ask a question.

"I know we don't know each other very well yet," he continues, "but the audience has to believe Mara and Trent are married. That we've been intimate for years."

I slide the first slip over my head. Is this the part where he tells me to get on my knees and put his penis in my mouth so I can understand my character better? He wouldn't be the first to try.

Men always think that type of shit is a power move, when really they're showing their hand. If someone wants to fuck you, then you've got leverage over them, simple as that. I thought his attraction to me was obvious at the audition (and at our impromptu callback at the school), but since then I haven't been able to get a clear read on him. He's not reluctant to touch me—he moves me around the stage sometimes like I'm a piece of furniture—but then there's his strange aversion to stage kissing. And the fact that he's looking me in the eyes right now, instead of the tits.

"What do you think of this one?" I ask.

"Too tight," he says. The first time a man's ever said *that* to me.

I shrug. "Feels okay to me."

"It might constrict your range of motion. For the fight scenes."

Fine. I pull it off and try the next one. Once the slip is on, I run my fingers through my hair, fluffing it up so it looks fuller, a little wilder. Malcolm isn't averting his eyes, but he's not ogling me, either. He's acting like I'm fully dressed, like this is all completely normal.

"So what did you have in mind?" I ask. "For us to get to know each other better."

"Are you free tomorrow?"

"I could be."

The second slip is looser fitting, but I don't like it. Too much scalloped lace trim scraping at my exposed skin. Malcolm has no reaction to it at all, so I take it off and try on the third.

As soon as the fabric settles over my body, Malcolm's mouth falls open. The low, wet sound of his lips parting shudders through me like a thunderclap.

"That one," he says.

He's as far away as he can be in these tight quarters, but in the mirror it looks like we're standing much closer together—as though if I leaned my head back, it would loll against his shoulder.

This is the reaction I was trying to provoke. But I'm still dreading what he's going to say next. It's usually some version of *Has anyone ever told you how beautiful you are?* Like he's the first man to ever really see me, like I'll be *so grateful* he's let me in on this secret about myself.

Malcolm steps closer, still silent. Maybe he won't say anything. To be honest, I much prefer it when they don't bother with words at all. Maybe he'll just grab me, spin me around, pull me into him. Slide the black satin straps off my shoulders and press his mouth to mine.

I'll let him get that far, at least. There's a trick to it, knowing the right moment to stop. I want him left panting, hopeful, like a dog waiting for a treat, but not insulted. Not angry.

I run through the scene in my mind. He'll kiss me—it feels inevitable now—and I'll kiss him back, for a few seconds, before pressing my hands against his chest to separate us. *I think it would be best if we keep things professional*, I'll whisper, so close he won't be able to see the lie in my eyes. *For now.*

And then I feel his breath on my spine, and for a second I let myself wonder if it wouldn't be better to get it over with, release the tension between us. Give in.

But he still hasn't touched me. I rock back on my heels, erasing a bit more of the space between us, and meet his eyes in the mirror. Let him take it as encouragement. Let him take it however he wants.

He smiles, his tongue darting out to wet his lips. What the hell is he waiting for?

"Thank you," he says. His tone is cool, casual. No trace of the heat I was so certain I heard before. "I'll let Joanna know which costume we're going with."

"You're sure?" I say. "I can try on some of the others if you—"

I start to undress again, slipping one strap off my shoulder. But he isn't interested. He isn't even looking at me anymore. In fact, he's already turning to leave.

"I'm sure," he says. "Turn the lights off when you're done."

16

JOANNA

WHEN I COME BACK UP FROM MY OFFICE, THE THEATER IS dead silent and pitch-black, aside from the greenish haze of a few pieces of glow tape still stuck on the stage from our last show. I make a mental note to pry them up before the *Temper* set is loaded in—or to make Bryn do it for me.

Mal must still be backstage. That, or he took off without bothering to tell me again. Bryn left a few minutes ago, and Kira will be gone by now too; it shouldn't have taken her more than a couple of minutes to try on those costumes.

I don't bother switching the lights back on. I know this space so well I can find my way just as easily in the dark. The door of the first dressing room stands open, showing nothing but shadows inside. A sliver of light shines underneath the closed door of the other. I hear Mal's voice coming from inside. Maybe he's on the phone?

But then I hear a woman's low alto.

Kira.

They're in there, alone, with the door closed.

Talking, I tell myself. Just talking.

I strain my ears, trying to make out what they're saying.

But now they've stopped speaking.

Is that—the rustle of fabric? The scrape of furniture legs against the floor? I try to extend my attention like a radio antenna, but there's nothing more to hear. Just a long, terrible stretch of silence.

Finally, the door opens. Mal slips out, leaving the door ajar behind him.

"Hey," he says. "Were you looking for me?"

Through the gap between the edge of the door and the frame, I can see Kira. She's wearing a black slip, like the one described in the stage directions. It fits her perfectly, skimming over her skin close enough to suggest the shape of her body underneath. Her hair is mussed, a dark halo around her head.

I imagine Mal's fingers in it, tugging at the roots. My hands curl into fists.

"I'm ready to head out whenever you are," he says.

So nonchalant. Hands in his pockets, half smile on his face. Nothing to see here.

Kira hasn't noticed me watching, doesn't even seem to realize the door is standing open. Or maybe she does realize, she just doesn't give a damn.

She's staring at herself in the mirror—almost as intensely as she stared at Mal during the audition. One strap of the slip has already fallen off her shoulder, and she tugs the other one down, letting the fabric glide off her body and puddle on the floor like water.

I force myself to look away. But not before I've gotten a glimpse of the soft curve of her stomach, the crease where her rib cage meets her waist.

"Yes," I say to Mal. "Let's go home."

17

KIRA

Meet me at the Shakespeare statue in Lincoln Park. 4pm tomorrow.

That's all the text from Malcolm said. No *please*, no *if you're free*, no explanation.

I ignored it when it arrived on my way home from the theater, and I kept on ignoring it this morning. If Spence had been around to slap some sense into me, I might have succeeded in blowing Malcolm off entirely. But Spence didn't come home last night, and I haven't seen him all day, either—he's probably still off running around with his new sex friend—and as the afternoon wore on, my curiosity got the better of me.

So here I am. I didn't bother dressing up, though; I'm wearing one of my less-flattering pairs of jeans and an old V-neck sweater of Spence's, no makeup beyond mascara and lip balm. I don't know what this is, but it sure as hell isn't a date. Malcolm made it crystal clear last night he has no interest in fucking me, and I'm not going to ask for further humiliation by tarting myself up on his account.

It's ridiculous that I let him rattle me so much last night. I don't even want to sleep with him. Not really. I just wanted to put him in his place, to feel like I had the upper hand for one brief, delicious moment. But to get the upper hand, you have to know which way is up, and with him, I'm never sure.

The Shakespeare statue in question sits on a narrow strip of parkland between the Lincoln Park Zoo and a line of luxury high-rises with lake views. It depicts the Bard reclining in a chair, his index finger stuck between the pages of a small book. He has a vaguely annoyed look on his face, like all the people passing through the park are interrupting his reading time.

It's already a few minutes past four, but I don't see Malcolm anywhere. If he summoned me out here just to stand me up, I swear to God.

I make a circuit of the statue, then take a seat on the bench behind it. I'll give him until quarter past the hour, and then I'm leaving.

I've been here before, but not for years. In fact, I think the last time was the night Spence and I saw *Hamlet*. We were supposed to meet up for drinks with some friends after the show. Spence's friends, not mine—a couple of colleagues from the day job he had at the time, working at a downtown gym catering to aging trophy wives. We had the bright idea of walking the whole way from Raven-swood to River North, to save money so we could afford more cock-tails. We'd only been in the city a few months then, and we were still learning our way around, so we ended up getting lost and wandering into Lincoln Park.

It was bitter cold that night—the kind of cold where your face aches and the hairs inside your nose freeze. I was used to harsh win-ters, growing up in Ohio, but the lashing wind off Lake Michigan took some getting used to. I've adapted now, bought the same North Face coat every other woman in Chicago wears from December to March, which renders me about as sexy as a walking sleeping bag.

When we stumbled across the statue, Spence dared me to climb up and sit in Shakespeare's lap. So I did, trying to strike a sexy pose while also grinding my teeth together to keep from shivering. Spence snapped a few pictures with his phone, and I still have a printout of one of the photos stuck to the vanity mirror in my bedroom. The image is grainy and washed-out, the flash rendering my pale skin ghostly, but I'm smiling so bright it's like I'm lit from within.

After Spence helped me down, he kept his arms around my waist and pulled me into a kiss. Anyone walking by would have thought we were young lovers, head over heels for each other. Or possibly drunk. I felt almost inebriated that whole night, even though we never made it to the bar. We were both giddy, high off the energy of the performance.

Before I saw Malcolm play the role, I wasn't a big fan of *Hamlet*—the play or the character. As far as I was concerned, he was a whiny little rich boy who deserved everything that befell him. But Malcolm's melancholy Dane wasn't mopey or indecisive, he was furious—at his murderous uncle, obviously, but also at himself, every time he faltered or failed to act. He brought out all of the character's charm and cunning and cruelty, his sharp wit a deadlier weapon than his rapier, and for the first time I could understand why Ophelia might love him, why she might go mad over losing him.

Usually, when I see a play, it's the other actresses I envy. I pick apart their performances, think about how I would have played the part better. But when I saw *Hamlet*, Malcolm was the one I wanted to be. His charisma, his physicality, his ease with the language. He made that daunting role look so effortless.

Ten years later, I still wish I could make someone feel the way Malcolm made me feel that night. Thrilled and fascinated and enraptured and devastated. So much, all at once. It was probably foolish of me, but I thought working with him might finally get me there. But maybe it's something that can't be taught.

"Mind if I sit down?"

The voice is familiar, and yet it isn't. I'm not sure it's actually Malcolm until I turn around and see him standing right behind the park bench, his hands braced on the top slat.

He's abandoned his usual uniform of slim-cut dark jeans and a black shirt. The jeans he has on today are a more relaxed fit, almost baggy on him, and he's wearing a flannel button-down, gray plaid shot through with greens and blues. His hair is messier, too, like he slept on it and didn't bother combing it afterward.

But it's not only his style that's altered. Malcolm is carrying himself differently, his feet planted wider, his shoulders rounded, his hands plunged into his pockets. I can't explain it, but he seems *younger*. Younger than his real age, certainly, and maybe even younger than I am. If I were meeting him for the first time, I might assume he was in his twenties, despite the salt-and-pepper hair. Even the crow's feet around his eyes seem to have vanished. I'll have to get him to teach me that trick.

"Hey," I say. "Did you just get here?"

I didn't hear him approaching on the sidewalk. Maybe he's been here the whole time, watching me from the small cluster of trees a few yards away. I wouldn't put it past him.

Malcolm doesn't answer me. He doesn't even acknowledge he heard me speak, just saunters around to the front of the bench and sits down. Not as close as he could have—he's left a good two feet of space between us.

"Sorry I was a few minutes late," I say. "I—"

"You like it here, don't you?" he asks.

"Uh, sure." What a weird fucking thing to say. "It's nice, I guess. This time of year."

I'm about to say something truly basic about the autumn leaves, but then he turns and locks onto me with those laser-beam eyes, and the words disintegrate in my throat.

"The last two Saturdays," he says. "I was walking by, and I saw you sitting here."

Now I'm really confused. I haven't been here since that night with Spence.

"You had a cup of coffee," he continues. "And you were writing in a notebook."

What the hell is he talking about? "I wasn't—"

"You looked so serious, I didn't want to disturb you." This, he says with a smile. It's open, friendly, sincere—the kind that's meant to put someone at ease. Nothing like any smile of his I've seen before.

Then it hits me: there's a line in the play, practically a throwaway, where Trent mentions meeting in a park. *That day in the park, I should have just kept on fucking walking.* Malcolm isn't talking about me, he's talking about Mara.

An improv exercise. Why didn't he just say so? I could have done some prep work before coming here. I've never been the kind of actor who has to write out a whole life story for every character I play. If I'd known that's what he wanted, though, I would have come up with something.

But I've answered my own question. He didn't tell me because he wanted to catch me off guard, so I'd have no choice but to react in the moment.

I smile back and stick out my hand for him to shake, like we're total strangers. Which we are, no matter how many hours I've already spent in his company.

"I'm Mara," I say. "And you're not disturbing me."

However far I may be from understanding the mysterious inner workings of Malcolm Mercer, I at least seem to have figured out the game he's playing right now. When I say my character's name instead of my own, his smile shifts. He's himself for a moment, rather than Trent, and he's pleased with me for playing along. A split second later, though, the mask of character settles back over his face.

"Nice to meet you, Mara," he says. "I'm Trent."

My turn again. Okay. What else do I know about Mara and Trent? They met in a park back when Mara was in graduate school, they've been married for several years—that's it.

Well, that and they hate each other's guts.

They must have liked each other at some point, though. At the start, when they got together. What would have made Mara want to talk to him that day in the park?

Don't have to dig too deep there, just look at the bastard. The careless hair and sloppy clothing somehow makes him even more attractive. I doubt my own purposely casual ensemble is doing me the same favors.

"What about you?" I say. "Do you come here often too?"

A lame line, but at least it tosses the ball back to him.

"Not really," he says. "You live around here?"

Goddammit. He's going to keep answering my questions with more questions.

I wish Spence were here to Cyrano de Bergerac some lines into my ear. He loves this improvisation shit. *It's so simple, Kira*—that's what he always said in college whenever I bitched about the improv exercises we had to do in our acting classes. As long as you commit, say *yes, and* instead of *no, but*, it's impossible to screw up.

Unless you freeze up and go mute, like I'm doing right now. Malcolm is watching me. Waiting to see what I'll do. If I drop character, stop the game, then he wins.

Not this time. This time, I'm going to play.

And I intend to win.

So I toss my head back and let out a bubbly sound that's nothing like my normal laugh. "I wish! No, I'm a grad student. I can barely afford coffee. What about you?"

THE LONGER WE PLAY, THE EASIER IT GETS.

We stayed on the bench until well after dark, then started walking—first wandering toward the lakefront, then slowly making our way down the paved bike trail that follows the coastline. Both of us refusing to break character. I've managed to make up a whole life for Mara: early memories, favorite foods, childhood pets. The first shitty job she held out of college, and the second, slightly less shitty one she had when she met Trent.

Most of what I've been saying to Malcolm is from my own life, just slightly altered. I'm from Delaware, Ohio, a little north of the state capitol, Columbus, so I make Mara from Marysville, which is a little south. I have a younger sister, so I give Mara an older one. Mara studied abroad for a year in Berlin, because I spent one inebriated weekend there with Spence during a backpacking trip we took for his twenty-fifth birthday, and I can still vaguely recall some of the major landmarks.

Until I saw the sun peeking over the silvery waves of Lake Michigan, I had no idea how much time had gone by. We're passing the imposing marble facade of the Field Museum now, heading onto the promontory that leads out to the Adler Planetarium and Northerly Island. Somehow, we've kept this up all night, and even though my feet ache and my voice rasps from overuse, I feel so *awake*.

Before we reach the planetarium, Malcolm veers off the path, taking a seat on the concrete steps leading down to the water. I follow. There was a slight chill in the air yesterday, but it's warmed up throughout the night, and now the weather feels almost balmy, like we're on the cusp of summer rather than winter.

We're far enough out into the lake for the noise of the city to fade away. All I can hear is the soft lapping of the waves and the sound of Malcolm's voice. I lean back on my hands, mirroring his posture, and my little finger brushes his knuckle. Neither one of us moves. We've been edging closer to each other all night, our arms bumping together as we walked, accidentally at first and then on purpose. Drawn like magnets.

"How long have you been a writer?" he's asking now.

The script never mentions what kind of writer Mara is—I've been assuming novelist, but she could be a playwright, an essayist, even a poet. At one point, when they're arguing, Trent says, *You're not going to use this, are you?* She doesn't answer him.

Okay. Substitute writing for acting.

"Since high school," I say.

"In class? Or on your own?"

"In class. Senior year English literature."

"And your teacher?" he asks.

My hands stiffen, fingernails scraping over the concrete. "What about my teacher?"

"Did he—" Malcolm stops himself. "Or, sorry, was it *she*?"

"He."

"He." Malcolm smiles. "Did he encourage you—your writing?"

Encourage. Yes, that's one way of putting it.

"He did," I say.

"So he was like a mentor to you."

"No. I mean, yes."

Shut up, shut up, shut up.

"A sort of father figure, then?"

My face screws up with disgust, and for a moment I'm not Mara any longer.

"What?" he says.

Malcolm doesn't need to know I dropped character. I can still play this off. I can still win.

"Nothing," I say. "It's just—he wasn't anywhere near old enough to be a father figure."

"I see," Malcolm says. "So he was closer to your age? How old were you?"

"Seventeen. When we first met."

It's taking all my mental energy to keep my face neutral. My brain suddenly feels like it's full of the same sludge that coats the bottom of the lake. I must not be as wide awake as I thought.

"Maybe you had a little crush on him?"

Malcolm's voice has a teasing lilt to it, but it doesn't match the look in his eyes. He leans closer, his shoulder touching mine. Like someone could overhear us, like we're not completely alone out here.

"I bet he had a crush on you, too."

I look away, casting my eyes down at my feet, then squinting out at the lake. His gaze seems to sharpen—the threads of a screw biting, twisting in deeper.

Say no. Change the subject. Laugh at him. Anything.

But how can he have any idea whether I'm telling the truth? This is just a game. I'm supposed to be my character right now, not myself. I can say whatever I want. He doesn't have to know.

"I started staying after class," I say. "To talk to him about my—my writing."

Malcolm nods, like he understands. "He took advantage of you."

"No."

I didn't mean for that to come out so harsh. Malcolm tilts his head a little. Taking note.

It's just, I've heard that statement before, so many times—from my parents, the principal of my high school, even Rob. He used to get so upset whenever I called David my ex-boyfriend or referred to our relationship as an "affair."

"He was really young," I tell Malcolm. "Almost as young as I was."

Fresh out of college, his first year teaching. And his last, thanks to me.

"But at some point, your relationship crossed the line."

He's leaning closer to me now. Too close. I can smell the coffee he drank before meeting me yesterday afternoon. His cologne. It has a smoky bite to it like the scent Spence wears, but there's no undertone of sweetness.

"Was he the one who stepped over the line?" Malcolm asks.

He was a predator, Kira. That's what Rob always said. *He should be in prison.* But I refuse to think of David as a predator, because that would mean I was his prey.

Besides, fucking me was the least damaging thing David Granville did.

The sun is higher in the sky now, orange light washing over us. It blazes in Malcolm's eyes, small flames barely contained by his pupils.

"No." Answering for me. He thinks he has all the answers. "It was you. Wasn't it?"

When I move to the edge of the step, my palms sliding up his thighs, Malcolm looks a little bewildered, like he has no idea what I'm about to do—which is how I know he's still in character. "Trent" may be confused, but Malcolm Mercer knows exactly what's about to happen.

I lean in. Now I can hold his gaze.

With the space of a breath left between us, Malcolm cups my face with his hands, his ring fingers hooking under the line of my jaw. He's holding me still, preventing me from closing the distance. Giving me another chance to stop, to call off this strange game we're playing.

I don't want to stop. I'm done talking. I close my eyes, exhale, let the tension melt out of my muscles. My lips come apart, and then his mouth covers mine.

I reach for his hips, my fingers slipping under his shirt, hooking his belt loops, hitching us closer together. I'm practically in his lap now, but he keeps his hands confined to my cheeks, my jaw, the sides of my neck. Very professional, but part of me is disappointed. I want his hands all over me. I want him to pick me up and wrap my legs around his waist and lay me back on the pavement and—

Malcolm is the one who ends the kiss. A good thing, too—I might never have stopped on my own. This type of improv, I could say *yes, and* to all day.

"This is what I was talking about before," Malcolm says.

He's himself now, no longer in character. When did he make the switch? The moment he pulled away from me, or sometime in the middle of the kiss?

"You feel the difference?" he says. "How the energy between us has changed?"

I nod. My face feels hot—it must be bright red. I'm afraid he'll think I'm blushing, that I'm embarrassed. It's more like I'm burning with fever. He still has one hand pressed against the side of my neck. I want to kiss him again, but it feels like crossing a different sort of line. We're not in character anymore. It would be me kissing him, not Mara kissing Trent.

Is that what I want? I thought I knew what I was doing in the dressing room the other night, but now I have no idea.

Malcolm stands up, smooths his hair, tugs his shirt back into place. Then he holds out his hand.

I take it, and without another word, we start walking back toward the city. I don't know where we're going, but I know we're not done. Whatever is going on between us, it's just getting started.

JOANNA

ALL NIGHT I WAS RESTLESS, MY MIND RACING, THINKING OF more things I need to do tomorrow, the next day, every day up until *Temper* opens.

I kept reaching for my notebook and phone, jotting down to-dos and writing emails to Bryn, which I sent with delayed delivery so her notifications wouldn't ping incessantly in the middle of the night. But who knows, maybe she was awake. I was positively vampiric at her age. Up until two or three, sleeping in until noon, with a nap between my afternoon classes and dinner.

These days, I can't seem to stay in bed past six, no matter how little sleep I get during the night. I pass Mal's room on the way to the bathroom. His door is open, which is strange. He usually sleeps with it closed. Could he already be awake? My stomach is growling. Maybe I can persuade him to go out for breakfast. Pancakes at Bongo Room on Clark Street, with a side of bacon and black coffee—that's his favorite. He always gets the gruesome-looking red velvet ones.

When we first moved in, we didn't even have doors to close. The place was a dilapidated husk—crumbling plaster, scorch marks on the kitchen ceiling, a fault line of cracked tiles running down the center of the bathroom floor—and even in that state, the rent was more than we could afford. But Mal made me believe it was worth it. He led me into the middle of the loft, circled behind me and put his hands on my shoulders. "Try to see the potential," he said. Then he started describing his ideas for the space, how we could turn it into both a performance venue and a home. He swiveled me this way and that, pointing things out, speaking so close to my ear his lips touched the lobe. His words conjured images in my head, and suddenly I could see it too—all the possibilities, everything he imagined for us.

Over the years, we've made improvements. Stripping and refinishing the floors to show the grain of the original oak, patching and painting over the walls. Like most of our furniture, all the paint colors were left over from theater sets: art gallery–white from *The Shape of Things*, steel blue from *Six Corners*. We could afford somewhere nicer now. We could afford to get our own places, too, but I don't see the point. I'm almost always at the theater anyway. Indifferent Honest is more my home than this place is.

I miss those first few lean years. We only had one pot in the kitchen, scoured dull from being scrubbed out after every meal, but we had five versions of the Complete Works of Shakespeare, which we kept stacked on our sloping mantel because we didn't own a bookshelf yet. Sometimes Mal would take one down and read from it for me. The Oxford edition was his favorite. Sonnets or soliloquies at first, then whole plays, a scene at a time, doing different voices for all the roles, his words echoing off the lead-glass skylight. We kept the lights off as much as possible to save on electricity, but we'd light clusters of candles and sit around them like we were casting a spell. In a way, we were.

The one and only time my mother came to visit me here, the magic was utterly lost on her. Within five minutes of her arrival, she found a rusty nail sticking straight up out of a loose floorboard in the corner. Mouth pursed, she pried it out with the multi-tool she always keeps in her purse, then spent the rest of the weekend looking at Mal like she wished she could do the same to him.

What do you know about this boy, really? That's what she said when I first told her about my plans to move to Chicago. As if Mal were just some guy I was following across state lines because of a crush. Her entreaties got more and more desperate in the weeks leading up to my departure. Finally, the night before I left, she told me if I went through with this, she'd have no choice but to cut me off financially until I came to my senses.

My whole childhood, she acted more like my friend than my mother. She adopted me on her own and made sure I knew that meant I was special, wanted. Chosen. As soon as I could speak in complete sentences, she started soliciting my opinions on the artwork in the gallery where she worked as a curator, and she took what I said seriously, too. A lifetime of *trust your instincts* and *do whatever you feel is right*, and all of a sudden she wanted to lay down the law? I almost laughed in her face.

We barely spoke, my first two years in Chicago. It wasn't until Indifferent Honest started to gain some traction with our production of *Hamlet* that I finally invited her to visit. I wanted her to see what Mal and I had created together. I thought once she saw him onstage, she would understand.

But after the show, all she had to offer were a few generic compliments about my directing choices. Her praise, however well intended, meant next to nothing to me by that point. My entire life, she'd told me every artistic thing I did, from finger painting to my two-week stint playing the flute, was *brilliant*, so how could I take her seriously?

The next morning, before she left to go back to Philadelphia, we went out for brunch, the way we used to every Sunday when I was a kid. One of us ordering a sweet dish, the other savory, taking bites off each other's plates. I made the mistake of asking her outright what she thought of Mal, and she reached across the table and squeezed my hand, with this tight, sad smile on her face. I used to think we looked so alike, even though I wasn't biologically hers, but in the harsh morning light spilling through the windows of the Chicago Diner that day, all I could see were our differences: the pinched tip of her nose, her translucent blond eyelashes, the wrinkles already cording her neck.

"You need to be careful with him, Joanna," she said. "I can't explain it, but . . . it's like he takes up all the air in the room."

I jerked my hand away from her and, after a few more minutes of arguing, threw my napkin down on my syrup-soaked plate and stormed out of the restaurant. We haven't spoken much since then. Just sporadic phone calls and emails that get shorter and more strained with every passing year. I know she still follows the theater company, though, because she texts me every opening night, without fail. I never answer. Mal agrees it's for the best. "I know you want her to understand, Jo," he told me at the time. "But she can't. She's not like us. She's not an artist."

I stop on the threshold of his room and peer inside. His bed is empty, the gray comforter pulled up, one side higher than the other.

My stomach churns—not with hunger anymore. I go inside and sink down on the corner of the mattress, running my hand over the space where Mal should be. It's smooth and cold.

He didn't sleep here last night.

IT'S NEARLY NOON WHEN MAL FINALLY SHOWS HIMSELF. I'M sitting at the kitchen table, trying to work but really just staring at my murky reflection in the laptop screen. He walks right past me anyway, like he doesn't even see me sitting here.

"Where have you been?" I hate him for making me ask. I hate myself for asking.

He's wearing the same clothes he had on when I last saw him yesterday—that hideous flannel shirt I'd never seen before. It's not him at all. It looks like a costume.

"Mal."

He still doesn't acknowledge me. He goes to the coffee pot, pours the remainder into the mug I was drinking out of earlier.

"Where were you last night? I was worried."

I should have been worried, I suppose, that something bad had happened to him. He could have been hit by a car. Mugged and shot. Left for dead in an alley. But that's not what I've been worried about, as I sat here stewing for the past few hours.

He tips his head back and drains the mug; I watch his throat move as he swallows. The coffee must be cold by now. Then he sets the mug on the counter and looks at me. Finally.

"I was with Kira," he says.

I didn't expect him to come right out and say it. I didn't think he'd lie—he wouldn't lie, not to me. I just thought he'd make me work harder to get at the truth. Chip away at him until I made a crack big enough for it to trickle out.

"All night?" I say.

Silence. That's a yes.

"And what exactly were you doing all night with Kira?"

"Just some character work."

That could mean anything. Mal has few limits when it comes to eliciting the performance he wants. *I can get it out of her*, he told me. Is that what he was doing last night?

"She's really coming along," he says. "I can't wait for you to see. You'll be there tonight?"

"No."

He looks at me blankly. Of course he would forget. It's the same weekend every year, but Mal doesn't keep a calendar. Why would he, when he has me?

"The fundraiser," I say. "You're still planning on meeting me there, right? After rehearsal?"

"Yes, yes, of course." He waves his hand like he's swatting a fly.

"What are you going to wear?" I give the flannel shirt a dubious once-over. It looks like something my Nirvana-obsessed college boyfriend would have worn. I want to rip it off his back and burn it.

"I don't know yet," he says. "Set something out for me if you're so concerned about it."

There's a hardness in his voice—like flint striking steel, about to ignite. I've heard him use that tone before, many times. But never toward me.

"If you don't want to come," I tell him, "then don't fucking come."

I start to walk away. He catches me by the wrist. It hurts, but that's my fault. I'm the one turning, twisting. All I have to do is relax and loosen my arm. Then it won't hurt anymore.

"Jo." He hunches down so he can look me right in the eyes. "I'm sorry I made you worry. But I'm fine. I'm here now. And I'll be there tonight."

He's still holding my wrist, but it's so gentle now. The loop of his fingers feather-light against my skin. If I tried to withdraw, his grip would break away like paper.

"I promise," he says.

19

KIRA

SPENCE BEAT ME TO THE THEATER. WHEN I WALK IN, HE'S IN the process of stripping off his shirt, revealing the sheen of sweat covering his torso.

"Hey." I set my bag down in the front row, one seat over from his.

"Hey," he says. "Sorry I couldn't meet you for dinner. I was—"

"Busy. I know."

His curt response to my text message asking him if he wanted to go to DMK Burger Bar before rehearsal was the first sign of life I'd seen from him since fight rehearsal two days ago. I'm not sure if he hasn't been home at all, or if we keep missing each other.

"Did you get something to eat?" I ask.

He lifts his eyebrows suggestively.

"Just couldn't wait until after rehearsal, huh?" I say.

"He's working the late shift tonight and tomorrow, so—"

Now it's my turn to raise my eyebrows. "So it's a guy?"

A look of panic flashes on Spence's face; he didn't mean to give that away.

"What about you?" Spence asks.

"What about me?"

"Anything you want to tell me?"

I take a pointed look at his bare chest. "You need a shower?"

He takes a clean T-shirt out of his bag and shrugs it on, then climbs into the second row so he's in the chair facing me, one riser up. He's grinning obscenely.

"You didn't come home last night," he says.

"I thought you spent the night with—"

"I did. But I came back this morning to get a change of clothes, *way* too early for you to be awake. And you weren't there."

I press my lips together. If he can be secretive, so can I.

"You were with him," he says. "Weren't you?"

My silence seems to be a sufficient answer for him.

"I knew it!" He leans forward and grabs my hands. "So tell me: Is Malcolm Mercer as good at actual fucking as he is at eye fucking?"

"I didn't have sex with him."

He drops my hands. "Liar."

"I'm serious. We were just walking around and talking."

"All night long?" Spence's facial expression somehow manages to convey both disgust and skepticism.

"I mean, we sat down for a while. And then we went out for breakfast together. Red velvet pancakes—scandalous!"

"I'm very disappointed in you, young lady," Spence says.

I roll my eyes. "I think you'll survive."

"But come on, you can't tell me you're not attracted to him."

Malcolm picks that moment to walk into the theater. Bryn is with him, but not Joanna. He's dressed up—all in black, shirt tucked in, suit jacket folded over his arm. As much as I'd like to believe it's for my benefit, I'm sure it isn't. Maybe he's going out after rehearsal? He has bruise-black circles under his eyes, but somehow on him they look handsome instead of haggard.

He greets Spence first. "Mr. Spencer, glad to have you with us again."

Spence gives him a tight smile and nod—wary, but staying on the right side of rude. It hasn't escaped my attention that the clean top Spence put on is his Steppenwolf T-shirt, from when he did the fights for one of their Garage shows. Which is the closest he can come to pinning his résumé to his chest and rubbing Malcolm's face in it.

Malcolm leans in, his hand on the small of my back. After I kissed him, the physical boundaries between us became so permeable it started to seem unnatural *not* to touch him. Another reason I'm glad we didn't sleep together. I've let too many walls fall already.

"I hope you were able to get some rest today," he says.

I haven't slept at all. I tried, several times, to take a nap, but I was too wired to keep my eyes closed for more than a few seconds at a time. I haven't stayed up all night since college, and back then I always felt flattened afterward, like the energy had been wrung out of me and poured down a drain. All day today, though, I felt like I had *too* much energy and no way to burn it off. At first I figured it was all the sugar and caffeine I consumed at breakfast, but the crash I anticipated never came.

"Don't worry," I tell him. "I'm ready."

20

JOANNA

I ARRIVE AT THE FUNDRAISER FASHIONABLY LATE. THAT WAY I only have to survive two hours of small talk without Mal while he's at rehearsal, as opposed to three.

This year it's at the Holiday Club, a faux-retro bar on the corner of Sheridan and Irving Park. The event is meant to raise money for Chicago non-Equity theaters in general rather than Indifferent Honest in particular, but it's an ideal place to meet people who love theater and have more cash than they know what to do with. A small company like ours can't survive on ticket sales alone. To have any hope of breaking even, we need donors. And every little bit helps.

When I pick up my name tag from the table at the entrance, I pocket Mal's, too. I laid out clothes for him at the end of his bed: a black button-down shirt, his best trousers. A suit jacket, too, but I doubt he'll bother with that. I thought about reminding him to shave, but telling him to would make him even less likely to do it. It works for him, though—that little bit of stubble, the wild hair. He looks romantic, poetic, like he could burst into a soliloquy at any moment.

When we first started Indifferent Honest, we shared a single black blazer between us for any occasion where we had to dress up.

It was tight across Mal's shoulders and couldn't be buttoned over my chest, and the lining was ripped out of the left armpit. But with the right posture—shoulders back and chin up, big strides like you own the place; Mal showed me how—that ratty blazer looked downright dignified. I still have it, folded up in the same box under my bed where I keep the stacks of birthday and Christmas cards my mother insists on sending me.

There's a band set up at the back of the bar, playing swingy Rat Pack covers, but no one is dancing yet. I recognize three of the five band members—including the singer, a curvy redhead wearing a cherry-colored wiggle dress—as local actors. I've never understood why so many actors are also in bands. Not enough rejection and disappointment in one artistic career, so they decided to add another?

I've been inside for less than five minutes when I see my ex-girlfriend, Lauren, perched on one of the piss-yellow vinyl bench seats lining the wall.

Girlfriend is maybe a bit of an overstatement. We went on a few dates, fucked maybe five times? It was good, I liked her, but she wanted more from me than I was able to give. The same reason most of my relationships go up in smoke. For me, the theater company is always going to come first. Maybe if I could find someone as obsessed with their job as I am with mine, we could make it work, but the only person I've ever known who meets that description is Mal. And he's not an option.

I give Lauren a polite smile from across the room, hoping that will be enough.

No such luck. She's walking toward me. This is going to be a long night. At least I look presentable. I put on lipstick, I blew my hair smooth, I'm wearing a low-cut blouse and a pencil skirt that cuts off some of the circulation to my waist.

"Joanna!" Lauren calls out. "How are you?"

I suppose it's nice of her, trying to sound like she's happy to see me. But there's a reason she went into administrative work instead of acting.

"Lauren. Good to see you."

She's wearing her hair shorter now, mussed up into little spikes. It's more interesting than the plain ponytail she used to have, but it doesn't suit her at all. She looks like a suburban mom who told her stylist she wanted an "edgy" new look to celebrate her divorce.

"How's the school program going these days?" I ask.

"Oh, you know," she says.

I really don't. My job has its fair share of tedium, but it's all in the service of creating actual art. I can't fathom having to listen to teenagers butcher the words of the best playwright in the English language day in and day out. I'd lose my fucking mind.

Lauren leans closer, her martini glass sloshing. It wouldn't surprise me if she's already a little drunk. She weighs all of a hundred pounds; she can't hold her liquor because there's nowhere to put it.

"I heard," she says, "that you just hired Kira Rascher."

It had occurred to me to call Lauren and ask her about Kira before agreeing to cast her. But whatever she said wouldn't have mattered to Mal, and I didn't relish the thought of talking to Lauren again if I didn't absolutely have to.

"Yes," I say. "She's playing the female lead in our fall production. I hope the rehearsal schedule hasn't been affecting her work."

"What do you mean?" Lauren asks.

"Well, we only rehearse at night, but I'm sure she has to get up bright and early to go to some of those schools outside the city."

"Kira doesn't work for me anymore."

"Oh. I didn't realize she'd quit."

A pretty stupid decision, if you ask me. Our company pays a decent weekly wage, but the show only runs through mid-December.

Truth be told, I was surprised Kira was part of the school program in the first place. She doesn't seem like she'd enjoy working with kids any more than I would.

"She didn't quit," Lauren says. "I fired her. I thought Malcolm might have told you."

She says Mal's name like it's an expletive. Lauren is the only person I've ever met, apart from my mother, who's completely immune to Mal's charms. It's not because she's a lesbian; I've seen him sweet talk plenty of gay women (and straight men, for that matter). But no matter what he threw at her to try and get in her good graces, it seemed to bounce off and clatter to the ground.

"Somehow," she continues, "he found out where Kira was teaching, and he came to the school."

My stomach drops. The day Mal decided to offer her the role, he disappeared for most of the afternoon. And then he came back so *sure*, like he'd been struck by a lightning bolt.

"I'm sorry, I had no idea." Apologizing for Mal comes as easy as breathing to me now. I can't tell if Lauren believes me. I wouldn't believe me, if I were her. "What did he do?"

"He didn't do anything, as far as I'm aware, besides sit in on the class. Kira's the one who decided to sexually assault her teaching partner in front of a room full of children."

"What?"

Lauren nods vigorously, eyes wide. She may have been horrified by Kira's behavior, but she's relishing telling this story again. I wonder who else she's told it to. Rumors tend to metastasize in the theater community.

"She completely changed the blocking, kissed him without his consent. Tim was *traumatized*. We'll never be invited back to that school again, that's for sure."

I do my best to continue to act horrified for Lauren's benefit, but this information feels like a puzzle piece slotted into place. What she's describing sounds exactly like something Mal would do. Fuck the venue, fuck the audience, fuck what's appropriate—all that matters to him is making the best, boldest, most authentic choice.

No wonder he was so certain about her.

21

KIRA

MY VOCAL CORDS ARE GETTING RAW, BUT THIS IS THE LAST run-through we have time for tonight. I want to do it perfectly this time.

"*Why?* Why the fuck would you—"

"*Because I don't want to have your fucking baby!*"

The line bursts from my throat like an explosion. Malcolm rounds on me, eyes flashing. He has his right index finger and thumb bracketed, pretending to hold the prescription pill bottle he'll have in his hand once we incorporate props. It's supposed to be Misoprostol, the drug Mara uses to induce the abortion she pretends is a miscarriage. Trent finds it in her purse and confronts her, triggering one of her imaginary violent outbursts.

We're in position for the slap—facing each other, angled so Malcolm's back is to the audience. I train my eyes on his. He meets my gaze. *Ready.* But then, I have no idea what he'd look like if he wasn't ready.

"How do I even know it was mine? We both know you've always been nothing but a—"

I rear back, then sweep my open palm across the space in front of his face. When my fingers pass his nose, I clap my left hand against my thigh—upstage, so the audience can't see. Spence traced an X on the side of my leg with his fingertip to show me the spot I should strike. "The thickest part, right here," he said. When I narrowed my eyes at him, he'd grinned and pinched my thigh. "Don't worry, doll— I know it's all muscle."

Usually the victim would do the knap rather than the attacker, but Spence assigned it to me because, once I'm in my costume, I'll be hitting bare skin, which will make the sound effect more convincing. The stretchy dress I'm wearing tonight is a few inches longer than my costume will be, so the knap is more of a muted *thwap* than a satisfying *smack*.

The rest is up to Malcolm. In time with the sound of the knap, he snaps his head to the side and raises his hand to his cheek, then shoots me a dark, stunned glare, like he can't believe what I just did. He plays his reaction a little differently every time—sometimes adding a yelp of pain or a sharp gasp, other times sticking with cold, menacing silence—but it's always convincing.

"Really nice work tonight," Spence says. "Both of you."

This fight rehearsal was so different from the last one, Spence seems suspicious. I can't blame him; Malcolm's change in attitude is giving me whiplash, too. For the past three hours, he's hardly said a word. He's been listening to what Spence tells us, and then doing it—flawlessly, every time, without complaint. His bizarre ban on stage kissing seems to have been lifted, too. Who knew all I had to do to get the guy to act like a normal human was talk to him for twelve hours straight and share some damn pancakes?

We could have broken for the night an hour ago if it weren't for me. It always takes me a little while to get the choreography in my body, so my muscles have it memorized instead of just my mind. That last run was the best one yet, but I still don't feel like I quite have it.

"I think I'm standing too far back," I say. "The people sitting on the ends of the first couple of rows might be able to see the distance between us."

"Better too far away than too close," Spence says.

Unlike the shove in Mara's first reverie, the slap is supposed to be strictly no-contact. If I touch Malcolm at all, I'm doing it wrong.

"What do you think?" I ask Malcolm. I can feel Spence bristling beside me, but he's not the one I have to satisfy here.

"I think it's fine," Malcolm says. "But if you want to stay a little longer and work through it a couple more times, I'd be happy to."

"You don't have somewhere you need to be?" I ask, thinking of his unusually dressy attire, and Joanna's equally unusual absence from rehearsal. Malcolm slung his suit jacket over one of the seats in the second row before we started rehearsing; now it's drooping off, the hem gathering dust from the floor.

Malcolm turns to Spence. "Don't let us keep you, Mr. Spencer. But Bryn, if you wouldn't mind, I'd like you to stick around, too."

She was already packing to leave, shoving her binder into her backpack and plugging her headphones into her phone. But when Malcolm looks at her, she nods and slumps back down in her chair, spreading the binder out on her lap again.

Spence glances at me. He'll stay if I ask him to, but I can tell he really wants to go.

"Get out of here." I smack him on the arm. "Say hi to your boy-friend for me."

Once he's gone, I take my mark for the top of the scene again and turn to Malcolm with a smile. I've been awake for something like thirty-six hours now. I should be ready to drop, but I know I have a few more runs in me, even if my energy is starting to flag a little. I want to get this right.

"Okay," I say. "Ready when you are."

22

JOANNA

I SHOWED UP TONIGHT PREPARED TO ANSWER QUESTIONS about *Temper*, the rest of our season, the renovations we did to the performance space over the summer. Instead the main question I'm asked, over and over and over again is: *Where's Mal?*

It's a good goddamn question. I wish I knew the answer.

I slip my phone out of my purse to check the time again. Quarter past eleven. Rehearsal should have ended an hour ago. Even if they ran a few minutes over, even if he took longer than usual to shut off the lights and lock up the building, even if he had to run home and change because he didn't wear his fundraiser clothes to the theater like I told him to, even if there were massive delays on the train, he should be here by now. I could text him, but he'd only ignore it. It took ages for me to convince him to get a cell phone, and he checks it so infrequently that people still call me when they want to reach him.

I've been making the rounds on my own, smiling and shaking hands and schmoozing with potential patrons, all the while keeping one eye on the door, watching for his entrance. He'll get here soon. He promised me.

I'm on my way to the bar to top off my drink when the marketing director at one of the more prominent Lincoln Park storefront theaters waylays me to ask, "Where's your husband tonight?"

"Mal and I aren't married," I remind her.

She cocks her head like a dog confused by a high-pitched sound. "Oh, I could have sworn you two were a couple. You look so nice together."

I hold the rim of my wine glass over my mouth so she won't see how tight and false my smile is. It used to thrill me when people would mistake me and Mal for a couple.

I know exactly how we look together. That's not the problem.

"I could *never* run a theater company with my husband." She laughs and sets her hand on my arm. "We'd murder each other!"

We part ways, with promises to set aside seats for each other at our companies' upcoming productions, even though I so rarely have time to see non–Indifferent Honest shows. I check my phone again. 11:23 p.m. No calls. If he doesn't get here soon, I just might fucking murder him.

I've talked to everyone I came to talk to, but I doubt I made any inroads. Mal may be atrocious at managing money, but he's great at getting people to give it to him. Another talent I don't possess. Last year, he spent most of the evening chatting up the well-preserved widow of a personal injury lawyer, who later made a truly obscene donation for our current season. I think Indifferent Honest might be in her will. (I also think he might have slept with her; I was afraid to ask.)

I wander back toward the bar, clutching my phone in one hand and the now-empty wine glass in the other. There's a tall, dark-haired man leaning against one of the bar stools, flipping through a menu with a winking Frank Sinatra on the cover. I've passed by him a few times while circulating around the room. Every time, he's been by himself, not speaking to anyone. He looks a bit miserable, to be honest, like he'd prefer to be literally anywhere else at the moment.

That makes two of us.

He looks familiar, too, now that I'm seeing him close-up, but I can't quite place him. Maybe he's an actor who's auditioned for us before? No, that's not it.

"Hi," he says.

Shit. Well, I *was* staring at him. Makes sense he'd take it as an invitation to talk. Based on the shabby sweater he's wearing, I don't think he's a person I can hit up for money, so at least I can relax about that for however long this conversation happens to last.

"Hi," I say.

He smiles. "You look like you hate these things almost as much as I do."

Is it that obvious? I thought I was putting up a good front, but I guess my percolating anger at Mal has started seeping out onto my face.

"I don't think we've met." I stick out my hand. "I'm—"

"Joanna Cuyler," he says. "Executive Director of Indifferent Honest Theater Company."

Okay, so we *have* met. And now he thinks I'm a bitch or an idiot or both because I didn't recognize him. This would never have happened if Mal were here. He remembers everyone. People come to our shows five years apart, and he greets them by name at the stage door.

I start to retract my hand, but the man reaches out and shakes it anyway.

"I'm Robert Kenmore," he says.

Kenmore. That's right—the *Tribune* reporter, the one who keeps hounding my inbox, trying to set up an interview with Mal. He looks different from his official newspaper portrait. There, his hair is combed forward to cover his overlarge ears, and the angle of his head disguises the size and slope of his knife-blade nose. No wonder I didn't recognize him.

Most of the other arts journalists in the city have gotten the message by now that Mal doesn't believe in doing press, but Kenmore is newer on the job. Still hungry, still trying to prove himself.

I can certainly sympathize with that. Indifferent Honest has been operating successfully for over a decade, but with every new season announcement, every opening night, I feel that same pressure, the familiar fear. This will be the year, I'm sure, that they find me out.

"Mr. Kenmore," I say. "So nice to finally meet you in person."

"Please," he says. "Call me Rob."

23

KIRA

WHEN MALCOLM OFFERED TO STAY "A LITTLE LONGER," I figured he meant twenty minutes, half an hour tops. But it's almost midnight, and we're still here.

We run the scene. I pretend to slap him. He stops and says, "Let's try that again."

So we do it again. And he stops again. At the same goddamn spot, so many times now I've lost count. It would be one thing if he gave me some direction, but it's like he's expecting me to figure out what he wants via osmosis or fucking telepathy.

He doesn't seem angry or frustrated or *anything* really. Ever since Spence left, Malcolm has been just . . . blank. It's like when he drops character, there's nothing there underneath. I don't know how else to explain it.

Maybe he didn't sleep today either, and this is how he gets when he's really tired? But if that's all this is, then why doesn't he call it quits, let us all go home and get some rest? The scene isn't getting any better. In fact, every time we do it, I'm pretty sure it gets a little bit worse.

We do the scene again.

He stops us again.

"One more time," he says, which means fuck-all nothing because he said the same thing six runs ago.

He goes back to his mark for the top of the scene. I stay where I am, hands on my hips. "Okay. Tell me what I'm doing wrong."

Malcolm turns and stares at me. It's nothing like the other times he's done it. There's no expression in his eyes, no spark of life.

"Did I skip a line, or . . .?" I look to Bryn for backup. She jumps a little in her chair, eyes widening like a frightened rabbit, and starts flipping back through the script pages.

I'm sure I didn't skip any lines, and I'm doing the choreography correctly too, but there must be a reason he keeps making me repeat the scene. The slap isn't forceful enough, or it's too forceful, or my stance is wrong, or the timing is off, or *something*. If he would just tell me what it is, I could—

"What makes you think you're doing something wrong?" Malcolm asks.

The space between my eyes throbs. I don't even know how to answer that.

"Let's do it one more time," he says. "From the top."

24

JOANNA

ROB KENMORE IS SO TALL, I HAVE TO TILT MY HEAD BACK TO look him in the face. My neck is starting to hurt, now that we've been talking for so long. But I don't want to stop. For the first time tonight, I've managed to go more than a few minutes without thinking about Mal.

Eventually, though, the conversation turns to him, as all my conversations seem to.

"So he seriously won't do interviews at all?" Rob asks.

"It's nothing personal," I say. "He prefers to let the work speak for itself."

Mal considers courting press coverage or favorable reviews akin to prostitution. He refuses to read reviews at all, even the ecstatic ones I print out and hang in the lobby.

Rob nods. Not satisfied but willing to drop the subject for the time being.

"I'm looking forward to seeing *Temper*," he says. "You open in, what, another couple of weeks?"

I nod. "The first weekend in November."

"I'd love to get my hands on a copy of the script, but it's not published anywhere, at least not that I could find."

"I might be able to help you out there."

"Really? That would be great. I find I enjoy plays more if I've read them first."

He smiles again and pushes his hair back. He keeps doing that, his fingers tracing the tops of his ears, exposing them. They're not *that* big, really. They just stick out at an angle from his head, like handlebars. It's kind of cute. Endearing, even.

I have had too much wine. I'm holding a half-full glass in my hand now—Rob grabbed it for me off the tray of a passing server—and I don't know how many this makes. I never drink this much. I rarely drink at all, just in social situations where it would be awkward not to.

"I did read the synopsis in your press kit," he says. "Sounds like a great role for Kira."

My grip tightens around the stem of my glass.

"You know Kira?"

25

KIRA

"YOU'RE NOT HAVING A MISCARRIAGE."

"No. I'm not."

"You did this on purpose."

"Yes."

"You didn't think I had a right to know?"

"The decision was already made."

"'The decision'? That's all it was to you? Just another decision, like what brand of mascara to buy or where to have dinner."

"I—"

My mind goes blank. Fuck. It feels like the words are right on the other side of a locked door and I don't have the key.

"Line," I say.

Bryn was zoned out, her eyelids at half-mast, so it takes her a few seconds of searching in the script to find where we are.

"'You're right, it—'" she starts.

My memory sputters back to life, and I take over.

"You're right, it wasn't even a decision. I knew what I had to do."

Malcolm pauses, pressing his lips together. "Let's take it back to the top again."

"No, I've got it now, we can—"

"The energy is gone," he says. "Let's start over."

Tears prick the corners of my eyes. I want to lie down on the stage and close my eyes, just for a second. I also want to pick up Bryn's binder and hurl it at Malcolm's fucking head. But he's already restarted the scene.

"You're not having a miscarriage."

"No. I'm not."

Hours ago, I spat those words, fire behind every syllable. Now they come out in a monotone. How does he do it? The same intensity, every single time, no matter how many times we do the scene.

"You did this on purpose."

"Yes."

"You didn't think I had a right to know?"

"The decision was already made."

"'The decision'? That's all it was to you? Just another decision, like what brand of mascara to buy or where to have dinner."

"You're right, it wasn't even a decision. I knew what I had to do."

"*Why?* Why the fuck would you—"

"Because I don't want to have your fucking baby."

He's going to stop me again, I know it, that line reading was so lackluster. He's going to make me do it all over again. I could lose my voice and he'd still want to keep going, mime our way through the scene—no words, just emotions.

I want to laugh, even though that's not funny, none of this is funny. But Malcolm hasn't stopped. He's still in character and about to deliver the cue line for the slap.

"How do I even know it was mine? We both know you've always been nothing but a—"

Just as I pull my hand back into position—it feels so heavy now, like there are weights wrapped around my wrist—someone's cell phone starts ringing.

No, not someone's. Mine.

Shit.

I drop my hand. "Sorry. I'm sorry, I—"

Malcolm gives me a look that could melt metal. Or is he still in character, still Trent? I don't know. I'm so fucking tired, I don't know anything anymore.

I swallow my apologies and rush to the seat where I left my bag. By the time I get there, the ringing has already stopped. I'm sure it was Spence, he's the only person who would even think of calling me at this hour.

"Let's take a break," Malcolm says.

I flick the ringer switch off and hold the phone up to show him. "It's off now, I—"

"Ten minutes." This he says to Bryn. He won't even look at me.

Bryn nods and jots down the current time in her binder. Malcolm is already walking out.

My hand tightens around my phone as I watch him go.

26

JOANNA

I'D NEVER HEARD OF THIS BITCH UNTIL SHE WALKED INTO MY theater a few weeks ago, and now it seems like Kira Rascher is turning up everywhere.

"We did a show together," Rob says when I inquire about how he knows her. "Back when I was still dramaturging."

I didn't know he used to be a dramaturg, but I can see it. The stories he writes are always detailed, well researched. His review of our *Edward II* mentioned several biographical details about Marlowe I wasn't aware of, and I wrote my undergrad thesis on him. For our shows, I usually end up doing any necessary research, since dramaturgs are yet another thing Mal doesn't believe in.

"We dated for a while, too," Rob adds, almost as an afterthought.

"What was *that* like?"

This is why I shouldn't drink unsupervised. Words go directly to my mouth without passing through my brain first. I glance at my phone again, more to hide the flush on my cheeks than anything else. I've totally given up on Mal showing his face tonight.

Rob nods toward the screen. "Expecting a call?"

"Sorry." I slide the phone back into my purse. "Someone was supposed to meet me here."

"Ah. The elusive Malcolm Mercer, I'm guessing?"

Elusive. That's a good word for Mal. He seems solid enough, but if you try to grab ahold of him, he slips through your fingers like smoke.

Where the *fuck* is he?

27

KIRA

MY EYES ARE SHADOWED, HOLLOW, THE DARK CIRCLES UNDER-neath them so pronounced they look like twin bruises. The lipstick I put on before rehearsal is faded and flaking now. The bits still left look like scabs around the edges of my lips. I pull a length of paper towel out of the dispenser and scrub at my mouth until it's bare and swollen.

I'm such an idiot. I actually let myself think we turned a corner last night—all those hours we spent talking, the easy way he smiled at me over the breakfast table. That kiss. Even though we were in character most of the time, some part of me thought I might finally be meeting the real Malcolm Mercer. But what did I really learn about him in all those hours we spent together? Nothing. We're still strangers.

I'm using the cramped bathroom backstage rather than the nicer one in the lobby, because it's the only place in the building I could guarantee myself a few minutes alone. There's barely enough room to turn around in here, but at least there's a lock on the door. The toilet is crammed into the corner, a notch cut into the drywall to allow the handle to move up and down.

The wall space—what little there is—is covered in snapshots from previous productions. Malcolm in a puffy white shirt holding a quill pen. Malcolm in a pinstriped suit, shaking hands with a woman in a voluminous fur coat. Malcolm lying on the floor, with his head pillowed in a young man's lap.

Jason Grady's lap, I realize, when I take a closer look. The photo is from the final scene of *Hamlet*, when, with his dying breath, Hamlet implores Horatio to stay alive to tell his story. Jason looks genuinely grief-stricken, his hand clutching Malcolm's collar, tears sparkling in his eyes.

But there's something else that catches my eye, in the background of the photo. I step even closer, my nose almost hitting the glass over the image, and squint into the shadows behind the stage.

It's me. I don't see Spence—he was there with me that night, so he must be standing just out of frame—but there I am, right at the edge of the picture.

How old was I when this was taken? Twenty-three, twenty-four? My body was slimmer, but my cheeks were fuller, my features prettier, more open. We'd only been in Chicago a little while, and so much still seemed possible then.

My younger self is looking at Malcolm like he just invented fire. That's how it felt, watching him for the first time—like I was witnessing something chaotic and consuming, so awe-inspiringly beautiful I couldn't look directly at it for too long or it might blind me.

The glow from the lights aimed at Malcolm and Jason caught enough of my face that I can tell my eyes were shining, just like Jason's. I was crying too.

There's a knock on the door. *"What?"* I snap.

"We're back in two," comes Bryn's voice from the hallway.

"Thanks." This comes out snappish, too, almost sarcastic. It wasn't intentional, I'm just so on edge. But explaining that to Bryn would take more energy than I have right now.

I splash cold water over my face, then stand up and let it run down the back of my neck and between my breasts. With my still-damp hands, I smooth my hair to tame the worst of the frizz and give myself a hard look in the rust-flecked mirror.

This is what I want. This is what I've always wanted. I have to go back out there.

Besides, making him wait will only make things worse.

Bryn is still loitering in the hall when I come out of the bathroom. She shrinks back a bit when she sees the look on my face.

"How much longer do you think we'll be?" she asks.

"Why?" I'm already heading back into the theater. She jogs to catch up.

"It's just, I have a midterm tomorrow, and . . ."

I nod toward Malcolm, who's standing on the stage, waiting for us. "Ask him."

"Ask me what?" Malcolm says. He's smiling now, but his eyes are scorching. When he turns his gaze on Bryn, she shrivels like burning paper.

"Nothing." She keeps twisting her hoodie's cord around her knuckles, wrapping it so tight her fingers turn red. "Never mind."

Bryn sinks back into her seat, leaning over her binder to hide the embarrassed blush painting her cheeks. But she's safe for now. Malcolm has turned his attention back to me.

He walks closer—close enough to touch me, though he doesn't do that yet. My pulse spikes and my shoulders clench.

"Are you okay?" he asks. The last thing I was expecting him to say.

"I'm fine," I say. "I just haven't slept since—"

"You haven't slept?"

"No. I mean, I tried—maybe I had too much coffee at breakfast, I don't know."

His eyes have gone soft and sweet now, like melted chocolate. Maybe he'll see reason. Now that he knows how exhausted I am, maybe he'll let me go home.

"So you're not prepared to work," he says.

You fucking bastard. For a second there, I thought he might actually be concerned for my well-being.

"I'm prepared to work," I say.

He turns away. "If you're not prepared, maybe it would be best if we—"

"I said I'm prepared." I take my mark for the top of the scene. He wants me to prove my dedication, I'll prove it. Whatever it takes. "Let's go."

Malcolm watches me. He's expressionless again, except for a subtle tension in his mouth.

"Fine," he says. "Lift up your skirt."

28

JOANNA

I CAN'T REMEMBER THE LAST TIME I WAS OUT AFTER MIDNIGHT and not hunched over my desk at the theater. Even in college, I didn't stay late at parties. I'd make an appearance, have a few sips of beer, then leave the half-empty bottle sitting on a windowsill and make an Irish exit.

The fundraiser has cleared out enough that Rob and I were able to grab one of the low, chrome-edged tables running down the middle of the room. The band finished up a while ago, and the bar's jukebox is playing something with jangly guitars and a horn section. Probably it's a popular song—one I'd recognize if I had a life outside of Indifferent Honest. The group at the next table over sings along, swaying so their shoulders knock together.

Rob has been nursing the same gin and tonic for the past hour. He seems completely sober; he might be the only person in the whole place who is. I'm not drunk, but my senses feel dulled. I have to concentrate to keep up my end of the conversation, which has turned to Rob's graduate work at Northwestern.

"Sorry," he says. "I'm talking too much."

My eyes must have glazed over. I was listening, but I was also trying—and failing—to picture him with Kira. I know I've only just met him, but Rob seems so quiet and serious. Old-fashioned, almost, and not solely because of the grandfatherly sweater he's wearing.

"No, you're fine," I tell him. The truth is, I like the way he talks. He's laconic, unassuming. He speaks to get his point across, not to ply or provoke or savor the sound of his own voice. Maybe that's why he likes women like Kira. Maybe he needs someone bold and brash, to counterbalance his subdued nature.

"What about you?" he asks. "Where did you go to school?"

"The University of Michigan, for undergrad. You know, I got into Northwestern for grad school too. MFA in Writing for the Stage and Screen."

"Oh really?" he says. "Where did you end up going instead?"

"I decided against it, actually. Mal and I started Indifferent Honest right after I graduated from college."

I got into a bunch of schools, even a few with full rides. And then I met Mal, and I turned them all down. I wonder what my life would be like now if I'd gone to Northwestern. Maybe Rob and I would have met each other back then.

"I didn't realize you were a writer, too," Rob says.

"I'm not." I've said this to myself so many times, the words come easily. "I mean, I was, back then. Or I was trying to be. I wasn't very good."

"That can't be true. Not if you got into Northwestern."

I can't tell if my face feels hot because I'm blushing or because of all the wine.

"So you started writing plays in college?" he asks.

"High school."

"What was your first one about?"

I shake my head. "It's stupid; you don't want to—"

"Try me."

Taken individually, Rob's features are all a bit odd, off-kilter, but somehow the overall effect is appealing. Especially when he smiles, the way he is now, one corner of his naturally downturned lips ticking upward.

I sigh and shake my head, but the truth is I want to tell him. I want to tell him everything about me. It's terrifying.

"Okay, fine. My first play—well, I had this friend. My best friend, since elementary school. But when I was, like, fifteen or sixteen, I realized I had a huge crush on her. So I wrote a play about her. About us."

I submitted the script to a local youth theater festival. I wasn't involved in the casting, but I'd described Nicole's physical appearance in such obsessive detail in the stage directions, the director ended up choosing a girl who looked almost exactly like her—the same wide hips, the same waist-length malt-brown hair. Even without the physical resemblance, though, anyone who knew us would've been able to recognize us in the characters.

"I had this fantasy that she'd see the play and realize she loved me, too."

"And did she?" Rob asks.

I laugh. It took me some time, but I can laugh about it now. "Not even close. She stopped talking to me."

Nicole wouldn't talk to me, but she was more than willing to talk to everyone else we knew. A semester later, classmates were still taunting me with lines from the play and sticking cheesy lesbian porn through the vents in my locker. I shouldn't have been as surprised as I was. Kids are cruel everywhere, even in crunchy-granola East Coast suburbs like Mount Airy. But my mother's unconditional love and validation had left me unprepared for that kind of public shaming. For the sensation of shame at all.

"I stopped writing after that," I say. "Until I had to take a playwriting class in college, and I remembered how much I enjoyed it."

I'd thought about going to college at Temple or even Penn (I had the grades for it), but after that experience, I wanted to get as far away from where I grew up as possible. My mother vetoed any school located outside the Eastern Standard time zone, and I ended up at the University of Michigan. There, everyone was just as accepting of my bisexuality as my mother had been when I came out to her.

"But then you gave it up again." Rob isn't smiling anymore.

"I guess I'm not cut out for it." I shrug. "You're a writer, you know how it is."

"It's not the same thing. I report facts. The kind of writing you do—sorry, *did*—that's baring your soul in public. I could never do that. I really admire it, actually."

He's staring at me now. It's nothing like the way Mal stares. I look down at the table.

"Maybe that's why the woman who wrote *Temper* keeps such a low profile," Rob says. "What was her name again? L. S. something?"

29

KIRA

"EXCUSE ME?"

"Lift up your skirt this time," Malcolm says. "For the knap."

As though his meaning was so obvious. I edge the hem of my dress up with my thumb so my palm is touching bare skin. He nods at me, and I hit my thigh.

"Again," he says.

I do. At this point, I'll do just about anything he wants if it means I can go home and go to sleep. While I'm waiting for Malcolm to speak or gesture or grunt or do something, *anything*, I start to imagine myself falling backward into the softness of my bed, pulling the covers up to my chin, shutting my eyes, drifting into darkness . . .

"Again."

"Do you want me to do it harder?" I ask.

He presses his lips together, eyes narrowed. I'm really starting to hate that look. Maybe he and Joanna have developed some sort of creepy mind-meld connection, but the rest of us mere mortals need him to use his fucking words.

"No, no, not harder—I don't want you to hurt yourself," he says.

Liar. I've done this so many times already, my arm muscles ache and the side of my leg is sore and throbbing.

"But it needs to sound like a real slap."

A real slap, by definition, would hurt, but okay, whatever.

"We should move on," he says. "It's getting really late."

Yeah, you think?

"No, I want to get it right," I say. "Show me."

Without giving Malcolm a chance to respond, I move so I'm standing right in front of him.

"Show me how you want me to do it."

At first, he's still as a statue. Then he takes a step forward, molding his body against my back. He runs his arm alongside mine and covers my hand with his own.

Malcolm brings my hand up, then smacks it back down. It's less forceful than the hit I was doing, but it stings more, leaving my palm buzzing. The sharp *crack* it makes bounces off the ceiling above the lighting grid, echoes back down. I see what he means—the sound is sharper, more like the real sound of an open palm colliding with someone's cheek.

"Try it again," he says. He lets go of my hand, but he's still pressed against me.

Bryn watches us, her eyes big as china plates behind her glasses. I close my eyes so I don't have to look at her. So I can pretend it's just us now, Malcolm and I alone.

I hit my leg again, trying to reproduce what Malcolm did. *Crack.* The pain reverberates through the whole left side of my body, spreading from the point of contact like ripples in water.

"Good," he says.

30

JOANNA

"Sedgwick," Rob repeats. "Like the street."

"Mmm-hmm. Like the street."

"And *Temper* is her first play?"

"In Chicago," I say. "I think she's had some scripts produced regionally. At festivals, mostly. Nothing published yet."

"How did you hear about it, then?"

"She submitted the script for season consideration. We have an open submission policy."

"Right," Rob says. "You must get a lot of garbage sent in."

I shrug. "A fair amount."

"And do you read all the submissions yourself, or do you have an intern do the first pass?" No one's ever bothered to ask me about this mundane part of my job before, but Rob sounds genuinely fascinated.

"I usually skim them myself, then print out the good ones for Mal. When there are good ones."

I narrow it down to ten options or fewer before involving him. We try to do at least one new play a year, plus a regional premiere if we can get the rights. Half the time, he ignores my list and makes his own choices. He thinks my selections are too "safe"—i.e. too likely to actually make money.

Rob nods. "So what stood out to you about *Temper* when you read it?"

"Well, it's a great part for Mal. And it's simple to stage, too—small cast, minimal set."

Mal is always in favor of keeping design elements simple, so they don't distract from the performances. But I'm sure he picked *Temper* mainly because he wanted to play Trent. We haven't done a show yet where he didn't take the lead role.

"Almost like it was created with Indifferent Honest in mind, huh?"

Rob is acting casual, swirling his finger through the condensation on his highball glass. But his questions are so rapid-fire, it's like he's reading them off a list. Like he prepared ahead of time for this conversation.

"About how old is Ms. Sedgwick?" he asks next.

"I'm not sure. Why?"

"Just curious. So you haven't met her, then? She's not involved in the rehearsal process?"

"No, she couldn't come out for rehearsals. She had other commitments, and she's not Chicago-based, so it wasn't practical."

"She's coming to see the show, though, right?"

"I'm not sure. I think her travel plans are still up in the air."

"So you have at least spoken with her?"

"She, uh—well, we haven't actually *spoken*." I tap my fingernail against the stem of my wine glass. I've been leaving one last swallow in there so I won't feel tempted to go back to the bar and get another refill, but now I'm having second thoughts. "She's not a big fan of the telephone, I guess."

"What about Mr. Mercer?" Rob asks. "Has he ever talked to her?"

"No. I always handle all the legal details for our shows."

Besides, I never let Mal interact with playwrights if I can prevent it. As much as he loves producing contemporary works, Mal hates having their writers involved in the process. Once the script is done and printed, as far as he's concerned, it no longer belongs to the playwright. It belongs to the director and the actors, and then to the audience.

A few years ago we were planning to produce *The Most Theatrically Corrupt*, a searing indictment of Chicago politics by a recent grad of the same Northwestern MFA program I turned down. He insisted on being hands-on, wanted to attend every rehearsal. By the second one, he nearly came to blows with Mal. A week in, he revoked the rights to the show. We lost a lot of money on that fiasco. All the playwright's fault, though, to hear Mal tell it, and he *has* told it, to anyone in the Chicago theater community who will listen. As far as I know, the poor guy hasn't had a single play staged since then. Last I heard, he was working in a ticket booth at Navy Pier.

"So," Rob continues. "You made the arrangements through a representative, or . . .?"

I smile at him and hope, in this dim light, he can't see how strained it is. "Oh, you don't want to hear about all those boring details, I'm sure."

"I love boring details." He gives me a lopsided smile in return. "Often when I'm writing a story, I find the most boring details lead to the most interesting angles."

He's not going to drop this. I have to tell him something.

"She has an agent," I say. "I dealt with him. She's a really private person."

"What was the agent's name?" He doesn't have a notebook or even a pen to jot the name down on his bar napkin, but something tells me he's logging every detail of what I'm saying.

This is more than curiosity. In fact, it's starting to feel like an interrogation. As if all our conversation up until this point was just a means of getting me to relax, to let down my guard.

Maybe Robert Kenmore has more in common with his ex-girlfriend than I thought.

31

KIRA

GOOD.

That single word gave me a jolt of energy like I'd just downed an espresso shot.

I was ready to go back to the top of the scene, do it again, do it as many times as Malcolm wanted. But we haven't said so much as a single line. Instead, he keeps asking me questions. Endless, elliptical questions, like a vulture circling some unseen point deep in my psyche.

I have no idea what time it is now. Well past midnight. Bryn disappeared a while ago. When I saw her get up, I figured she was going to the bathroom, but she hasn't come back. Her things are still here—her binder open on her seat, her pinback button–covered backpack slumped underneath—so she must still be somewhere in the building.

"Have you ever hit anyone before?" he's asking now. "A lover, or—"

"No."

My answer was too automatic, too defensive. He can tell I'm holding something back.

"I mean, no, not a lover."

I can't help saying the word "lover" with a hint of sarcasm, like I'm putting air quotes around it. I've always found that term vaguely ridiculous. Spence likes to refer to me as his "lover" whenever he wants to piss me off.

"Who, then?"

"My sister."

My little sister, Anastasia—Stacy. That beautiful Russian princess name, and she preferred to be known by the abbreviation associated with lame 1980s pop singers.

"How old were you?" Malcolm asks.

"I was seventeen. She was fifteen."

"And you were angry with her."

I nod.

"Why?"

It's a long story, I want to say, but I know he won't accept that answer.

"Because she told a lie?" Malcolm asks. "Or because she told the truth?"

"Because she threatened to tell the truth, about—"

No no no, stop, what are you doing?

"What was his name?" Malcolm asks.

"Who?" But I know who he means, what he's getting at.

"Your teacher," he says. "The one you slept with."

Of course he could tell I wasn't making that up.

I'm so tired. Maybe if I give him what he wants, he'll let me go home. Maybe honesty would be easier than manipulation.

"David," I say. "His name was David."

Malcolm is pacing now, his hands clasped behind his back, like a professor giving a lecture. "So your sister, she threatened to tell people about you and David."

"Yes. She saw us together."

It was the spring of my junior year of high school. Opening night of my first-ever show. I played the lead role, so I got to take the final bow, and then David came onstage to present me with a bouquet of flowers. They were nothing special—carnations from the grocery store, dyed various shades of neon—but his hand brushed mine when he gave them to me and the card said *For my brilliant leading lady,* so as far as I was concerned, they were better than a Tony.

Our school didn't have a proper auditorium, just a stage on one end of the gymnasium, so our "dressing rooms" were the same locker rooms we used to change for gym class. I was the only girl in the play, so I got the girls' locker room all to myself. I had several different fantasies in rotation about David finding me there. They all started with him bursting through the door and gathering me in his arms, like we were a couple reunited after a long war.

When he did finally enter the locker room, that night after our first—and, though I didn't know it then, our only—performance, he did it quietly. I heard the squeak of the door hinge and turned to find him sliding his slender frame into the room with a furtive glance down the hallway to make sure no one was watching.

He knew he shouldn't be there. I knew it too, but to me it was more proof of how much he wanted me. Boys hit on me all the time, but here was a man willing to put himself on the line to steal a few moments alone with me. When I was seventeen, David Granville seemed like a man, but looking back, I can see how young and immature he truly was.

He told me I was wonderful, the best part of the play. He told me how proud he was of me. He didn't tell me how beautiful I looked, face shining under my stage makeup, hair smoothed into perfect 1940s waves, cleavage swelling over the bodice of my thrift-store costume, but his eyes said that part loud and clear. He wanted me, just as much as I wanted him. I was sure of it.

So I stood up on my toes in my nude character shoes, looped my arms around his neck, and kissed him. He put his hands on my waist, like he was going to push me away. But he didn't. His fingers dipped into the small of my back and he pulled me closer. Close enough to feel him getting hard, pressing against the front of his pants.

I felt so powerful. I wanted him, and now he was mine.

Then I opened my eyes and saw Stacy staring at us from outside the cracked-open locker room door.

I didn't tell David, and I didn't go after her. I knew she wouldn't tell our parents or anyone else right away. She'd want to rub my nose in it first. We never got along, though our grudges had gotten more complex as we grew up.

"When you hit her," Malcolm says. "Was it an act of passion? Or did you make a decision to do it?"

Stacy confronted me while I was wiping off my stage makeup with our mother's jar of cold cream. We had our own rooms but shared a bathroom in between. It was the site of most of our arguments, the battleground between two enemy territories.

She didn't say anything at first, just shut the bathroom door behind her and stood there, staring at me, this self-satisfied little smirk on her face.

"Well," she said finally. "At least now I know how you managed to get the lead in the play."

I turned off the water. I laid the washcloth over the lip of the bathroom sink. I screwed the lid back on the cold cream. And then I turned around and slapped my sister across the mouth.

I think I'd been waiting for an excuse to hit Stacy in the face since the day she was born. When I slapped her, her head whipped to the side, her other cheek smacking against the door. Saving me the trouble, I thought at the time. She didn't cry out, and she didn't try to strike me back. But she did something worse—she ran down the hall to our parents' room to tell them what she'd seen in the locker room that night.

"I decided," I tell Malcolm.

"You decided. Okay," he says. "So what about Mara? When she hits Trent, is it an act of uncontrollable passion? Or something else?"

Mara could be played as a miserable woman trapped in a toxic relationship, standing by silent and passive, capable of fighting back only in her fantasies. But when I read the script, that's not what I thought of her at all. She's full of fury, dangerous, a fuse nearly burned down to nothing. She's been waiting, for years probably, for Trent to do something that will justify her attacking him—and whenever it finally happens, she intends to be ready. The reveries are mental rehearsals for future, inevitable violence. If anyone in *Temper* is a victim, it's Trent.

I haven't answered, but Malcolm seems satisfied.

"Let's try the slap again," he says.

He moves into position. Starts the cue line. I draw my hand back.

"You're nothing but a—"

I try to sweep my hand through, but there's something in my way.

The hard edge of Malcolm's jaw, meeting the tips of my fingers.

32

JOANNA

I MANAGE TO PLACATE ROB WITH A PROMISE TO SEND HIM the name of L. S. Sedgwick's agent first thing Monday morning.

Which I guess is technically now. It's nearly 2:00 a.m. The bar will be closing in a few minutes. I'm dreading going home. The feeling is like a chunk of ice caught in my rib cage. I don't know if it's because I'm afraid Mal will be there, or I'm afraid he won't be.

Is he wondering where I am? Is he worried about me at all? Has he given me a single goddamn thought this entire night?

Rob and I walk out together. The temperature has fallen—that tart bite of autumn in the air. He stops on the sidewalk and turns to face me, hands shoved into his pockets, braced against the wind.

"Where are you headed?" I ask. "We could share a cab."

It's not until the words leave my mouth that I realize how they might sound. Like I'm propositioning him, asking him back to my place. I'm so tired, I'm not thinking clearly.

Then again, why *shouldn't* I ask him to come home with me if I want to? I don't owe Mal anything. He could be fucking Kira right now. He is fucking her; of course he is, it was inevitable. I knew it would happen from the moment she walked into the audition. That's what he was doing last night, and that's what he'll be doing every night until he tires of her, too. If I'd gone home earlier, I would have had to spend the night listening to her screaming through the wall between our bedrooms. Just like all the others.

Mal never makes a sound in bed. I used to fantasize I would be the one to make him lose control. I thought about it all the time. What his voice would sound like crying out my name.

I let myself fantasize now, about the look on Mal's face—and on Kira's—if I brought Rob home with me. The wind ripples through the sequined Holiday Club sign, scattering winking gold lights in Rob's hair, and I wish I knew: Do I really want him, or do I just want to hurt Mal?

Ridiculous. As if anything I do is capable of hurting Mal.

33

KIRA

I ONLY GRAZED HIS JAW. AND AS SOON AS MY FINGERTIPS made contact, he turned his head, following through the motion of the slap.

No one's injured. Everything's fine.

And Malcolm is smiling.

"That was better this time," he says.

"You didn't turn your head."

He stares at me. "Yes I did."

"I mean, you did it too late."

"All those other times," he says, "you were just going through the motions. That was the first time I really felt something from you."

Yeah, my hand fucking hitting you in the face. Maybe it was my fault—I might have been standing too close to him. I don't know.

Malcolm steps even closer. "Don't tell me you didn't feel it too."

Spence likes to say the reason stage combat is so difficult is that you're asking actors to be at their most precise when they're also at their most passionate. Letting go, giving in to emotion—that's what leads to people getting hurt. Or worse.

It's not passion I'm feeling right now. I don't know what it is. But I know I can't be precise, not anymore, not without some sleep. We shouldn't be doing this. It's dangerous. I didn't hurt him, but I could have. One more inch closer and—

"I want you to do it again," Malcolm says. "And this time, don't think about the choreography. Just be in the moment. Feel what Mara is feeling."

I open my mouth to protest, but he's already back in character.

"*Why?*" he says. "Why the fuck would you—"

It takes me a second to find my place, to catch up with him.

"Because—because I don't want to—"

He stops. "No. Do it again. Make me believe you."

I squeeze my eyes shut, frustration exploding behind my eyelids like fireworks. "Because I don't—"

"I don't believe you. Again."

"Because I don't want to have your fucking—"

"Dammit, Kira." He's circling me now, both character and blocking abandoned. "You act like you're watching yourself in a mirror. Look at me."

I look up at the ceiling instead and let out an exasperated sigh.

"Look at me."

Malcolm takes my chin between his thumb and forefinger, forces my face level with his. It's the first time he's touched me in hours, but it doesn't feel that way. It feels like his hands have been everywhere, like there's no part of me left untouched by him.

"I'm your mirror," he says. "Stop thinking about what you look like, stop trying to be sexy. I don't give a damn about that."

I've always wanted to hear that sentiment from a director, but not like this.

"That day at the school," he says. "What impressed me wasn't your cleavage or all that vampy bullshit you were doing—I mean, Lady Macbeth as a seductress? How fucking original."

Blood burns in my cheeks, and I hate myself. I want to slap my own face to make it stop. "Why the hell did you cast me, then?"

"Why do you think I cast you?"

Because you wanted to fuck with me. Because you wanted to fuck me. Because all I am to you is a body, an object you can move around the stage and bend to your will.

Because I was stupid enough to stare back.

Malcolm lets go of me, resumes his circuit around the stage. He's somewhere behind me when he stops. I can feel his breath on my neck. I'm too tired to turn around, to face him. So I don't see the moment when he drops back into character.

"*Why?*" he says, speaking lower than before. "Why the fuck would you—"

I try to put some power behind the words this time. But my voice is nearly gone, and they come out weak, a plaintive whine instead of a defiant shout.

"Because I don't want to have your fucking baby!"

He's going to stop me again, I'm sure of it—and I deserve it this time, that was pathetic. But he stays in character, moves on to his next line.

"How do I even know it was mine? We both know you've always been nothing but a—"

I don't make eye contact before the slap this time. I don't take note of the distance between us. I just rear back and go for it.

Malcolm catches my wrist in mid-swing. "You're still holding back."

I have nothing left to hold back. I'm spent. Empty. Why is he doing this to me?

I shake my head. "I'm sorry, I—"

"Don't apologize. Tell me: What is Trent about to call her?"

"I don't—"

"Yes you do. What's the next word he's going to say?"

Whore. You're nothing but a—

My hand curls into a fist. He lets go of my wrist.

"You've been called that before," he says. "Haven't you?"

I don't answer. I don't have to.

"And Mara doesn't want to hear it, does she? She wants to slap that word right out of his mouth. Why?" He leans in, locking his eyes on mine. "Because it's a lie, or because it's the truth?"

"We both know," he says—Trent's line, but he's not in character, he's saying the words in his own voice, looking at me like he can see straight through to my spine.

He's too close. He's not close enough. I don't know anymore.

"You've always been nothing but a—"

34

JOANNA

"ACTUALLY, I THINK I'M GOING TO TAKE THE TRAIN," ROB SAYS.

The Red Line runs twenty-four hours a day, and we're right across the street from the Sheridan station, but at this time of night he could be waiting for thirty minutes or more for the next train.

So he'd rather stand in the freezing wind on a train platform than spend any more time in my company. Got it. All these years of mixed messages from Mal, and now I can't even tell whether or not a man is attracted to me anymore.

"Well, it was nice talking with you," I say. Of course he's not interested in me if he likes women like Kira Rascher. I was deluding myself. As usual.

"Likewise." He's squinting across the street at the El platform. Already planning his escape.

"No promises, but—I can ask Mal again, about the possibility of an interview. If you want."

Stop it. Stop talking. Walk away while you still have a shred of dignity left.

"That's okay," Rob says. "You know, I think I'd much rather interview you."

At first I'm not sure I heard him right. Another group of stragglers from the fundraiser have spilled out the front door of the Holiday Club; they're standing a few feet away from us, one of them mugging his way through some elaborate anecdote while the rest shriek with laughter. Actors.

"Me?" I ask. "Why would you want to interview me?"

I've given interviews to local press outlets before, but only as a mouthpiece for Mal and the company. I'm the consolation prize they'll accept when they can't get him to return their calls.

Rob smiles at me and leans in close. I take a step back, but he isn't trying to touch me. He just wants to make sure no one else can hear.

"Because," he says. "We both know there's no L. S. Sedgwick."

35

KIRA

MY HAND FEELS DISCONNECTED FROM THE REST OF MY BODY, beyond my control—a bullet loosed from a gun, impossible to take back. Malcolm's head snaps to the side, fast and hard as a slammed door, and he drops to his knees.

I blink like I've been startled awake from a nightmare. But this is real. My palm is stinging, prickling, and I'm shaking and oh my God, this is real, I actually hit him.

"Fuck."

I'm the one who spoke, but my voice seems distant, distorted, buried somewhere under the echoing *crack* of my hand colliding with his face. My skin burns from my palm to my fingertips, where I scraped over the stubble on his cheek.

"Fuck."

Malcolm hasn't said a word, or moved from his position on the floor, head bowed, supporting himself with steepled fingers. I reach out to touch him on the shoulder.

"I am so sorry, are you—"

I blink, and suddenly he's standing, advancing on me, so fast I stumble backward, but I don't fall because he has ahold of my wrists.

This is the rest of the blocking, the part we haven't gotten to because we kept repeating the slap. Trent is supposed to push Mara up against the hotel room door and hold her there until the blackout signaling the shift out of her reverie and into reality.

But the set is still under construction, so there's no door yet, only a bare wall. The base of my spine hits it first. Then the back of my skull, then my knuckles, scraping over the brick as Malcolm forces my hands above my head. He's gripping the narrowest part of my wrists, right over the pulse points, exactly where Spence told him not to.

The slap split his lip. There's a thin line of blood trickling down the center of his chin. His eyes are blazing, but his breathing is calm, steady as a metronome. The opposite of mine, which is growing more ragged by the second, like it's trying to win a race with my pounding heartbeat.

Malcolm inhales again—deeper, deliberate, almost meditative, his ribs expanding to press into mine, pinning me tighter against the wall. I twist, testing his grip. He holds firm.

We're so close, I swear I can taste copper on my tongue. If we kissed now, his blood would run into my mouth, down my throat, settle in the pit of my stomach.

His gaze bores into me, hollowing me out.

There's no blackout coming.

Nothing to stop him.

But all he does is take another deep breath. I force myself to breathe in too. The air hitches and rattles in my throat, but it works— my heart rate starts to slow.

Inhale. Exhale. Over and over until we're breathing as one, synchronized, staring at each other, unblinking, our diaphragms rising and falling in time, hearts beating the same rhythm.

After the next inhale, Malcolm stops. He lets go of my wrists, but I keep my arms right where he pinned them. He smiles, and the wound in his lip stretches wider.

His eyes are enough to hold me now.

36

JOANNA

"HOW DID YOU KNOW?" I ASK.

Something flashes in Rob's eyes. He's trying not to gloat.

He didn't know, at least not for sure, that L. S. Sedgwick wasn't real. But now he does.

Because I just admitted it.

He doesn't know all of it, though, he can't possibly know—

"It was you, wasn't it?" he asks. "You wrote *Temper*."

I was so careful. Paranoid, even. I wrote the whole play in secret, in stolen moments when Mal was asleep or out of the apartment. I went to the library downtown to type it up and print it out so there was no way Mal could come across the script until it was right where I wanted it: in the season shortlist pile, with a fake name on the cover.

"Why did you decide to use a pen name?" Rob asks. "The initials L. S.—do they have any particular significance to you?" He's interviewing me already. He can't help himself.

"They're . . ." No reason not to tell him this; not if he's already figured out all the rest. "They're my mother's initials."

He nods. Filing this away, too. "Does Malcolm know?"

"Of course he does," I say, but I can tell Rob doesn't believe me. Why would he? I've always been a terrible liar. The only reason I've gotten away with this lie for so long is that Mal never had any reason to suspect, to call me out on it. If he'd looked me in the eye and asked if I was, in fact, L. S. Sedgwick, like Rob is doing now, I would have crumbled immediately.

I catch him by the forearm. He looks down at my fingers digging into his sweater, but he doesn't try to shake himself free.

"Please don't write about this." I'm begging. I hate myself. If only I had other ways of persuading him. I'm sure Kira would have no problem handling this situation. She'd turn it around so he was the one who had to beg.

Rob looks hurt that I would question his integrity. But I don't know this man. And he doesn't know me, either, no matter what he thinks he's figured out.

"I won't," he says. "Unless you decide to let me interview you. That's why I came here tonight—to talk to you about what I suspected. But I won't write the story without your consent. It wouldn't be much of a story anyway if you're not willing to confirm anything on the record."

So he already knew about my writing background. He sought me out on purpose. Lulled me into a false sense of security and then sprung this trap. How long has he been looking into me? I imagine him googling my name late at night in his Tribune Tower office, taking notes on my life, saving pictures of me into a file.

I'm shaking my head, and my mouth hangs open, but I can't think of a thing to say.

"Sleep on it," Rob says. "I'll give you a call tomorrow. If you're not interested, don't answer, and I promise I'll leave you alone."

He takes my hand and presses something into my palm. A business card, thick cream-colored paper with embossed black lettering. His office extension is printed on the front, but he's written his cell phone number on the back in blue pen.

A taxi slides up to the curb. Did he wave it down for me? I didn't notice. I feel numb. Even the cold slap of the wind on my face seems remote, like it's happening to someone else.

Rob opens the taxi door for me. "Get home safe," he says.

I climb inside. Without saying goodbye, without even looking at him again.

His card feels so heavy in my hand. I could open my fingers, let it flutter into the footwell for the next passenger to find.

Instead I slip it into my purse. All the way to the bottom, burying it like I wish I could bury this night. Bury the truth.

37

KIRA

I STAY THERE, BACK PRESSED AGAINST THE WALL, LONG AFTER Malcolm leaves me. He just walked away without a word. I let my eyes fall shut for a moment—I could feel his hot breath on my face, and I was bracing myself for anything, a kiss or a blow or his hands pushing up my skirt to bare more of my skin. But he didn't touch me. When I opened my eyes again, he was gone.

My palm burns, my leg throbs, the muscle underneath pulsing faster than my heartbeat. When I finally lower my arms, I expect to see raw red marks braceleting my wrists, but there's nothing. I can still feel the imprint of each of his fingers, exactly where he touched me.

Finally, I peel myself off the wall and gather up my things. The lights are still on in the theater. Backstage, too. I make a slow trip through the building, switching them off one by one. I half expect Malcolm to jump out of the shadows at me like a ghoul, but there's no sign of him.

When I enter the dressing rooms, I keep my gaze cast down at the floor. I don't want to look at myself in the mirror. Not right now.

I find Bryn curled up on the floor of the second dressing room with her head pillowed on her balled-up black hoodie, an open text-book slanted against her stomach.

Her hair is loose, spilling over her shoulders. She always keeps it tied back in a ponytail or up in a messy topknot, so I didn't realize how much it looks like my own, dark and wavy and wild. It's a few inches longer than my hair, though—long enough that if she were naked, the strands would cover her breasts, like a nymph in a classical painting.

I nudge the sole of her shoe with my toe. She starts awake, push-ing her glasses up on the bridge of her nose so she can rub her eyes. Her fingers come away smudged soot-black with eyeliner.

"What time is it?" she asks.

It's not until she asks this that I realize I have no idea. Sometime between midnight and dawn. Though I haven't looked outside since before rehearsal. It could be noon, for all I know.

"We're done," I tell her. My voice scrabbles around the back of my throat like a small animal trying to claw its way out. "Lock up when you leave."

IT IS, IN FACT, STILL NIGHTTIME. A LITTLE PAST TWO, ACCORDING to my phone, which has about 5 percent battery life left. I could have sworn I was stuck in there with Malcolm for much longer. The moment after I hit him, when I watched him go down—that alone felt like an eternity.

I don't remember most of my walk to Belmont. I'm the only one on the platform. The lights above me drone like cicadas. I've never noticed them before. Usually I'm standing here at a decent hour, with lots of other people around me, talking, blasting music from their phone speakers.

It's not even that cold out, but I keep shivering. Violently, clench-ing every muscle from my toes to my jaw.

Finally, a northbound Red Line train pulls in. It's one of the shorter trains they run in the middle of the night, so I have to jog to catch up with the last car. Once I'm on board, I lean against one of the poles by the door, my temple resting on the cool stainless steel. Staying alert is physically painful, almost nauseating, but if I sit down, I'm sure I'll fall asleep and end up riding the train all the way to the end of the line at Howard.

There's only one other passenger: a guy eating corn chips, lifting his phone away from his mouth so the person on the other end of the line can't hear him crunching. It's all I can hear—each chip shattering between his teeth. I think of bones snapping.

Malcolm could have broken both his wrists, bracing his fall against the concrete floor. I could have burst his eardrum. I could have ended the show in that one moment, that one lapse of control. I could have ended my career.

I should never have told him about David—even obliquely, in the guise of character. I shouldn't have told that man one true thing about me.

He still doesn't know the whole story. No one does.

The night my sister told my parents about me and David, I didn't hang around to witness their reaction. I snatched the keys to my mother's SUV off the hook by the garage and drove straight to David's house. I knew where it was, because I'd gone over there once to borrow a biography of Vivien Leigh. He told me I reminded him of her, which I thought was romantic until I read it.

David didn't live in one of the Stepford-esque housing developments in town, like my family did. His house—a snug and shabby Craftsman with blue shutters and built-in bookshelves—was out on one of the country roads closer to the school.

The first time, he hadn't let me inside; I'd waited on the porch while he went in to get the book. But that night—the night everything ended for him, and started for us—I had no doubt he would let me in. I parked around back, in the gravel driveway that curved behind the house. When I got out of the car, he was standing on the back porch, so he must have seen me coming. He didn't ask what I was doing there. He didn't seem surprised to see me at all.

As I was climbing the porch steps, I caught a glimpse of my own reflection in the windowpane on his back door. With my face scrubbed bare and my hair falling limp again, I looked much younger than I had an hour earlier, but David stared at me with the same glint of guilty desire in his eyes.

"My sister saw us," I told him. He sucked in a breath—not shocked. More like he was psyching himself up, preparing for what we both knew was about to happen. "It's all out in the open now—or it will be soon. So there's no reason . . ."

He took a step back. The shadows on the porch made his cheeks look hollow, and for a moment he seemed decades older than me rather than a few years. I waited until his shoulders hit the closed door, and then I put my hands on his chest. I slid them up around the sides of his neck, into his hair. I was about to kiss him again, but he did it for me.

I didn't tell him I was a virgin. I didn't want him to be careful with me—concerned, tender, any of that. Even at seventeen, I had no patience for that type of attention.

By noon the next day, he was fired. We were still naked in his bed together when he got the call. The Sunday matinee of the play and the second weekend of performances were all canceled.

My parents thought that was the end of it. Everyone did. But David and I kept seeing each other in secret for months afterward. And we made a plan: as soon as the school year was over, we were going to move to New York City together, try to make it as actors. That had always been his real dream, he told me, and by then it had become mine, too.

The night before graduation, I told my parents. I shouldn't have bothered, I already knew what they would say. *I thought we'd put this whole business behind us, Kira. It's bad enough, the things people have been saying these past few months, and now you want to make it worse?* And underlying all of it, the unspoken implication: *Why can't you be more like your sister?* My perfect little sister with her straight As and her age-appropriate, abstinence-pledging boyfriend. Compared to her, I could never hope to be anything more than a cautionary tale.

But I was eighteen by then, and they couldn't stop me. I snuck out of the house before dawn to meet David. By the time my classmates were trudging across the football field to collect their diplomas, we were halfway to New York.

The train pulls into Addison. There's a pack of drunk guys wearing backward baseball caps and Blackhawks jerseys waiting on the platform, but they pile into the car ahead of mine. Must be my lucky night.

David and I had only been in New York a few days when I got the callback for my one and only NYC stage credit: the role of Abigail in a way-off-Broadway production of *The Crucible*. David's face split into the widest grin when I told him. "That's so amazing, baby, I knew they would love you."

"I don't have the part yet," I said, chewing on my bottom lip.

"It's still something to celebrate," he insisted, and he started kissing me all over, the way he used to then. Working his way from my shoulder to my collarbone to the hollow of my throat, and finally my mouth. Within minutes, we were fucking against the kitchen counter, David apologizing every time he accidentally bumped my head against the cabinets.

It all seemed so romantic, at first. I liked to imagine David and me years later, as successful, award-winning actors in a well-appointed apartment with a Central Park view, laughing about our first summer in the city. *You could reach the coffee pot from the bed. We kept all our clothing in our suitcases. The window air conditioner died, and we had to sleep naked for two weeks before the landlord fixed it!* And then we'd squeeze hands and look into each other's eyes and say, *We didn't mind, though. We had each other, and that was enough.*

I don't even know where he lives now—whether he's alive at all. We haven't spoken since I was a teenager, but he sent me opening night flowers a few times, for shows I did in Ohio that made it into the local papers. Not just garish grocery store carnations. Red roses, tied with ribbon.

The train leans hard to the left as it steers around the curve before the Sheridan station. The guy with the chips stands up, brushing crumbs off the front of his jacket onto the speckled gray floor. I shut my eyes and press my forehead against the pole. The car lurches a little on the track, knocking my skull against the metal, keeping me awake.

Another passenger gets on. My eyes are still closed, but I can hear footsteps, coming through the door at the other end of the car and then moving down the aisle. Closer and closer, stopping just a few inches away from me. Close enough I can hear the person breathing, until the train pulls away again and the rumble of the wheels on the track drowns out the sound.

Are you fucking kidding me? A completely empty train car, and this motherfucker is going to stand right next to me? The last thing I need right now is to see some creep's sad, wrinkly dick sticking out of his fly. If he touches me, I swear to—

As the thought crosses my brain, I feel fingers brushing my shoulder blade. I whirl around, swinging my arm wide. My eyes don't open until I make contact.

38

JOANNA

AS MY TAXI SPEEDS DOWN IRVING PARK TO RAVENSWOOD, I think about what I should have said when Robert Kenmore called my bluff about the play.

Nothing, that's what. I should have kept my damn mouth shut.

No, I should have laughed at him. Acted like what he was saying was so absurd, it didn't even deserve a response. That's what Mal would have done.

I've never lied to Mal before. I mean, in small ways, certainly— the white lies we all tell every day to maintain civility. *It's fine, I don't mind. Of course I'm not mad.* But nothing like this.

I didn't think it would go this far. I figured he would read the script and reject it and that would be that. I assumed he wouldn't even get through the whole thing. Mal reads until he gets bored, which could happen in the last scene or two lines from the start.

When he first read the play, I was there watching him—pretending to do bookkeeping work, but really peering at him over the lid of my laptop, looking for any clues about what he was thinking.

The last time I'd let him read something I wrote was almost a decade ago. That play was about a poet who used her painful personal experiences to fuel her creative process. I wrote it as a one-act originally, and he wanted me to expand it into a full-length play. I wasn't sure how to go about it, but Mal told me not to worry. He would help me.

At first he would just brainstorm with me, let me bounce ideas off him. Then he started suggesting his own. I began to lose track of what was mine and what came from him. I told myself it didn't matter. We were partners, collaborators. Equals.

But soon, whenever I sat down to write, I started hearing Mal's voice in my head. Not the way I'd fantasized about when we met, him reading the words as I wrote them, but criticizing, berating me. Shouting over every line I wrote, even though he'd never raised his voice to me in real life.

With every new draft I produced, I tried harder to please him. And the harder I tried, the less satisfied he seemed. First he corrected my grammar. Then he told me it was *too* polished. One day he thought the characters were mundane. The next they were unrealistic, inauthentic. Finally, he decided the problem was me. *You're holding back, Joanna. I know you're capable of better than this.*

He suggested putting it off another season, so I could keep working. Get it right. We decided to do another show instead, cut the company's teeth on some Shakespeare. I wanted to start with one of the lesser plays, maybe *Taming of the Shrew* or *Measure for Measure*, but Mal insisted on *Hamlet*. It was a gamble. Indifferent Honest would either go down in flames and be remembered, if at all, as yet another fledgling Chicago theater company that flew too close to the sun, then crashed and burned. Or, if we pulled it off, we would be legendary. There was no in between. In between was mediocre, and we were going to be great.

I should have known he would be drawn to *Temper*. A tough, strange little play, with a playwright so obscure no one had heard of her before? Total catnip for Mal. He had an excited light in his eyes from the first scene, but I was afraid to get my hopes up. Afraid he'd hate it, and just as afraid he'd love it. He kept reading, turning the pages faster and faster. When he stood up and started pacing around our living room, curling the pages of the script back in his fist, I knew I had him.

I didn't even mean to write it, not really. In college, after that playwriting class sparked my creative imagination again, I wrote all the time, and I always planned every aspect of each new project before putting down a word. I had outlines and character biographies and beat sheets and bulletin boards covered in inspirational images. But *Temper* was different. It started with just a line, scribbled in the margins of a notebook. *The decision was already made.* Then a scene. Then another. Every time I sat down to work on it, I told myself I was playing around, this wasn't serious; it was an exercise and nothing more. After about a year, I had to admit to myself it was a play. And a good one, too. The best thing I'd ever written.

I wanted to show it to Mal, but I couldn't even bring myself to tell him I was writing again. Slipping the script in with the other submissions for our new season seemed like a perfect plan. If he hated it, he'd never need to know it was mine. I could forget the whole thing ever happened.

But now the play—*my* play—is opening in a few weeks, and soon my secret will be out, too. Rob said he wouldn't publish anything without my approval, but I don't believe him. Of course he'll write a story; he can't pass up a scoop like this. And then everyone will know. *Mal* will know.

None of this would have happened if he'd just showed up when he said he would.

When I get home, the loft is dark. Mal's door still stands open, everything inside exactly the way it looked this morning. I should feel relieved that I don't have to see him lying there, draped with Kira Rascher's naked body. But instead all I feel is white-hot rage.

I've been swallowing my anger all evening. Little sips of it, every time I checked my phone screen and it was blank, or looked at the door and saw someone other than Mal walking in. Now all I want to do is spew every last bit of it out again. I hurl my purse to the floor, but it isn't enough. I want to overturn furniture. Shatter glass.

That's how I felt when I was writing *Temper*—like I had to get the words out of my body or I would explode. I didn't want to write it, but I couldn't stop myself. There wasn't enough space left inside me to contain it any longer.

I sink into a seat in the living room. Not on the sofa, where I usually sit, but in Mal's favorite chair: a scarlet upholstered wingback with wobbly clawed legs we've used as a throne for several of Shakespeare's kings. I dig my nails into the carved wooden arms, marring the finish.

He has to come home sometime. I don't care what hour of the night it is. I've been waiting for him all evening, what's a little more time?

39

KIRA

THE MAN STAGGERS BACK, HANDS UP IN SURRENDER. IT TAKES a second for my eyes to focus, to make out his features, and another to realize I recognize him.

It's Rob. My ex-boyfriend. And I thought this night couldn't get any stranger.

I wish I'd given myself a once-over in the dressing room mirror after all. From what I can make out in my dark, distorted reflection in the train windows, I look like hell heated up in a microwave.

"Hey." My voice comes out flat as sandpaper and twice as rough.

"Nice to see you, too," he says. He's trying to sound sarcastic, which he's never quite been able to pull off.

It's been a while—a year, maybe more. The last time we ran into each other was at a show a mutual friend did, some interminable fantasy epic full of fake swords and puppets shaped like dragons. The theater was in an alley configuration, audience on both sides. Spence and I sat right across from Rob, and our eyes kept meeting. He was always the first to break eye contact. It became like a game, almost. I think I may have watched him more than the show.

"You startled me," I say.

"I said your name, like, five times."

I must be even more out of it than I realized. Thank God it was Rob who snuck up on me and not an actual stranger. I generally feel pretty safe in Chicago—despite all the terrifying local news stories about rapes and muggings my mother likes to forward to me from the safety of her suburban Ohio McMansion—but shit does happen. Last year I heard about a girl who got stabbed in the neck on the Red Line and bled out on the platform before the paramedics could get there. I think of the blood seeping from Malcolm's split lip again.

The train shudders, and I stagger back. Automatically, Rob reaches out to steady me, but his hand stops before we touch. I don't need his help anyway, my grip on the pole keeps me upright. Both of my hands ache.

"You okay?" he asks. "It's awfully late."

He's out and about at this ungodly hour too, I'd like to point out, but I know what he means. It's different for men—especially men who are six foot two with broad, hulking shoulders. Rob isn't all that muscular, unless he's been hitting the gym since we split, but he wears his clothes so baggy it's easy enough to imagine he might be ripped under there. Though he's nowhere near as intimidating as Spence, not many people would chance messing with him. The two of them are the same height, but Rob always stoops a little, like he's apologizing for his size.

"I'm fine. I'm just getting out of rehearsal."

"What? It's—" He checks the exact time on his watch. Rob may be the only person I know who still wears a watch that isn't in any way smart. "Two twenty-seven in the morning. Isn't that illegal?"

"It's not a union theater."

"Still." He studies my face like he's looking for signs of damage.

"So what's your excuse for being out so late?" I ask. "Hot date?"

It's impossible to glean any clues from his clothing. No matter the occasion, Rob dresses like a college professor—and not a cool young one, either. Tonight he's wearing a cardigan sweater with suede patches on the elbows, one of at least three I know he owns, which should really be outlawed before the age of forty.

"Boring fundraiser," he says.

"So business, not pleasure." I'm a little relieved, which is ridiculous. We've been apart now for longer than we were together. It's none of my business what—or who—Rob does.

"Could have been worse—last night they sent me to cover this experimental performance piece in a warehouse out in Northwest Indiana."

I make a face. "How was it?"

"Like being trapped in theatrical purgatory."

That must be a line he's going to use in his review. Rob doesn't just think before he speaks, he composes each sentence, sometimes going through multiple drafts in his head. Which was great if he was thinking of the perfect romantic phrase to whisper in my ear, but beyond infuriating whenever we argued. Those long pauses, when I knew he was editing himself, striking through all the things he really wanted to say to me. I wished I could read his mind, get at the unfiltered truth. But maybe there's something to be said for that—a person who loves you enough to lie.

The train slows. We're at Argyle now, the stop before mine. Rob is holding on to one of the plastic straps hanging from the ceiling, and the swaying of the train brings him so close to me I can feel the heat coming off him. I'm so exhausted, all I want to do is fall into bed, but now I'm imagining Rob in bed with me—not fucking him, but the way we used to lie together afterward, his body curving around mine, his long nose brushing the nape of my neck, his fingers fitted into the crease of my waist.

"You want me to walk you home?" He's almost whispering, like he's concerned someone could overhear us.

It isn't too far out of his way. Last I knew, he lived in Rogers Park, one neighborhood north. I've only seen the outside of his building—a pretty brick six-flat covered in ivy—once, when Spence drove me there to drop off the last box of Rob's things I found lingering around my bedroom after we broke up. When we were dating, he lived in a dilapidated Evanston bungalow with three other guys he went to Northwestern with, so we spent most of our time at my place.

"No, that's okay. I'm—"

The train lurches, and I almost lose my grip on the pole. Rob touches me this time, his fingers spreading across the small of my back. Even after it's clear I'm not going to fall, he doesn't let go. I lean into him—just a little, subtle enough it could be an accident. I forgot how huge his hands are, almost spanning the width of my waist.

"It's no trouble," he says.

No trouble. Somehow I doubt that. With Rob and me, there's always trouble.

40

JOANNA

IT'S NEARLY THREE IN THE MORNING WHEN I FINALLY HEAR Mal's key in the door. I'm pacing beside the kitchen table to keep myself awake. Despite my simmering anger and the stiff back of Mal's chair, I kept drifting off.

He's fumbling at the lock, metal scratching metal. I wonder if he's drunk. I've only seen Mal intoxicated on one other occasion. He's not a cruel drunk, he just goes quiet, his eyes hollow like the lights are switched off inside him.

If I'm going to tell him about the play, it has to be now. Otherwise I'll lose my nerve.

The door swings open. The lights from the stairwell glow around the borders of his body, but his face stays in shadow. His hair is wild—whipped out of place by the wind, or . . . the image comes, unbidden: Kira straddling his lap, her fingers crawling like spiders over his scalp. Pulling his head back, exposing his throat. I wonder if I'll find her lipstick there, or if he had the decency to scrub it off before coming home to me.

"Mal, we need to talk."

He doesn't seem to hear me. He's turned away, busying himself with doffing his jacket, emptying his pockets, slipping out of his shoes.

"Mal." Nothing. It's as though I don't exist. "Mal, where the *fuck* were you tonight?"

I slam my hand down on the table. The items he's removed from his pockets jump. He doesn't.

"At the theater." His voice is even, mild. Maddening.

"At the theater. Doing what, exactly?"

"Rehearsing."

"It's almost three in the morning. You were supposed to finish at ten. You promised to meet me at—"

"We ran long."

"'We'? You mean you and Kira."

And now we're back to the silent treatment. He's unpacking his bag now—a leather messenger, embossed with his initials. I bought it for him the first Christmas after the theater started bringing in real money. He starts stacking papers on the table. Making sure the piles are neat, which he's never bothered with before in his whole goddamn life.

"I know you're fucking her."

He stops. Exhales. Still won't face me.

"Just admit it," I say.

"Joanna."

"I know you are, you've been fucking her this whole time, you—"

"Listen to yourself."

I can't. My pulse thunders in my ears. When he's calm like this, placid and reflective as still water, I want to plunge my hand into him, force him to churn and splash, to *react*.

I reach for his shoulder. If he doesn't have the decency to turn around and look me in the eyes while he lies to me, I'll fucking make him.

But before I can touch him, he whips around to face me, and I finally see him in the light.

There's red smeared over his mouth, but it isn't Kira's lipstick. It's fresh blood.

41

KIRA

ROB PUTS HIS HAND ON MY BACK AGAIN AS WE DESCEND from the train platform, steering me around a sour-smelling wet patch on the second-to-last step.

The air is a few degrees cooler this far north and so close to the lake. Rob sees me shiver and takes off his sweater, handing it over without a word. It's way too big on me, so the suede patches line up with my forearms instead of my elbows.

"Sorry," he says. "It probably smells. Long day."

It does smell, but only like him, the books he collects and his hopelessly untrendy aftershave. Sometimes I catch a whiff of that same spicy scent on another man—usually someone much older than Rob—sitting next to me on the bus or passing me on the sidewalk, and I miss Rob so much my chest hurts.

I fold the sweater over my front, crossing my arms to hold it in place. The wind coming off the lake chases us west down Berwyn Avenue.

We had our first kiss on a night like this one. I can't remember the exact date, but it must have been around the same time of year—October, not freezing yet, but a chill in the air, the smell of smoke and decay on the wind. We were standing outside the Music Box, the marquee lights making our eyes dazzle, and he'd just wrapped his herringbone coat around my shoulders. He took two whole weeks after our first date to kiss me, which is longer than most of my relationships have lasted in total. It was worth the wait. Rob uses his body as precisely as he uses his words.

He walks me to the front door of my building. I don't say *good-bye* or *thank you* or *would you like to come upstairs?* I just turn my key in the lock and go inside. I know he'll follow.

People are always impressed when they see where Spence and I live, at least until they get inside our apartment. The surrounding blocks are a historic district, full of painstakingly preserved turn-of-the-twentieth-century homes—the kind of neighborhood where you have to apply for a permit to change the color of paint on your shutters. The three-flat greystone we live in looks impressive from the outside, but the interior is dilapidated. The skylight in the entryway leaks every spring, and sometimes you can taste rust in the tap water.

We climb the stairs to the third floor, Rob's shadow looming larger than mine even though he's a few steps lower. Keeping a respectable distance. That's Rob for you—always so fucking respectable.

The door to Spence's room stands open, which means he isn't home. We're alone.

"So you and Spence still live together?" Rob asks.

"Yeah." I bristle a little at that "still." Rob found my relationship with Spence perplexing, even before he knew the full extent of it.

"Is he out of town?"

"I think he's at his boyfriend's."

"Spence has a boyfriend? Seriously?"

I shrug. Spence would chafe at that term, but he's not here to contradict me.

"What about you?" I redirect. "How's . . . Lisa?"

"Liz. She's fine. We broke up a couple months ago, actually."

"Oh. I'm sorry to hear that."

Usually I would be able to make my performance of that line more convincing, but I'm too exhausted for dissembling.

"It's okay," he says. "It was amicable. She's going to grad school in California, so."

Rob prides himself on staying friends with all his exes. I'm the one who ruined his perfect streak. The earth between us isn't scorched, but I'd definitely consider it singed. This is already the longest conversation we've had since we parted ways.

Rob slips off his shabby leather loafers and sits down on the sofa. Still at home here.

There's a hole in his left sock, the tip of his big toe peeking through. I feel a surge of affection for him, so sudden and violent it's like bile rising in my throat.

"So aside from the crazy hours," he says, "how's it going at Indifferent Honest?"

I'm surprised for a second, but I shouldn't be. It's literally his job to keep tabs on what's going on in the Chicago theater community. Of course he would have heard I was cast in *Temper*. I wonder if he was surprised. I don't think Rob considers me a bad actress. Limited, maybe. He had me pegged as a specific type, and I don't know if I could have ever changed his mind. After a while, I wasn't interested in trying anymore.

"Great. It's going great." I slip out of my shoes and kick them under the coffee table. "Well, except for the fact that I hit Malcolm Mercer in the face tonight."

Rob's mouth falls open. "You *what?*"

I try to laugh, to pass my statement off as a joke, but the sound comes out strangled, hysterical. I must seem insane to him right now. His crazy ex-girlfriend, always causing drama.

This was a bad idea. He shouldn't be here. I should thank him for walking me home, tell him how exhausted I am, and send him on his way.

Instead, I scrunch up my face and squeeze my eyelids shut until tears start to seep through. As soon as he sees I'm crying, Rob stands up again.

"Come here," he says.

But he comes to me instead, folding his body around mine. One hand on the small of my back, one on the back of my head, stroking my hair. It's better than I remembered.

At some point—I can't identify the exact moment—my weeping turns real. It's like I pried the floodgates open, and I'm not strong enough to force them closed again.

I'm so fucking tired.

Rob kisses the part in my hair, the tip of his nose dragging over my scalp, then leads me over to the sofa, sits, and pulls me down beside him.

"Tell me what happened," he says.

So I tell him—about the play, Mara's reveries, the slap. How Malcolm made me do it over and over again for hours until I felt like I was losing my grip on sanity, my grip on everything, until finally—

"Did you hurt him?" Rob asks.

"I mean, he was bleeding. He just made me so mad, I—"

I raise my palm in the air, like I did before the slap. Rob flinches, as if he's afraid I might actually strike him. Maybe he should be afraid of me, of what I might do.

Rob takes my hand, pulling it down into his lap like he's disarming me of a deadly weapon. "I'm sure he understands it was an accident."

I'm not certain of much in the wake of tonight's events, but I do know this: that slap was no accident. Malcolm wanted me to hit him. I wanted to make him bleed. On some level, we both knew exactly what we were doing.

I pull my hand away from Rob and stand up. "I need a drink. Do you want a drink?"

I already know he doesn't. Rob's never been much of a drinker, and he probably has to be at work in a few hours. He's one of the only people I know with a real job—a desk and business cards and everything. But he'll hold the glass and pretend for my sake.

Spence keeps a Don Draper–style bar cart in the living room—for "entertaining," he claims, but mostly the two of us partake alone while watching bad movies on Netflix. I take his best bottle of Scotch and two vintage tumblers off the cart and pour generous helpings for Rob and myself.

As I'm preparing the drinks, I can sense Rob looking at my bare legs. It isn't his usual subtle glance; even when we were dating, he was shy about ogling me. But now he's outright staring.

"Do you want ice?" I ask. "Or—"

His fingertips brush the side of my thigh, lifting the hem of my skirt. I freeze, the neck of the Scotch bottle tapping the rim of the glass.

"What the hell is this?" he says.

Rob almost never swears, and his voice is shaking. I set the bottle on the coffee table and look down at the spot he's touching.

It's the place on my thigh where I do the knap. The skin is already starting to purple with a massive bruise, the size of my palm.

"Did he do this? Did he—"

Rob shoots to his feet, knocking his shins into the coffee table, rattling the glasses.

Most people who know Rob don't know about his temper. I didn't either—not until the night we broke up.

He's pacing the length of the sofa now, like a caged tiger, and his hands are curled in fists, his nostrils flaring. I had no idea he still cared this much. No idea he *ever* cared this much, to be honest. I can't tell whether he's trying to keep himself from shaking me so hard my teeth snap together, or finding Malcolm Mercer and beating his beautiful face to a bloody pulp.

"It wasn't him," I say.

"Then how did—"

"It was me. I did it."

Rob stops and looks at me. His eyes spark like sliced wires. "What do you mean, you—"

"That's where I do the knap. We did it so many times, I guess I must have . . ."

He shuts his eyes and takes a slow, deep breath in—some sort of meditative exercise I've never seen him do before. Maybe he learned it from Liz. I saw them together once, across the lawn at a concert at the Pritzker. She had on Lululemon leggings that matched the trim on her picnic basket, and her freckled face was as bright and sunny as the summer sky. It seemed impossible to me that a man who loved her could ever have loved someone like me.

"It's okay." I take a step toward him. "I'm okay."

Rob opens his eyes.

He seems startled to find me standing so near to him, and he shifts back on his heels. I take another step forward. This time, he doesn't move away.

Most of my other exes I've fallen back into bed with at least once after we were supposedly over. Not Rob. Once we were done, we were done. Maybe that gave him closure, but for me it made him feel like unfinished business.

I wasn't expecting this, it's not why I let him come home with me, but even that brief touch of his fingertips on my thigh sent a rush of pleasure straight to my core, and I can't help imagining it, how easy it would be to turn around, push him back onto the sofa and straddle him, sink down . . . I wouldn't even have to take off my dress.

A fraction of an inch farther, and we'll be kissing, for the first time in years. But Rob has to be the one to do it. He has to choose to close the distance between us.

He puts his hand on my neck, pressing his thumb into the hollow of my throat.

"Kira . . ." He hasn't pushed me away yet, but he won't let me get any closer, either. I lean into his hand. "Kira. Stop."

I don't. His fingers tighten, squeezing my throat.

"I said *stop*."

Rob lets go, so fast I stumble forward a little and nearly collide with him. He rakes his fingers through his hair, turning away from me, then back again.

"I should never have come here." He's looking down at the floor, speaking more to himself than to me. "I should know better by now."

I move toward him again, hands out to touch his face. "Rob—"

He reaches for my wrists like he's going to grab me and fling me away. But he stops himself and builds a barrier between us with his voice instead.

"No."

He's already moving toward the door. Getting away from me as fast as he can.

"Good luck with the show," he says. "Or, sorry, I should say: break a leg."

"Wait." I'm still wearing his sweater, he'll have to come back for it. I start to undo the buttons. My fingers are trembling.

Rob stops on the threshold, his hand on the doorknob, but he doesn't look back at me.

"Keep it," he says.

As soon as the door shuts, I wrap the sweater around myself again, holding my rib cage. More tears threaten, but I blink them back. No point now, without an audience.

I down my drink and Rob's and take the bottle with me to bed.

42

JOANNA

MAL LETS ME TOUCH MY THUMB TO HIS LIP AND SWIPE AWAY the blood beaded there.

"What happened?" I ask. More blood has already welled up to take the place of what I wiped off. The split is deep; I can see the tissue underneath his skin, pink and pulsing.

"We should go to bed," he says.

"But you're hurt." I reach toward his mouth again. This time he stops me, taking my hand, covering it with his own. "Tell me what happened. Did someone mug you, or—"

You know who did this. The thought comes to me with such sudden, declarative force, it's like someone shouting in my ear.

He's still holding my hand. He threads his fingers through mine. "Come to bed, Jo."

He leads me into my own room, dragging me along beside him like I've never been there before, like I don't know the way. It's too dark to make out his expression, but I can see the whites of his eyes shining. He lies down on the bed, still wearing the shoes I picked out for him to wear to the fundraiser, the polished leather stark against the field of faded blue flowers on my quilt.

We used to sleep next to each other all the time. Back when we couldn't afford real beds, just twin air mattresses laid out on the floor of the loft. Whenever we needed to make room for rehearsals or performances, we'd deflate them and stow them in the bathtub. But most nights, we pushed them together and stayed up until all hours, talking about plans for our next show like girls whispering in their bunks at summer camp. We'd fall asleep side by side, surrounded by books, papers, half-eaten plates of food. Sometimes touching each other, sometimes not.

Mal's eyes are shut now, but he finds my waist, pulls me down with him. One of my shoes slips off, clattering to the floor beside the bed. My pencil skirt has ridden up, wrinkling around my hips, exposing a swath of pale skin above my knees.

I don't even remember what I wanted to say to him. All the speeches I wrote and rewrote in my head. The second I saw he was bleeding, my rage burned off like fog.

He ended up bleeding during the first performance of *Hamlet*, too. Our replacement Laertes accidentally scratched him while they were grappling over Ophelia's grave, and by the end of the scene, Mal had blood leaking into his eye.

But he wasn't upset. In fact, he liked the way it looked, the edge it lent to the scene. So much so that he reopened the wound himself every night, digging his thumbnail into the spot until red seeped out again. He has a small scar there to this day, cutting through his eyebrow.

Mal rests his head against my shoulder, breathing already slowing as he slips into sleep. I don't need him to tell me a thing, I already know.

Kira is the one who made him bleed.

43

KIRA

WHEN I FINALLY DRAG MYSELF OUT OF BED ON THE WRONG side of noon, I don't feel even remotely rested. Only the jump forward in time convinces me I slept at all. That much Scotch would usually knock me out, but my sleep was shallow and scattered.

At some point during the night, I stripped off Rob's sweater, along with the rest of my clothes, and now I'm covered in goose bumps so pronounced they look like welts. I hate this in-between time of the year, when it's cold but not cold enough for our landlord to switch on the heat.

This is the time of year Rob and I broke up, too. Two whole years after we started—my longest relationship to date, unless you count Spence.

The last time my family took any interest whatsoever in my life was when I started seeing Rob. My mother dropped out of college to get married, and Stacy tied the knot before the ink on her diploma was dry, so they both treat my continued singleness like it's a deadly wasting disease. They seemed to take my relationship with Rob as a sign I was finally coming to my senses.

The minute Stacy saw my social media relationship status switch back to *Single*, she called me—the first time we'd spoken on the phone in years. She didn't even say *hello* when I answered, just "What happened?" By which she meant: *What did you do this time?*

What happened was, I got pregnant and I didn't tell Rob. I decided long ago I have no interest in motherhood, so I didn't see the point of burdening him.

When I was a teenager, the only option was the vacuum-cleaner approach, but now they give you a choice—at least, if you catch it early like I did. That's what it felt like to me: a cancer, something I needed to stop before it could spread.

Spence drove me to my clinic appointment, where I took the first dose of pills and left with another dose, to be taken at home the next day. The second dose had just started to kick in when Rob stopped by the apartment unexpectedly, to pick up a book he'd forgotten.

He could tell immediately something was wrong. I tried to play it off, and I might have gotten away with it, if my body hadn't betrayed me. A nasty cramp twisted my gut, and I couldn't stop myself from grimacing. I insisted I was fine, I had a little stomach bug, that was all, and he should go before I infected him. He wouldn't hear of it. "Kira, please," he said. "Let me take care of you."

So he stayed—set me up on the sofa with a soft blanket over me, made me soup from scratch, rubbed my feet. Every time he looked at me with those liquid-brown eyes like a loyal dog, I felt something worse than the pain: guilt, settling inside me heavy as a pile of stones. It wasn't the abortion itself I felt guilty about; that was a necessary medical procedure, like getting a tooth pulled. But I could no longer deny that my mother and sister were right about Rob: he was too good for me. I didn't deserve this treatment, and I didn't deserve him.

Eventually I drifted off to sleep, nestled in the sofa cushions, my feet still propped up in Rob's lap. I woke up to him shaking me by the shoulders. Blood had started to leak out between my legs, soaking into the blanket, and since he had no idea what was really going on, he was frantic. He wanted to take me to the hospital.

At that point, I had to tell him. I figured he would be angry, for the deception if not the act itself. But I wasn't at all prepared for the pain in his eyes. He kept asking me *why*—not why I didn't want to have his baby (or any baby at all, ever), but why I hadn't told him earlier, why I didn't want him to come with me to the clinic.

The truth is, I always thought Rob and I were temporary. He was having fun with me, and then he'd settle down with a woman who was more like him. Serious. Responsible. *Nice.* But that day I realized: he loved me in a way I wasn't sure I could ever return. It would be better, I reasoned, to let him go before he wasted any more time.

So I thought of the most unforgivable thing I could say, and I said it. I told Rob the baby probably wasn't his anyway, because I'd been fucking Spence the whole time we were together. Part of me wished he would see through the lie, call me on my bullshit (and it was bullshit, I didn't so much as hold Spence's hand while I was with Rob), shake his head and say *I don't believe you, you wouldn't do that.* But of course he believed me. It seemed like exactly the kind of thing I would do.

And then Rob did get angry. He was looming over me, eyes darkening like thunderheads, and I realized something else: he wanted to hurt me. Backhand me across my smart mouth, maybe, or shove me into a wall. It was taking every scrap of his self-control to stop himself, to keep that spark of menace from growing into an inferno.

I should have been frightened. I should have been horrified. But instead I thought: *there it is.* Underneath his sweet, unassuming surface, Rob was dark and twisted and fucked-up, too. I finally understood why he wanted me, at the exact moment when he decided he no longer did.

I didn't tell my sister any of this. I mumbled some generic explanation about how Rob and I weren't right for each other, how we wanted different things. She sighed, and I could practically hear her shaking her head through the phone. "Kira, you know you might never find a guy like him again, right? You should call him, try and work things out. Maybe it's not too late."

But it was too late. I'd made damn sure of that.

I dig Rob's sweater out of the gray tangle of my bedding and hold it up to my nose. The smell of his aftershave has faded from the material slightly, but it's still enough to make my chest ache.

Every damn part of me is aching right now, so much worse than the usual head-throbbing of a hangover. I feel like I've been in a fight. And it's not over yet. I might be able to avoid running into Rob for the foreseeable future, but in a few short hours, I have to walk back through the doors of Indifferent Honest and face Malcolm again.

I need coffee before I can contemplate this any further.

When I open the bedroom door, something rushes at my feet. I'm so foggy, I don't manage to react until it's already slammed into my ankles.

It's a dog—a stubby little one with vampire-bat ears and a face like smashed road kill. It gapes up at me, tongue lolling out the side of its mouth.

What the fuck?

The television is on in the living room, so Spence must have finally come home, but that doesn't explain the dog. If he got a pet without telling me, I'm going to fucking kill him.

I pull Rob's sweater back on, wrapping it around my body to cover up my bra and underwear, then head down the hall to investigate. The dog follows me, close enough to slobber on my heels.

Spence is stretched out on the sofa, and he's not alone. There's a young man with curly brown hair sitting beside him, Spence's bare feet resting in his lap.

The dog scurries past me with a yelp and jumps up on the sofa with them, snuffling around the rim of the cereal bowl the guy has balanced on Spence's ankles.

So this must be his mysterious gentleman friend. At last we meet.

But then he turns around, and I realize he's not so mysterious after all.

It's Jason Grady.

44

JOANNA

WHEN I WAKE UP, MAL'S ARM IS STILL SLUNG ACROSS MY WAIST. In the daylight, I can see it there rather than just sensing the weight of it, but that doesn't make this feel any less unreal.

The clock on my dresser says it's after twelve p.m. I can't recall the last time I slept in this late or got so many hours of sleep in a row. I can't remember the last time Mal set foot in my bedroom, either. I'm embarrassed, suddenly, by how childish the space is, how much of its contents are left over from my college dorm room or childhood bedroom. Posters from theater department productions I stage-managed—*Cabaret, Into the Woods*—in cheap plastic frames from Target. The sagging bookcase by the closet, stuffed full of playscripts left over from undergraduate classes and novels I may never have the time to read. The quilt underneath us, hand stitched by my mother to match the canopy bed I slept in as a little girl.

I roll over to face Mal. He exhales, and I breathe it in.

Pathetic, the tiny morsels of intimacy I accept from him.

The split in his lip has scabbed over, but it still looks red. It must hurt. I want to know what happened between them. What provoked her. Kira Rascher seems like the kind of woman prone to passionate love affairs, throwing dinner plates in the heat of anger, and having make-up sex that snaps the legs off the kitchen table. I wonder if she ever fought like that with Rob. He seemed so reasonable and even-tempered. But you can't tell what a person's like, after only a few hours. Sometimes even after you've known them for years. We all play our parts.

I've never hit someone. Never injured another person at all, unless you count stepping on a fellow passenger's toes on the train. But of course I've wondered about it. Not only when I was writing *Temper*, but before that. What it would feel like to make a person bleed, hurt, suffer through nothing more than the contact of my skin to theirs.

I did do research when I was writing the play, on what happens when you strangle someone. It takes less time than I might have thought, and less strength. The trachea is a fragile thing. Cartilage only, no bones to protect it. Thirty-three pounds of pressure to close it off entirely. Seconds before loss of consciousness. Brain death within five minutes.

Mal told me once about an ex-girlfriend of his—someone he dated during his single year of drama school at Carnegie Mellon, well before he met me—who liked to be choked in bed.

"Isn't it dangerous?" I asked him. The wrong question. He wanted me to be curious. Intrigued.

"Not if you do it right." He showed me the correct place to press, the carotid artery on either side of the neck. Cut off the blood to the brain, and the person passes out. As soon as you let go, the blood flow starts back up again. No permanent injury, supposedly.

He showed me her signal, too—the one she would use if she wanted him to stop. A pinch on the side of the wrist. Hard enough to hurt.

I asked him if she ever had to use it, and he smiled—fond, reminiscing.

"No," he said. "Not with me."

I press my fingertip into the hollow of Mal's throat, feeling the edges of the bone. Waiting, to see if he'll wake up. He doesn't, so

I keep going, tracing up over the lump of his Adam's apple, to the point of his chin, the line of his jaw.

He hasn't shaved in at least three days. How could he have? He hasn't been home. He's been with her. At the theater and wherever else they went together.

My fingernail digs into the soft flesh under his jaw, and I catch myself, retract my hand. He still doesn't wake, but he turns his head away from me. Exposing his throat.

I watch the flutter of his heartbeat for a while. He seems so innocent when he's asleep. Vulnerable. I suppose we all do.

He looks younger, too. The lines around his eyes slackened into oblivion. They've been etched deeper over the years, but even back when I met him, he had those lines. I used to fantasize about running my fingertips over them. Smoothing them out, then watching them form again as he smiled at me. I'd never wanted to touch another person so much in my life.

I wasn't then, and I'm still not, a touchy-feely, physical person. I prefer handshakes to hugs. I don't like to cuddle after sex. But with Mal, from the first day I knew him, I felt like I had to sit on my hands to keep myself from brushing back his hair or caressing his cheek. It was a totally alien feeling to me, that magnetic pull, the sense we were already familiar. As if we'd known each other for years even though we'd only just met.

I had a serious girlfriend at the time and being in the same room with Mal was enough to make me feel guilty, like I was cheating on her just by looking at him. Jess had a jealous streak anyway, set off whenever I spent time alone with my male friends. When she'd make noise about it, I'd remind her it was just as likely I might be fucking my female friends. *So you think bisexual people shouldn't be allowed to have any friends at all?*

That usually shut her up, but I knew Jess would have preferred to pretend my bisexuality didn't exist. She treated it like a sordid secret. A defect she had to overlook in order to be with me. She was paranoid I was secretly straight, just engaging in a little college-era experimentation. When I told her I was moving to Chicago to start a theater company with Mal, she'd shaken her head and said, "I knew it. I always knew you'd leave me for a man."

By the time I graduated from college, I'd met plenty of other people who identified as bi, but Mal was the first one who treated bisexuality like it was the most natural thing in the world. He assumes people are bisexual unless they tell him otherwise. One of our favorite pastimes after I arrived in Chicago was sitting on a bench in Lincoln Park sharing a single Intelligentsia pour-over coffee between us and talking about which passersby we found attractive—male, female, and everyone in between.

Mal is still asleep, breathing softly through parted lips. We're lying so close, all I'd have to do is tilt up my chin, and our lips would meet.

I used to be so obsessed with the idea of kissing him. When we first met, I was too shy to act on my desires, so I waited for him to make the first move. And then I kept on waiting, far past the point when I should have realized it was hopeless. Mal didn't want me that way, and he never would.

But I can't help wondering: How would he respond? If he woke up and found me pressed against him, my mouth on his, my fingers twining in his hair. Would he push me away?

Then again, he might not wake up—not right away, not entirely. He might stay like this. Eyes closed, half-conscious. Muddled enough to mistake me for someone else.

He might even think I'm her.

45

KIRA

SO THIS IS WHAT SPENCE HAS BEEN DOING FOR THE PAST FEW weeks.

When he sees me standing in the doorway, he starts, jostling Jason's cereal bowl. They obviously thought they were alone. A few pieces of granola fall to the floor, and the dog hops down to vacuum them up.

Spence swallows. "Kira, you remember—"

"Jason. Hi."

"Good morning," Jason says. "Well, afternoon, I guess."

He's not wearing pants, but he still has that stupid leather cuff on his wrist. The T-shirt he's got on over his boxer briefs is Spence's—an old OSU theater department shirt, the front stretched out because it used to be one of my favorites to steal and wear to bed.

Jason's dog finished all the scattered cereal and is now back to investigating my feet. Its cold, slimy nose touches my toe, and I jerk my foot away.

Jason snaps his fingers. "Lafayette, here."

The dog jumps up on the sofa and seizes the space on Jason's lap previously occupied by Spence's feet. It's still staring at me, its dim black eyes bulging.

"If I'd known you didn't like dogs"—Jason pauses to give Spence a pointed *why didn't you tell me?* look—"I would have left him at my place."

"Don't mind her, Kira detests most living things. I'm one of the rare exceptions."

Spence smiles at me. I do not smile back.

"There's some coffee left if you—" he starts, but I'm already on my way to the kitchen.

Spence sprung for the good Metropolis coffee for his guest. I noticed, too, that Jason was drinking out of Spence's favorite mug: a gold-and-black mid-century modern antique I've been forbidden to touch on pain of death since I shattered its mate in the sink a few years ago.

Jason Grady. All this time he's been sneaking around, it was so he could fuck Jason Grady?

I'm not surprised Spence slept with him, just by how long it seems to have been going on. Spence has had plenty of hookups with sweet-looking young guys like Jason, but they always end in tears—and never Spence's.

And it's almost unheard of for him to bring dates back to the apartment. Our downstairs neighbors have no doubt overheard the two of us going at it plenty of times, but I've never walked in on Spence screwing someone else, let alone snuggling with them on the sofa like he was with Jason. Spence would probably claim it's out of respect for me, but my theory is he's afraid the rack of weapons beside his bed might make his sexy serial killer vibe seem a little too literal.

Jason must be fine with it. Spence and his sharp edges.

Spence follows me into the kitchen, like I figured he would. Rob's sweater falls open as I reach into the cabinet above the coffee maker to get one of our not-off-limits mugs. He's staring, but at the sweater, not me. My body is as commonplace to him by now as the dish drainer.

"That's a hideous sweater," he says.

"Thanks." I pour myself some coffee—too much, splashing over the side—and take a sip.

"Where'd you get it?"

"It's Rob's," I mumble into the lip of the mug.

"You robbed someone?" He looks impressed rather than scandalized.

"It belongs to Rob."

"Rob. As in your ex-boyfriend Rob?"

"I ran into him last night. On the train, after rehearsal. He walked me home."

Spence's eyes widen. "You two didn't—"

"No, you're the only one getting laid around here. Congratulations." I glance down the hall toward the living room, where Jason has wisely stayed with his dog. "So when did *that* happen?"

"A few weeks ago. I got his number from you, actually."

"What?"

"The napkin he gave you at Lady Gregory's."

"You went through my bag?"

"It was sticking out of the top! Fair game."

I roll my eyes and take another drink of coffee. "So am I allowed to talk to him? Or should I go back into my room and pretend this never happened?"

"Up to you," Spence says. "I think you two would get along, actually."

Not fucking likely. "So why all the sneaking around, then?"

"Jason wanted to keep things just between us for a little while. He asked me to—"

"He asked you to lie to me?"

"No, not—he thought it might upset you, that's all."

I told Spence about Jason accosting me and warning me about Malcolm. I didn't mention the way he gripped my arm, how fast the warmth drained from his eyes. Maybe I should have. Though, knowing Spence, that would have made him *more* likely to pursue Jason. He loves a little damage, as long as he's not expected to fix it.

"Does he know about—"

"Us?" Spence says. "Yes. I told him on our first date."

Now I'm really surprised. Usually when Spence is seeing someone, he waits until the perfect moment to tell them about our long-standing friends-with-benefits arrangement—i.e. when he's over them and ready to slam down the self-destruct button. I take the opposite approach: I tell guys right from the start, so they don't get the wrong impression about what I'm looking for. It's not my fault so many of them don't listen.

"And how did he take it?" I ask.

"He thanked me for my 'honesty.'" Spence laughs, like he's told a joke, but the smitten smile playing across his lips tells a different story.

"Oh yeah, he's big on honesty."

Spence bristles. "He was just worried about you."

"You're working with Malcolm, too. Is Jason worried about you?"

"Just try to be nice to him, okay?" Spence grabs the hem of Rob's sweater and tugs me closer—though not as close as he would if we were truly alone. "For me."

I hold out my mug. "I'm going to need a hell of a lot more caffeine in my system if you want me *nice*."

He tops me off, and we head back into the living room. The television is silent now, set back to the Netflix menu, but as I cross the threshold, Jason's dog gives one short, sharp *yap*, like I'm an intruder in my own home.

Then Spence grabs my arm, sloshing hot coffee onto my thumb.

"What the *fuck*," he says, pointing at my leg, "is that?"

46

JOANNA

I NEED TO GET OUT OF THIS BED BEFORE I DO SOMETHING I regret.

Mal's fingertips drag across my stomach as I slide out from under his arm, but he doesn't stir. He's still asleep, or doing a good job of pretending.

He's so good at pretending.

As soon as I stand up, my head feels clearer. Clear enough to realize I don't need Mal to tell me what happened last night, because someone else was there. Maybe Bryn will turn out to be good for something after all.

She answers on the second ring. There's traffic noise and a blast of wind into the receiver, then her frantic voice.

"Joanna, I'm so sorry, I'm on my way now, I'll be there as soon as—"

"It's okay." I forgot she was supposed to work today; on Mondays, all her classes are in the afternoon, so she usually comes into the office for a few hours in the morning.

"I'm sorry, I'm such a—"

"Bryn. It's okay. I don't care that you're late. I'm not even at the theater yet myself."

Quiet on the other end of the line now, except for Bryn's panicky breathing. She might be crying, I'm not sure. It doesn't matter. Her agitation is all the opening I need.

"You sound upset. Are you all right?"

"I'm . . . I'm fine. I overslept."

"You guys were at rehearsal pretty late last night, huh?"

She hesitates. "I guess so."

"I'll talk to Mal," I say. "Make sure it doesn't happen again."

"It wasn't his fault." This spills out of her so fast, I can tell she's been thinking about it, planning what to say to me.

"Then whose fault was it?" I ask, although the answer is obvious to both of us. I just want to hear her say it.

But she's gone quiet again. Probably gnawing her lip. She's always doing that when she's nervous, when she doesn't know what to do. Which is most of the time she's at the theater. She sinks her teeth in so deep, sometimes I think her flesh will split like ripe fruit.

"Bryn, it's okay, you can tell me."

"I shouldn't—I mean, I don't really know what happened. I fell asleep. They were still rehearsing, but I had to study, so I went to one of the dressing rooms, and . . ."

"And before that?" I prompt her. A police siren screams somewhere in the distance; I'm not sure if it's outside our building or carrying over the cell line. I press the phone closer to my ear.

Bryn exhales. "She just . . . she wouldn't stop."

47

KIRA

SPENCE GAPES AT THE BRUISE ON MY LEG. IT LOOKS EVEN worse now than it did when I went to bed. The skin's turned mottled crimson, like crushed berries smeared over the side of my thigh.

"That's the leg where you do the knap," he says. "Please don't tell me that's from the fucking knap!"

I don't answer him. He can see the truth all over my face anyway.

"Fucking hell, Kira."

He crouches down on the floor to get a better look at the damage. Jason's dog thinks Spence is trying to play, and it rams its head repeatedly into his kneecap.

"How many times did you do it?" Spence asks.

"I don't know," I say. "A lot."

"He kept you there until, what, like one in the morning?"

Jason. I almost forgot he was here. Spence is still studying the side of my thigh, running his thumbs around the borders of the bruise. I swat his hand away and turn to face Jason.

"Two in the morning, actually."

Jason nods knowingly. "Classic Malcolm Mercer. He's trying to dismantle you."

"What?" I say.

"That's what my therapist calls it, anyway. He's breaking you down so he can build you back up again the way he wants you. You've been working with him for a few weeks now, right?"

I nod, moving away from Spence to perch on the arm of the sofa next to Jason.

"Well then, I hate to break it to you, but the honeymoon's over." Judging by the look on Jason's face, he doesn't hate breaking this to me at all. He hasn't actually said the words *I told you so* yet, but it's implied. "Mal's going to be a tyrannical nightmare from here on out. He pulled the exact same shit during *Hamlet*."

"I thought Joanna directed *Hamlet*." To my knowledge, though, she hasn't directed another show since, at Indifferent Honest or anywhere else. I always wondered why. As great as Malcolm's Hamlet was, Joanna's direction was what set off his brilliance, made him shine.

"I mean, sure, in theory," Jason says. "The thing about Mal is, he's a theatrical power bottom. Even if he had the smallest part in the show—even if he was, like, a stagehand—he'd still find a way to take control. And he *loves* to push people."

"What do you mean?" I ask, though after that rehearsal I'm pretty sure I know exactly what he means.

"Like when we were working on the big sword fight at the end of *Hamlet*—Joanna thought it was good, but Mal kept insisting we do it over and over. He said he didn't believe Chris—that was the guy playing Laertes—really wanted to kill him."

Spence goes to stand behind him, squeezing his shoulders. He's heard all this before, I realize. Guess it's more serious between them than just fucking.

"So what happened?" I ask.

"After a couple of hours of that, we all wanted to kill him. I'm guessing you can relate. And finally Chris snapped. Slammed him into the wall so hard it punched a hole in the plaster. Mal ended up with a concussion and a dislocated shoulder."

"Jesus," I say. "He must have been furious."

Jason shakes his head. "No, that's the thing—he wasn't mad at all. He acted like he wasn't even hurt. Joanna and I had to drag him to the hospital, and the whole way there he kept going on about how amazing Chris's performance was, how real it felt."

His eyes are glazed over now, like he's reliving the memory as he shares it. "Chris quit the next day. I should have quit, too. We all should have."

"Why didn't you?" I ask.

"I was nineteen, and I thought we were making 'great art.'" He makes a brief, bitter sound that's not quite a laugh. "I was a fucking idiot."

"It wasn't your fault," Spence says. His voice is so low and tender, I almost don't recognize it.

Jason nods, with a little hitching inhale like he's holding back tears. But his eyes aren't glazed and distant anymore. He holds my gaze as he leans back against Spence's broad chest and reaches up to thread their fingers together. Then a smug little smile tugs at the corners of his lips.

Spence can't see it. That smile is just for me.

48

JOANNA

AFTER MAL FINALLY WOKE UP, WE SPENT ALL AFTERNOON together. Late lunch in Wicker Park, the same place he took me the day we met.

That day, I was supposed to attend a formal dinner at a downtown steakhouse, where they would announce who won the top prize of the playwriting contest. Instead, I ditched it to get beer and greasy burgers with Mal at a diner tucked under the El tracks. After dinner, we walked down Milwaukee Street to Myopic Books. The store reminded me of my favorite bookshop in Ann Arbor, the Dawn Treader, except Myopic was on several rickety levels, while the Dawn Treader extended back and back from the street until it felt like you'd passed into another dimension.

We went up to the top floor of the store and sat down at a little round table between the bookshelves (it's still there, the finish flaking off more with each passing year). All evening I'd been watching the way his mouth moved as he spoke. I imagined leaning across the table and kissing him. The kind of bold action I liked to write for my characters, because I could never take it myself.

We stayed there for several more hours, talking. It took me that long to get up the courage to ask him what he thought of my play.

Honestly, I expected him to say he liked it, even if he didn't. That's what everyone else who'd read or seen it had done when I asked them some version of the same question. My mother went so far as to call the play *magnificent*. Instead, Mal got a strange, pensive look on his face. Lips pursed, eyebrows pinched.

Then he asked me if I'd ever been in love before.

I nodded automatically. Of course I had. In fact, the play was about my first love, Ryan, a philosophy major I met during freshman orientation. We dated for two years, and then he broke my heart by splitting up with me over the phone during the first month of his study abroad year in Prague. I had been devastated, and writing the play helped me get through the pain. And then, of course, there was Jess. We were definitely in love, and she was far more serious about me than Ryan had ever been. At the time, Jess and I were even thinking about going to the same graduate school—or at least schools close enough together for us to visit each other on weekends.

But Mal didn't accept my answer. He locked eyes with me and leaned closer, almost like he was going to kiss me. My breath stopped in my throat.

"No," he said. "You haven't. Not really. Not yet. You've read about it in books, but reading about something isn't the same as experiencing it."

My cheeks burned. I was furious at him—his arrogance, his presumption—but I also knew he was right. The two feelings were like threads wound together so tight I couldn't unravel them.

"You're writing from here." He tapped his temple. "When you should be writing from here."

He reached under the table and touched my stomach. The first time he ever touched me. His palm pressed into my belly, gentle but expectant, like I was pregnant and he was trying to feel the baby kicking.

I wanted to shove him away. I wanted to stand up and storm out. But mostly I wanted him to keep touching me, for his hands to be somewhere on my body, always. I thought again about kissing him, but what I was imagining had turned violent, almost an assault. I wanted to draw blood. To take something from him, too.

The next day, I found out I'd won the playwriting competition. I got a check and a little trophy with shiny gold plastic comedy and tragedy masks stuck on top. But I spent the whole bus ride back to Ann Arbor rereading my script and thinking about how right Mal was—about the play and about me. I thought I'd poured my heart out on those pages, but the emotions I wrote about were shallow, cliché, childish. The play had no depth, no substance, no soul. Because I didn't either.

I had so many openings today, so many opportunities to tell Mal the truth. This secret has felt like a ticking clock lodged inside my chest since I wrote the first word of the script, but now that Robert Kenmore has found me out, I know I'm running out of time.

After lunch I needed to run a few errands, so Mal went to the theater ahead of me to check on how the set build was coming along. When I arrive about half an hour before rehearsal, he isn't in the performance space—though pieces of the scenery are, the walls of the hotel room and the frame for the bed taking shape—so I head backstage to look for him. The door to Dressing Room B is open, the lights above the makeup mirror casting a golden glow into the hallway.

I expect to find Mal inside—trying on some costume pieces, or pacing back and forth running his lines. Or even sleeping. We've both caught catnaps in here more than once. It's the bigger of the two dressing rooms, more room to stretch out on the floor.

Instead, when I look through the dressing room doorway, I see a naked woman, sitting in the folding chair that's usually pushed under the makeup table. Her back is to the door. Head lolling. Some of her dark wavy hair spilling over the chair, the rest caught between the metal and her shoulder blades.

Mal's head is moving between her legs.

He looks up, but he doesn't see me standing in the doorway. He's too busy staring at her. The split in his lip has opened up again, a little blood trickling down. His tongue darts out to lick it away, then continues around the edges of his mouth. Tasting her.

He kisses her, starting at the knee and working his way in. She writhes, moaning, and he clamps down harder on her thigh, holding her still. Heat prickles across my face, between my legs. But I can't tear my gaze away.

When she comes—only a few seconds later; he knows exactly what he's doing—she arches her spine over the back of the chair, and he grips her ass, his fingers digging in. He must be leaving marks.

His eyes fall closed, and he rests his cheek against the inside of her leg.

I have to go before he sees me. Before—

My phone buzzes in my hand. I'm so startled, I almost drop it. Mal's eyes flick open again as I retreat into the shadows of the hallway.

I answer on the last ring before it goes to voice mail. By then, I've made it far enough away from the dressing room that they shouldn't be able to overhear me. Unless Mal caught sight of me and decided to follow.

"Hello?" I push open the back door and step into the alley behind the theater. Just in case.

"Hi, Joanna." It's a man's voice; not one I recognize.

The door falls shut behind me. I don't have my keys, so I'll have to go around to the front to get back in. Maybe I can pretend I just arrived. Mal doesn't have to know I saw him. Or her.

"It's Rob. Kenmore?" he adds, when I don't answer. "From the—"

"I remember." I slump against the wall, squeezing my eyes shut, but that only makes me see them clearer. The slickness around Mal's mouth, the way his tongue traced the line of his lips, and—

"Oh, uh, good, I—is this an okay time to talk?" Rob says. "I can call back later if you—"

"No."

I knew Mal and Kira were fucking. So why did seeing it with my own eyes make me want to rush into the room and drag her out by her hair?

He's not mine.

I have no right.

"Okay, no problem," Rob says. "Is there a time tomorrow that would—"

"No, don't call me back. I'll call you."

I hang up and press the edge of the phone to my forehead, sinking down lower on the wall. The bricks snag at the back of my shirt.

Another lie, easy as breathing.

KIRA

ON THE WAY TO REHEARSAL, I STOP IN TO OSMIUM AND BUY the largest coffee they have on offer, partially because I'm still operating at a substantial sleep deficit, and partially to kill time so I won't get to the theater early. After my conversation with Jason, I made a decision: from now on, I'm going to keep things 100 percent professional between me and Malcolm. No more after-hours excursions. No more confessing personal details as a substitute for character development. I'm not even going to talk to him unless it's related to the play.

It seems like a solid plan. Until I come through the front door of Indifferent Honest at precisely 6:59 p.m. and find Joanna waiting for me in the lobby, arms folded across the front of her tailored black blouse.

Fuck. She knows. She's going to rip me a new one. She might even fire me.

No, wait—she's smiling. Or maybe that's a bad sign? I don't think I've ever seen her smile before.

"Kira!" she calls out. "Do you have a minute?"

I gesture toward the theater doors. "We're just about to—"

"Don't worry, I'll deal with Mal. Let's go to my office."

Joanna takes me by the elbow, jostling the coffee cup. It's still full—too hot to drink yet—and a trickle of scalding liquid travels down the heel of my hand to my wrist. The only way I can keep from crying out is to bite the inside of my cheek.

I've never been to her office. It turns out to be in the basement, accessed by a door tucked into the back corner of the lobby. I didn't even notice the door was there before; it's painted the same dark gray as the walls. While we descend, I lick the coffee off my hand, then suck up the excess pooled in the lid of the cup. The lower level of the building feels like a dungeon: cold, oppressively dark, with a faint smell of standing water. I'd go crazy if I had to work down here.

Joanna sits behind her desk and motions for me to take the metal chair across from it. The chair's twin is pushed into the corner, beside a flimsy folding table. Bryn's sticker-covered laptop sits on top, but Bryn herself is nowhere to be found.

The room is claustrophobic to begin with, but the framed posters hanging from floor to ceiling make it feel like the walls are closing in. There's one blank spot left, in the bottom corner of the wall behind the desk, right next to the dented green filing cabinet. That must be where she's going to hang the poster for *Temper*.

I point at the one for *Hamlet*, which hangs right above Joanna's head. It shows Malcolm's face in profile, his cheekbone sharp as a guillotine blade.

"I saw that show. I don't know if I ever told you."

"Oh?" she says flatly. She probably thinks I'm bullshitting her, sucking up. Though what good that would do me at this point, I don't know.

"I thought it was brilliant. The way you staged the *get thee to a nunnery* scene, so the audience could see Claudius and Polonius watching the whole time—I loved that, I always wondered how you came up with it."

"I don't remember." She folds her hands on top of her notebook— the same black spiral one she seems to carry everywhere. "It was a long time ago."

Joanna usually keeps at least one side of her straight blond hair tucked neatly behind her ear, but it's all fallen forward now, emphasizing the hard line of her jaw. She has one of those faces that's only beautiful from certain angles. I've wished for a face like that before. I'm sure I would have a more interesting career looking like her than looking like me.

"Look, Kira," she says. "About last night's rehearsal."

I shift in the chair, my bruised thigh throbbing against the metal. I wore jeans today so the mark wouldn't show. It should be gone by opening night, as long as I don't do any more damage in the next two weeks.

I feel like I'm back in high school, summoned to the principal's office. Ironically, the first time I got sent there, David was the teacher who sent me, because my skirt was supposedly too short for the school dress code. This was well before our affair, back in the first month of the school year. He was desperate to prove that, even though he was only a few years older than us, he wasn't a pushover. I was so furious when he ordered me out of the classroom. I even tried to argue with him, right there in front of the other students. It didn't occur to me until much later that I should have wondered why he'd taken notice of the length of my hemline in the first place.

"I know we're not a union house," Joanna continues, "but it's still important to me that we respect people's time."

Tell that to your artistic director, I want to say. Instead I take a sip of my coffee. It scorches my tongue, but I swallow it anyway.

"How late did rehearsal go last night exactly?" she asks.

"I'm not sure," I say. "We were working on the scene with the slap, and—"

"Yes," she says. "I wanted to speak to you about that as well. I'm sure, given your . . . relationship with Mr. Spencer, you understand the importance of performing fight choreography safely."

"Of course I do, I—"

"Because if you're having trouble with the choreography, I'd be more than happy to bring him in for an additional session or two."

She smiles again, wider this time. Her top teeth are crooked, just enough to make her look slightly feral.

My hands tighten around the coffee cup, denting in the Dark Matter logo on the sleeve. "That won't be necessary."

Spence was riled up enough when he saw my self-inflicted bruise. The last thing I need is for him to find out about Malcolm's split lip, too. As Spence is fond of saying, the first rule of stage fight club is *NO ACTUAL FIGHTING.*

But this is such bullshit—yeah, okay, I hit Malcolm, but he drove me to it by keeping me up all night, keeping me at the theater until two in the morning, pushing me and pushing me until the only place left to go was off a mental cliff. If Jason Grady is to be believed, he's pulled this crap before. And Joanna has stood by and let him.

Joanna comes around to the front of the desk and leans against the edge. Her legs almost touch my knees, crisp designer denim clashing with my faded H&M jeans.

"Hey, I get it," she says. She's shifted into a bright, faux-friendly tone of voice, like a woman out to brunch in a prescription drug commercial. I'd prefer to be yelled at. "I'm a perfectionist too, and I know sometimes Mal can be . . ."

Infuriating? Manipulative? Fucking psychotic?

"Passionate," she finishes. "So while we both appreciate your tenacity, what happened at last night's rehearsal can't happen again."

Now there we're in agreement. "I don't know what Malcolm told you, but—"

She smiles. No teeth this time. "Mal didn't tell me anything."

Bryn must have, then. But she doesn't know about me hitting Malcolm, she was asleep by then. Unless he filled her in after the fact.

"Okay, fine," I say. "But he was the one who—"

This time, Joanna doesn't need to interrupt me. I stop myself midsentence, wracking my brain, trying to remember. Was Malcolm the one who suggested staying later?

Or was it my idea?

If you want to stay a little longer . . . I'd be happy to.

But even then—it was Malcolm who made us do the scene over and over, Malcolm who kept stopping and starting and twisting my mind into knots. I never asked to leave, but if I had, it wouldn't have mattered. He would have found a way to make me stay anyway. I'm sure of it.

At least, I *was* sure.

50

JOANNA

I'LL SAY THIS FOR HER: KIRA RASCHER IS A MUCH BETTER actress than I thought.

I can't get over how easily she lied. The way she looked me right in the face with those cold, indifferent eyes and acted like she had no idea what I was talking about. Trying to blame the whole thing on Mal, when he came home bleeding and she doesn't have a mark on her.

And I suppose she thought she was going to be able to butter me up with all that bullshit about *Hamlet*. The directorial choice she mentioned wasn't even mine, it was Mal's. He's the one who suggested having Claudius attempt to intervene on Ophelia's behalf, and letting the audience see Polonius holding him back, choosing to let Hamlet keep on brutalizing his own daughter.

Clever of her, too, to leave the theater after her assignation with Mal. Getting coffee, so she could make it look like she had just arrived. She might have fooled me, if I hadn't seen what I saw. I don't understand why they're trying to hide their relationship from me in the first place. Mal has fucked actors in plenty of other shows we've done, but he's never bothered to keep it a secret before. Not from me.

Bryn walks by in the hallway, carrying a cardboard box balanced against her hip.

"Bryn," I call out. She stops and backtracks, coming to stand in the doorway.

The long night at rehearsal left her with dark circles under her eyes, but her cheeks are flushed pink. She's wearing knee-high boots under a black dress instead of her typical Chuck Taylors with duct tape on the soles and pen drawings of skulls on the toes. She still has her omnipresent hoodie on over the dress, but I can almost make out the shape of her body for once.

"Are those the programs?" I ask.

"Uh-huh." She comes in and sets the box down on my desk. "I finished with them yesterday."

I pick up one of the programs and examine it. Bryn takes a hair tie off her wrist and starts twisting her hair up into her usual sloppy ponytail.

"Sorry, but I'm going to need you to redo some of these."

"What?" She lets go of her hair, sending it tumbling back over her shoulders. "Why? What's wrong with them?"

"The fold is uneven. The staples, too." I hold it up to show her.

Bryn presses her lips together and looks up and to the side. The beginnings of an eye roll, but she's smart enough not to follow through.

"Is there a problem?" I ask.

"Mal said they were fine."

Since when does she call him *Mal*? When she first started working here, she addressed him only as *Mr. Mercer*. Then she stopped referring to him by name at all, like he was Voldemort or something.

Besides, Mal hasn't bothered with anything as mundane as programs in years. Usually I fold and staple every last one of the fucking things myself and end up with paper cuts all over the pads of my fingers.

"Do you need me to show you how to do it again?" I ask her.

"Can we talk about this later?" she says. "I'm late for rehearsal."

"Hey." But she's already turning to go. I slam the flat of my hand on the desk. *"Hey."*

Bryn flinches and turns around to face me again. But I can still see that spark of rebelliousness in her eyes. Maybe I made a mistake, going easy on her for showing up late today.

"How about you cut the fucking attitude," I tell her. "Or I'll make sure you don't have to worry about being late to one of our rehearsals ever again."

Bryn shrinks and sucks her lower lip between her teeth. She looks legitimately frightened of me.

So that's what it feels like.

51

KIRA

I'M PREPARED TO WORK.

I leave Joanna's office in a daze, still trying to pick through the shards of my memory. I didn't attempt to argue with her any further. What would be the point? It's my word against Malcolm's—and Bryn's, though she slept through the worst of it.

I should have told Spence what really happened. He would have chewed me out, but he also might have had some decent advice. (Not that I usually take his advice.) I just couldn't stand it, that smug look on Jason's face. He warned me, and I didn't listen, and now here I am.

If you're not prepared . . . Maybe it would be best if we—

I find Malcolm alone in the theater. He's sitting on the foot of what will eventually be the hotel room bed. So far, it's just a piece of plywood balanced on some black-painted blocks.

He looks up when I enter. The split in his lip looks angry, but he doesn't. He doesn't look anything, really. That hollowness in his eyes again, the abyss staring back.

Let's go.

He's as adept at using silence as a weapon as he is at using words. Maybe there's nothing he can't weaponize, turn against me. Or make me turn against myself.

I wonder if he's expecting me to apologize. Did I say I was sorry, afterward? I remember reaching for him, trying to lay my hand on his shoulder, but I can't remember what I said, or if I even spoke at all. The whole night is such a blur.

Well, I'm not going to give any ground by talking first. I already made that mistake with Joanna. I hold my coffee cup in front of my mouth like a shield.

Our standoff is interrupted by the entrance of Joanna and Bryn. "Good, you're both here," Joanna says. Her voice still has that fake flash to it. "Are we about ready to get started?"

"Actually," Malcolm says. "Could you come back in a couple of minutes? Kira and I need to talk about something."

Joanna looks at me, and our eyes lock for a second. As unsettling as that conversation in her office was, I don't want her to leave. I'm still trying to get my bearings, and whatever Malcolm is about to say now is sure to confuse me further.

"Alone," Malcolm adds.

"Of course," Joanna says. "We'll come back in ten."

"Thanks, Jo." He gives her a smile but doesn't get one in return. I try to catch her eye again—*don't go, please, I need witnesses*—but she's already turned her back. Bryn follows suit, staying a few feet behind her, slouching so much she's almost cowering.

Jason said things were only going to get worse from here on out, and I believe him. But that doesn't mean I have to lie down and take it. I'm not going to quit like that actor who played Laertes did. I'm not going to let myself fall apart or break down or whatever the hell happened to Jason that's left him so damaged a full decade later. Malcolm may have done this type of shit before, but I'll bet he's never done it to someone like me. I've already made him bleed once, and I'll do it again if I have to.

As soon as we're alone, Malcolm moves over and pats the empty spot beside him. I take a seat, but as far away from him as possible.

"Before we get started," he says. "I wanted to take a moment to apologize for last night."

"This morning."

I had that snarky comeback on deck, and it shoots out of my mouth before his words have a chance to sink in. Of all the things I expected from Malcolm when I walked into the theater tonight, an apology sure as hell wasn't one of them.

"This morning," he repeats. "Yes, I suppose you're right. In any case, I shouldn't have pushed you so far, so fast. You weren't ready. I see that now."

There it is. The condescension I was expecting, delivered with a smile so indulgent, any lingering guilt I might have had about hitting him dissolves like acid-eaten flesh.

"What's that supposed to mean?" I ask.

Malcolm hesitates, acting like this is hard for him, like he doesn't want to criticize me. Like he hasn't been waiting all day to say these things.

"I expect a lot from my actors," he says.

"Yeah, so I've heard."

"Really?" Malcolm asks. As if he isn't well aware of his reputation. After all, he's spent years crafting it as carefully as any of the roles he's played onstage. "From who?"

"Jason Grady, for one."

I toss the name out into the room like a grenade. Malcolm has no reaction to it. For a second I think maybe he's forgotten all about Jason by now—must be tough for him to keep track of all the actors he's tortured over the years—but then he asks, "How do you know Jason?"

"He's—" I almost say he and Spence are dating, but I don't know what Malcolm might do with that information. "A friend of a friend."

"I see," Malcolm says. "And what did he have to say about me?"

"Well, he told me I shouldn't work with you."

Another smile, almost serene this time. "But you didn't listen to him."

"Obviously not."

"Jason is a very troubled young man," Malcolm says. "Or at least he was when I knew him."

I shift in my seat. The plywood bites into the backs of my knees. "Troubled how?"

"We had—well, I suppose I thought it was a fling, but Jason took it more seriously. When it ended, he didn't handle it well."

"Meaning what?"

"Meaning he broke into my apartment and sliced his wrist open with a kitchen knife."

Malcolm says this so matter-of-factly, my first reaction is that he must be making it up. But then I remember the leather cuff Jason always wears. And the way he looked at me the night we met, that hint of hostility shining in his eyes.

"If we're going to do this, Kira," Malcolm says. "We need to trust each other. We need to be able to say anything, do anything, if it's honest, if it's right for our characters. This morning, you were holding back and holding back, and then you exploded."

I thought that's what he wanted—why else would he have gone to such lengths to provoke me?

Because he enjoyed it, that's why. Seeing me detonate, knowing he was the one who built the bomb and lit the fuse.

What I don't want to admit to him—or to Rob, or to Spence, and certainly not to Jason Grady—is there's a part of me that enjoyed it, too. I wanted to hit him, so I did. There was no pause, no moment of decision, like when I slapped my sister. A direct line from desire to action. The moment my hand met Malcolm's jaw, the boundaries between myself and my character dissolved. I became Mara. She became me. My performance stopped being a performance at all.

Malcolm's words echo in my mind again. *I really felt something from you. Don't tell me you didn't feel it too.*

That's the problem: I did feel it. The raw power in my performance, when I finally lost control. And as much as it scared me, there's a part of me that's even more afraid I'll never be able to get that feeling back again. At least not on my own.

"I want you to ask yourself something during tonight's rehearsal." Malcolm pauses, staring me right in the eyes, making sure I'm listening. "We know Mara's angry, that she fantasizes about violence. But is she actually capable of committing it?"

I think everyone is capable of violence under the right circumstances, but I doubt he'll accept that response. It's too safe, not specific enough. It doesn't have teeth.

"Don't tell me your answer," he says. "You have to decide for yourself: what your character is capable of. Whether she could really hurt her husband, or even kill him."

"Whether the end of the play is reality," I say. "Or another one of her reveries."

Malcolm smiles. This time it's real. "Exactly."

Just like when he held me against the wall, my breathing starts to sync with his. The difference is, now I'm not trying, it's just happening.

"Whatever you decide, you have to commit to it. Believe in it. Not just here." He taps his temple. "But here, too." He reaches toward me, hovering his hand over my stomach. I feel a pulsing heat there, in the space between his palm and my body.

"So." He bites his lip—teeth pressing right on the split, like it doesn't hurt at all. "Are you ready to get started?"

The energy between us is taut as knotted rope. I let it wind around me, tug me forward.

"I'm ready."

52

JOANNA

BLOOD RUNS DOWN KIRA'S FOREARM, POOLING ON THE FLOOR between her and Mal.

"That's too much," he says. She nods in agreement.

They're testing the blood packs for the end of the first act, when Mara's medical abortion kicks in, and making a mess of the set in the process. Someone will have to clean it all up before we start the run-through.

Mal holds out his red-streaked palm, and I hand him the next blood pack. During the show, he'll have to break the pack against Kira's inner thigh and smear the contents down her legs. He can't do that now, because she's wearing leggings. She always seems to be wearing leggings. Bending over in them so the material stretches over her soft round ass and the seams of her underwear show.

Kira offers Mal her arm again. He takes her by the wrist, pulling her arm out straighter, then presses the blood pack into the crook of her elbow. When it bursts, a little bit splashes up on Mal's face, making a red teardrop near the corner of his right eye. Kira swipes it away with the pad of her thumb. Mal smiles at her. He doesn't say thank you. He doesn't need to. They're communicating just fine without words. Communicating not only with each other, but with the rest of us, too.

They've been like this all week. Ever since he kicked me out of my own theater so he could have a private conversation with her. Whatever he said, it worked, at least in terms of her acting. She's improved so much in the past few days, it seems almost like magic. But I know it's not magic, it's just Mal. He said he would get a great performance out of her, and he is.

Kira still hasn't admitted to hitting him, but she keeps injuring him. Nothing so serious as the split lip, at least not on the parts of his body I get to see on a regular basis. But he has thin lines of scabs decorating his back, scrapes on his knees and elbows, mouth-shaped bruises where his neck meets his shoulder. The more she hurts him, the closer they seem to get. It's like she has him under a fucking spell.

Mal twists her arm one way and then the other, examining how the blood looks under the stage lights. He keeps stroking her wrist with his thumb, spreading the red liquid farther.

"I wasn't sure how much blood there should be," I say.

I brought in several different options: some with a more watery consistency, some more viscous, colors ranging from poison-apple red to clotted crimson.

"Not quite this much," Kira says. "More like a heavy period."

I blink at her. So matter-of-fact. Unashamed. Not that she should be ashamed. But I would be. I'm ashamed of so many things less significant than ending a pregnancy.

Kira swirls her finger in the blood and shoots a devious grin at Spencer, who's seated in the second row, typing out something on his cell phone. Tonight is the last full run before we start tech, and I extended an invitation to all the designers. Only Spencer and Austin Hutchinson showed up.

Austin is going to be our board op for the run, too. The technical elements of the show are so straightforward, it's really far beneath his skill. I almost felt bad asking him, and I couldn't understand why he said yes to the gig. Until I noticed the way he looks at Bryn during

212 ||| LAYNE FARGO

our production meetings. He's sitting with her now, in the front row, and he keeps staring at the curve of her neck as she bows her head to write notes in her binder.

Kira leans across the seat in front of Spencer's, her shirt riding up to show the small of her back, and dabs some stage blood on his nose. He recoils, swiping at the spot with his sleeve.

"You're gonna pay for that," he says. "I know where you live."

He's only pretending to be annoyed. His fondness for her shines out of him like a spotlight whenever they're in the same room. She must know. It's so obvious it's almost embarrassing. Which means she knows exactly how he feels about her, she just doesn't give a damn.

A low buzz sounds. Mal pulls his phone out of his pocket, smearing sticky red fingerprints on the screen.

"He's here," Mal says to me.

"Who's here?" Kira asks.

"Just a guest we invited to watch the run. Why don't you head backstage and get cleaned up, and we'll say—what?" He looks to Bryn. "Ten minutes to places?"

Bryn nods. I stand up and head toward the lobby.

Mal and Kira may be getting along better now, but he doesn't tell her everything. There are still plenty of secrets he shares only with me.

Mal's guest is waiting outside the front door of the theater, pacing and stamping his feet against the mat. At first glance, he looks too young to be the person Mal said he was. But then he looks up at me and smiles, and I see the deeply-etched lines around his blue eyes.

I push open the door with one hand and extend the other one for him to shake. He's not wearing gloves, and even though his grip is light, the cold lingering on his skin is sharp enough to sting.

"Hi, I'm Joanna Cuyler. And you must be David."

53

KIRA

MY SKIN STILL FEELS STICKY, EVEN AFTER SPENDING MOST of the last ten minutes in the bathroom scrubbing at my arms. Whatever was in those blood packs is stronger stuff than the concoction Tim and I used for our classes.

With Spence and Austin, plus whoever Malcolm's special guest is, I suppose this is technically our first performance in front of an audience, even if it's a small one. We had our final fight rehearsal last night, to learn the choreography for the strangling scene. It was supposed to be a few days ago, but Spence had to reschedule for some reason. Some reason to do with Jason, I'm sure. That's all he does lately: hang out with Jason, or text Jason, or tell me he'd love to chat, but Jason is waiting.

At least pushing the fight rehearsal back allowed enough time for Malcolm's lip to heal before Spence saw him. There's still a small raised line where it split—I can feel it during our deeper kisses in the last scene—but it's not apparent unless you know where to look.

The bruise on my leg took the better part of the week to disappear, fading from ripe berry purple to a sickly mottled yellow, and then finally to a faint golden hue like tea spilled over the pages of a book. Sometimes I could swear there's still an ache under the skin there, embedded deep in my muscles.

While we wait backstage for the run-through to start, Malcolm keeps tracing his thumb over his jawline, and my mind goes to the way he touched me during the last rehearsal. Every time we do the final scene, something changes. Intensifies. Last night, we went even further than we had before. He started it, by sliding his thumb under the trim of my underwear, tracing the curve of my ass. It was only fair for me to dip my hand past the waistband of his pants to do the same.

Did I dig my nails in, when I grabbed him back? I think I might have, but I don't remember. I was so caught up, it's a blur. This whole week has been a blur. It's like something takes over me when we're onstage together. Something primitive. His body says *I dare you*, and mine can't resist the challenge.

Bryn calls out the first cue, and I make my entrance through the hotel room door, Malcolm following right behind me. The set is basically complete now, just missing a bit of paint and other cosmetic touches. It's finally starting to feel like a real show. I know my lines and blocking so well I'm on autopilot—which is the perfect place to be before tech week starts, when the light and sound cues confuse everything again.

Austin is sitting next to Bryn, leaning on the armrest between them. The two of them seem cozy together, almost flirtatious. A showmance in the making, perhaps. Or maybe they're already fucking, but attempting to keep up a professional appearance around the rest of us.

I've always loved that part: the sneaking around, finding ways to be intimate without being obvious. When Rob and I first started seeing each other, before we were ready to go public with it, I'd find excuses to sit as close to him as possible while the director was giving notes at the end of rehearsal. Sitting beside him seemed too blatant, so I usually opted for the seat right in front of him instead. I'd let my hair tumble over the chair back so it accidentally-on-purpose brushed against his shins.

Spence has moved down to the front row, in the seat Joanna usually occupies. So where is Joanna? The next time my blocking allows for it, I do a quick scan of the audience.

There she is: in the back row, the only part of the space still cast in shadow when the stage lights are on full. She's sitting next to a man—Malcolm's mysterious guest, I assume. He looks familiar. In the dim light, from this distance, he almost looks like—

My breath catches. But it can't be him.

I used to notice men all the time who looked like David in some way. The same narrow, stooped shoulders, sitting in front of me on the bus. The same fine, curly hair, somewhere between brown and blond, catching the sunlight as I walked down the street. The same long, delicate-boned fingers handing me my credit card and latte over the coffee shop counter. It used to make me clench, freeze, feel like fleeing. But after a while, I stopped worrying about running into him, stopped rehearsing the scene in my head, imagining what I would say. Obsessing over all the things I should have said to him before.

It can't be him. He has no reason to be here. He doesn't even know I live in Chicago. I have him blocked on every possible form of social media. Besides, this guy is wearing glasses, I can see the stage lights flashing off the lenses, and David doesn't wear glasses.

Or at least, he didn't when I knew him. But it's been almost fifteen years. Maybe he wears them now.

No. It's not him. I'm being ridiculous. *Don't get distracted.*

I force myself to focus on the scene, on Malcolm, and for a few minutes it works. We've made it to the part where we're getting dressed for the wedding, which is a fairly intricate dance of blocking, overlapping dialogue, and simultaneous onstage costume changes (which we mime for now; we'll start incorporating costumes next week).

There aren't a lot of laugh lines in this play, but there's a potential one in this scene. I'm talking about our mutual friend, the one who's getting married (and who it's strongly hinted, later in the play, Trent has been fucking on and off for years), and I say, "Hope she's not as much of a control freak in bed as she is about this fucking wedding. Though who knows, maybe her fiancé is into that."

It's not exactly a gut-buster, but it made Spence snicker the first time we ran lines together, so I've been prepared to take a brief pause after it once we're in front of an audience.

As soon as I get the line out, I hear it: laughter, from the back row. The sound is whispery, soft—more like a sigh than a laugh. But I'd know it anywhere.

The first time I heard David laugh was in English class, when he had us read a scene from *Midsummer* aloud. He assigned me the role of Puck, and he laughed at my reading of the lines mocking the rude mechanicals. When the bell rang and all the other students were filing out, he asked me to stay behind so he could compliment my comic timing. *You have an excellent feeling for verse*, he said. The first time a teacher had ever praised me for anything. I smiled the whole way home. When I walked into the house, my mother saw the look on my face and asked me what was wrong with me.

So it is him. He's here, sitting a few yards away from me. Watching me, right now.

I press my hands together to hide their shaking. It doesn't make any sense. I told Malcolm David's first name, that's all. Unless there's something I'm forgetting, some other crumb I dropped.

I shouldn't have told him anything, I should never have mentioned David to him, what was I thinking, I—

The space has fallen silent. The next line must be mine, but I don't even know where we are in the script. I squeeze my eyes shut for a second, hoping somehow when I open them again, David will be gone. I'd prefer losing my shit and full-on hallucinating to accepting the fact that he's really here.

"Line," I say.

Bryn opens her mouth, then hesitates, looking down at her binder again. I glare daggers at her. This is humiliating enough without her gaping at me like that.

"I know, I know, I'm supposed to be off book, but—"

Malcolm interrupts me. "It's not a line."

"What?"

"You're supposed to cross downstage," he says. "That's what I'm waiting on."

He has the balls to sound annoyed with me. This must be what he wanted, to throw me off, to fuck with me. What I don't understand is why.

I've been trying so hard not to look in David's direction, but finally I have to, I can't help it. He's leaning forward in his seat now, elbows propped on his knees. When our eyes meet, he smiles, gives me an awkward little wave like we're neighbors who've run into each other at the supermarket, and I feel like I'm going to be sick.

Spence twists around in his seat to see what I'm staring at. He wouldn't recognize David, I don't have any pictures of us together. Spence turns back, then furrows his brow into an *are you okay?* look.

I'm not. I'm not okay. But I can't tell Spence that without telling Malcolm and Joanna and everyone else in the room.

I press my fingers to my forehead. "I'm sorry, can we just—take it from the top?"

"Let's pick up where we stopped," Malcolm says.

"But we're only a few minutes in, and—"

"And we're already running behind. Take it from your last line."

The night I slapped him, he made me restart that scene so many fucking times I lost count, but now he's concerned about keeping to a schedule?

I retake my place. My teeth are gritted together so hard it feels like I'll grind my molars to dust. It's the only way I can keep myself from screaming.

Out of the corner of my eye, I see David sit back and cross his legs. *Ignore him. Pretend he's not there. Pretend he doesn't exist.*

But all I can think of is the last rehearsal of mine he attended.

While I spent that summer dashing between my day job and *Crucible* rehearsals, David kept going on auditions. Audition after audition, sometimes dozens in a week, and he never got so much as a callback. It started to get to him, to sour him—and not only on acting.

We barely had enough money to buy ramen noodles at the bodega, so I have no idea how David was paying for all the bottles of whiskey I kept finding around our apartment. He was drunk when I left that morning to go to my shift at the touristy coffee shop where I worked, and still drunk when he showed up at the theater that evening.

I didn't realize he was there until intermission, when the stage manager came into the dressing room and asked who the hell the guy sitting out in the house was. I went with a couple of the other girls in the cast and peeked around the curtain. David was sitting in the third row, glowering. I could smell the booze on him from where I stood.

I assured the stage manager I would take care of it. But when I approached David and told him he had to leave, he refused. Aidan, the twenty-something pretty boy with cut-glass cheekbones who played Reverend Hale, came to my aid, and together we were able to get David to head for the door.

On his way out, David turned and said to me, "He's the one you're fucking, isn't he?"

It wasn't the first time David had implied I might be cheating on him, but it was the first time he'd been so blatant about it. Aidan blushed and looked down at his shiny black shoes. He was attracted to me, and I was well aware of it, but we'd done nothing more than a bit of harmless backstage flirting.

"Or is it the director? I saw the way he was looking at you."

I folded my arms over my stiff Puritan frock, trying to narrow my eyes into a glare so I wouldn't cry. "Go home, David," I told him.

He took a staggering step toward me. "For all I know," he hissed, "you're fucking all of them."

That was the first time I felt afraid of him.

54

JOANNA

WHEN I TOLD MAL ABOUT THE STRANGE EMAIL I'D GOTTEN from a man claiming to be Kira's old acting teacher, I figured he'd tell me to ignore it, delete the message without replying. Instead he said to write back and invite him to the show.

I didn't ask why. I could guess, though. Mal never does anything without a reason, and usually that reason is to get a rise out of someone.

If that was his plan, it's working. Kira hasn't spaced on any more blocking or flubbed her lines, but her performance tonight has been just short of unhinged. Sometimes it works; she's never been more terrifying in the reverie scenes. But then it seems like she can't come down again.

In moments when she's supposed to be still, I've noticed her trembling, like she's tensing every muscle, trying to keep herself under control. She's sweating, too, despite the chilled air of the performance space. It started as a thin sheen on her forehead and her upper lip, but now that we're almost to the end of the play, she's slick with it, the back of her shirt darkened, tendrils of her hair sticking to her neck.

It's almost over now. Mal and Kira are on the bed, kissing, ramping up to Mara's final reverie. God, the way he kisses. With his whole body, not just his lips. It looks so spontaneous, passionate, real, but, like the rest of the play, every movement is choreographed.

Or at least, it's meant to be. Kira is taking liberties again. When Mal pushes her thighs apart with his knee, the way he's supposed to, she slides her hands under his shirt and scratches her nails across his back, leaving red streaks along his spine. Then she tugs the shirt off over his head, so hard I'm shocked the fabric doesn't tear. He goes along with it, pulling his arms through and tossing the shirt on the floor. He won't be wearing one, once they're in costume, but she's still not following the blocking.

Their lips come together again—more collision than kiss, rough enough to bruise—and she wraps her legs around him and squeezes, lifting her hips off the bed to meet his. Another improvisation. What the hell does she think she's doing? Is this for David's benefit?

I looked him up online, after he'd accepted our invitation. His social media accounts are buried under an avalanche of newspaper articles, chronicling the ignominious end of his education career. The stories referred only to *a female student*, *a young woman in the high school's drama club*, or simply *Mr. Granville's victim*. It might not have been Kira. But *something* clearly happened between them.

My search turned up her senior class yearbook picture, too. She had frizzier hair then, and a fuller face, but the same sultry, defiant expression. She looked like a grown woman who knew exactly what she was doing, while David Granville looked the part of a sweet-natured schoolboy. He still does, really, despite the wrinkles around his eyes. Probably how he escaped any punishment beyond losing his job. He's leaning forward in his seat again, his chin cupped in his hands, but the expression on his face is unreadable. I can't tell if he's aroused or angry, burning with jealousy, or just plain bored.

Kira rolls Mal over so he's flat on his back, keeping her thighs clenched around his waist. She's supposed to slide her hands up his chest and put them around his throat. Instead, she bends down and kisses him again, opening her mouth so wide it looks like she's trying to swallow him whole. Her fingernails rake across his sternum, ripping at his skin. Drawing blood.

"Stop."

I don't realize I've said this out loud until David starts and turns to look at me. Bryn and Austin twist around too. Not Spencer. He keeps his eyes fixed on Kira and Mal. If he wasn't already aware they were sleeping together, he sure as hell is now.

They're still going at it, like they didn't even hear me. Mal's hands tangle in her hair, and she digs her nails in deeper, gouging the skin around his clavicle.

"*Stop.*" This time I stand up, and my voice cracks the air like a whip.

That gets their attention. They're both breathing hard, Kira's chest heaving. Mal's mouth looks bloody, her lipstick smeared over him. The same color as the blood on his chest.

"What's the problem, Jo?"

He sounds irritated. He has every right to be. I've never interrupted one of his rehearsals before. But I couldn't continue to stand by while—

"You're bleeding," I blurt out.

"What?" he says.

I've made it to the stage now. I point at his chest. He looks down, sees the red streaks.

"Jesus, Joanna, it's just a scratch. We were almost to the end."

"She was hurting you."

"It's nothing, I didn't even feel—"

"She *keeps* hurting you."

"Joanna."

His eyes flash. A warning I would usually heed, but not tonight. Tonight I've had enough.

"What about the other night? Your split lip?"

As soon as I mention this, Kira's eyes narrow, and she darts a look toward Spencer. He's standing now too, hands on his hips.

I turn toward him. "Oh, didn't she tell you about that?"

The answer is clear from his expression. Well, at least it's good to know Kira Rascher lies to everyone, not just me.

"Hey." Kira climbs off the bed. "How about you stop talking about me like I'm not *right fucking here.*"

Mal gets up too and comes to stand between me and Kira, putting a hand on each of our shoulders. Kira scowls and shrugs off his grip. I have to tense my whole body to keep from leaning into him like a grateful, attention-starved pet.

"Look," he says. "It's been a long week. Obviously, tensions are running high. Let's finish the play, and then we'll go out and get a drink. All of us, together."

He looks up toward the back row of the theater, where David has been sitting. Watching this whole scene play out like it's another part of the show.

"You'll join us too, won't you, Mr. Granville?" he asks. When David nods, Mal grins and squeezes my shoulder. "Great. I think we all need to blow off a little steam."

We take our seats. They get back into the bed. Kira drags the kiss out even longer. For my benefit this time, I'm sure of it. The moment seems to stretch on forever, but finally she puts her hands around his neck.

Mal's eyes widen in shock—*like he's trapped in a nightmare and desperate to wake up*, that's what I wrote in the stage directions— and he grabs ahold of her wrists. It looks like she's pressing down, but really she's trying to move her arms out to the side, away from Mal's neck. His grip is the only thing keeping her hands in place, maintaining the illusion. If he let go, so would she.

After a few moments, Mal goes still, releasing Kira's wrists, letting his hands flop to the side. He's still bleeding where she scratched him. Beads of red decorating his chest, glistening under the lights. He slows his breathing so much, he really does seem dead. He's always been good at that. Even after the exertion of the sword fight in the last scene of *Hamlet*, the rise and fall of his belly was barely visible during Horatio's play-ending speech.

Mara is supposed to look dazed when she lets go of Trent's neck. Like she can't believe what she's done. But Kira looks triumphant, power-drunk. Defiant, just like in that old class photo. Like she knows *exactly* what she's done, and she can't wait to do it again.

55

KIRA

I COULD HAVE JUST GONE HOME. BUT THEN MALCOLM WOULD'VE won. And even worse, David would have known just how much seeing him again rattled me.

So now I'm in a dive bar a few blocks east on Belmont, standing next to the only man who's ever broken my heart. Not my idea of a fun Saturday night.

I've been to this place once before with Spence—for some storytelling open mic he pretended to be interested in because he was fucking one of the performers. Tonight the small stage tucked against the far wall of the space seems to be set up for a musical act instead, one wan spotlight pointed at a drum set and a few standing microphones.

I'm trying to talk as little as possible, and Joanna has been silent since we left the theater. She keeps staring down at the table and chewing on the insides of her cheeks. When she's not drinking, that is. She's downed two drinks since we arrived, and her green eyes are already starting to look a bit glassy. Bryn and Austin were the only ones smart enough to stay behind. To test out a couple of sound cues, they claimed—a likely story, but even if that's really all they're up to, I envy them right now.

Malcolm seems more than happy to fill the silence for us. I've never seen him this chatty. First he was talking David's ear off about *Temper*, and now they're trading acting class anecdotes. David apparently found himself another education job, teaching introductory theater classes at a community college outside Indianapolis. That's his excuse for being in Chicago: an annual conference on performing arts in higher ed held at the Palmer House Hilton. At least if he still fucks his students, they're all over eighteen now.

David keeps catching my eye from across the high-top table, giving me these shy little smiles like we're sharing a secret. It used to make my stomach flutter when he looked at me like that. Now I feel like throwing up.

Spence is being no help at all. He's standing on my other side, but he keeps staring at his phone. Right now he's typing something with his hands hidden under the table, like we can't all tell what he's doing from the blue glow on his face.

I told Spence about David, early on in our friendship. Well, I told him the basics: I had an affair with my teacher, we ran away to New York together, it didn't work out. He responded by giving me a high five—*You little slut, I love it!*—and confessing to me he'd been hot for one of his teachers in high school too. *But alas, he was tragically heterosexual. No offense.*

Malcolm and David have gone quiet—both staring at me, waiting for some response, but I tuned out their conversation a while ago. I pretend I don't notice them and start picking at my fingernails instead. There's still some blood caked underneath them. I can't tell if it's from the blood packs or Malcolm's chest. I didn't mean to scratch him so deep, but I can't say he didn't deserve it.

"Mr. Granville was just telling me how much he enjoyed your performance tonight," Malcolm says.

I'll bet. David probably loved that little showdown with Joanna, too. More proof I'm the vindictive bitch he thinks I am.

"You were fantastic," David says. "You've really come a long way."

"Thanks." I tack on a smile. Let him think I didn't notice that dig.

"I saw an article about the show online," David explains, even though I didn't fucking ask. "So I emailed the theater—I wanted to send you flowers or something, for opening night. I used to get you roses, remember?"

I remember. The bolt of panic in my chest when I saw his handwriting on the card. The way the thorns stung when I closed my fist around the stems and threw the whole bouquet in the trash.

"I'm just thrilled the timing worked out so I could see you. Thank you again for the invitation," David says—not to Malcolm, but to Joanna. She gives him a tight little smile and nod, then stares into the dregs of her beer glass, refusing to meet my eyes.

Of course Malcolm made Joanna do the dirty work for him. But it was his idea, inviting David to the theater, I'm sure of it. Joanna may be a bitch, and she may not like me very much, but she's too busy to play these kinds of mind games. She wouldn't think to do something like this, not without Malcolm urging her on.

David leans in to make sure I hear him this time. It's loud in here, a cacophony of overlapping conversations, but he doesn't need to get this close.

"It's so good to see you again, Kira. You look great."

He doesn't. Those glasses make his face look even narrower, and they do nothing to conceal his crow's feet. His hairline is receding, and his shirt is doing a poor job of hiding the stomach paunch protruding from his thin frame like a tumor. It's hard to believe he and Malcolm are around the same age.

The silence stretches. I tap my fingers against the edge of the table. David drains the last of his beer.

"I'm going to go get another round," David says. "Do you want anything?"

"Oh, no, that's okay."

"Come on," he says. "Let me buy you a drink."

I really don't want a drink—I'd prefer to keep my inhibitions raised as high as humanly possible tonight—but it'll get rid of him for a few minutes, so I say, "Sure."

"You still drink Crown Royal?" he asks.

I never cared for Crown Royal, I just pretended to because it was David's drink of choice, and when I was a teenager it seemed sophisticated. But if I let him order me something I actually like, I might be tempted to drink it. I nod and smile at him again—lips tighter this time, blinking too much. He doesn't seem to notice.

"I'll join you," Malcolm says. Joanna goes with them too, wobbling a little. As soon as they've turned their backs, I let my smile drop like a glass shattering against the floor.

56

JOANNA

I SPLIT OFF FROM MAL AND DAVID AND STUMBLE TOWARD THE bathroom. Another drink would be a bad idea. But I'm full of those tonight.

I shouldn't have interrupted the rehearsal. But Kira shouldn't have been acting that way—ignoring the blocking, ripping off his shirt, clawing at him like an angry cat. And now she's standing there scowling while Mal, David, and Spencer vie for her attention like a trio of performing monkeys. No one forced her to come with us.

Mal has been acting like a different person since we left the theater. Smiling, laughing, clapping Kira's teacher on the shoulder like they're fraternity brothers. And going on and on about what a genius L. S. Sedgwick is. How he knew from the first page he had to do her play; he's never read anything like it before. No matter how many times he does each scene, he keeps finding new levels to explore. A far cry from what he said about the last play of mine I let him read.

I'm expecting the bathroom to be dank and claustrophobic, covered in Sharpie graffiti and bodily fluids, but instead it's all white subway tile. Too bright. I lock the door and bend over the sink, splashing cold water on my face. I feel like I could throw up, but I want to hold it all inside me—all this toxicity, all this rage. Churning in my guts, burning at the back of my throat.

When I submitted the *Temper* script, I had this fantasy that maybe if Mal fell in love with my words, he might finally fall in love with me, too. But would he be talking about the play like that if he knew I was the one who wrote it? Maybe he only loves my words when he doesn't know they're mine.

The hallway was empty when I went into the bathroom, but when I come out, there's a young man leaning against the pockmarked green wall across from the door. He's smiling—soft, to himself rather than at anyone around him—but as soon as he sees me, his expression curdles. And that's when I recognize him.

Jason Grady.

It's been years since I've seen him. I've thought about him often, though. Every time I clean our living room and see the stain he left on the floorboards, I can't help but flash back to the moment I found him there. Lying in a pool of his own blood.

57

KIRA

"SO THAT'S THE FAMOUS DAVID GRANVILLE," SPENCE SAYS. He's still looking at his phone—no longer typing, but he keeps clicking the button on the side so the screen strobes on and off again. "I thought he'd be bigger."

David is only a couple inches shorter than Spence, but he's much slighter. I used to wrap my thumb and index finger around one of David's slender wrists and joke that I could break him right in half. I felt so safe with him at the beginning. From the first day I saw him standing at the front of my English classroom, I thought he seemed gentle, sweet—sensitive, like a consumptive Victorian poet. I was certain he would never hurt me. He didn't seem capable of hurting anyone.

"And less . . . Midwestern," Spence continues. "I don't know why, but I always imagined him with a British accent."

"He's from Kansas City," I say.

But Spence is back to ignoring me and fiddling with his phone.

"I'm sorry, am I keeping you from a very important booty call or something?"

"Jason's band is supposed to play here later tonight," he says.

Now I almost wish I had a drink, so I could spit it out. "He's in a *band*?"

This is the sort of thing Spence would usually delight in mocking with me—just the kind of distraction I could use right now—but he only nods.

"What's the name of this band?" I ask.

"They don't have one yet. It's kind of a new thing."

"Well, what time are they going on?"

"I don't know." He frowns at the blank screen. "I need to make sure he knows first."

"Knows what?"

"That we're here."

That Malcolm is here, he means.

"Jason's a grown man," I say. "I think he can handle running into his ex."

I'm handling it, aren't I? I may have let my anger boil over a bit during rehearsal, but I'm keeping my shit together now. If it's a scene Malcolm wants, I'm not going to give it to him.

Spence shakes his head. "You don't understand."

No, I don't fucking understand, because my best friend doesn't tell me anything anymore. This is the longest conversation we've had all week.

Malcolm makes his way back to the table, holding a glass of dark beer. He must have left David and Joanna behind at the bar. Well, at least Spence is here as a buffer.

But as Malcolm sets his beer down on the table, Spence's phone buzzes again. A shadow falls over his face when he reads the screen, and he turns to leave.

"Where are you going?" I ask.

All Spence says is, "Backstage." And then he's gone.

It's not fair of me to be angry at him. I haven't been entirely honest with him, either. If Spence knew what really happened the last time I saw David, he'd probably have sent him back to Indiana already with a black eye and at least one broken limb.

"They're out of Crown Royal," Malcolm tells me. "I think he's getting you another kind of whiskey instead, but if you want something else, I can—"

"Don't pretend you give a damn about what I want."

My voice is razor-wire sharp, but Malcolm only smiles.

"Why did you bring him here?" I ask.

He pretends to consider for a moment. Maybe he doesn't have a reason, except he suspected seeing David would bother me. This is another one of his fucked-up games, and I'm tired of playing.

"I could tell you have a lot of unexpressed anger toward him," he says finally.

"I never—"

"You didn't need to tell me. You tense up whenever you talk about him. Here especially."

Malcolm presses his fingertips into the hinge of my jaw. I grit my teeth, flexing the muscle there, pushing back against his touch.

"So?" I say.

David is on his way back from the bar now, holding two matching glasses. When he sees me looking at him, he smiles. The muscles in my jaw jump again.

Malcolm moves behind me, squeezing my shoulders. This time I let him.

"So," he says, his mouth next to my ear. "I want you to express it."

58

JOANNA

"JASON. HI." MORE WORDS SWIM BY IN MY BRAIN AND I'M trying my best to catch them, put them in the right order, but they're slippery and writhing like fish. "What brings you—"

He scowls and pushes away from the wall. "Fuck off, Joanna."

I take an unsteady step back. The heel of my shoe catches on the baseboard. There's a strand of wet hair sticking to my jaw like a worm, but I don't try to fix it.

I'm a lot drunker than I realized.

"Mal's here, too," I tell Jason. I should go find Mal. Warn him. As far as I know, the two of them haven't spoken since before the night Jason made that bloody mess in our apartment.

"I know," Jason says. "Spence told me."

I had no idea he and Spencer were even acquainted with each other, let alone that they knew each other well enough for Jason to call him by the same nickname Kira does.

"So you're still cleaning up Mal's messes for him, huh?"

I look down. The floor seems to tilt. I think about throwing up all over his shoes.

"Who knows," Jason continues. "Maybe your patience will pay off one of these days. Once he's fucked over every single person in Chicago, he might finally resort to fucking you."

"I'm sorry," I say. "I—"

"You're sorry?" He rolls his eyes and scoffs. "Good. You should be fucking sorry. Because it's your fault, too, you know."

Jason is unstable. He's always been unstable. Mal made sure to remind me of that, over and over, in the days following the incident. *Don't beat yourself up, Joanna. How could you have known he would do something like that?*

But I did know. I could see it in his eyes, from the day he auditioned. The way he looked at Mal, like a lost puppy who still trusted humans even though he'd been kicked by every single one he'd met. I should have known it would end in tragedy.

While we were doing *Hamlet*, I kept working on my play about the poet, trying to contort it into a shape that might meet with Mal's approval. I'd take care of company business during the day, run rehearsals at night, and then stay up until all hours writing and rewriting.

By then, Mal's ideas for the play had tangled around my own like brambles. Cutting off their circulation, bleeding them dry. The protagonist changed so much I didn't recognize her anymore. She'd started out as a flawed but sympathetic heroine. After Mal's input, she became a sociopathic monster, someone who intentionally generated pain so she could channel it into her art. In the final draft, the plot turned on her pushing her boyfriend into committing suicide, just so she could write about it.

Mal was finally satisfied with that version of the script—except he wanted me to make the main character a man instead of a woman, so he could play the role. He had no interest in being the sweet and fragile boyfriend. But he suggested another actor, someone he thought would be ideally suited for the part: his devoted Horatio, Jason Grady.

If I'd just agreed to cast him, everything might have turned out all right. But I wanted Mal all to myself.

"I'm sorry," I say again. "I hope you've been able to get the help you—"

"Mal's the one who needs help," Jason says. "And you're just as bad as he is. You see him pulling this shit over and over, playing with people like fucking chess pieces, and you run interference for him, make excuses, act like he should be able to get away with murder because he's some *artistic genius* or whatever."

Jason stabs his finger at my chest like he wishes it were a blade. His voice sounds angry, but in his eyes there's a glint of something else: hysteria, cornered-animal panic, even though he's free to walk away. Just like he was then. The leather cuff on his wrist shifts, and I can see the edge of the gnarled scar it's hiding.

"Don't be 'sorry,'" he says. "Fucking *do something*."

59

KIRA

have—"

"It's fine." It's horrible, it tastes like furniture polish. I took a single sip for show, then set the glass back down on the table.

"So how long have you been in Chicago?" he asks.

"Since right after college."

"Ah. So you did decide to go to college after all."

He'd love to take credit for that, wouldn't he? Before his class, I showed no academic aptitude whatsoever, so I assumed I'd be stuck in small-town Ohio all my life, working as a chain restaurant waitress or a receptionist for a car salesman who pinched my ass and called me "sweetheart."

When we were found out and David got fired, I was so worried I'd ruined his life. He insisted I'd done no such thing. "If it weren't for you," he told me. "I'd still be stuck working a job I hate, sleepwalking through my life. You saved me, Kira."

He said such pretty things, at the start.

The music playing over the bar's speakers fades out, and a woman with acid-green pigtails comes out and takes a seat at the drum set. Then a guy with horn rim glasses, carrying a bass guitar. And following right behind them, Jason and Spence.

Jason doesn't look toward our table. And if Malcolm notices him, he doesn't give any indication. He's watching David and me like this strained conversation of ours is a one-act play we're putting on solely for his amusement.

"And that guy," David says. "The one with the eyebrows."

"Spence."

"He's your boyfriend?"

"No." I'm not in the mood to explain any further. Besides, if David turned around and took a look at the stage right now, he'd have his answer. Spence has been holding Jason's guitar, and when he hands it to him, Jason gives him a smile like a wide-open window. Doesn't look to me like he's the least bit traumatized by Malcolm's presence in the audience. But he's got Spence right where he wants him now: standing by his side, far away from me.

"I see." David laughs and shoots a conspiratorial look at Malcolm. "It's kind of tough to tell with her sometimes, you know what I mean?"

Malcolm doesn't respond—not even a twitch of his lips. But he lays his palm against the small of my back. Under the table, where David can't see, but in full view of Joanna, who's just returned from the direction of the bathrooms. Her face turns even paler and more pinched when she sees Malcolm's hand on me. I don't give a damn, let her think what she wants.

Jason strums a few chords to make sure his guitar is in tune, and then the band launches into their first song.

You said it's not love unless it makes you bleed
You showed me where to cut and I said "how deep"
I was the more deceived

Spence takes up a position at the foot of the stage, his back to us. I guess I'm on my own.

Jason's singing voice is a sweet baritone, deeper and more pleasant than his speaking voice. Under different circumstances, I might find it soothing, despite the lame lyrics. But right now it's just one more thing in this room that makes me want to scream.

"Why did you really come here, David?" I ask.

He has the gall to seem taken aback by the question. "I told you, I was here for the conference anyway, and—"

I scoff and roll my eyes. He used to hate it when I did that. It was childish, he said. This pathetic excuse for a man, who only wanted me when he thought I was a pliable young thing, so impressed with his intellect, his passion, too naive and foolish to ask questions. To push back.

"Fine," he says, and I can see it flickering in his eyes now: the contempt, the loathing he feels for me, burning off all that false friendliness. He's trying to hide it, but there's a reason he never made it as an actor. "I wanted to see you. Not only that, Kira, I wanted . . ."

He reaches across the table and lays his hand over mine. I tense every muscle in my body. The heat from Malcolm's fingers spreads farther on my back, turns throbbing.

"I wanted to apologize." David huffs out a breath, like this is the hardest thing he's ever had to do in his whole miserable life. "I'm really sorry if I hurt y—"

"You did."

"What?" David says.

"There's no 'if.' You did hurt me. And you know it."

My other hand, the one he's not touching, clenches around my whiskey glass. I imagine tossing the drink in David's face, watching the amber liquid stream out of his eyes like tears.

David was never one of those men who were too macho to cry. He cried all the time. He cried at the theater, he cried after sex (or should I say *lovemaking*, since that's what he preferred to call it). And he cried the day I told him he'd gotten me pregnant.

He didn't believe the baby was his, of course. He'd convinced himself by then that I was cheating on him with half the cast of *The Crucible*. I stopped trying to deny it, because it only made him more upset. "Just tell me the truth," he'd say. Over and over, that same demand. "Tell me the truth, Kira, if you care about me at all, tell me the truth." I wished he would just get it over with, call me a lying whore and kick me out. At least that would have been honest.

I wanted to leave him. But I had another week of the show left, and nowhere else to stay, so I decided to stick it out. I made an appointment to have an abortion the morning after closing night. It would cost me my whole *Crucible* paycheck, but what other choice did I have? David, of course, refused to help pay for it.

That last week was pure torture. Everything I did pissed David off. I got a call from the clinic confirming my abortion appointment, and he was convinced it was another man phoning me. ("Was that the father?" he asked, then muttered, just loud enough for me to hear: "If you even know who the father is.") He was perpetually drunk, moping around the apartment. At least he didn't want to fuck me anymore. I was revolted by the sight of him. His face looked red and swollen all the time, from weeping or drinking or both, like you could puncture the bags under his eyes and pus would ooze out.

"I feel awful about what happened that night," he continues, his hand still covering mine.

Our last night together, he means. He cried then, too. After he screamed at me and threw me to the floor of our shitty East Village studio apartment, he couldn't stop crying.

"You feel awful." My voice is flat, metallic. A lid set on top of something volatile, steam escaping the edges. Malcolm's thumb starts making slow circles over the base of my spine.

"Of course I do. I'm so sorry, Kira. You have to know that."

Of course he saved his insincere apology until he could deliver it in front of an audience. Of course he would show up now—now, when I'm finally doing well for myself, finally having some small measure of success. How like David, to wait until I had something in my life worth ruining.

He picks my hand up off the table and traps it between his. I try to pull away, but he presses down harder.

"Stop it." My voice spikes over the mellow music.

People are turning to look at us now. But not Spence. He only has eyes for Jason, up onstage crooning that insipid melody like he doesn't have a care in the world.

You're not honest, you're not fair
There's emptiness behind your stare
I was the more deceived

I can still feel it, all of it: David's tears seeping into my shirt, soaking down to my skin, the way his arms knotted around my stomach, holding me down on the sweating green linoleum. He was stronger than he looked—stronger than me, despite those skinny arms of his, those delicate fingers. *I'm so sorry, it was an accident, I love you, you know I love you, Kira, baby, please forgive me, please.*

His eyes are pleading the same way now, tears at the corners, glistening behind his glasses.

I'm not going to placate him, the way I did then. I'm not going to force my body to go limp and stroke his hair and tell him it's fine, everything's fine, of course it was only an accident.

I wish I'd fought, instead of pretending to forgive him. I wish I'd slapped him or kneed him in the groin or scratched bloody lines into his cheeks. Maybe he would have attacked me back, seriously hurt me, or worse—but at least I would have left a mark.

Malcolm presses his hand harder into my back, urging me forward. He's been silent this whole time, but I hear his voice in my head again.

Express it.

"Let go of me," I say to David.

He looks wounded. "Kira—"

"I said let go."

He's still holding my hand, flattened like a flower between his palms. Until I rip it away, with so much force I would have staggered backward if not for Malcolm steadying me. I don't have to look at Malcolm's face to know he's smiling.

"Please, Kira—let's not leave things this way."

David reaches for me again, and that's when I finally explode.

"Don't fucking touch me!"

My knuckles ram into the bridge of David's nose. I don't even remember closing my fingers into a fist.

The music sputters out. David doesn't go down, but his glasses do, clattering on the dusty hardwood floor a few feet away. Everyone in the bar is staring at us now—including the bouncer from the front door, a burly guy with arms covered in blackwork tattoos, already pushing through the crowd to reach us.

"Ma'am," he says. "I'm going to have to ask you to leave."

I don't even acknowledge him. I'm watching David as he fumbles around on the floor, trying to find his glasses. Joanna finally crouches down and retrieves them for him. When he takes them from her, his hands are trembling. He looks terrified.

Good. He should be.

"Ma'am," the bouncer repeats. When I still don't acknowledge him, he reaches for my arm. Malcolm steps between us.

"We're going," he says. He puts his hand on my lower back again, steering me toward the door. "If you could settle the tab, please, Joanna."

Joanna stares at me like I'm a poisonous snake about to strike. I brush past her as Malcolm marches me toward the door, bumping my shoulder into hers on purpose.

Malcolm pauses, right before the threshold, and beams a smile back at the stunned bar patrons. "Sorry for the disturbance."

He looks toward the stage as he says this. Right at Jason. Jason's face goes white, and his hand closes around the neck of the guitar.

Footsteps trail us out of the bar, and I assume it's Spence. But once we're on the sidewalk, I see it's David who followed us.

Spence stayed inside. With Jason.

David looks dazed, bewildered, like he still can't believe what just happened, what I did. His glasses sit crooked on his nose now, and there's a spiderweb of cracks on one of the lenses, glittering in the sickly orange glow of the bar's neon sign. But he's barely bleeding, nothing but a sliver of red leaking out of one nostril.

I should have hit him harder.

"Kira, I—" he starts, his voice breaking.

"Don't cry." I take a step toward him, both hands curling into fists this time. He shrinks away from me. "Don't you dare fucking cry, David."

Malcolm catches me by the wrist, holding me back, keeping me in check. "Why don't I walk you to the train station, Mr. Granville? We should give Kira some space."

But then he leans in to whisper in my ear, too low and close for David to hear.

"I knew you had it in you."

JOANNA

AFTER MAL LEFT WITH KIRA, I DIDN'T SETTLE THE TAB LIKE HE instructed me to. Instead, I sat down on a bar stool and waited. I told myself I was waiting for him, but it was just an excuse. To order another drink, and then another, until my thoughts blurred to static. I knew he wasn't coming back.

I'm not sure how late it is when I finally leave the bar and start walking back toward the theater, steps unsteady, street lights swimming in my vision. Waiting for the light to change at Belmont and Greenview, I squeeze my eyes shut for a second and all I can see is the look on Kira's face when she lunged. She seemed almost feral, like she wanted to rip her former teacher's throat out with her teeth. Smile around the sinew.

Mal could have stopped her. But he stood there and let her do it. A little grin tugging at the corners of his lips the whole time. That attentive, merciless amusement. Like an animal playing with his food. That's the reason he brought David Granville here—the only reason. He wanted to see what Kira would do.

I've never seen her as unnerved as she was tonight. She scared me, and she should scare Mal. But I can't say I didn't enjoy it, watching her squirm.

You're just as bad as he is.

Bryn said she would lock up before she left, but I want to check for myself because she always seems to leave something undone. A dead bolt unlatched or a light turned on. Sure enough, when I walk in the lobby is dark, but at least a few of the lights in the performance space are still switched on, outlining the door in a soft yellow glow.

I drag my hand along the wall—not to find my way but to steady myself. My head is pounding like I'm already hungover, and I'm so tired I can hardly focus my eyes. If I can navigate the stairs, maybe I should go down to my office, lay my head on my desk and sleep for a little while. It's not as if Mal will miss me if I don't come home.

I cross the threshold. Feel for the light switch. One more step and I'll be standing in the light. But then there's a sound from the stage, and I freeze, my hand hovering over the switch.

The lights are still on because Bryn is still here, perched on the desk downstage left. And standing between her spread legs, with a hand plunged deep under her skirt, is Mal.

I SHOULD HAVE LEFT THE SECOND I SAW THEM. BUT I COULDN'T make myself move. Besides, it was almost like they *wanted* someone to see. A building full of dark corners, and they were onstage, bathed in light, on full display.

So I stayed to the end, hidden in the shadows at the back of the space. Watching the muscles in Mal's forearms flex as he moved his fingers inside her. The way Bryn pressed back against him when he flipped her around and bent her over the desk. Listening to every moan, every squeak of the furniture legs against the floor. The wet slap of their skin.

Mal didn't cry out when he finished, but he bent over Bryn's back and pressed his cheek against her spine. That was the part that made my chest burn the hottest.

He didn't kiss her, after. At least not by the time I slipped out into the lobby again, while Bryn was still straightening her skirt, cleaning the smudged lenses of her glasses off on her sleeve.

I left the building without locking it, walked straight to the near-est El station at Southport and Roscoe. If it weren't so cold, I'd be tempted to stay out all night, wandering the streets. I haven't done that since I was as young as Bryn.

She's not so young. Not really. She's an adult, and based on what I just witnessed, she's clearly consenting. It's none of my business.

It could have been her, too, with Mal between her legs in the dressing room that day. She and Kira look enough alike, from behind. The wide pale hips, the unruly dark hair. Maybe all this time, Bryn's the one he's been fucking. It's far more likely he's screwing them both, though—the same way he juggled Jason Grady and the woman who played his mother in *Hamlet*.

I go and stand under one of the heaters hanging over the train platform. They always make me feel like I'm an egg in an incubator. About to crack open.

There must have been signs. There are always signs. But the only difference I've noticed in Bryn is her change in wardrobe, suddenly dressing like she had someone to impress. Well, that and her attitude the other day in my office, the way she tossed her hair and rolled her eyes like she thought I was the most pathetic person alive.

With Jason, it seemed so obvious in retrospect. He started out a little shy, nervous—playing our Horatio was his first major role out-side of school plays, after all—but he had this vitality about him. He was excited, bright, eager, a ray of light in rehearsals. But day by day, the light started to dim from his face. He got paler, thinner. Drawn. I never saw him cry, but I often saw the aftermath. The swollen skin, the red-rimmed eyes—eyes that followed Mal's every movement. By opening night, Jason was a shadow of himself, haunting the theater, but his Horatio was heartbreakingly brilliant. I remember thinking that whatever Mal was doing to him, it was working.

Jason may have started to crack during *Hamlet*, but it was what happened after that shattered him. I wasn't there when Mal told him he couldn't have the part in my play. The aftermath, though, I couldn't avoid: Jason showing up at our apartment at all hours, bang-ing on the door. Sobbing, begging, refusing to leave. And Mal coolly denying him. *I don't know what I was thinking, you're too immature to handle a part like this. You're not willing to go far enough.*

But Jason was willing to go further than I ever imagined. Seeing him tonight, standing in the sallow light outside the bar bathroom, all I could think about was how he looked when I found him. White wax skin, bruise-blue lips. Red everywhere. Flowing out of his wrist, wound between his fingers like ribbon.

Even then, even as I was screaming my throat raw, jabbing my fingers under his jaw to feel for a pulse, punching 911 into the phone with shaking, blood-soaked hands, I knew it wasn't a suicide attempt. It was an audition. He did it exactly the way I wrote it in my script: a curving cut with a kitchen knife, on his right wrist only. He just sliced too deep.

Mal wasn't there. He didn't come to the hospital, either—another administrative detail he was all too happy to leave to me. I scrubbed the floor clean myself. For days afterward, no matter how many showers I took, I still smelled copper.

After that, I couldn't even look at my play. Every page seemed stained with Jason's blood.

A train arrives. I watch it slide in, stare at the doors as they open, then close again.

I rummage in my purse for a piece of candy, a stick of gum, *anything* to take the sour taste out of my mouth. Something sharp slices under the nail of my pointer finger.

The corner of Robert Kenmore's business card. I stick my finger into my mouth, then pick up the card and hold it up to the bilious light.

Don't be sorry.

I turn the card over. Smudges of my blood mar the space where he wrote his cell phone number, but I can still read it.

Do something.

I take out my phone and tap in the numbers. Before I have a chance to change my mind.

One ring. Two. I can still hang up. It's not too late.

"Hello?"

He sounds groggy, like the call woke him up. Of course it did. It must be after midnight by now.

I open my mouth, but my voice feels lodged in my throat. Like I could choke on it.

"Who is this?"

"It's . . . I'm . . ."

I press my fingers between my brows and squeeze my eyes shut.

"It's so late, I shouldn't have . . . I'll just—"

"Joanna?"

He recognized my voice. This pleases me, more than it should.

"Yes. I'm sorry, I shouldn't have called you at this hour, I don't know what I was—"

"No, no. I'm glad you called."

Rob sounds much more lucid now. I hear the creak of mattress springs—him sitting up in bed. I wonder if he's alone, or if there's someone there beside him. He isn't whispering, so maybe he's alone. Or just rude. But he didn't seem rude when I met him at the fundraiser. He seemed like one of the kindest people I've ever met. And he's kept his word, so far at least. It's been a week, and he hasn't revealed my secret, or tried to contact me again. He's leaving it up to me, like he promised he would.

"Does this mean you've reconsidered?" he asks.

There's another train approaching. I keep staring at the third rail, thinking about what happens when someone touches it.

"Yes. When can we meet?"

61

KIRA

I WALK THE WHOLE WAY HOME, AT LEAST AN HOUR STRAIGHT north on Ashland Avenue, taking in gulps of bracing air, waiting for the adrenaline to burn off, for guilt to overtake my exhilaration. Malcolm's voice echoes in my head, keeping time with the crisp slap of my shoes against the frozen pavement.

I knew you had it in you.

When I get home, Spence is already there, slouched on the sofa, sipping something amber from the bar cart. He stands up as soon as he sees me.

"There you are," he says. "Are you okay?"

Now he asks. At least he's here, though—I figured he would spend the night at Jason's again. A night alone with Spence is exactly what I need right now. Even if we do nothing other than sit side by side on the sofa and drink until our eyes blur.

But then the water turns on in the bathroom, and I realize we're not alone after all. Of course not.

"Jason's taking a shower," Spence says. "We're going to watch a movie or something if you—"

"I'm really tired," I tell him, even though I'm not tired at all, I'm so spun up I feel like I may never be able to sleep again.

"Why don't I fix you a drink," Spence says. "And we can talk."

The last thing I want to do is talk. I want him to take me into his bedroom and throw me down on the mattress and fuck me until my inner thighs are bruised, until my thoughts turn to nothing but white heat.

"I told you, I'm tired, I just want to—"

"You know I'm generally pro punching asshole ex-boyfriends. But giving your boss a split lip? That's another matter entirely."

Spence's tone is still teasing, but he's not joking around anymore. I'm surprised it took him this long to bring it up. I expected an earful the second rehearsal ended.

"Would it help if I told you he deserved it?"

"I'm sure he did," Spence says. "But you can kick Malcolm Mercer's ass on your own time. When you're onstage, you need to stick to my choreography."

"How did the slap look tonight?"

Spence shakes his head. "That's not the—"

"How did it look?"

"It was perfect—tonight. But it has to be perfect every time." He takes my hand and squeezes it. His warmth makes the rest of my body feel even colder. "I just want you to be safe."

"Don't worry about me, I can take care of myself. As you saw earlier—if you were even paying attention."

Spence's eyes soften. "He needed me, Kira."

I needed you, I want to say. But that's not how our relationship works.

"Yeah, well, Jason isn't as fragile as he wants you to think."

"You're right," Spence says. "He's not fragile. In fact, I think he might be the strongest person I've ever met."

I can't stop myself from rolling my eyes. "How much has he told you, anyway—about him and Malcolm?"

"Enough."

Both an answer and a warning. Spence clenches my hand harder. My sore knuckles throb, but I don't pull away.

"Look," he says. "You know I don't care if you're fucking the guy. He's hot as hell, believe me, I get it, but—"

"I am not fucking him. Not that it's any of your business." I can feel the rage rising again, blood pounding in my ears. "God, Jason's really got you tied by the dick, doesn't he? I thought you hated all this relationship bullshit, couldn't stand to be tied down or—"

"No, Kira." He lets my hand drop. "That was you."

I'm done. I'm so done tonight, with everything and everyone. I turn on my heel and start to walk away, but Spence comes after me. When he reaches for my shoulder, I'm already spinning around to shove him. Then I shove him again, harder, so he stumbles into the back of the sofa.

He stares at me, stunned. For all our flirtatious roughhousing, I've never hit him anywhere near that hard before.

My hands are still flat on Spence's chest. Jason switches off the water in the bathroom. The shower curtain *snick*s back.

I fist the front of Spence's shirt and pull him in until our lips slam together—rough, my mouth open. The same way I kissed Malcolm onstage tonight.

He's not forceful about it, when he pushes me away. He's so much stronger than me, he doesn't need to be.

"Hey Spence, is it okay if I borrow—"

Jason appears in the bathroom doorway, steam curling around him, wearing one of our ratty red towels tucked around his waist.

His scar is bright red from the hot water—or maybe it always looks like that, like a gruesome little smile. When he sees me looking, he presses the inside of his wrist against his thigh to hide it.

Spence drops his hands from my shoulders. "Take whatever you want," he says. "I'll be right there."

Jason looks from Spence to me and back again, suspicion flickering in his eyes. He didn't see the kiss, but the tension between us hangs heavier in the air than the humidity from the shower.

He heads toward Spence's bedroom, leaving wet footprints in his wake. Spence follows without so much as a glance back at me.

"Spence," I say. "I'm—"

"For God's sake, Kira." He turns his head just enough that I can see the scowl twisting his features. "Just fuck him already."

62

JOANNA

TONIGHT IS THE INVITED DRESS REHEARSAL. MAL DOESN'T believe in previews. He thinks it's disrespectful to the audience, pretending some performances "count" less than others. Why an invited dress is any different, I have no idea. But I gave up on that argument years ago.

The programs have been proofread and printed. I confirmed and paid for all the local marketing—the full-page ad in the *Red Eye*, the banners on the sides of CTA buses. The props are in place, the costumes hung up in the dressing rooms, the wrinkles steamed out. The house opens in a little over an hour, and we're ready. I've even stolen a few minutes to sit down in my office and triple-check the to-do list in my notebook.

But I can't shake the feeling I'm forgetting something. Something small and insignificant that's slipped my mind and could bring the whole show crashing down.

My phone buzzes, rattling against the desktop so loud I jump in my seat.

At first I think it might be my mother. But she always texts on opening night, never any other time. Always the same words, too: *Good luck tonight. I love you.*

I flip the screen faceup and read the message. It's from Rob. I'm not stupid enough to have his contact information saved in my phone, but I recognize his number by now.

The story will run in tomorrow's paper.

So official. The period at the end of the sentence and everything. I thought I had a few more days. Before I would have to face the consequences of my actions. He must have gotten them to rush it, to coincide with opening night.

The story is sure to reach my mother in Pennsylvania. I wonder if she'll still love me and wish me luck, when she finds out what I've done.

This is it. The point of no return. Except that point already passed me by when I snuck away from tech rehearsal yesterday afternoon to meet Rob.

He was waiting for me outside the Heartland Cafe, even though it had been pouring rain all day. His pant legs were soaked halfway up his shins, glasses fogged so I couldn't see his eyes. He had a sport coat on. Brown wool, suede patches on the sleeves, like the ones on the sweater he wore the night we met. And there I was in my sloppy tech-week clothes with a constellation of stress acne on my jaw.

Sorry, I said. *I didn't have time to put on makeup.*

He smiled. *That's okay. Neither did I.*

A knock on the office door startles me back to awareness.

"Come in."

The door opens a crack, and Bryn peers around the edge. I knew it had to be her. Kira wouldn't come to my office willingly, and Mal wouldn't knock.

"They're starting the fight call," she says.

We don't have a proper fight captain; usually that role is assigned to a cast member with stage combat experience, who isn't part of the fight scenes in the show. With a cast of two, we have to improvise. Which means me sitting in on the preshow run-through of the fight scenes, to make sure they aren't missing anything.

When I look at Bryn now, I don't see *her* anymore. I see the places Mal touched with his hands, his lips, his—

"I'll be right there," I say.

Rob had ordered hot tea for both of us, then took out a steno pad and a silver pen, jabbing the pen against his chest to click it open. I brought my notebook, too, but it stayed shut on the table between us. The first few questions were easy. Warming me up.

How did you and Malcolm Mercer meet?

I send my last batch of emails, switch off the lights in my office, and shut the door behind me before following Bryn up to the performance space.

Most theaters of your stature have administrative staff, a board of directors. But Indifferent Honest is just you and Mr. Mercer. Why haven't you expanded the company?

Mal and Kira are already on the second part of the fight call, working through the slap. They're both barefoot, and Kira is in her black slip, though she has yet to do her hair and makeup. I take a seat in the front row, right as Mal says the cue line.

After Hamlet, *you moved into a more administrative role. Why is that?*

Kira brings her hand back. The stage is bathed in red. Austin is running a last check of the lighting effect he designed for Mara's reveries. He brings up the red light so gradually it's almost imperceptible at first, but by the time Mara lashes out at Trent, they look blood-soaked.

I see. But you didn't tell anyone, about what really happened?

Mal grabs Kira's wrists and walks her toward the wall. Slow, controlled. They're doing everything at three-quarter speed, making sure all the details are right.

"Hold please," comes Austin's voice from the booth. "Going dark."

They freeze in place, staring into each other's eyes. Austin kills the lights. When he brings them up again, Kira and Mal are in the same position, but even closer together. His hips urging hers back against the scenery flat.

Was that your decision, or Mr. Mercer's?

They do the strangling next, skipping over the kiss leading up to it. Austin leaves the lights stark white this time. I can see every quiver of Kira's bare thighs, every flutter of Mal's eyelashes as he struggles then falls still.

What inspired you to start writing again, after giving it up for so long?

By the time fight call finishes up, a few audience members are already waiting in the lobby. The last thirty minutes before the show pass in a haze. I take tickets, hand out programs, show people to their seats. Answer questions, make small talk. All the things I always do before a show, but I feel like I'm standing outside my body, watching myself go through the motions.

Soon Austin's preshow playlist of sultry jazz tracks is winding down. I shut the door after the last couple of audience members and lean back against it. The low drone of overlapping voices rumbles through the metal.

There's a seat for me in the front row—on the far end, so I can slip in and out during the show if necessary. Bryn hung a little *Reserved* sign on the chair.

This is the moment I've been waiting for. The first time a script I wrote will be performed in front of an audience in over a decade. It doesn't matter that no one in there knows it's mine. They'll know tomorrow. Everyone will know.

I should go inside. Sit down. I'm running out of time.

Instead, I take my phone out of my pocket and look at Rob's message again. I haven't responded yet. Maybe it doesn't require a response; he already has everything he needs from me.

I type out the word Okay. Stare at it for a moment, my thumb hovering over the send button. Then I delete it and write something else instead.

What are you doing tonight?

KIRA

USUALLY THE TIME LEADING UP TO A PERFORMANCE IS A whirlwind of activity, but since our behind-the-scenes crew is pretty much just Bryn, it's so quiet backstage, it's almost eerie. Austin is in the booth, and Joanna is probably out in the lobby, handing out programs and chatting up the audience members.

Bryn passes me in the hallway as I'm walking from the dressing room to the wings. In her backstage blacks with her dark hair braided down her back, her pale face looks like it's floating, disembodied.

"I set the suitcases," she tells me.

"Thank you."

"Have you seen—"

I shake my head. The door to Malcolm's dressing room is open, but the lights inside are off. I know he's in the building, because he was here for fight call half an hour ago.

He hasn't mentioned the incident with David again. I haven't brought it up either, mostly because I'm afraid he'll be able to tell I'm not mad about it anymore. I know I should be—I tried to be, did my best to stoke the flames of my rage, replaying each and every one of

Malcolm's manipulations, forcing myself to dredge up some of my most painful memories of David. But it's as though some tight knot inside me unfurled when my fist met his face. Even with the slow grind of tech rehearsals and the fact that Spence and I are still barely speaking, I've felt lighter all week, more at ease with myself and my performance.

Bryn wanders off again, worrying her lower lip with her teeth, and I press my eye to the crack in the door leading to the stage, looking for Spence out in the house. He likes to come early so he can be sure to get his seat of choice: dead center in the back row. Once rehearsals are done, he hates sitting in the front—says it makes him feel like he's part of the show rather than an audience member.

His face is in shadow, but I recognize him by the way he's sitting, his legs splayed wide like one of those obnoxious men who take up three seats on the train. He's alone. Not that I really thought he would bring Jason.

I can see Spence's hands, too, leafing through the program in his lap—looking for his own photo and bio, no doubt. Everyone who sees the cover image will probably assume those are my hands scratching across Malcolm's back, even though they're nothing like mine. The fingers are too long and elegant, the nails flawlessly manicured.

A hand slides under my hair to touch the bare skin at the base of my neck. I start, my shoulder blades pinching together.

Malcolm. I didn't even hear him approach, but now he's standing right behind me. His fingers are icy, as though he's been outside in the cold.

"How are you feeling?" he asks.

"Fine."

As soon as the word leaves my lips, though, I realize I'm not fine at all. I'm sick with nerves, my stomach thrashing. I haven't felt this way before a show since my very first play, all the way back in high school. Even for the *Crucible* opening in New York, I was too anxious about dealing with David afterward to get properly nervous about the performance itself.

"It's okay," Malcolm says. "When we did *Hamlet*, I threw up before every show."

I remember the bathroom in that loft. I try to picture him there, hunched over the toilet, retching, his knees grinding into the grimy floor tiles. It's difficult, imagining him vulnerable, weak. Human.

He slides his hand down my spine to the small of my back, then moves it to my abdomen.

"Just try to breathe."

Malcolm inhales and exhales, his breath rustling the coils of my hair. He presses down until I inhale, too, expanding my stomach into his palm.

Another flash of memory, involuntary this time: my first moments alone with David. I stayed after rehearsal to ask for help with speaking my lines louder, supporting my voice from my diaphragm. He stepped behind me, as close as Malcolm is now, and hovered his hand over my stomach.

That's not what gave him away, though—it was the instant after, when I took a deep breath, like he'd told me to, and the fabric of my shirt brushed David's palm. He took a breath then too—not a calm, measured intake of air, but a shuddering gasp. I was thrilled by it. All I thought was: *he wants me, just like I want him.* I didn't realize until much later how stupid I was, how naive, to have ever believed he wanted to teach me, to help me become a better actress, when of course all he wanted was to fuck me.

I feel dizzy all of a sudden, tangled up in the memory. Instead of Malcolm's calm, steady breathing, my head is full of the ragged sound of David sucking in the air next to my ear, trying to control himself, willing himself to step away from me, to stop this before it was too late.

I take a step backward—right into Malcolm. He presses his hand harder into my stomach, holding me steady. His fingers are warm now, the chill banished by my body heat.

As much as I want to believe Malcolm sees something special in me, something I bring to this role no one else could, for all I know I'm nothing but a prop to him, an interchangeable body, and the woman in that photo on the program, whoever she is, could just as easily be playing Mara tonight.

"Curtain in five."

Bryn's voice comes from somewhere behind us. My eyes are shut. I don't remember closing them. I don't open them, don't turn to look at her. I know how this must look. Malcolm lifts his hand off my stomach, but he doesn't step away from me.

"Thank you, five," Malcolm tells her.

Then he leans in again, his lips touching my ear, and gives me one final piece of direction, more command than encouragement:

"You're going to be brilliant tonight, Kira."

64

JOANNA

I WALKED RIGHT OUT THE FRONT DOOR. EAST ON BELMONT to Clark Street. Caught the 22 bus up to Andersonville. Waiting for the bus was the hardest part. Once I stopped moving, the urge to run back to the theater was so strong, the muscles in my legs kept contracting in painful spasms.

Mal and Kira are onstage, speaking my words, and I'm not there.

On the bus, I keep looking at the time on my phone, tracking where they are in the play. Now he's exiting to the bathroom. Now she's taking the pills.

Rob is waiting for me under the striped green awning of the wine and spirits store at Clark and Foster. He has earbuds in, but as soon as he sees me step off the bus, he takes them out, wrapping the cord around his phone and stowing it in his pocket.

Now Mal is zipping up Kira's dress. Now she's turning to him and kissing him.

We go out for a late dinner at Andies, a cozy Mediterranean restaurant I've walked past many times but never tried. The host seats us by the fireplace.

I haven't eaten anything since the buttered toast and black coffee I had for breakfast. No time, and my stomach is too unpredictable on opening nights. I don't usually throw up, like Mal used to, but I feel on the verge of it all day.

Rob orders an appetizer for us to share, a plate of cheese the waitress sets on fire with a flourish of her hand, like she's performing a magic trick. I take a small bite, to be polite, but then my stomach twists and I realize it's with hunger instead of nausea. I rip off a corner of warm pita bread and scoop the cheese into my mouth.

We don't talk about the play. But every time Rob's sleeve shrugs up far enough to uncover the watch on his wrist, I think about what's happening right now at Indifferent Honest.

Now she's slapping him. Now he's shoving her into the wall.

After dinner, Rob suggests we go to a late-night show a few blocks away. I've heard of the theater before—they're a Chicago institution, an experimental company that does a rotating selection of short plays, trying to squeeze as many as thirty of them into an hour-long performance—but I've never been. Too busy making art of my own. At least that's what I always told myself.

Despite the chilly weather, when we arrive, there's already a line wrapping around the corner. Rob explains how their unusual admission system works (first come first served, cash only, ticket price determined by the roll of a die) and tells me about some favorites among the plays he's seen there before.

Now she's straddling him. Now her hands are closing around his throat.

"They open the doors at eleven," Rob says, pushing his sleeve back to glance at his watch again. "So less than an hour now. You're not too cold?"

I shake my head. He's getting the worst of the wind, standing on the outside of the sidewalk. I huddle closer, letting him shelter me.

Now they're taking their bows.

65

KIRA

MALCOLM TAKES MY HAND AND PULLS ME TO THE EDGE OF THE stage.

The invited dress is over, and I barely remember the performance. Only small details, shards of moments. All of Malcolm—the heat of his breath on my neck, the spidery shadows cast by his eyelashes, the sound of his fingers raking through his hair—like I was somehow both onstage with him, and watching him from a distance, just one more member of his audience held in thrall.

Malcolm lets go of my hand to take his solo bow, sweat gleaming on his bare back under the spotlight, then smiles at me and applauds, motioning for me to take a bow on my own, too. When I straighten up again, flipping my hair over my shoulders like I'm surfacing in water, I finally look toward Spence's seat in the back of the house.

He's not there. The place he was sitting is empty, a crumpled copy of the program left on the chair. He must already be backstage, waiting for me.

The spotlight is hot on my face, and my cheeks hurt from smiling. My hands ache, too. Malcolm stretched the strangling out this time, taking longer than usual to pass out. Or maybe it just seemed that way to me. I can still feel the places on my inner thighs his torso touched as he was moving underneath me, but I can't remember anything else.

Malcolm takes my hand again, and we bow together one final time. He gives a little wave to someone in the audience on the way out. Not Joanna—as far as I know, her reserved seat in the front row stayed empty through the whole show, and I didn't see her backstage at intermission, either.

I've never lost track of my time onstage like this before. I feel as if I sped through the whole thing, but also like it lasted an eternity. Usually I'm aware of every moment when I'm performing—aware of my body in space, the other actors around me, and the reactions from the audience. If someone shifts in their seat or laughs a little too loud or whispers something in their date's ear, I notice.

But right now I have no sense of even whether I fucked up or did well—not until Malcolm pulls me close, pressing his mouth against my ear so I can hear him over the applause.

"I told you."

At first I'm not sure what he means. Then his words from before the show come back to me: *You're going to be brilliant tonight.*

Was I?

Just as I suspected, Spence is already backstage, pacing back and forth across the hallway between the dressing rooms. The space is so narrow he can only take a few steps in each direction before he has to double back. His leather oxfords screech against the concrete floor.

I smile wide when I see him. There's been tension between us since our argument after the run-through, but at the moment I can't even remember what we were fighting about.

"Spence!" I call out. I feel almost giddy, light, like I could float over to him, gliding above the ground.

He looks up at me. I'm expecting him to give me one of his devilish grins, gather me in his arms and spin me around, tell me he thought I was brilliant, too. But his expression is dark, and when he sees Malcolm coming up behind me, it turns into an outright glower.

"What the fuck was that?" Spence says.

His voice is loud enough to carry out into the theater, where the audience is still gathering up their coats and bags, filing out, chatting about the show or where to go for late-night drinks.

"What are you talking about?" Malcolm asks.

Spence scoffs and puts his hands on his hips, flaring out his black suit jacket like a cobra's hood. "I don't even know where to fucking start."

Malcolm gives him a sliver of a smile. "Please try."

Spence looks to me for support. But I don't know what to say. I remember so little of what happened out there, I have no idea what we could have done to upset Spence so much. I didn't hit Malcolm again, did I?

Surely I would remember that.

"Well, for starters," Spence says when I don't jump in, "you know damn well the slap is supposed to be no-contact."

"Her hand barely grazed me," Malcolm says.

"That's still contact, though, isn't it?"

Did I really touch him again during the slap? I must have, if Spence says I did.

"Fine," Malcolm says. "We can correct it during fight call tomorrow." He turns to Bryn, who's been hanging back in the shadows watching us. "Bryn, could you please make a note to—"

Spence interrupts him. "That's the fucking least of it, and you know it."

Malcolm just blinks at him, eyebrows canted upward. Spence puts his hands out, mimicking the stranglehold.

"Kira's hands were pressing down on your throat."

"No they weren't," Malcolm says. "Were they, Kira?"

I look from him to Spence and back again. Speechless. Helpless. Why can't I remember?

"I saw it," Spence says. "Her hands were around your neck. They were pressing right—"

"You were sitting all the way in the back, so maybe—"

"I know what I fucking saw! Her fingers were like this."

Spence steps toward me and seizes me by the neck. There's no tension in his fingers, until I try to step away. Instead of letting go, he holds firm. As if I'm an inanimate object, some fucking stage prop that exists only to help him make his point to Malcolm.

"Spence." I've found my voice again, but it sounds low, dangerous. Like it belongs to someone else. "Let go."

Spence releases my neck and steps back, hands up in surrender. Malcolm moves between us and puts his hand on my shoulder.

"Are you all right?" he asks.

I nod. "I'm fine. He didn't hurt me."

"Kira," Spence says. "You know I would never—"

"Look," Malcolm says, turning back to Spence. "I'm the victim, right?"

Spence doesn't answer. He's focused on me now, trying to get me to make eye contact with him, to wordlessly reassure him we're still on the same side.

"So I'm in control the whole time," Malcolm continues. "If what we're doing feels safe to me, then what's the problem?"

"It doesn't fucking matter how you 'feel,'" Spence says. "What I saw on that stage tonight was objectively dangerous."

"That's your opinion."

"Any decent fight director would tell you the same. Why did you even bother hiring me if you were just going to ignore every fucking thing I taught you?"

"We're using the choreography you taught us," Malcolm says. "But sometimes in the moment, things change. I know you're not an actor anymore, but surely you can understand that?"

Spence steps closer to Malcolm, looming over him. Malcolm doesn't look intimidated in the least by Spence's height or the murderous expression on his face. In fact, he looks almost amused, a strange little smile tugging at the corners of his lips.

"I want my name out of the program," Spence says.

"Spence, come on," I say. "Don't be ridiculous. We're opening tomorrow, you know all the programs have already been printed."

"Do whatever the fuck you want. But I'm not going to have my name on it."

"You'll take your fee, though, I'm sure." The first thing Malcolm's said with some bite behind it.

"I did my work," Spence says. "If you idiots choose to ignore it, that's on you."

Malcolm cocks his head, looking at Spence like he's really seeing him for the first time. "I can see why he likes you," he says.

Spence's hands curl into fists. "Don't you dare bring him into this."

"Jason's told you a lot about me." This isn't a question—he's certain of it. His voice is low and cold, his words slithering out like a snake moving through grass.

Spence's nostrils flare, his eyes pitch-black. "Don't even fucking say his name."

"Has he shown you his scar?" Malcolm asks. "I don't know why he insists on covering it up. I think it might be the most interesting thing about him."

That does it. But it doesn't matter what he said, anything out of Malcolm's mouth would have been enough to set Spence off at this point. He was waiting for an excuse.

Spence advances on Malcolm and shoves him hard—the heels of his hands smashing into Malcolm's collarbone, exactly the way he told us not to do in the show.

Malcolm rocks back on his heels but maintains his balance. He's keeping his hands behind his back, the fingers of one circling the wrist of the other. Even when Spence grabs him by the shoulders, he makes no move to defend himself. If Spence wants to turn this into a fight, he's going to have to throw the first punch.

"For fuck's sake, you two." I step between them and try to press them apart, one hand on Spence's shirt, the other on Malcolm's bare sternum. Bryn keeps her back against the wall, watching us nervously, twisting the end of her braid.

The stubborn bastards won't budge, so I start prying at Spence's fingers, still clamped around Malcolm's shoulder. Finally, Spence releases his grip, throwing his hands back in disgust.

And smacking right into my eye socket.

The impact sends me reeling to the floor. I catch myself on the heels of my hands, and pain shoots up from my wrists to my shoulders, but it's nothing compared to the punishing throb of my eye.

"Fuck!" Spence says, somewhere above me. "Jesus fucking Christ, Kira, are you okay?"

I keep my gaze trained on the floor. Blinking and blinking, until the spots in my vision mix with the tears welling in my eyes.

Spence crouches down beside me, putting his arm around my shoulder. "Kira, are you okay? Let me see."

He tries to tilt my face up toward the light so he can get a look at my eye. I raise my arm, pushing him away, shielding myself.

"Kira, I'm so sorry, it was an accident, I—"

Spence reaches for me again. This time it's Malcolm's voice that stops him.

"She doesn't want you to touch her."

Now Malcolm kneels beside me. He threads his arm around my waist.

"Isn't that right, Kira," he says. The sentence should be a question, but there's no upward lilt at the end.

I know Spence didn't mean to hit me. But all I hear is David's voice, repeating the same pointless words.

I'm so sorry, it was an accident . . . Kira, baby, please forgive me, please.

"We should get some ice on that eye," Spence says. He's speaking to me only, acting like Malcolm isn't even here. "Let's go home and—"

"No."

I look up at him now. My eye is already swelling, I can feel it. The pressure.

"I don't want to go home with you."

Spence looks stricken, almost panicked. "Where the hell else would you—"

"You can stay with me," Malcolm says. He stands up and brushes off his pants, then holds a hand out to help me up. "Stay with me tonight."

I stare at his outstretched fingers. My vision is starting to clear, and so is my memory. I'm recalling snippets of the show now, like Spence somehow knocked them loose from wherever they were locked away in my mind.

Malcolm was gentle with me tonight. He held me against the door with feather-light pressure. He was there for me every moment—listening intently, like he was hearing everything I said for the first time. We were good together. Better than I could have hoped for, could even have imagined. *Brilliant*, like he said. While we were onstage, I felt like we'd known each other forever, and like I wanted to keep doing this with him for at least that long.

I know which coffee cup is Spence's favorite and the sound he makes when he finishes masturbating in the shower, but we don't share anything real, anything significant. We never have. He doesn't understand how important this show is to me, how much I want to be the actress Malcolm believes I can be. The actress I was tonight.

I take Malcolm's hand and let him pull me to my feet.

66

JOANNA

I CAN'T REMEMBER THE LAST TIME I HAD THIS MUCH FUN. THE performers onstage seem as though they're enjoying themselves even more than the audience. They're so energetic they practically bounce off the walls, dropping characters and picking up new ones like they're juggling balls in the air. I can see why Rob loves this, why he brought me here. It's the opposite of what we do at Indifferent Honest: casual, playful, *free*.

After the show is over, Rob offers me his hand to help me out of my seat. When we reach the street, our fingers stay intertwined. I'd forgotten how good this could feel. His hand nearly enveloping mine, soothing and electric at the same time.

He says he'll walk me to the train, but instead of turning toward the station, we keep going straight, heading down Foster Avenue toward the lakefront. I don't know where Rob lives. It could be near here, or miles away.

We cross into the park, streetlamps winking off the mirror shards in the mosaic decorating the Lake Shore Drive underpass. We're talking about the play that closed out the performance—a sardonic exchange between two rival writers in a coffee shop—and Rob laughs, even louder than he did during the actual show. No reason to hold back now.

I love the sound of his laugh. My own is almost always silent, my shoulders shaking, lips pressed together. Keeping my amusement safely contained. And Mal—well, he has a different laugh for every occasion, and none of them mean he's amused.

On the concrete path by the water, it's freezing, the wind much bolder without any buildings around to block it. Points of light line up over the black horizon: airplanes, not constellations. Late-night flights coming in to land at O'Hare. It's been at least an hour since I've thought about *Temper*, but it starts to bleed into my mind again.

The newspapers have probably been printed by now. My confessions in black and white, indelible. Rob told me they were running it on the front page—his first-ever front-page feature. A milestone in his career, and possibly the end of mine.

I don't know what scares me more: the possibility Mal might be furious with me, or that he won't care at all, about any of it. My vanishing act tonight, or my months of subterfuge, or the fact that I told all my secrets to a stranger instead of to him.

Rob and I are the only people in the park. It feels like we're the only people on the planet. We sit down on a bench facing the lake, and Rob lays his arm across the back. He's not touching me, but I want him to, so I slide closer, notching my shoulder under his. We've gone silent now, almost reverent, like we're in a cathedral.

We sit like that for a long time, listening to the white noise of the waves and our own breathing. Then, before I even realize I've decided to speak, I hear myself, voice just loud enough to carry over the wind. Confessing one more secret.

"I don't want to go home."

Rob cinches his arm tighter around me. His lips move against my hair when he speaks.

"So don't."

67

KIRA

ALL THE LIGHTS IN MALCOLM'S APARTMENT ARE OFF, AND he leaves them that way. I can make out the shadow-draped shapes of the furniture, but no other details, as he leads me back to his bedroom. He took my hand when we left the theater, and he hasn't let go of it since.

There's no overhead light fixture in the bedroom, only a lamp on the bedside table, and another standing in the corner. Malcolm switches on the one by the bed, creating a small spotlight in the darkness. I remove my coat, and he takes it from me and hangs it up in the closet, along with his own.

His bedroom is blank and clean, as stark as the dark clothes he wears. No artwork on the walls, no books on the bedside table, no shoes or clothing or anything else cluttering the floor. It looks like an undressed set.

There doesn't seem to be a mirror anywhere either, which is a relief. So far I've been able to avoid seeing the full extent of the damage Spence did to my eye. I turned off my phone so I wouldn't have to look at his steady stream of apology texts, either.

Malcolm turns and stares at me, examining my face. He brushes his fingers near my eye socket—not touching, but close enough.

"I'll go get some ice," he says.

I'm struck with a sense of déjà vu, but it takes me a second to figure out why: this is one of Trent's lines in *Temper*. After Mara starts bleeding and tells him she's having a miscarriage, he goes offstage and returns with a bucket of ice cubes—the only thing he can think to do to help her.

No hotel ice bucket here, so Malcolm returns with a plastic bag full of ice instead. He seals off the top of the bag and sits down on the bed.

"Come here."

Another one of Trent's lines—though it's innocuous enough, something people say every day. It's never occurred to me before, but the first thing he ever said to me is also a line in the play.

You're bleeding.

I sit down next to him on the bed. He motions for me to lean back against the wall—there's no headboard, just flat gray paint—then presses the bag against my eye. He's near enough to me now I can feel his breath on my cheek.

"I'm so sorry about this," he says.

I take the ice out of his hand and hold it in place myself. "Yeah, well, you're not the one who hit me."

"You know," he says, settling back beside me with his shoulders against the wall, "when Joanna hired him to do our fights, I recognized him—from an audition a few years ago. He's a much better fight choreographer than he is an actor."

Spence never told me he auditioned for Indifferent Honest. I'm guessing it didn't go well, or he definitely would have bragged about it after.

But Malcolm's right about his acting abilities. I could never admit this to Spence, but there were times when I hated performing with him. He tended to be showy, always trying to make himself the center of attention even if he was playing a minor character. He never seemed genuine. The complete opposite of Malcolm.

I shift the bag against my eye. The ice is already starting to melt, rivulets of cold water tracing over my palm and running under my sleeve. "Was I really . . ."

"What?" he asks.

"Brilliant. In the show tonight."

He pauses, lips pursed—the same expression he had right before my audition. I don't know what he's about to say, but it's definitely not *yes, of course you were*. I hate myself for how much I wanted to hear that response. It's a gnawing hunger, this need for his approval. Tearing open new spaces inside me only he can fill.

"You were the best you've ever been," he says finally. "But you were also . . . far away somehow. I didn't feel like you were fully there, in the moment with me. Do you know what I mean?"

I do know. I still don't entirely understand what went on in my mind during that performance, but I know I retreated—into myself, away from the audience, and from Malcolm, too. I wasn't present, not the way he is, onstage and also right now in this bed, his body curved toward mine. He'd hardly have to move to put his hands on me.

"You were so close tonight, Kira," he says. "But you're still holding something back."

We've kissed each other countless times now, touched each other almost everywhere, demolished so many of the boundaries between us. What's one more?

It would be the easiest thing in the world, natural as breathing. But letting Malcolm inside my body wouldn't really be letting him in. I'd still be holding back, trying to appease him with an easy answer, staying safe behind the walls I've built, when what I need to do is raze them to the ground.

I set the ice down on the bedside table. I turn back to Malcolm, meet his eyes, lace my fingers through his again. And then I start talking.

I tell him about David, the parts I left out before—the school play, the kiss in the locker room, the first time we fucked. Our months of sneaking around, our plan to run away together. How quickly things soured between us, the weeks of insinuations and accusations and arguments.

Malcolm listens, silent, staring into my eyes. The way he's holding my gaze now feels like a comforting embrace rather than a challenge. A safe space, a place I want to stay.

So I tell him the part I haven't told anyone. Not Spence, not Rob, not my family. I think finally letting it out will be difficult, but the words flow from me like an exhalation of breath.

Things were so bad between David and me by closing night of *The Crucible*, when he told me he wanted to come, I lied and told him it was sold out. He showed up to the cast party afterward anyway—already drunk, and there was an open bar at the event. Instead of being cruel to me, though, he all of a sudden started acting clingy, overly affectionate. Which was even worse. He kept at least one hand on me at all times, on the small of my back or around my shoulders, so everyone would know we were together, that I belonged to him.

I put up with it until the moment he planted a sloppy kiss on my neck and reached under my skirt to grab a handful of my ass. Then I told him to stop, and when he didn't, I pushed him away.

David didn't like that at all. "What?" he slurred. "I'm not allowed to touch my own girlfriend now?"

Finally I fled him entirely, slipping outside into the sultry night air. There was a man standing off to the side of the entrance, smoking. I'd seen him in the audience, and then backstage afterward, talking to the actor who played John Proctor.

He introduced himself as a "filmmaker," which probably meant he had six-figure art-school debt and a couple of shitty short films under his belt. He was wearing glasses with blue-tinted lenses, even though it was dark outside, and a scarf wrapped around his neck in a way that was supposed to look careless. He stared at my tits while talking to me and didn't even try to hide it.

He asked me if I smoked. I didn't, but I said yes and accepted a cigarette from him. David hated smoking, and that night I would have done just about anything to spite him.

Which is how I ended up back at our apartment with the filmmaker. It was so easy. All I had to say was, *I live a couple of blocks from here*, and he was practically erect. We started making out on our way up the stairs, and I looped that ridiculous scarf around my fist and imagined pulling it tight enough to turn his face blue. He was so eager, I was afraid he'd finish before David came home and caught us.

But David walked in just in time. He flipped out, of course—and the filmmaker ran out of our apartment with his pants still unzipped, leaving me to fend for myself. Usually when David and I fought, I shouted right back at him, but that final time, I stayed still and silent, pretended my skin was made of armor, able to deflect every insult he threw at me. He'd been calling me a whore in so many words all summer, and now I'd proven it was true. What else was there to say?

My silence only infuriated him more. He started shaking me, screaming in my face. *Say something, say something, Goddammit, Kira!*

I don't think he meant to push me as hard as he did. He was so drunk, his balance was off, and he lost his bruising grip on my shoulders and flung me down instead. When I hit the floor, relief shot through me along with the pain. Finally, he'd made the toxicity between us tangible, something I could feel in my body. But the blood between my legs a few hours later—that felt like salvation.

"I suppose I should thank him," I tell Malcolm. "If he hadn't shoved me like that, I might not have miscarried. And then I would've had to spend the last of my savings on an abortion, instead of on a bus ticket to get myself the fuck away from him."

"Don't do that," Malcolm says. The first thing he's said, since I started talking about David.

"Do what?" I ask.

"Make light of what happened. Pretend you don't care."

He reaches toward my face again. This time he touches me, pressing gently into my temple, then running his thumb over the curve of my brow. Pain pulses in my eye.

"He hurt you," he says. "You're allowed to be angry."

I'm not sure whether he's talking about David or Spence. It all feels the same to me now.

Malcolm's hand moves down to cradle my chin, tilting my face toward his. The same way he did the night I slapped him, but the gesture is tender now, more intimate than any kiss.

Look at me. I'm your mirror.

"That doesn't make you a victim," he says.

If he kisses me now, I'll let him. It takes all my remaining will-power to keep myself from doing it first, breaking through the only boundary we have left.

But we hold still, until he turns away to switch off the lamp. We can still see each other by the pale shine slipping through the mini-blind slats, like we're caught in the moment between when the stage lights start to dim and when they fade to full black.

Malcolm loops his arms around my shoulders and pulls me down beside him on the bed. I lay my cheek against his chest, and our breathing starts to sync again. Our pulses, too, his heartbeat keeping time with the throbbing of my swollen eye.

It must be after midnight by now. In just a few short hours, we'll be onstage together again, and I'm not going to hold anything back. I really will be brilliant.

68

JOANNA

I WAKE UP TO THE SMELL OF COFFEE AND SOMETHING ELSE. Spicy cologne. The scent is threaded through the fibers of the blanket around my shoulders.

Rob.

I'm on his sofa. Alone. Sunlight streaming through the windows. Not the watery light of morning, but the harsh glare of the afternoon sun. Rob's apartment building is right next to the lakeshore, set back on a quiet cul-de-sac. The sidewalk in front was dusted with drifted sand; it crunched under my feet as we approached the front door late last night. No, early this morning.

We huddled so close to each other on the park bench, but once I accepted his offer to spend the night, he didn't touch me again. Not even a brush of my lower back as he ushered me inside his building and up the shadow-swathed staircase.

I wanted to kiss him, there by the lake. I thought about it again with every step we took closer to his apartment. Then in the stairwell I let my imagination go further, pictured myself scaling his body like a tree, wrapping my legs around his waist, pushing my fingers through his hair. The sounds he would make against my mouth in the dark.

He continued to play the gentleman, even after we were inside. He told me I could have the bed, and he would sleep on the sofa. He gave me a T-shirt to sleep in—heathered gray cotton, soft and faded, so large on me it hung nearly to my knees. It looked old; I wondered if Kira had ever worn it when they were together. It would look very different on her, the width of her hips and the weight of her breasts straining against the fabric, hiking up the hem.

He shut the door between us so I could change, and he didn't open it again. I tried to sleep. But I can never sleep the night before a show opens; with the newspaper story looming, too, I was sure it was a hopeless endeavor. I stared at the ceiling for a while, then opened the door and peered around the edge.

Rob was stretched out on the sofa, facing the cushions. He didn't quite fit; one foot dangled off the side. He wasn't snoring, but I could hear the soft, steady hush of his breathing.

I could have said something, tried to wake him up. But we'd spent all night talking, and I was done with words. I crawled over the arm of the sofa and fit myself into the narrow space between his body and the cushions.

He didn't wake up until I pressed my lips to the hollow of his throat. He swallowed once, against my mouth, and then tilted his face down so we were a breath away from kissing. His hands were in my hair, and I could feel him getting hard already, pressing against my stomach. But he let me be the one to decide what would happen next.

After I kissed him, once it was clear I wanted to do more than that, he tried to pull the T-shirt off over my head. I tugged it back down. He accepted this, wordlessly, and stopped trying to undress me, even as I peeled his clothes off and let them fall to the floor beside the sofa.

They're not there anymore. He must have picked them up. Maybe at the same time he laid the blanket over my shoulders.

Now, in the daylight, I take in the details I couldn't see last night. Across from the sofa, there's a bricked-over fireplace with built-in shelves on either side. The shelves are packed full of books, leather-bound antiques mixed in with mass market paperbacks. The spines on all of them are striated; he's actually read them. The blanket around my shoulders looks handmade, stretched and soft.

Everything seems carefully chosen and well cared for. Curated. A real home, rather than the glorified storage space where Mal and I live, surrounded by old set pieces and other reminders of fictional worlds we've created together while I was ignoring my real life.

I could leave. Before Rob comes back in. I could take off the shirt he gave me, pull on my own clothes, and slip out the door. Pretend this never happened. He might call, but surely if I ignored him he'd get the message. He's tenacious when it comes to his job, but he doesn't seem like the type to press his luck after personal rejection. He would just move on with his life. Forget about me.

I roll over on the sofa, tugging the blanket higher so it covers my mouth, my nose. Trying to disappear. But when I glance over at the old steamer trunk he uses as a coffee table, I see my own face staring back at me.

Today's *Tribune*. My picture is on the front page, above the fold.

69

KIRA

I WAKE UP ALONE IN THE MIDDLE OF A BROAD GRAY BED. The room looks almost like the *Temper* set—the dark walls, a small desk in the corner. For a moment I'm disoriented.

Then I hear the shower running, and I remember: I'm in Malcolm Mercer's apartment. In his bed, in fact. And today is the day.

Today we open.

Lying down, my eye didn't hurt much, but sitting up makes it throb again. Standing is even worse. The pain radiates out to my temples, down the line of my jaw.

I wander out of the bedroom and into the living area—my first look at the loft during daylight hours. The rest of the space isn't as spare and monochromatic as Malcolm's room, but it doesn't quite look lived-in either. All the furniture seems mismatched, the ornate red velvet chair out of place next to the brass and glass coffee table, the busy Persian rug clashing with the sleek modern sofa (which I swear looks just like the one from Indifferent Honest's production of *The Real Thing*).

As haphazard as the decor is, it's hard to believe this is the same space where they put on that scrappy, spectacular production of

Hamlet. Now the hardwood floors are polished and sealed, the walls are painted uniform white, and nothing looks likely to electrocute you or give you tetanus.

Fine by me, since the sun streaming through the slanted skylights in the ceiling is painful enough. It must be well past noon by now. The brightness sinks into the socket of my injured eye like fangs.

There's another door, on the opposite side of the living room, which I assume leads to Joanna's bedroom. It's shut, so she could be inside, asleep or awake. Aware I'm here in her home or not.

Low on the wall next to the doorframe, there's one spot that hasn't been painted, that's still the crumbling, dingy plaster I remember. And there's something written on it. I crouch down to take a look.

Names, scrawled in black pen. Joanna's is there, along with Malcolm's signature—two large *M*s with slashes after them.

Slightly below Malcolm's name is Jason Grady's. His handwriting is neat, almost pretty, each letter clearly and carefully formed. He wrote a quote, too, one of Hamlet's lines: *To be honest, as this world goes, is to be one man pick'd out of ten thousand.*

"That's from *Hamlet.*" Malcolm's voice comes from somewhere behind me.

I freeze, like he's caught me at something, even though I'm not doing anything wrong. When I stand up and turn to face him, I do it too fast, and my head reels.

He's just come out of the bathroom, dabbing the last remnants of shaving cream off his jaw and neck with a white hand towel. He's wearing jeans, but no shirt.

"Closing night," he says. "We all wrote our names there. Jo still won't let me paint over it. She's more sentimental than I am, I suppose. How did you sleep?"

"Fine. Thanks."

Somehow it feels like we had a one-night stand, even though sleeping was all we did—and fully clothed, on top of the covers, at that.

"Is she—" I start to ask, my eyes darting toward the closed door.

Malcolm shakes his head. "She didn't come home last night. I would have heard her."

I don't know Joanna as well as he does, obviously, but based on what I do know, this seems completely out of character for her. Malcolm doesn't sound the least bit concerned, though.

"How's your eye?" he asks.

"Not too bad," I lie. If it feels this bad, I know it must look even worse. I have no idea what I'm going to do for the performance. Mara and Trent's marriage is fucked up, to be sure, but it changes the whole dynamic if I come out onstage with a black eye.

"Thanks for letting me crash," I tell Malcolm. "But I should head home, get a change of clothes at least. I'll see you later at the—"

"I'll come with you." He's wiping his hands off on the towel, already heading into his bedroom.

"That's okay," I call after him.

He comes back out, wearing a black sweater now. He's carrying our coats, too, slung over his arm.

"I don't mind," he says, handing me my coat. "You shouldn't have to face him alone. We'll go to your place, and then we'll get something to eat before the show."

Spence might not even be there. Maybe he spent the night at Jason's. Besides, what happened last night—it *was* an accident. Spence would never hurt me, not intentionally.

"I know he overreacted," I say. "But if I really was pressing down on your throat, or—I mean, he's right. I could have hurt you."

Malcolm shrugs on his own jacket—the same gray canvas one he wore the day he came to the school. "But you didn't."

"Still."

"Look," he says. "If you're really that concerned about hurting me, we can come up with a signal or something."

"What, like a safe word?"

Despite my not-insignificant number of sexual partners, I don't have any experience with safe words or the sex acts that require them. Spence and I are too lazy for anything more involved than fuzzy handcuffs, and Rob's idea of adventurous sex was doing it in the shower.

"Exactly like a safe word," he says. "Except I won't say it out loud. How about this: during the stranglehold, if I want you to stop, I'll pinch your wrist."

He demonstrates, squeezing the skin over my wrist bone between his thumb and forefinger. It stings—enough to distract from the painful pulsating of my eye, so it should get my attention onstage. Unless I space out the way I did last night.

Malcolm lets go of my wrist but keeps ahold of my hand, running his fingertips over the ridges of my knuckles. "We won't need it," he says. "I trust you."

He shouldn't. I'm not even sure I trust myself.

70

JOANNA

I LOOK VERY SERIOUS IN THE PICTURE THEY CHOSE—A portrait I had taken for our season announcement two years ago. My arms are crossed over my chest, and I'm looking straight into the camera, not even a hint of a smile on my face.

Maybe Mal hasn't seen it yet. I briefly entertain a fantasy of buying every copy of the *Chicago Tribune* and making a bonfire. But the paper has been out for hours, and the story is online now, too. Probably being passed around the email accounts of everyone in the theater community, posted on social media. Liked and commented on, corroborated and debated.

Rob comes in carrying a tray with two coffee mugs and a French press. He's dressed now, in different clothes than he was wearing last night, though I don't think he's showered based on the state of his hair, which sticks out from the sides of his head like fanned-out fingers. I want to smooth it down, tuck the strands behind those absurd, wonderful ears of his.

"Hey." He sets the tray down on the trunk, pinning one corner of the newspaper.

I tug the blanket around my shoulders. "Hey."

If he's used to women like Kira, I'm sure I was a disappointment. In the heat of the moment, keeping my clothes on felt like armor, a way of holding him at arm's length even while he was inside me. But in the cold reality of day, it seems hopelessly childish. Like I was a teenager making out in my mother's basement, afraid of getting caught, rather than an adult woman enjoying no-strings-attached consensual sex. I'm too accustomed to my relationship with Mal, where there's no sex, but strings attached to everything.

Rob starts to pour coffee from the French press, then stops with an inch of space left in the mug. "Sorry, I should have asked: Did you want sugar or cream?"

"No, I prefer it black. Thank you."

He fills the mug the rest of the way. As he hands it to me, he nods toward the newspaper. "Did you read it yet?"

I shake my head, dragging my lower lip across the rim of the mug.

"You don't have to," he says. "Not if you don't want to. I won't be offended. I mean, you already know what it says."

"How much did you use?" I ask.

"Everything."

When we sat down together at the Heartland, I asked why he wasn't recording the interview. I hated the idea of him sitting in his office, listening to my voice over and over as he composed his story, but I hated the idea of him misquoting me even more.

"I prefer the old-fashioned way," he told me. "I find that if I use the recorder, people talk to it instead of to me. I just want to have a conversation."

He had a whole folder of notes, though—research he'd done on me. He even found copies of some of my plays from college and the few years after, when I was still writing. That's part of how he guessed I was the real author of *Temper*. The writing style, the word choice.

Rob sits down next to me and goes to put his hand on my bare knee, but stops before actually touching me, his palm hovering a few inches above my skin. An absurd courtesy, considering. His brown eyes search me and not for weaknesses.

"I know how hard it was for you," Rob says. "Telling me . . . all of that. So I understand if you'd rather—"

"I want to read it."

I have to, so I'll know just how much damage I need to control. I remember his questions, and I remember the substance of what I said in response, but I can't recall my exact words. The interview felt the way writing sometimes does, when it's going well: a dam let loose, words spilling out like water, drowning my cautious, conscious mind so I can confess what I never could otherwise.

He starts to stand up. "I can leave you alone if you—"

"No." I catch his hand in mine, interlacing our fingers. "Stay."

Rob squeezes my hand as he sits back down beside me. His thigh presses alongside mine, like it did when we were sitting on the park bench.

I pick up the newspaper and start to read.

71

KIRA

THE TEMPERATURE DROPPED OVERNIGHT, COLD ENOUGH TO cover the city in a fine layer of frost. The air seems to crackle, and the wind cuts right through my thin coat.

The closer we get to the apartment, the more anxious I feel, and by the time we're climbing the stairs to the front door, my pulse pounds so hard Malcolm must be able to hear it.

I turn my key in the lock, but Malcolm reaches around me to open the door. He enters the apartment first—like he owns the place, even though he's never been here before.

Spence and Jason are sitting on the sofa. They both stand at the sound of the door. Like me, Spence is dressed in his clothes from last night—wrinkled now, his shirt untucked. His bloodshot eyes match the red fabric.

Jason's dog is here, too. It lets out one sharp bark and bounds over to the door to greet us. I ignore it, but Malcolm smiles and crouches down to scratch between its ears.

"Lafayette." Jason's voice is tight with panic. He snaps his fingers, but the dog doesn't respond. It's sniffing Malcolm's sleeve now, leaving little smudges of drool.

"Kira, I—" Spence starts. Then he stops, staring at me. "Jesus. Your eye."

I've still managed to avoid looking at it. It was tough, on the train—all those windows—but I kept my eyes focused on the floor or on Malcolm.

Spence approaches, reaching toward me. I edge my face away from him, turning so the shadows in the entryway hide the fucked-up side of my face.

"I'm so fucking sorry, Kira."

"You said that already."

"I'll say it as many times as it takes. You know I would never hurt you on purpose."

He's showing off, even now, playing his pain and remorse to the hilt. It's more for Jason's benefit than for mine. When he went after Malcolm last night, that was more for Jason's benefit, too.

I brush past him, heading in the direction of my bedroom. Malcolm stands up and follows me, his hand on the small of my back.

"Kira, please," Spence calls after us. "Just talk to me!"

What disagreements we've had over the years, we've never resolved with words. No, Spence and I have only ever been able to work out our differences in bed, and that's not an option this time.

The way Jason looked at Malcolm, as if he thought Malcolm might pick up his stupid little dog and rip its throat out with his teeth. Ridiculous. Jason's the one who staged a dramatic scene that nearly cost him his life because he couldn't handle being dumped.

Spence comes after us, striding down the hall. As soon as Malcolm and I are inside my room, I slam the door and turn the lock.

"Kira." Spence is right outside the room, his feet casting shadows under the door.

I can't avoid looking at my eye any longer. The mirror on top of my vanity faces the door, and the dusty glass seems to magnify every detail: the purple arc sweeping down the bridge of my nose to my cheekbone, the jaundiced haze around the edges.

"Kira," Spence says again. "Please."

The biggest opening night of my career, and I look like I've been in a fistfight.

Thanks to him.

Spence smacks the doorframe. I tense, my back teeth clacking together.

"Kira, for fuck's sake!"

"Fuck off, Spence!"

I didn't mean to scream so loud. But once the words erupt from my mouth, rage rushes up behind them. Malcolm is still touching the small of my back. He slides his fingers up my spine, and I almost turn on him, tell him to take his fucking hands off me. But as he presses between my shoulder blades, my breathing begins to steady again.

"What do you need?" he asks.

I can't look at him. I want to punch the wall. I want to punch Spence. I definitely want to punch Jason Grady.

I strip down and change into a clean sweater and jeans, not even pretending at modesty in front of Malcolm anymore. Just in case, I grab another change of clothes off my closet floor and sweep some of the cosmetics strewn across the vanity into the mouth of my bag. I feel like I'm running away from home.

By the time Malcolm and I leave my bedroom, Spence has abandoned his post outside. He and Jason are at the other end of the hall now. Jason has his head in his hands, and Spence is holding onto the backs of his arms, leaning in so close his hair brushes Jason's forehead.

When Jason sees us, he scoops his dog off the floor and ducks into Spence's bedroom. Spence stays where he is. Between us and the exit.

"Kira, come on," he says. "I said I was sorry. Please don't leave like this."

I stop, white-knuckling the strap of my bag. "Move, Spence."

He doesn't. In fact, he turns so his broad shoulders take up even more of the hallway. Malcolm isn't touching me anymore, but he stays close, hovering a step behind me.

"Not until you talk to me," Spence says.

"She doesn't want to talk to you," Malcolm says. My jaw tightens—how dare he speak for me—but I can't deny that it makes me feel bolder, having him at my back. "I'm not sure how much clearer she can be. So how about you—"

"How about you shut the fuck up?" Spence is seething again, that black look in his eyes, fingers curling into fists. "This is between me and Kira."

"Well, when you gave my leading lady a black eye right before opening night, I'd say it became my business, wouldn't you?"

Malcolm's tone is calm and conversational, like he can't sense the tension in the room at all. He's enjoying this, the way Spence's face is morphing from desperation to bewilderment and back again. The truth is, so am I.

"She's not *your* anything, you piece of shit," Spence snarls. "Now why don't you get the fuck out of my apartment before I give you a black eye to match?"

"It's my apartment, too."

At least it is for now. If Spence and I don't patch things up, I know I'll be the one to move out. There's no way I could afford this place on my own.

We've lived together for more than a decade. Longer than a lot of marriages—and happier, too, until now.

"If Malcolm being here upsets you so much," I say, "why don't *you* go?"

"I'm not leaving you alone with this—"

"Oh, now you want to protect me? I know what I'm doing."

"Do you, Kira?" Spence reaches for me, trying to grip my shoulders. "Are you sure?"

"Get your hands off me."

The venom in my voice seems to work on him like a slap across the mouth. He looks stunned and stung, and his hands drop to his sides.

But he's still blocking my way to the door. I'm considering trying to battering-ram my way past, when Jason bursts out of the bedroom, rushing into the narrow space separating Spence from me and Malcolm. He's trembling, his eyes brimming with held-back tears.

And he's brandishing one of the daggers from Spence's rack of stage weaponry, the blade pointed right at Malcolm's chest.

72

JOANNA

THE FURTHER I READ, THE MORE ROB FIDGETS. HIS HEEL TAPPING against the floor, his fingers drumming on his knee. He's nervous, about my reaction to the story.

He should be nervous.

Because even though my face is front and center, even though my name is emblazoned across the top of the page, his story isn't about me.

In fact, it's not an interview at all. It's an exposé. Painstakingly researched. It must have taken him months to put together. Longer.

When he said he used everything, he meant it. Rob talked to Mal's high school girlfriend. His stage movement professor from Carnegie Mellon. The artistic director of the Shakespeare company he toured with after dropping out of college. Dozens of Indifferent Honest costars and colleagues, including the actress who worked with him on several shows before having a nervous breakdown and quitting the theater entirely. She lives in Milwaukee now, and she's married with twin boys and a different last name, but Rob managed to track her down.

He didn't interview Mal's parents, but he found out their names, their professions, where they lived. All the places Mal lived before he settled in Chicago. Things even I didn't know about him, like the fact that he spent his first year in the city shacked up with an acting teacher more than twice his age. Things I didn't want to know.

When I reach the end of the article, I go back to the start and read it again. To let it all sink in, and to make Rob suffer in silence a little longer.

There are quotes from Jason Grady, too. I recognize his comments, even though he chose to remain anonymous. That heartbreak-tinged spite in his words. I talked about him in my interview, too, but I didn't use his name. That night we ran into him at the bar, I wonder if he'd already spilled his guts to Rob or if that's what drove him to it. Seeing me and Mal. That infuriating smile on Mal's face when he left with Kira.

When I finally lower the paper and turn to Rob, he looks apprehensive. But not guilty. Not sorry.

To think I trusted him. I should have known better. A dozen years with Mal ought to have taught me at least that much.

He's waiting for me to say something. To pass judgment. I pick up my coffee cup and take a sip. It's cold now. Rob's mug still sits on the tray, untouched.

"Well?" he says finally. "I understand if you—"

"All those people you interviewed from Indifferent Honest."

Rob swallows. "Yes?"

"What did they say about me?"

He shifts on the sofa. His thigh isn't touching mine anymore.

"Surely they must have said something." Jason, at least—he would never miss a chance to savage me, to make sure the whole world knew about my complicity in Mal's manipulations.

"The story is about Malcolm," Rob says.

"Yes, I can see that." I've been twisting the edge of the newspaper; it tears a little, a jagged gash cutting through the headline.

"The things he's done, they're not your fault." Rob lays his hand on my knee, the newspaper flat between his palm and my skin. "You couldn't have known. You were—"

I stand. The paper slides off my lap and onto the floor. Rob's hand falls away, too.

I don't know what word he was about to use. Some synonym for *innocent*, I assume. I'm a lot of things, but that's not one of them.

"I thought you would be . . ." Rob trails off, his jaw working. He passes his fingers through his hair, making it stick out at even wilder angles, casting spiky shadows on the wall behind him. "I mean, is that what you wanted? For him to take you down with him?"

I don't respond. I'm trembling now, my fingers pressed into fists.

Rob stands, too, and moves toward me. "You don't deserve that, Joanna. You're nothing like him."

He has no idea. Who I am. What I deserve.

I stare up at him. My hands may be shaking, but my gaze is steady. "I'm done talking about this."

Rob shuts his eyes for a second, breathing in. "Joanna, please, let's just—"

I seize the hem of the T-shirt. Pull it off over my head, toss it onto the floor. It lands on the newspaper, covering my printed face.

Rob gapes at me. At everything I didn't let him see last night. He's speechless, but I can see the hunger in his eyes. I plant my hands on my hips, nails digging into the soft flesh there. Steadying myself.

"I said I'm done talking."

73

KIRA

"GET OUT," JASON SAYS. EVEN THOUGH HE'S SHAKING, HE somehow keeps the hand holding the dagger steady, the point close enough to Malcolm now to slide between the weave of his sweater.

The dagger is only a stage weapon. The blade is dull. But it could still do plenty of damage. With enough force, almost anything can kill.

Strange he didn't take one of the swords, if he really means to hurt Malcolm. Spence even has one with a sharpened blade. He keeps it tucked away in a studded leather scabbard. Maybe he didn't tell Jason about that one. Maybe for good reason.

"Jason." Spence keeps his voice low, steady, like he's trying to soothe a frightened animal. "What do you think you're doing?"

"He won't leave. He shouldn't even be here." Jason tightens his grip on the handle of the dagger.

I'm afraid to make any sudden movements, but I can't help glancing over at Malcolm. He's the only one of us who isn't drawn taut like a bowstring. He's just standing there, hands in his pockets, looking almost relaxed, not at all concerned about the weapon leveled at his heart. He actually looks a little impressed, like he didn't think Jason had it in him.

A smile starts to creep across Malcolm's face. Daring Jason, egging him on, as if he wants him to do it, just so he can find out what it feels like when the blade sinks in.

It makes sense, in a way, the dagger. That's a weapon for when it's personal, when you want to look someone in the eye as you kill them. When you want to feel their blood spilling out over your hand before it flows to the floor.

Jason jabs the blade closer, tears streaming down his cheeks. *"Get out!"*

I flinch. Malcolm doesn't. He seems certain Jason won't hurt him. I wish I could be so sure.

"Jason." Spence switches to his stern teacher voice, the one he uses whenever fight rehearsals start to get out of hand. "Give it to me, now."

Jason's hand is tremoring along with the rest of his body now, but he doesn't lower the dagger until Spence grabs his wrist and twists it around behind his back to disarm him. The weapon clatters to the floor. Jason slumps against Spence, sobbing, and the way to the door is finally clear.

Malcolm moves ahead of me, stepping over the dagger. He opens the door, then stands aside so I can exit first. He starts to follow me, but on the threshold, he pauses and turns to smile at Jason again. A different sort of smile this time: friendly and warm and all the more chilling because of it.

"Good to see you again, Jay. You look well."

Jason sucks in a breath like he's been punched in the stomach.

I can see it in his eyes—he doesn't want to hurt Malcolm anymore. He's fighting the urge to follow him, to heel at his side like a dog. I think of Helena's lines in *A Midsummer Night's Dream*: "Use me but as your spaniel, spurn me, strike me, neglect me, lose me; only give me leave, unworthy as I am, to follow you." Spence's grip is the only thing keeping Jason from doing just that.

Jason might not want to admit it to himself, but he still loves Malcolm, on some level. Otherwise he wouldn't be able to hate him this much.

Spence has both of his arms wrapped around Jason now, restraining him and comforting him at the same time. Malcolm starts to close the door between us, but I hold it open, my palm flat against the peeling paint under the peephole.

Spence looks up at me. Jason goes limp, sagging to the floor, dead weight.

"I'll see you at the theater," Spence says. There are tears in his eyes now, too.

"Don't bother," I say. "Looks like he needs you again—and I sure as hell don't."

74

JOANNA

WE END UP IN THE SHOWER, INSTEAD OF HIS BED.

It's the first time I've tried to kiss Rob standing upright. He nearly has to bend double to fit his mouth to mine, to put his hands around my waist. To slide them lower.

I don't make it easy on him. I don't stand up on my toes, tilt my head back. I make him come to me.

The water sputtered cold at first, but now it's turned so hot it feels like needles pricking my skin. The pain helps, but it isn't enough. My mind keeps wandering. Returning to the story. To that actress, the one who had the nervous breakdown. I'd almost forgotten about her. Tried to, anyway. But now it's all rushing back. Amelia Wellington. Pretty girl. The auburn hair and luminous skin of a Pre-Raphaelite painting, and a perpetual stick up her ass. Just like with Kira, I could tell Mal wanted to fuck her from the first, but he waited. Unusual restraint, for him.

They always played couples. Sometimes happily married, sometimes tragically torn asunder. In the last show she did with us, their characters were supposed to be in a miserable, sexless relationship. So Mal ordered her to cease all sexual activity for the duration of the play. No masturbation, no sex with her boyfriend.

She was already tightly wound, but by the end of the run she was pulled so taut she was ready to snap. On closing night, she actually came onstage. I saw it, the little shudder, the swallowed gasp. Mal barely touched her. Nothing outside what the script called for, nothing that could be considered inappropriate. But in her sex-starved state it was more than enough.

I remember how red her cheeks burned while she was taking her bows. But then her skin was flushed all over when she and Mal showed up (an hour late) to the cast party, hand in hand.

I hated her. I hated her so much it could have burned a hole in my chest. I hated her, when I should have hated him.

Rob is kissing my neck now, but I barely feel it. I feel the shower spray more than his touch. Spilling over my breasts, sluicing between my legs.

I press down on his shoulders. Push him to his knees.

When he looks up at me, water streaming from his eyes, there's a fire there I haven't seen before. Maybe this is how he used to look at Kira. Like he wasn't sure if he wanted to screw her or scream at her.

I smooth his hair down, slicking it against his skull. Tracing the bone underneath.

"You were going to run the story today no matter what," I say. "Weren't you?"

He nods. A drop of water plummets off the tip of his knife-blade nose.

I can't look at him anymore. So I lean back against the steam-slick tile and pull him toward me.

75

KIRA

MALCOLM STILL INSISTED ON GETTING SOMETHING TO EAT before the show, but after the scene with Jason and Spence I wasn't hungry. So I watched him down a whole bowl of Furious Spoon while I pushed my ramen noodles around with chopsticks. When we arrive at the theater, Bryn is standing outside the front door, right under the red awning, pacing back and forth. Her jeans have slashes across the thigh, and the freezing air has pinched her exposed skin pink.

"Oh, thank God!" she says when she sees us.

"Where's Joanna?" Malcolm asks.

Bryn's eyes go wide. "You haven't seen it yet?"

"Seen what?"

"Oh my God."

"Bryn," I say. "Seen what?"

Bryn takes her phone out of her back pocket and pulls something up on the screen, then passes it to Malcolm. I lean close so I can see it too.

A picture of Joanna, on the *Chicago Tribune* website.

My first thought is that she's dead. But someone would have contacted Malcolm, surely. They probably list each other as emergency contacts, like Spence and I do.

When I look closer, though, I see it's not an obituary, it's a story. By Robert Kenmore.

Malcolm starts scrolling. I try to read the text, but he's going so fast I only catch a few words. Then he stops, lifting his thumb away from the screen.

> There is no L. S. Sedgwick. I'm the one who
> wrote *Temper.*

My mouth falls open. She wrote the play? Buttoned-up, all-business Joanna Cuyler wrote *this* play?

"Did you know about this?" I ask Malcolm.

He tries to control his face, but I can tell—he didn't know. He had no fucking idea. I can't see his real feelings, but I can see the work he's putting in to hiding them.

I take Bryn's phone out of his hand and skim through the rest of the article myself, picking Joanna's quotes out of the screed.

> Mal was never supportive of my artistic ambi-
> tions. He wants to be the star, the center of
> attention. The only real artist.

"She's coming tonight, right?" Bryn asks.

> He's provocative, but not in the way he thinks.
> He provokes other people to violence, cruelty,
> acts they would never consider without . . .

Malcolm is silent, his jaw working, his eyes unfocused.

> Yes, I think he does enjoy it.

Bryn isn't crying yet, but I can hear it building. "She has to come."

Why am I still working with him after all these
years? That's a good question.

Joanna is ballsier than I thought, going behind Malcolm's back
with the play, talking to Rob on the record, and who knows what
else. But it would take a whole other level of bravado to show up
tonight after dropping a bombshell like this.

I hand Bryn's phone back. "I don't think she's coming."

Bryn makes a sound halfway between a sob and a squeak. "But
she's supposed to open the house and hand out the programs, and I
don't even have the keys to the box office, and—"

Malcolm grabs her by the shoulders. She goes still.

"We don't need her," he says. It seems like he's talking to himself
more than to Bryn. His grip on her is so tight his knuckles blanch as
pale as her face. "We'll figure it out. Okay?"

There are tears welling in Bryn's eyes, but she nods.

"What time is it?" he asks.

Bryn looks at her phone. "Six twenty-two."

"Then we'd better get to work."

76

JOANNA

I DIDN'T WANT TO GO BACK TO MAL'S PLACE (ALREADY I'M thinking of it only as his; did I ever really consider it mine?), so I went to the Macy's on State Street and bought myself a new outfit to wear to opening night.

Rob came with me. Waited outside the dressing room, holding my purse. Like we're an actual couple. I wonder if we'll even see each other again after today.

When I see my reflection in the front window of Indifferent Honest, I hardly recognize myself. The outfit I picked out looks nothing like my normal clothing. It looks like something I imagine sophisticated debut playwright L. S. Sedgwick would wear: a black sheath dress with seams emphasizing my waist and the flare of my hips, designer pumps with heels that could puncture a lung. I even smell different, Rob's citrus shampoo and sandalwood soap lingering on my hair and skin.

I wonder if he can still taste me.

Rob and I are early enough the door is still locked, though the lights are on in the lobby. I take my keys out of my purse, but my hand stops halfway to the lock.

"You okay?" Rob asks.

My fingers tremble, rattling the keys. "I just—"

"Need a minute?"

I nod and drop my arm, clenching my fist around the keys to keep them still.

"No problem," Rob says. "We have time."

Not much time. An hour before curtain, half an hour until the house opens. Audience members could start arriving at any moment.

This morning, after we dried off and got dressed, Rob asked me whether I was still going to the show tonight. It never occurred to me not to. How could Indifferent Honest possibly open a play—*my* play—without me there to see it?

My phone buzzes in my purse. I take it out and glance at the screen, but I already know what I'll find. A text message from my mother, the same one she sends every opening night.

Good luck tonight. I love you.

When I was a teenager, when half my high school was mocking me for the play I wrote about my friend, my mother told me to just ignore them. She was full of bumper sticker–style platitudes on the situation. *Don't let them get to you. Stand up tall and walk right past them. Pretend they aren't even there.*

It never worked. I never stopped noticing their stares. I never stopped caring what they thought. Her approval wasn't enough for me. Not even close. I wanted what I couldn't have, what was just out of reach.

Rob touches my shoulder. The first time he's touched me since this morning in the shower, though we spent all day together.

"You're sure you want to do this?" he asks.

I answer him by turning my key in the lock and pushing open the door.

77

KIRA

WE MIGHT JUST MAKE IT. MALCOLM AND I SET OUR OWN PROPS, and Bryn's been bustling around taking care of the rest, giving him as wide a berth as she can in the close quarters of the theater. I keep catching her staring at him with a strange dread in her eyes.

Still digesting the newspaper story, I suppose. I pulled it up on my phone and read the rest while Malcolm was running a light and sound check with Austin. After reading through to the end, the fact that Joanna is the true author of *Temper* no longer seems so strange. None of the people Rob interviewed had anything nice to say about Malcolm, but Joanna's comments were absolutely scathing—a catalog of ruined careers, broken hearts, broken bones, curdled with years of pent-up rage. All the shadowy rumors about Malcolm Mercer dragged into the light.

Joanna didn't use his name, but I know it must have been Jason she was referring to with that story about the young man who nearly bled himself dry trying to impress them. Unless more than one actor has opened up a vein in the middle of her and Malcolm's apartment—not out of the question, I suppose. I know all too well what he can drive people to do.

But I still can't wait to take the stage with him tonight.

Malcolm comes down from the booth, taking the steps two at a time. Bryn's shoulders shrink up when she hears him coming. She's sitting in the front row, blotting out Spence's name in the programs with thick lines of Sharpie, the tips of her fingers tinged black like they're frostbitten.

"We don't have much time," he says. "So are you okay with skipping fight call?"

"Can we run the slap at least?"

The shove is simple, and we have our "safe word" for the strangling now. But I'm still concerned about the slap. One inch off, and I might make contact again—and make him bleed in front of a full house of patrons this time. Though, if they've read today's *Tribune*, they might just cheer me on. If even a quarter of what Rob reported is true, Malcolm's got much worse coming to him than a slap across the cheek.

"Sure," Malcolm says. "Take it from 'How do I even know it was mine?'"

Right as I'm rearing back for the slap, the lobby door swings open. I freeze, my hand still raised.

Joanna walks in. In that sexy dress, with her lips painted the color of fresh blood, it takes me a second to recognize her. But I recognize her companion right away: Rob, wearing a wary expression and the same drab sport coat he always trots out for opening nights. He keeps a step back from Joanna. Not like he's hiding behind her, more like he's serving as her bodyguard.

Bryn and I both stay frozen in place—my hand still raised in mid-air, the tip of her marker poised over the program page—watching Malcolm, waiting for his reaction. I don't even know if he recognizes Rob, but once he figures out who he is, I doubt he'll give him a warm welcome either.

Malcolm turns toward them, but he doesn't scream or seethe. Instead, his face splits into a wide grin.

"Well, what do you know?" he says. "The playwright is here."

78

JOANNA

"SO NICE OF YOU TO JOIN US THIS EVENING, MS. SEDGWICK."

Mal makes a sweeping gesture like he's announcing the arrival of royalty. He's dressed for the first scene, but the dark jeans and black shirt are so close to his typical offstage clothing, you'd have to know him as well as I do to tell it's a costume.

He approaches Rob, sticking out his hand. "And you must be Mr. Kenmore."

Rob doesn't take the bait. He's not even looking at Mal—he's staring past him, at Kira, as she rakes her hair off her face. Exposing a purple bruise around her eye.

Rob tenses like a dog with its hackles going up. "What happened to your eye?"

"Oh, just a little accident," Mal says. "Last night, after the invited dress—"

"I'm asking Kira."

Rob shoulders past Mal to reach her. He tries to brush her hair back again to get a better look, but she swats his hand away. There's a casual intimacy in both gestures that makes my stomach ache.

"Did he hit you?" Rob demands.

Kira scowls. "What the hell do you care?"

"Answer me, Kira." Rob's voice slips through his gritted teeth like a knife blade. He sounds like a different person than the man I've spent the last twenty-four hours with.

"It was Spence, actually," Kira says. Rob rocks back on his heels, confusion contorting his face. "You wanna try this white knight bullshit with him? Because I think he can take you."

Spencer hit her? It really must have been an accident, then.

Rob comes to stand beside me again, but he can't seem to tear his eyes away from Kira. Mal watches them, recalculating. I am, too. I knew they had a relationship, but I didn't have any idea Rob still had such strong feelings about her.

"You were with him last night?" Mal asks. Not bothering to look at Rob.

"Yes." In my perilous high heels, I'm still much shorter than Rob, but I'm almost the same height as Mal. It's a strange feeling, standing eye-to-eye with him. "I'm—"

I was going to say *I'm sorry*, out of politeness, out of habit. But I'm not sorry. Not for this.

"I should have told you," I say instead. I'm not sure that's true, either.

"Well, now you have." Mal's voice is so sharp I could lacerate myself on it. "You told me, and the rest of the city, all at once. How efficient of you."

"You never would have wanted to do *Temper* if I'd told you the truth. You would have found something wrong with it, something to criticize, some reason why—"

"How do you ever expect to be a real writer, Joanna? If you're so afraid of criticism you have to hide behind a fake persona to protect yourself from it."

My jaw tightens. I'm not letting him do this to me. Not again.

"I think what Joanna did is incredibly brave," Rob says. "She told the truth. That's more than someone like you could ever—"

Mal laughs. "People have been saying awful things about me for years. You think anything's going to change because you bothered to write some of it down?"

He turns back to me. "And really, Joanna, using poor Jason's suicide attempt to try and smear my name? That's low, even for you."

"It wasn't a suicide attempt, Mal."

The words I've tried to say to him so many times, but they always got stuck in my throat. He's not going to own up to any of this. Not now, not ever. But I know the truth, and I've said it out loud. It's not enough, but it's a start.

"You're too hard on yourself, Jo."

A moment ago he was insulting me, and now Mal's voice sounds sympathetic. Tender. He makes these shifts all the time, but I've never been so aware of it before.

"Jason is a very troubled young man," he continues. "I couldn't have known—"

"You did know," I say. "And so did I."

Rob sucks in a breath and looks at me. "You said he was the one who pushed Jason to—"

"She's been lying to everyone for years," Kira says to him. "What makes you think she told you the whole truth and nothing but?"

"Stay out of this," I snap. "It has nothing to do with you."

Kira turns toward me. "What the hell is your problem with me, Joanna?"

"Right now?" I say. "Or in general?"

She looks so furious, for a second I think she's going to haul off and hit me. I want her to, almost. I deserve it. Or maybe what I really want is to find out whether I have it in me to hit her back.

But Kira doesn't come any closer, just folds her arms and fixes me with a vicious glare.

"You know what I think?" she says. "You're jealous."

I scoff. "You think I care if you're fucking him? He fucks everyone."

"Really, Joanna?" Her voice drips with acid. "Does he fuck *everyone*?"

My cheeks burn, and I'm certain then: I could do it. I could hit her. Blacken her other eye, pull her pretty hair, push her down on the concrete floor. I wonder if Rob would try to stop me. I know Mal wouldn't.

But Kira doesn't deserve my hatred or my rage. She's Mal's victim too. She just doesn't know it yet.

"Excuse me, but—"

Bryn. I almost forgot she was here. She may even have slipped out to the lobby while we were arguing. She's standing by the door now, twisting a lock of hair around her finger.

"It's seven thirty-five," she says. "The house was supposed to open—"

"Just a minute," I say.

"But there are people waiting already, and—"

"*Just a minute*, Bryn."

"We don't have a minute," Kira says. "We have a show to do. *Your* show, apparently, so—"

"Look, I know you don't want to believe me, but—"

"Oh, I believe you," she says. "I just don't give a fuck."

Mal puts his hand on the small of her back. He's gazing at her now with something like admiration. The one thing I've always wanted from him, even more than his love.

"We should go get ready," he says. "Bryn, you can open the house in another—"

Rob interrupts him, but he's speaking only to Kira again. "You don't have to go through with this," he says. He reaches for her face again, cupping her jaw. "You have to see now—he's dangerous, Kira."

When I get angry, I burst out in red splotches like a rash, my eyes bug out, I look grotesque. Not Kira. Rage suits her. It lights up her whole face.

She grabs Rob's hand and flings it away from her. "So am I," she says.

KIRA

I FEEL LIKE PUNCHING SOMETHING AGAIN, BUT THIS TIME I settle for sweeping everything off the makeup table with a frustrated scream.

Malcolm eases the dressing room door shut and leans against it, watching me.

No, I don't want to punch something. I want to punch *her*—ruin her precisely applied lipstick, see the sharp line of her haircut shatter as her head whips to the side.

"Tell me how you're feeling right now," Malcolm says.

"How does it look like I'm feeling?" I say through clenched teeth.

"Define it," he says. "Put it into words."

"I'm feeling fucking *pissed off*."

He won't stop, will he, not even for a second. Telling me what to do, how to act, directing my rage like it's just another scene.

"That's generic." Malcolm stoops to pick up a tube of lipstick that rolled into the toe of his shoe. "Be specific."

He keeps picking up the items I scattered, placing them back on the pockmarked surface of the makeup table. He's arranging them much neater than I had them originally, lipsticks lined up like little soldiers, compacts arranged by size, everything symmetrical.

"It feels like . . . burning."

"Where?" he asks.

"Excuse me?"

"Where exactly in your body? Locate it."

"In my chest," I say. "And my hands."

They're curled into fists—how long have I been holding them like that? I force my fingers to unfurl, and several knuckles crack at once.

"My eye," I say. "It's really bad, isn't it?"

Malcolm examines me. "Nothing a little makeup can't fix."

He switches on the lights above the makeup mirror. I sit down, and he kneels on the floor between my legs, propping his elbows on my thighs. He touches his index finger to my chin, tilting my face toward the light.

While he's tending to my eye, I'm free to stare at him—the scab near his ear from where he cut himself shaving this morning, the vein on his forehead that sticks out when he's thinking. His long, dark lashes, the curve of his lower lip.

"You're shaking."

I am, but I had no idea, not until he told me.

"You're letting your anger distract you," he says.

Of course it's distracting me. After everything that went down with Spence and Jason, then I have to come here and deal with this bullshit? Not just that damn story, but Rob—the way he looked at Joanna, the way his body tilted in her direction, even when he was talking to me. They're sleeping together, or about to. He rejected me, literally pushed me away, and now he has the gall to show up here, with her, on the most important night of my fucking life, and talk to me like I'm some confused, helpless child.

I wince as Malcolm starts spreading a bead of concealer under my eye. He lifts his hand away.

"Hold still."

He takes my chin in his other hand, holding me in place as he blends the concealer in, dusts some powder on top of it. He's quick—practiced at this.

Joanna is jealous of me, I see that now. Not because she thinks I'm sleeping with Malcolm, or at least not only that. She's jealous because I see what I want and I take it, while all she can do is sit by and watch. She wanted to be a writer, a director, whatever, and she wants to blame Malcolm for forcing her to give it all up. But he didn't force her to do anything, any more than he made Jason Grady drag that knife across his wrist.

"There," Malcolm says. "Good as new."

I check myself out in the mirror. Aside from some minor puffiness, which the eyeshadow and mascara I'm about to put on should camouflage, my injured eye looks just like my uninjured one. As though nothing happened at all.

I wish I could pretend nothing happened. I wish Spence was here tonight, even though the thought of seeing him makes me want to put my fist through the glass in front of me. Since our freshman year of college, he's been at every single one of my opening nights, either backstage with me or sitting in the audience. Even when the stage lights are too blinding for me to make out faces in the crowd, I can always find him. I know his laugh, the sound of his breathing, the rhythm of his applause.

I could still call him. He might miss the first act, but he could make it in time for the second. I didn't bother telling my parents or my sister about the play, because Spence is more my family than they've ever been. He'd come if I asked him to, no matter what I said before, no matter what's happened between us.

Or maybe he wouldn't. Maybe he'd tell me Jason needs him too much. Maybe he wouldn't even bother to pick up the goddamn phone.

Malcolm is standing now, leaning over me, his hands on my shoulders, his eyes on mine in our reflection. "All this anger, all this energy," he says. "It's a gift. You can use it tonight onstage. Channel it into your performance."

His voice is so calm, so assured, it makes me want to scream again, flip the makeup table, smear all his careful work off my face.

This is how Mara feels. When she looks at Trent, this is exactly how she feels. Fire in her bloodstream, burning to the ends of her fingers, prickling her scalp, her muscles tense, her molars grinding together. Mara has to work every moment to keep her rage and hatred bottled up inside, to keep it from spilling out.

But I only have to keep mine contained until I step out on that stage.

I watch my face harden, my cheeks tensing into flat planes, lips pressing together, eyes clouding. Malcolm bends down to speak right into my ear. In the mirror, I see his lips moving, his tongue between his teeth.

"Save it for the show," he says. "Don't waste it on them."

80

JOANNA

I THOUGHT ABOUT OFFERING TO HELP BRYN OUT IN THE LOBBY, but she seems to have it under control. We never assign seats anyway, so all she has to do is tear tickets and hand out programs.

Usually regular patrons come up to me for a handshake and some small talk before the show. But tonight the people filtering in are keeping their distance, regarding me as though I have a contagious disease. Lauren at least looked at me on the way to her seat, though her lips puckered tight with disapproval. Rob may have had a story to run regardless of my involvement, but my betrayal is what made it front-page news.

They're still here, though. They still came to see the show. To see Mal. I'm not sure whether I'm relieved or disappointed.

Most of what they're saying stays buried in the general hum of conversation, but I catch a few words.

I told you, I always knew there was something—

It's appalling, just absolutely—

And she knew the whole time, can you—

Rob shifts in his seat and puts his arm around my shoulders as if to shield me, but his body language is even stiffer than before.

He seems far away. Probably wondering what else I neglected to tell him. Or still worrying about Kira.

When Mal led her offstage by the elbow, she glared back at both of us like she wished she could strike us dead on the spot. But in Mal's eyes, there was nothing. No anger, no love, no malice.

I may never have cut myself open like Jason, but I know what it feels like to be desperate for Mal's approval, willing to do anything to get a moment of his attention. It's like a drug; you get addicted, and then he takes it away from you. He'll do it to Kira, too, soon enough.

The lights start to dim.

Showtime.

81

KIRA

THE AUDIENCE IS QUIET. I'VE TAKEN MY PLACE BESIDE MALCOLM in the dark.

He's right. I have to use my anger. I can't let it distract me, but I also can't let it dissipate.

So I grit my teeth until the throbbing of my injured eye comes to the forefront of my awareness again. Then I summon the events of the last twenty-four hours in my mind—a looped tape: Spence's knuckles colliding with my eye socket, Jason wielding the dagger, Joanna's smug expression when she walked into the theater, the fond way Rob looked at her, and the pity in his eyes when he turned them on me. The infuriating calm of Malcolm's voice, pouring like poison into my ear.

I wait for my cue—the recorded beep of a hotel key reader— then turn the door handle and walk onto the stage. Malcolm follows right behind me.

He deposits our prop luggage at the foot of the bed, making a good show of pretending the bags are heavy, even though all but one is empty, stuffed with wads of newspaper to hold their shape. I start inspecting the room like it says to in the stage directions, but I can't help stealing sidelong glances at the audience during my slow walk around the set.

It's a full house. Bryn must have given Spence's ticket away to someone. Lauren's here, a few rows up, and I recognize a few other faces, too. Actors I've auditioned with, directors who didn't deign to give me a callback. Joanna and Rob are sitting together in the front. He has his arm slung across the back of her seat.

Rage rises in my throat. I swallow it, concentrating on the sensation of it scraping and burning down my esophagus, settling in the pit of my stomach.

I try to train my attention on Malcolm, really listen to his lines, react in the moment like I'm hearing the words for the first time, but I'm too aware of the audience. Not a single one of them is here to see me. Everyone's here for Malcolm. Not just to see him act, but to see what he'll do.

They must be wondering about what Malcolm has done to me. Whether we're fucking—no, how *long* we've been fucking, if we were doing it from the start or if it took me a little while to give in. If he's pushed me to the brink of a nervous breakdown too. Thanks to Rob and Joanna's stunt, my performance tonight might not even matter.

Finally, we reach the moment when I'm alone onstage for the first time. It's only about fifteen minutes into the show, but it feels like we've been out here for hours already.

Malcolm exits through the false door in the scenery flat, which is meant to lead to the hotel room's bathroom. I cross back over to the desk and unzip Mara's purse, taking out the prop prescription medication bottle. I tilt the contents out onto my palm—there are four pills, small white circles—then stare at them. I try to concentrate on what I should be feeling right now. Determination, trepidation, fear that Trent will catch me.

But I'm not feeling any of those things. I'm just standing still, waiting for the next cue—a toilet flushing, offstage in the imaginary bathroom. It seems to take forever to come, but finally the sound plays. I act as though I've been startled back to awareness, but the reaction feels forced, as fake as the pills in my hand.

I put them in my mouth—two on each side, between my gums and my cheek—and shove the bottle back into the purse. The pills dissolve with a wan mint-flavored fizz, the sweet taste coating my tongue and twisting my stomach. I should have listened to Malcolm and eaten something before the show. Too late now.

I'm supposed to change my costume, into the clothes Mara wears to the wedding. I'm thinking of her as separate from me, when I should be settling into her skin.

By the time Malcolm returns, I'm down to my bra and underwear. He's not supposed to look at me—Mara and Trent have been together for years, so they aren't excited about seeing each other undressed anymore—but his gaze roams over my bare skin anyway.

I put on the slip, then a black sheath dress over it, and gather my hair in my fist, turning my back so Malcolm can zip me up. He goes slower than he should. I can hear the metallic bite of the zipper's teeth as they connect, one by one.

I let my hair fall over my shoulders again as I start to walk away. Malcolm catches me by the elbow and reels me back in, pressing his palm to my stomach.

"You're sure you don't want to tell anyone?" he says.

"We talked about this." I'm supposed to sound a bit weary and annoyed, to make it obvious we've discussed this subject not once, but many times. Instead my voice sounds flat, monotone, like I'm reading the line off a cue card.

"I know," he says. "But when are we all going to be together again? It's the perfect time."

He pulls me even closer, looping his arms around my waist. I put my hands on his arms, almost like I'm pushing him away, trying to escape, but I keep a smile on my face.

"I just want it to be our secret for a while longer. Okay?"

I kiss him—a quick, perfunctory peck, like we've practiced so many times—and start to pull away. Malcolm is supposed to let me go so I can cross to the desk, take a pair of earrings out of the clutch and put them on, but he doesn't. He tenses his arms, holding me in place.

Then he leans in and kisses me again. Not a peck this time. The kiss is forceful, possessive. I stiffen at first, but it only makes him press down harder. What the hell is he doing?

I want to shove him off me and scream. But that would be out of character—until the lights turn red for one of the reverie scenes anyway. The only thing I can do now, without going against the script, is to kiss him back.

But that doesn't mean I have to be nice about it. I cup Malcolm's jaw in my hands and dig my nails in, right under the bone so I can feel the thrum of his jugular through my fingertips. Hard enough to hurt, but not to break the skin. Not yet.

I feel him smile against my mouth, and then he lets me go.

82

JOANNA

I WAS CONCERNED ABOUT KIRA BEING RECKLESS, UNPROFES-sional, going too far. But right now, she's not going far enough.

Her performance is listless, flat, distracted. She's dull—the lus-ter gone even from those just-bitten lips of hers—and she's making my play sound dull, too.

The only interesting thing that's happened so far is that unscripted kiss Mal laid on her, but now she's alone onstage again, and people in the audience are shifting in their seats, folding the pages of their programs back and forth. The man seated on my other side stifles a yawn.

Mal re-enters, his face smeared white with shaving cream. It's the same kind he uses at home, I can smell it.

"I think I forgot my razor," he says to Kira.

"No, I packed it for you," she says.

Not my most thrilling bit of dialogue, I'll admit. But the last time I saw this scene, there was a crackle in the air between them. Mara's on edge after spending hours in a car alone with Trent, and this is yet another instance where he's expecting her to do things for him he should have taken care of himself.

Kira unzips an outer pocket on one of the suitcases, pulling out a silver razor. She turns it over in her hand, the blade glinting under the stage lights. The razor is real rather than a bladeless prop, because Mal doesn't actually use it. He's supposed to take it from her, go offstage again, and return with his face wiped clean.

But she doesn't give him the razor. When he reaches for it, she keeps ahold of the handle. She takes a step toward him. The shine is back in her eyes now, and she wets her lips with the tip of her tongue.

I can almost feel the shift in the air, the moment when the audience reengages again. Mal is watching Kira, waiting to see what she'll do, and now they are, too.

She steps even closer. So close there's only a sliver of space separating them. Then she touches the blade to his cheek and drags it down.

Mal doesn't flinch, doesn't react in any way. But when he presses at the spot under his cheekbone where she's scraped the shaving cream away, red wells up around his fingertip.

83

KIRA

NOW I'VE DONE IT. I MADE MALCOLM BLEED, AND WE HAVEN'T even gotten to the slap yet.

It's far from a gushing wound, but it's obvious, a bright red line snaking down his cheek. Maybe the audience will think it's part of the show—a clever makeup effect, rather than a real injury.

Or maybe they'll take it as proof that I'm unstable, unprofessional. Another one of Malcolm Mercer's poor innocent victims, no different from Jason Grady.

I can't stop to wipe it off or ask him if he's okay or apologize. Besides, I don't want to apologize. I don't care if he's okay. He deserves this. He deserves worse than this. I have to keep going, stay in character. And I've never felt more in character than when that blade broke his skin.

Malcolm takes the razor from me like he was supposed to in the first place—why didn't I just let him? what the fuck was I thinking?— and he presses his fingertips into my palm. The slightest touch, too subtle for the audience to notice.

He's trying to reassure me. He doesn't care that I made him bleed. That's what he wanted, for me to react, in the moment. To forget about the audience and the blocking and even the script and feel something real. That's why he grabbed me and kissed me the way he did.

I meet Malcolm's eyes and let everything else drop away, the way I did before playing Lady Macbeth for him all those weeks ago. But I'm not retreating into my imagination now. I'm falling headfirst into him.

Don't waste it on them. Fuck Joanna and Rob. Fuck the rest of the audience. Let them think what they want about me, and about us. Let them think Malcolm is using me, ruining me, destroying me. I'm using him, too. There's no reason we can't both get what we want.

I have no idea what he might do next. But he doesn't know what I'll do either. I haven't even begun to show him what I'm capable of.

84

JOANNA

MINUTES FROM THE END OF THE FIRST ACT, AND MAL IS STILL bleeding where Kira cut him.

He pushes her against the back of the door, runs his hand over her shoulder, along the curve of her waist, coming to rest on her hip. He stares at her for a moment, like he's waiting for her to stop him. Then he slips his fingers under her skirt.

She closes her eyes and bites her lip, leaning her head back against the door, leaving it ambiguous if Mara is feeling pain or pleasure in this moment.

Exactly the way she should be playing it. Her performance started to improve the moment she pressed the razor into his cheek. I can't take my eyes off her. I wrote the damn play, and I'm still tense, stomach churning. Wondering what's going to happen next.

I hear the pop of the blood pack, because I'm listening for it. Mal draws his hand out from between Kira's legs, holding it up so the audience can see the red painting his fingers. The woman sitting behind me gasps.

"You're bleeding," he says.

Kira doesn't answer him. She's staring down at her stained thighs, the shock of red leaking out from under her black dress.

"Why are you bleeding?" he says. "What—"

"It's okay," she says.

Mal stands up, casting about for something he can use to wipe off the blood.

"We're going to the hospital."

Kira holds her hand out in front of her as if the red drops on her fingers are jewels. She doesn't look shocked or frightened. Only fascinated. That's the word I wrote in the stage directions: *fascinated*, like Mara wasn't sure her plan would work until she saw the proof flowing out of her body.

"It's okay."

"Stop saying that."

"It's okay," Kira says again. "I'm just having a miscarriage."

Mal takes his time with Trent's reaction. He lets a few seconds go by, so what Mara has said can sink in. And then his face *breaks*. He's not crying, not screwing his features up into an ugly mask. Nothing so obvious. Every individual muscle in his face seems to tense and then go slack, and the light drains out of his eyes. It's masterful. So much better than what I imagined when I wrote this scene.

The lights go out. The end of the first act. Everyone around me bursts into applause. Even Rob, though his is more of the polite, golf-clapping variety. I try to move my hands and realize they're crooked almost into claws, my fingernails digging into my thighs. I edge up the hem of my skirt and see the marks I've left, little red half-moons in my skin.

This is even harder than I thought it would be.

85

KIRA

THE STAGE BLOOD BETWEEN MY LEGS MAKES IT HARD TO walk. My thighs keep sticking together. I think I'm leaving a trail of red drips in my wake, but they're impossible to see backstage with the black floor and the dim lighting.

I feel like I'm half-conscious, like I left a part of my mind out on the stage. The way Malcolm touched me during that last scene felt almost *too* real. When he maneuvered the blood pack into place, his thumb brushed the spot where my thigh meets my hip, and I wanted to arch my back, move against his hand.

Usually Bryn is waiting for me backstage with a wet washcloth so I can clean the blood off my legs. When I reach my dressing room, though, there's no sign of her. Then Malcolm appears in the doorway.

He has a white towel wrapped around his hands, just like this morning at his apartment. The towel is already streaked red with the stage blood he scrubbed off his fingers.

I sit down on the edge of the makeup table and part my knees.

Malcolm slams the dressing room door shut behind him and closes the distance between us with two long strides. He starts wiping away the blood, starting at my knees and working his way higher on my thighs, pushing up the hem of my skirt. I spread my legs wider.

Everything outside the dressing room has faded into a low buzz at the back of my mind. All I can hear is the ragged sound of my own breathing. Malcolm's breath is still steady and calm, but I can see the pulse point below his jaw throbbing. I lay my hand over his.

He stops, looks up at me. I hold his gaze. Guide his fingers deeper.

His fingertips brush over my underwear, then start to tease up the edges of the fabric. He's dropped the towel. I can see the place where it lies on the floor, at the very edge of my vision. It's soaked through with red now.

I move against his hand, the way I wanted to onstage. I might come just from this, I'm so close, just a few more seconds . . . but then he stops, drawing his hand away.

A flare of anger scorches my chest. I grab him by the wrist, try to pull his hand back. In a flash, he's on his feet, flipping me around so I'm facing the mirror. He leans in so his chest presses against the length of my spine, pinning me in place. His hands rest on the makeup table, one arm on either side of me, caging me in.

"Use it," he says, his mouth hot against my ear.

"Fuck you." Every part of me is throbbing, from my scalp to the soles of my feet. From arousal or hatred, I'm not sure. When it comes to Malcolm, the two are so mixed I no longer know how to separate them.

"Use it," he says. "Use everything. Leave it all on the stage."

"I need to get ready." I try to buck back against him, but he holds firm, pressing my hips against the edge of the table. His hands move to my waist. The fabric of my dress bunches under his palms, lifting the hem higher.

He kisses me on the shoulder, his teeth dragging over my bare skin. "You are ready."

I meet his gaze again in the mirror. My eyes are still sparking with anger. But the longer we stare at each other, the calmer I feel. I nod, once—a slow, controlled motion of my chin.

It's not until then that I notice the dressing room door is open again, and Bryn stands on the threshold, twisting a spotless white towel around her hands. Her lips are pressed together, trembling, like she's on the verge of vomiting, tears, or both. Malcolm doesn't seem to see her.

"Five minutes to places," Bryn says.

I move nothing except for my eyes, which I slide over to meet hers in the mirror.

"Thank you, five," I say.

86

JOANNA

THE STAGE STARTS TO BLEED RED. STILL TOO SUBTLE FOR THE rest of the audience to notice, but I'm aware of the exact moment the lighting shifts.

"You didn't think I had a right to know?" Mal says.

Kira stares at him. The red light shows up in her hair first, a bloody haze around her skull.

"The decision was already made." The line comes out in a low hiss. Her performance shifted again after intermission. Like a switch was flipped somewhere inside her. She's not acting anymore. She is Mara.

I thought I saw Spencer slip in during intermission, seconds before the lights dimmed again. The seats are all full, so he must be standing somewhere at the back.

I wish I knew what happened, how he ended up giving Kira that black eye. I'm sure Mal had something to do with it, even if he wasn't the one to land the blow.

Or maybe it's my fault. If I hadn't run off last night, I would have been there to supervise, and then—

No. I'm not taking responsibility for Mal's mistakes anymore. Only my own.

" 'The decision'?" Mal says. "That's all it was to you? Just another decision, like what brand of mascara to buy or where to have dinner."

"You're right, it wasn't even a decision. I knew what I had to do."

This might be the last time I see Mal onstage. Maybe even the last time I see him at all. On some level, I knew when I told Rob those things, when I let him write them down, it would be the end of Mal and me. The end of Indifferent Honest.

"*Why? Why the fuck would you—*"

"*Because I don't want to have your fucking baby!*"

They're in position for the slap. Mal's back is to the audience, but I can picture the look on his face. That smug, triumphant glint he gets in his eyes when he's about to say something that cuts to the quick of you, makes you react in a way you couldn't have foreseen.

I fucking hate that look.

"How do I even know it was mine?" he says. "We both know you've always been nothing but a—"

Crack.

Kira strikes. Mal sinks down to the floor.

She really hit him. The lights are so red now I can't see the place on his cheek where her hand made contact, but I'm sure of it. That wasn't the sound of a knap, it was the sound of her skin on his. The real thing.

My face feels warm, tight, and I realize: I'm smiling. It's the same rush of queasy exhilaration I felt when she sliced his cheek with the razor.

My anger toward Mal spilled over every page of this play. I had to write it all down. Get it out of me. But only now, seeing the words brought to life before my eyes, does it feel like I'm truly expelling it. All that built-up, clotted rage, gushing out of my body. Splashed across the stage for everyone to see.

I look at Mal, hunched there in the red light, and I imagine him soaked in it.

My smile stretches wider.

87

KIRA

MALCOLM SLAMS ME INTO THE DOOR SO HARD MY TEETH clack together.

It feels incredible. Almost as good as slapping him did.

I could have gotten myself off as soon as he left my dressing room, in the few minutes we had left before going to places. My skin was humming, my head pounding, every square inch of me swollen with desire. It would have taken so little, a few quick motions to relieve the pressure.

But I know how I'd feel now if I'd given in: the tingling limbs, the drowsy languor, the fuzzy sensation in my head like my skull is stuffed with cotton. I wouldn't be sharp, I wouldn't be on edge.

He was right: everything I'm feeling now can be used onstage. It would be a shame to waste it.

I struggle against his grip—more than I usually do, not just for show, but so he'll have to clamp his hands down harder. So he'll have to hurt me, too, give me more pain, more rage, more to work with, so much it's spilling out of me, overflowing the boundaries of my body, my mind, pouring out on the stage like blood.

Blackout.

I freeze. Then I feel his lips pressing against mine—so quick I wonder if I imagined it.

That kiss was not in character, not for the benefit of the audience. I've almost forgotten the audience exists, ever since intermission. That kiss was for him, and for me, alone here in the dark.

That was Malcolm, not Trent.

My palm still tingles. I curl my fingers into a fist and flex them out again as I move to my mark for the next scene. When Malcolm brushes past me in the blackness, the air moving around him sweeps over my skin, sending a shiver down my spine.

The lights come up again, showing the pink outline of my palm on Malcolm's cheek. I didn't make him bleed this time. But I bit the inside of my own lip when I hit the door. I press the tip of my tongue to the spot and taste copper.

This is what it feels like to be fully in the moment. To make what happens on stage *real* rather than a bunch of rote, memorized words and actions. Last night was an expressionistic blur of pure feeling, and I thought I was giving a great performance, losing myself in my role, but I had no idea.

I didn't understand, not until now.

I never want to stop.

88

JOANNA

HE'S KISSING HER, AND I FEEL NOTHING. THE SPACE WHERE my love and hate and longing and jealousy used to reside is empty. A drained abscess.

Rob called me brave, but that's a lie, too. If I were really brave, I would have stood up to Mal years ago instead of swallowing my rage and contenting myself with his scraps. Worshiping his talent while sublimating my own. I would have put my name on the play from the start. Or maybe I wouldn't have needed to write this play at all.

Working on *Temper* let me spend hours imagining, in vivid, luxurious detail, all the ways I wanted to lash out at Mal but couldn't bring myself to act on in reality. Screaming at him, hitting him, choking the life out of him. He must have known, on some level. Must have sensed how much I hated him, no matter how deep I tried to bury it. Maybe he doesn't care whether I hate him or love him, as long as he has power over me.

I'm looking at him now, writhing around on that bed with Kira, their limbs tangled up like snakes, and all I see is a fictional character. A person I created out of my own imagination. Twelve years in his company, and I don't know anything about him. I couldn't figure out his thoughts or feelings or motivations, so I made them up. I liked the mask he wore for me, so I didn't try to look underneath. If I had, I would have seen what I saw before the show tonight: there's nothing behind it. Mal only changes character, he never drops it. He's a cipher, different for everyone he meets.

This hollow man. This is who I've built my existence around. I've tossed my entire adult life into the abyss of him, one moment at a time. Watched them all sink out of sight, lost forever.

Not anymore.

89

KIRA

THERE'S NOTHING BEYOND THIS BED, HIS BODY AND MINE, bathed in red light.

Malcolm pushes his fingers through my hair, his tongue searching deep in my mouth. I slide my hands down his back, grip the flesh below his ass, dig my nails in.

We're in character, but I know we both understand: this is a rehearsal, too. For later. For tonight, after the show. I have no doubt now that Malcolm and I will sleep together. But it won't be some cheap fuck, offering my body in exchange for something I want. It will be a consummation, a celebration, of every desire we've had since we first laid eyes on each other, just as raw and brutal and brilliant as what we're creating here on this stage.

I can't wait.

I push him onto his back, swing my leg over his waist. When he inhales, his stomach expands to touch the space between my legs. I feel like he's inside me already.

I know Joanna has thought about this—about kissing him, fucking him, possessing every part of him. I bet she's fantasized about what happens next, too. Imagined exactly what it would be like to put her hands around his throat and squeeze, to feel him go still under her, the beat of his pulse fading out like the end of a song.

I slide my hands toward his neck. I look into his eyes, but not to check in, to see if he's ready. I already know he is. We've both been ready for this since the day of the audition. Since the moment he stared at me, and I stared back.

90

JOANNA

MARA PUSHES HIM BACK DOWN ONTO THE MATTRESS. HER HANDS are around his throat.

Trent looks shocked, but he doesn't struggle.

Mal takes ahold of Kira's wrists, stares up at her, eyes wide and pleading.

She squeezes harder.

My hand tightens around Rob's. I'm probably cutting off his circulation, but he doesn't complain, doesn't try to withdraw. I imagined this. I conjured it in my mind, and now it's really happening. Kira's hands standing in for mine. Her rage eclipsing my own.

Mal is writhing underneath her now, his legs wheeling, kicking at the bedding. The fitted sheet starts to creep up, exposing the white corner of the mattress.

She's killing him.

His chin juts up. Tears streaming from the corners of his eyes. He's gripping her wrists so tight his knuckles have turned white. Pinching her skin between his thumb and forefinger.

She's killing him. She's—

I lurch forward in my seat. Only an inch, and then I freeze in place again. Rob looks at me. I can feel his eyes on the side of my face. Searching, questioning, wanting to know what's wrong.

I could stop her. It's not too late yet.

Kira is shaking, goose bumps on every part of her body. Her eyes are shut, and she looks so beautiful. That's not in the stage directions. But it works. Maybe she decided that's the only way she could go through with it. If she didn't look him in the eyes while his life drained out.

Trent's eyes close. His head falls to the side. The only sound is Mara's ragged breathing.

I can hear my own heartbeat, too, pounding in my ears.

Lights out.

91

KIRA

THE APPLAUSE ROARS THE SECOND THE LIGHTS GO OUT.

I'm still astride Malcolm, gently cupping his jaw now, my fingers curving around the sides of his neck. I bend down and kiss him. Usually he lolls his head to the side when he pretends to pass out, but tonight he's facing up. Our lips meet in the darkness.

I whisper his name against his mouth. "Mal."

The audience rises from their seats. They must be giving us a standing ovation. The first of my career. And now someone is rushing toward the stage. Not from the risers, but down the aisle, from the back of the house.

Spence.

I can barely see him—just his eyes, the whites shining red in the glow of the emergency exit light, the only source of illumination in the space during the blackout—but I would know him anywhere, the way he moves, the slope of his broad shoulders.

Of course he came. Of course he wouldn't miss tonight. He must have been standing somewhere the lights didn't reach. I'm so glad he was here to see this.

The best performance of my life.

Spence walks onto the stage—what does he think he's doing? We still have to do the curtain call, Malcolm and I have to stand up and clasp hands and take our bows. I imagine the way he'll smile at me, the light shining in his eyes.

Spence grabs me by the shoulders. Dragging me off the bed.

Away from Malcolm.

I try to resist, to hold on, but my hands are too stiff, I can't get a solid grip. My fingernails rake across Malcolm's chest, rending his skin again.

Spence is shaking me—or is he the one shaking? Screaming in my face, but I can't hear him. The applause is too loud, it fills my head, the sound rushing like water.

The lights come up. The red ones, then switching over to stark white. Everyone in the audience is on their feet, but their hands are still. Frozen at their sides, or covering their mouths. Eyes wide and staring.

Like Malcolm's eyes. I could have sworn he closed them, he always closes them, so it looks like Trent might just be sleeping, like Mara might have imagined the whole thing. But this time they're still open. Open and staring, up into the blackness above the stage. Gazing at nothing.

It's not applause I hear. Just the thunder of blood in my ears.

And Bryn's sobs, from the shadows at the edge of the stage. Lauren tripping down the risers, shrieking for someone to do something. Rob's calm, low voice speaking into his cell phone. Spence swearing, the heavy stomp as he stalks away.

Only Joanna comes into the light with me. She stands on the other side of the bed, her back to everyone else, Malcolm's prone body between us. We stare at each other for a long moment—silent, unblinking. There's no anger in her eyes. No horror, no shock, no tears. She's almost as still as he is.

I'm her audience now, the only one who sees the look on her face when she turns her gaze down on Malcolm. The way her lips curl back, as she closes his eyelids. Not quite a snarl or a smile, but something in between.

The stage lights dim again, and we're alone in the dark.

ACKNOWLEDGMENTS

THANK YOU FIRST AND FOREMOST TO MY KICKASS AGENT, Sharon Pelletier. It's such a dream to get to work with you, after years of admiring your angry feminist tweets from afar. And to my amazing editor, Kate Dresser—after just a few minutes on the phone, I knew my book would be in the best of hands with you. Thanks also to Lauren Abramo and Dana Spector, for taking *Temper* places I never imagined it could go, and to Molly Gregory, Stacey Sakal, Jen Bergstrom, Chelsea Cohen, Monica Oluwek, Caroline Pallotta, Abby Zidle, Diana Velasquez, Mackenzie Hickey, Anabel Jimenez, and everyone else on the Scout Press team for all your hard work.

This book is what it is today because of the Pitch Wars mentoring program, so thank you to Brenda Drake for creating Pitch Wars and changing the lives of so many writers. Thank you to my mentor, Nina Laurin, for seeing the potential in my messy manuscript and also for forcing me to torture my characters more. (It's good for them.) A huge thanks as well to everyone who cheered me on and commiserated with me during Pitch Wars, but especially Hannah Whitten. We'll always have Adam.

I might never have started writing in the first place if it weren't for my good friend Anna Geletka, who is one of the most talented writers I know. Thank you for showing me it was possible. Someday our books will sit side by side on a bookstore shelf, alphabetical order be damned!

Thank you also to Christina Gorman, for teaching me how to strangle someone over tea and scones like the badass bitch you are. To Katharine Hannah, for helping me look the part. To Gillian Flynn and Jessica Knoll, for making writing about angry, fucked-up women cool (and marketable!). To Kellye Garrett, Andrea Somberg, Margarita Montimore, Jennifer Udden, and all the other people who sent me rejection letters that made me want to keep going.

And finally, thank you to my family. To my mom, who encouraged my love of books by reading to me, taking me to the library all the time, and even illustrating my earliest writing attempts (there was one about a manatee; it was epic). To my furry writing assistants Byron, Roxie, Jada, and Finn. And to Nate: I could not have done this without you. Thank you for supporting me, always talking about my characters like they're real people, and just generally putting up with my bullshit. You're one of the good ones, babe.

TEMPER

Layne Fargo

This reading group guide for Temper *includes an introduction, discussion questions, and ideas for enhancing your book club. The suggested questions are intended to help your reading group find new
and interesting angles and topics for your discussion. We hope that
these ideas will enrich your conversation and increase your enjoy-
ment of the book.*

INTRODUCTION

Two ambitious women are drawn into the mind games of a manipulative theater director in this feminist psychological suspense novel set against the backdrop of the Chicago indie theater scene.

When struggling actress Kira Rascher finally lands the role of a lifetime—starring in a new play called *Temper*—the gig comes with a catch: working with Malcolm Mercer, a mercurial director who's known for pushing his performers past their limits, onstage and off. While Kira's convinced that she can handle Malcolm, the theater's cofounder Joanna Cuyler sees Kira as a threat—to her own thwarted artistic ambitions and to her twisted relationship with Malcolm. But as opening night draws near, Kira and Joanna both start to realize that Malcolm's dangerous extremes are nothing compared to what they're capable of themselves.

TOPICS & QUESTIONS FOR DISCUSSION

1. Reflect on your first impressions of both Kira and Joanna. How did your understanding of (and feelings about) these two main characters evolve over the course of the novel? Do you recall the key moments at which your impressions of either (or both) character(s) changed?

2. Kira is aware of how often she's under the male gaze. How does she use this to her advantage, and in what ways does this make her vulnerable?

3. Kira and Joanna often feel mistrust, jealousy, and even hatred toward those whom they see as competition—including each other. Discuss the nature of female competition as it's portrayed in this novel. In your mind, why do such intense feelings arise from competition among women? Have you experienced this in your own life?

4. When Kira is first warned about Malcolm's intensity by Jason—whose backstory at this point in the novel is still unknown to the reader—what did you imagine awaited her? How did your initial theories align or conflict with Mal's behavior throughout the novel?

5. The playwright behind *Temper*, L. S. Sedgwick, is first introduced as the play's mysterious writer in Chapter 5, and the reveal of the play's true authorship comes later, about halfway through the novel. Was there a moment when you suspected that Joanna might be the play's author, and what was your reaction to this revelation?

6. How would you characterize Joanna and Mal's relationship? Were you surprised to learn about Joanna's unrequited feelings for Mal?

7. Which act of violence leading up to the novel's shocking final scene did you find the most foreboding, and why? Discuss the ways in which acts of violence serve as foreshadowing through the novel.

8. Revisit Kira's paragraph-long reflection on the Mara-Trent dynamic on pages 135–136: "Mara could be played as a miserable woman trapped in a toxic relationship, standing by silent and passive, capable of fighting back only in her fantasies. But when I read the script, that's not what I thought of her at all. She's full of fury, dangerous, a fuse nearly burned down to nothing. She's been waiting, for years probably, for Trent to do something that will justify her attacking him—and whenever it finally happens, she intends to be ready. The reveries are mental rehearsals for future, inevitable violence. If anyone in *Temper* is a victim, it's Trent." In what ways does this relationship parallel elements of the Joanna-Mal dynamic, or the Kira-Mal dynamic? Do the gender pairings (i.e., Joanna/Kira as Mara, and Mal as Trent) align?

9. On page 189, Jason warns that Malcolm aims to "dismantle" the actors whom he directs. Which characters are "dismantled" in this novel, and by whom?

10. Consider how sexuality is both presented and deployed in this novel. What is your response to the ways in which sex and sexuality are used by characters to assert power or dominance?

11. Do you consider Kira and Joanna to be feminist characters? In what ways do they combat sexism in their careers, as well as in their relationships?

12. Joanna reveals her imposter syndrome on page 228, saying: "Maybe he only loves my words when he doesn't know they're

mine." Do you think these feelings of insecurity stem from Mal's treatment of her, or from Jason's dramatic act of self-harm, or from somewhere else entirely?

13. On page 333, Joanna describes Mal as a "hollow man." Do you read Mal as a manipulative and unfeeling sociopath, or a boundary-pushing genius, or neither? Could Mal be considered a tragic character?

14. Discuss the role of the audience in this novel. How often are these characters performing (whether on- or offstage)—even when the audience is just a single person?

15. Consider the story from Malcolm's perspective; what if his point of view were introduced, or the entire story were told from his first-person perspective, in his own voice? What would you title the novel, and how do you think the female characters would be portrayed?

16. What do you think of the author's choice to alternate between Kira's and Joanna's perspectives, keeping both in the first person? How would your impression of Kira change if we saw her only through Joanna's eyes, rather than having access to her thoughts? How about Joanna?

17. In the play, red lighting indicates that Mara is shifting from the real world into a "reverie." Do you interpret the final scene of the play to be real, or a reverie? How about the final scene of the novel itself?

18. Author Layne Fargo has a background in theater and used to work as a dramaturg. Which behind-the-scenes revelations of a theatrical production did you find the most interesting, or the most surprising?

ENHANCE YOUR BOOK CLUB

1. **Serve a Shakespearean Cocktail**: Mal's performance in *Hamlet* is referenced throughout the novel as an example of his intensity onstage. Pay homage to the Bard at your book club discussion by serving a Shakespeare-inspired cocktail! Check out *Shakespeare, Not Stirred: Cocktails for Your Everyday Dramas* by Caroline Bicks and Michelle Ephraim for a wide range of recipes, or go with the Hamlet Cocktail itself: mix 2 parts vodka, 1 part Campari, and 4 parts orange juice.

2. **Cast the Movie**: Who do you envision taking on each of the main characters in a cinematic adaptation of the novel? Distribute slips of paper and ask each book club member to cast the main players (Mal, Kira, Joanna, and Spence). Once everyone has chosen their four lead actors, share your selections and see if any overlap! Now, how about the supporting cast of David, Jason, and Bryn?

3. **Explore Other Difficult Women**: Author Layne Fargo cohosts a podcast about challenging heroines called *Unlikeable Female Characters*. Choose an episode (or go right to Episode 1: "Favorite Unlikeable Female Characters") and circulate it among your book club members to deepen your discussion of Kira and Joanna in the context of a broader literary trend in female characterization.

4. **Take an Improv Exercise for a Test Drive**: Channel your inner Kira! Head over to http://improvencyclopedia.org and challenge your book group to one of their recommended improv games before diving into your discussion of *Temper*.

Keep reading for a sneak peek at Layne Fargo's next "raw, ingenious, and utterly fearless" (Wendy Walker) novel

THEY NEVER LEARN

Available from Scout Press in October 2020

1

SCARLETT

I'LL KNOW IT'S WORKING WHEN HE STARTS TO SCREAM.

But for now, I wait. I snuck into the garage an hour ago, when it was still pitch-black outside. I'm dressed to match the shadows, a hood pulled up to hide my vivid red hair, face scrubbed clean of makeup. No need to look pretty for this.

There aren't any vehicles in here, just some old exercise equipment sitting on scraps of carpet, stale sweat and mossy body spray hanging in the air. I'm pressed into the back corner behind a set of warped metal shelves. Enough to conceal me, if I stay extremely still. I keep my breathing steady, focusing my gaze on the peeling red vinyl of the weight bench, the small gashes in the material like open wounds.

Footsteps slap the pavement, and the side door to the garage swings open. Right on time. A young man comes in, swabbing the sweat off his brow with the hem of his T-shirt.

Tyler Elkin. Star athlete, and one of the worst students I ever taught in my Intro to English Lit class. As starting quarterback, he took the Gorman University football team all the way to the conference championship last season. That was before the rumors started.

He tugs his earbuds out and swipes his thumb across his phone screen. Music starts blaring from a small speaker set up on a crate beside the weights, a screamy white-boy wannabe punk rocker whining about some girl who broke his heart. That bitch, how dare she.

It sets my teeth on edge, but I don't move a muscle. I can't risk Tyler seeing me. Not yet.

Tunelessly humming along, Tyler walks to the dented mini fridge in the corner and removes a glass bottle. He tosses the cap onto the floor and takes a long pull of the liquid inside. It's an energy drink he makes himself, with activated charcoal, cayenne, and several raw eggs. Smells awful, and tastes even worse. I tried it myself, after brewing up a batch based on the instructions on his Instagram. Then I added my own special ingredient, mixed right in with the rest of the bitter grit at the bottom.

He made a video on his "kickass morning routine" too. He starts his day the same way, even on weekends: up at 5:00 a.m., hours before his fraternity brothers, for a brisk run along the path by the river at the edge of campus. He always pauses to take a photo of himself with the sunrise saturating the background. Then he comes back here, to the garage behind the frat house, for weight training. He'll down half his energy drink now, the other half once his workout is done, while he captions his sunrise selfie with some inane motivational message. *Rise n grind. Make 2day yr bitch.*

Tyler polishes off another gulp and wipes his mouth. He has full lips and long eyelashes, which renders his face almost feminine from certain angles. He could be a model, one of those sun-burnished Abercrombie boys tossing a ball back and forth in matching madras shorts. It's clear from his social media he considers that his backup plan, if the whole football thing doesn't work out. A boy like Tyler, he could have any girl he wanted. But where's the fun in that? It must get boring after a while. Not that that's any excuse.

Tyler lies back on the weight bench and starts raising and lowering the barbell in time with the music. Until his rhythm slows, stutters. His fingers wrap tighter around the bar. Then they spasm, and he almost lets go of the weight, dropping it on his catalog-perfect face.

My breath catches. That would ruin my whole plan.

He barely manages to keep ahold of the barbell. With quivering hands, he sets it back on its stand and shuts his eyes for a second. He sits up, shaking out his wrists, his arms. But now his legs are spasming, his calf and thigh muscles clenching and unclenching like fists.

Tyler stands, trying to walk it off, rolling his neck, cracking his vertebrae. I shrink deeper into the darkness. It's almost time, but not yet, not—

"Fuck," he says, raking a hand back through his sweat-soaked blond hair. He picks up the bottle again, taking another swig, Adam's apple bobbing as he swallows.

Still holding his drink, Tyler leans against the weight bench, trying to stretch out the strange cramps in his legs. It's only a few seconds before he seizes all over and collapses. The bottle goes with him, landing beyond his outstretched hand. The glass doesn't break, but the remaining contents flow out onto the concrete floor.

That's fine. He's had more than enough now.

Tyler's body is no longer under his control. He's twitching, contorting, spine arching, lifting his back off the floor so he's supported only by his head and heels. He finally lets out a scream—throaty, guttural at first, then keening higher, turning into a sob.

If it weren't for his obnoxious music, someone might hear. If he gets much louder, they might anyway. I step out of my hiding place, but he's in so much pain it takes him a few seconds to put it all together—to recognize me in the first place and then to wonder why his literature professor is standing over him in his own garage at six in the morning, smiling while he screams.

"Please," Tyler manages to choke out. "Help me, please h—"

Another convulsion takes hold of him. Soon he won't be able to speak at all. This is the most I've ever heard out of Tyler Elkin's mouth. When he bothered to show up to my class, he grunted one-word answers, slumping down in his seat with his legs sprawled across the aisle like he didn't give a damn how much space he took up.

They never do, men like him. Well, he's more of a boy, really.

The garage's fluorescent overhead light emphasizes all the still-adolescent features of his face: the downy excuse for a mustache on his upper lip, the pimple swelling in the crease between his nose and his cheek.

He's a boy, and he'll never become a man. Because in a few more minutes, he'll be dead.

It's risky for me to be here. I know that. I could have left the tainted drink in the fridge for him and slipped away while he was still out running. But the truth is, I enjoy this too much to miss it. It's my reward, for all the hard work. Besides, there's one more step in my plan.

I pick up Tyler's phone and hold it in front of his face. At first the device doesn't recognize him, his features are so twisted with agony. I wait for the convulsions to ease again, his body giving up the fight even before he does. After a few more seconds, the lock screen blinks away.

I open Instagram and crop Tyler's latest selfie so only the sunrise in the background is in the frame, applying the filter he uses for all his posts. For the caption, I imitate the appalling grammar and spelling he employs.

last run last sunrise, so sorry 4 everthing

Tyler lies there panting, soaked through with sweat, blinking up at me as I methodically wipe all traces of my fingerprints from the device.

"Why—" he starts, but his throat is too constricted to speak.

I put the phone in his twitching hand and lean over him, my body casting his in shadow.

"Megan Foster," I say.

Tyler's eyes widen—and *this*, this is my favorite part. The abject terror that takes over their faces. That's how I know they're finally seeing me, realizing what I truly am.

I imagine what Tyler might say, if he were still capable of forming words. *It wasn't just me*—that's probably where he'd start. He wasn't the only one who held Megan down on that filthy frat house mattress. They all did it—Tyler and four of his closest friends, half the starting lineup of the football team.

I didn't start it. Who knows, that might even be the truth. Maybe Tyler was the second to take his turn, or the third, or the fourth, or the fifth. Maybe by the time he got there she'd given up fighting back, so he could almost pretend she was willing. He didn't have bruises and scratches on his arms afterward, like his teammate Devin Caldwell did. But the police didn't do a damn thing to Devin Caldwell either. They claimed there wasn't enough proof.

For me, what Megan said was more than enough proof. True justice would have been bolting the fraternity house doors and setting the whole place on fire, burning every one of those boys in their beds. I might not even have needed to douse the place in kerosene first, considering every surface is sticky with spilled alcohol. But I can't kill them all, not unless I want to get caught. I've spent the past sixteen years murdering men who deserve it, and I'm not about to get sloppy now.

So I made the logical compromise: pick one man and make an example of him. Tyler was the clear choice. Not because he's the quarterback or the alpha male or any of that macho bullshit, but because, even though he and his four teammates all did something abhorrent that night, Tyler's sin was the worst.

It was his Instagram that tipped me off, actually: photo after photo of Tyler at parties, leaning against walls and doorjambs and tree trunks, holding a bottle like the one oozing out on the floor beside his soon-to-be corpse.

Tyler believes clean living means a stronger game. So while his frat brothers got wasted on cheap beer and skunk weed, Tyler restricted himself to sipping his homemade energy drinks. Five boys raped Megan Foster, but only one of them did it while stone-cold sober.

Looking back, the signs were there from the first week of class— the way Tyler always picked the seat right behind Megan's, flicked her curtain of brown curls back while she was trying to read. Told her, even as she shrank away from him, *You'd be so pretty if you smiled.*

He's seizing again, but he's gone silent now, eyes rolled back into his head. I crouch down beside him, careful not to touch anything else. It's just a matter of time. No hospital could help him at this point, not with that much strychnine in his system.

There. Finally. Tyler's body goes through one more bout of clenching convulsions, and his lips stretch back from his teeth, fixing his too-handsome face in a gruesome parody of a grin.

Who's smiling now, motherfucker?